CW01206971

Tethered by Hannah Calver - The first book in the Elementals Series.

Dedicated to

Sarah, Stacey & Kate

N, O, P, E & M

Copyright @ Hannah Calver 2024

This book is a work of fiction and any resemblance to actual persons, living of dead, is purely coincidental.

Part 1

> She is coming, my dove, my dear,
>
> Its lips in the field above are dabbled with blood-red heath,
>
> The red-ribb'd ledges drip with a silent horror of blood,
>
> And Echo there, whatever is ask'd her, answers 'Death.'

Maud: A Monodrama, Alfred, Lord Tennyson

Chapter 1

Last day of the full moon cycle.

His world was stopped as suddenly as a clock that had run out of time, leaving him in a silence that echoed with the absence of everything he once knew. The vibrant colours of his life faded into a monochrome blur, and the once familiar sounds became distant memories, like whispers carried away by the wind.

The dagger flew towards him. It cleaved the air in two as it made its way to his heart. A part of his mind marvelled at its beauty. The golden blade, so sharp it could cut the very fabric of reality, shimmered with an almost ethereal glow. Time seemed to slow as he watched its deadly arc, a mixture of awe and dread filling his thoughts. The dark red rubies in its hilt and blade shone in anticipation of the feast they would have as it made his body its bloody sheath. He could almost hear the sinister whisper of the weapon, promising pain and finality. Yet, in that fleeting moment, he found a strange sense of clarity, a calm acceptance of the inevitable.

He saw his soul come to him as a dragon, her swirling blue eyes crying out as the one he loved best went somewhere she could not follow. She was his other half, the better half. Without her, he was incomplete, just as she was without him. How could she possibly survive if he were no longer there?

Her voice in his head, always comforting, always there, silently begged him to stay. The cord of bright blue light that connected them, was weakening and fraying, dimming as the darkness crept in, like ink spreading through water.

And then he saw her, the one who held his heart, eyes a honeyed brown, sparkling with tears still to be shed. Eyes he would have happily drowned in for the rest of his days. The world around him faded, leaving only the intensity of her gaze, a beacon of love and sorrow that anchored him to life as he had once anchored his other half, his soul. In that moment, he knew he wanted to fight, not just for himself, but for the promise held within those tear-filled eyes.

He wanted to fight against the darkness threatening to engulf him for them, for the two people he loved best in the world. But the pull of the shadows was too powerful. As he felt the darkness spread from his mortal wound, icy tendrils wrapped around his heart, squeezing the life out of him. His pulse, a faint echo in the void, beeped around him. Someone was shaking his shoulder, calling his name, a distant echo in the encroaching silence.

"Tenney…"

The voice and the rhythmic beeping grew louder, the shaking harder, hands digging into his shoulder.

"Tenney!"

He opened a groggy eye. His back ached from the position he had fallen asleep in, his head resting awkwardly on the bed, his hand on hers, his backside propped up by the hard chair he had pulled over. As he moved, he felt the bruises he had received – and given – each one painfully reminding him of the events of the past two days.

Blinking away the remnants of his dream, he looked up to see her face, pale but alive. Her eyes fluttered under their lids. Tenney's heart pounded with a mix of anxiety and hope as he watched her. The beeping of the monitors around them seemed to synchronise with his racing pulse.

Running a hand through his tousled brown hair, he groaned as he sat up and stretched, rubbing a thumb and a finger in the corners of his eyes. His hand still gripped hers as she lay sleeping peacefully, at last. It was her heart he could hear as it made its staccato beat across the machine, its wires snaking beneath her hospital gown. The sounds of the hospital grew and banished the last vestiges of his dream away.

"Tenney, love, we're going to get some coffee from the café." He turned to look into the eyes of his mother. Her usual happy, relaxed face was drawn with worry. "Will you be ok, love?" she asked. Her soft Massachusetts accent sounded like a balm as she whispered to him, stroking his hair back from his face as she had done when he was a small boy. He saw her pale as she revealed the purpling bruise under his eye, marring the face she was sure had been blessed, or cursed, by the gods. His father, standing like a guard at the doorway, his face haggard, was waiting to usher his wife away.

He nodded his head. He would be fine. He wasn't going anywhere. As his parents left the room, his attention went straight back to the person in the bed.

"Hey," he whispered softly to the sleeping figure, his voice cracking with emotion. "You're going to be okay. I'm right here." Relief washed over him, mingling with the pain and exhaustion. She was safe, and for now, that was all that mattered.

Her long blond hair spread out around her small, pixie-like face as if it was a halo. Her naturally pale skin finally felt warm to his touch again as she breathed unaided once more. He knew that when she wakened from her sleep, her eyes would blaze momentarily, a swirling miasma of blues and greys. They seemed to whirl like a strong wind, spiralling leaves until finally deciding on what colour they would be that day. Hers was a face he knew better than his own, a face he treasured above all else. He cursed his decision to leave her. And the events which led to her flatlining in this cold hospital room.

Tenney sighed deeply, the weight of the past days pressing heavily on his shoulders. He traced the lines of her face with his eyes, memorising every detail as if afraid she might slip away again. The rhythmic beeping of the heart monitor was a constant reminder of her fragility, yet also a beacon of hope. The connection between them, forged through shared pain and unwavering love, was palpable. Despite the bruises and the exhaustion, Tenney felt a renewed sense of purpose. They had survived the storm, and together, they would face whatever came next.

**

<u>Two days earlier. The first day of the full moon cycle.</u>

Tennyson Wiseman woke up excited, having slept soundly, for which he was grateful, knowing what the day would bring. Rolling on his side he faced the wall, on the other side of which he knew Aura would be stirring. He waited for her to pad into his room, knowing he would not have to wait long. Through a crack in his curtains, he could still see the full harvest moon as it battled with the dawn.

Quietly, his door opened, but it wasn't Aura who stuck a sleepy head around the door. Instead, it was the small, wet black nose of his dog, Bo. At three years old, he still behaved like an over excited puppy, as he launched his small terrier-cross body at Tenney's head. Laughter followed Bo into the room.

"Oi!" he said. "Stop lollygagging and help me get this mutt off!" Small hands wrapped around Bo's body, carefully lifting him away and earning a licking of her own, Aura kept laughing.

"Stop it," Tenney said, trying hard to hide the smile that he knew was spreading across his face and eyes.

"Shove up," said his twin sister.

Tenney obliged, moving closer to the wall and making space for her and the dog under the covers. As they laughed together, they fell into the easy companionship that only they could share. The room filled with warmth and the soft glow of the early morning light, casting a golden hue over everything.

Bo, now settled between them, wagged his tail happily, enjoying the attention from both sides. Aura snuggled closer, her laughter subsiding into a contented sigh.

"Did you have your nightmare last night?" Aura asked, although she felt she already knew the answer, just as he would know she hadn't had her recurring dream. To affirm her, he shook his head.

"No. Did you?"

Aura thought back over the last few weeks, where every night seemed to be filled with a flight and bright green eyes shining out of a pitch-black face. Last night had been mercifully dreamless for them both.

Changing the topic, she asked him, "Are you excited?"

Tenney could sense the underlying question she wouldn't utter – '*Are you ready to leave me?*' He considered his answer carefully, knowing that she could tell if he was lying easier than she could read a book.

"I am," he replied. "And I am not. I have looked forward to going for so long, deferred so many times. I know this is my last shot, and if I don't take it, I may never get the opportunity again. But," he paused, pulling her in closer again, "I will hate to leave you."

Aura smiled weakly up at him, a single tear falling from her eyes that were the brightest blue he had seen in a long time. Carefully, he wiped it away, watching as his thumb pad absorbed the sparkling droplet.

"Promise me you will return for our 21st birthday, Ten?" she asked.

"Wouldn't miss it," he said, kissing the top of her head.

They stayed like that for a moment, wrapped in the comfort of each other's presence. The day ahead was filled with uncertainty, but in that instant, they found solace in their bond. Tenney knew that no matter where his journey took him, a part of him would always remain with Aura, and he would carry her strength and love with him, until it guided him back home.

**

The Wiseman family lived in a middle house of a terrace called The Barracks in the Forest of Dean, between the lane leading to an ancient Celtic hill fort and the village of Denebury. The house had been in their father's family for many generations, with Samuel himself being a true Forester, born within the St. Briavels Hundred. They moved in shortly after the twins' birth in America.

As parents often do, they loved to tell the story of how Tenney came out fighting, his small body red, his tiny hands in fists as if ready to take on anyone who crossed him. Their eyes would grow misty as Martha recalled the feeling of knowing she had a second baby to birth, a twin hidden from scans and tests. Samuel would effusively mimic the shocked faces of the medical staff as they realised another baby was being born. Unlike her brother, Aura was born blue and barely breathing. Martha, her new maternal instincts kicking in, begged for her new daughter to be reunited with her brother, and within seconds, Aura pinked up and mewed while Tenney calmed down, his small hands relaxing as he felt his sister beside him.

Four years later, they welcomed a second son, Sam, and their family was complete. They lived happily in their forester's house. A large kitchen was the heart of their home. Stretching the length of the house, a round table big enough to seat 6, divided the space into two. At the far end, over the kitchen sink and beside the aga, a window gave them a view of their long garden. At the end was a gate leading into the thick woodland surrounding them. They could see the trees as they made their gentle slope up the hill, a bed of spiky evergreens pointing to a crown of ancient oaks.

At the front end of the kitchen, they could see their driveway, and, across the lane, half hidden within the tangles of brambles and the overgrown hedge, an old, abandoned shed. They were shielded from the lane that ran the short distance to the village.

Along one wall of the kitchen, a large floor-to-ceiling bookcase was filled to bursting with different texts. At the bottom were old children's books they were loath to part with. Above them, a couple of shelves were dedicated to books on archaeology and anthropology, including some authored by Samuel Wiseman. There were also popular fiction books they had enjoyed - adventure and intrigue stories, fantasy fiction, and the occasional romantic novel that both Aura and her mother took guilty pleasure in reading. Entire sets of old and modern classics including those by Tolkien and Goodkind. The complete stories of Cadfael were squeezed between George RR Martins works and Star Wars compendiums. One length of the vast bookshelf was dedicated to books of poetry and prose, a significant portion dedicated to Tenney's namesake. Their Barrack was *wum*, home, a haven from the outside world.

Aura thumbed the small blue book in her hand. It was tatty and well-read, its pages annotated, lines and verses underlined or highlighted. She knew he was behind her without looking, could sense his presence anywhere in the house.

"Wotcha doing?" Tenney asked, taking the book from her hand. He smiled, his megawatt smile, a smile that had charmed many and seemed to light up a room as he read the title: *Maud*.

Closing his eyes as he pictured the words, he recited a verse from heart:

> *"All night have the roses heard*
>
> *The flute, violin, bassoon;*
>
> *All night has the casement jessamine stirr'd*
>
> *To the dancers dancing in tune;*
>
> *Till a silence fell with the waking bird,*
>
> *And a hush with the setting moon."*

"I want you to take it, Ten," she whispered. "Think of me when you read it."

In the warmth of their kitchen, as they waited for their family to join them, he pulled her to him again, wrapping her in his arms and wishing she was coming with him. A bit of his soul fractured, knowing she would not leave the Forest. As he held her, he spotted his favourite photo on the large American-style fridge. It was of Aura holding Bo as a tiny wriggly puppy, laughing as his tongue was caught perfectly on camera mid lick of her nose. Carefully, he removed it and placed it as a marker within the leaves of their favourite poem.

**

"Are you ready, son?" Samuel asked, a drop of maple syrup hanging precariously from his beard. Tenney gave his half smile and nodded.

At 6'4", Tenney towered over his father. He had adopted the older man's motto of "family first." He held his father in high esteem, hating to disappoint him and wishing he was more like him—wishing he was slower to anger like him. Samuel was passionate, but unlike Tenney, he seemed to know how and when to channel it. His rarely flappable nature made him feel like the safest person in the world.

People said Tenney favoured their mother, Martha. With hazel eyes and curly brown hair, Tenney was often unaware of the admiring gazes he received. He presented a confidence in himself, and his enigmatic, dismissive attitude only added to his charm and appeal. When he gave his full attention to a person, it was like they were staring into the face of a deity— all-consuming and overwhelming. But this masked the times when he couldn't control himself, when he would rage at the world or sink into a deep depression. Only Aura could still him, her calmness and nearness shaking him from his reveries. In truth, her opinion of him was the only one that mattered.

"What are you two going to do before we have to leave?" asked Martha, her "r"-less dialect often at odds with the locals' propensity to add the extra phoneme. She often rolled her eyes when her children called her 'Mar' instead of 'Ma'. Despite having lived in the Forest for over twenty years, she was fiercely proud of her Eastern New England accent. Carefully, using a spatula, she flipped the pancakes and bacon, the only meal she could reliably not burn.

Aura, watching their mother cook, replied for them. "We're going to head up to the fort, give Bo a good run, and remind Tenney of the good points of living here before he swaps trees for endless blue skies." She smiled at him then, mischief dancing in her eyes.

"Just be sure that you are back by noon, so we don't have to rush to get you to the train at Gloucester!"

Hearing his name, Bo perked up, disturbing the elderly spaniel beside him. Jess tolerated the younger dog and was happiest in her bed by the range, warming her old, tired bones.

"Looks like that's our cue then," Tenney laughed, pushing back from the table and stuffing the last of his pancake into his mouth.

Samuel looked at his younger son, a quiet boy who preferred to spend time alone in his room, usually on his computer games, his music thumping around the house. He saw how this son longed to be close to his older siblings and ached when he saw his rejected looks time after time as the twins closed ranks against the world.

"Hey, Sam," he said, pointing once again with his fork. "Why not go with them?" Samuel felt the temperature in the room drop, the atmosphere thick with unsaid things. He caught the look Tenney and Aura shared between them—he swore they communicated telepathically sometimes. He immediately regretted his question.

"Sure, Sam. You're welcome to come if you want to," Aura said diplomatically. Samuel silently blessed her as he saw Tenney's jaw clench and unclench as his hands fisted around the dog's leash.

Sam was looking forward to Tenney's departure—not that he would or could tell anyone in his family that. He was looking forward to not being 'Tenney's younger brother,' or being misjudged by his teachers and peers at school when he didn't show the same athletic prowess as his older sibling. He was looking forward to a few weeks of not feeling as though he was the lesser brother, the outcast of the family.

Staring daggers at his father, Sam simply shook his head before excusing himself from the table and returning to his room. *Maybe Theo will be online?* he thought to himself.

"Come on then, Aur," Tenney said, his jaw now relaxed, the tension dissipated. He seemed indifferent, almost cold, to Sam's reaction as he pulled on his hoodie. "Let's go."

Chapter 2

Watching from his conservatory of his house at the end of the Barracks, the old man watched the twins leave through their back gate, the small, noisy mutt yipping at their heels. As they waved to him when they passed, he forced what he hoped was a suitable smile on his leathery, sagging face.

He fidgeted in his chair as though his skin didn't sit quite right on his bones. He would wait a while longer.

**

The walk up to the fort didn't take them too long. They followed the path they both knew as well as the lines on their hands, winding through the trees. They scrambled up the ancient embankments, long reclaimed by nature, until they reached the summit.

The summit was protected from all but the harshest of winds on three sides by a ring of ancient oaks, with a gap affording them the best view from the Forest. They looked out across the landscape. On this side of the hill, the climb was steeper, the embankments higher. From here, they could see the River Severn winding through its valley on its way from the Welsh mountains to the Bristol estuary, where it merged with its sister rivers, the Wye and the Avon. The silvery snake passed the city of Gloucester, its tall cathedral tower standing as a sentinel.

Behind it, hemming the large valley in on three sides, were the Cotswolds and the Malvern Hills, their forest making up the third side of the triangle. On a clear day, they could see into Wales, catching a glimpse of the Sugar Loaf Mountain. Tenney took in the views, knowing that he would soon be in a county famed for its flat fen lands, agricultural fields, huge green houses and polytunnels filled with tulips and the immense, unending, unbroken sky.

Throwing Bo's ball, they whiled away the time in companionable silence, revelling in just being the two of them together, knowing it would be a month before they would be together again when Tenney returned home for their birthday.

Finally, they sat on the moss-covered rocks at the centre of the summit, where once stood a building from the Dobunni tribe who had called the hill home two millennia before.

"What are you most looking forward to?" asked Aura.

"Girls," Tenney answered quickly, laughing and feigning moving away as Aura swatted him with her hand.

"Seriously," she gently rebuked. "Tell me."

"I'm looking forward to the course," he answered in more measured tones. "I have wanted to study animal behaviour forever, you know that. Lincoln has one of the best degrees in this field, with the best chance of going out into the world to study animals in their natural habitat. So, I guess that, and…" he smiled cheekily at her once more. "The girls!"

After receiving another loving rebuke from his tolerant sister, he whispered, looking away from her across the view below, "But I wish you were coming with me."

She felt everything he did. Sometimes, she didn't know where he ended, and she started. The thought of him leaving filled her with a mix of pride and sadness. Aura wished that she could go too, that she had even an ounce of the courage that he had to leave this place.

She felt a deep connection to the land, to the long history of the Forest. Despite the difficulties she had experienced and the heartbreak she had suffered at the whims of others, being here, at their favourite spot, gave her focus. The sounds of the woodlands, the smell of the earth, the buzzards that glided both above her and below in the valley, helped bring her harmony. She hoped that this place would have the same effect after Tenney left. A part of her was afraid that she would just disappear on a breeze without him here, grounding her.

"Dads offered me a place on his dig team," she said. Tenney looked wide-eyed at her. "He starts a new dig at the Manor house in the village and has said that I can be on his team, learn from the 'best.'" She made air quotes with her fingers when she said "best." "I really want to do this, Ten. And I don't want to let Dad down."

"That's amazing, Aur," Tenney said, struggling to sound genuinely pleased for her. He had hoped that she would change her mind and join him, at least for the first few weeks.

Aura could sense his disappointment, but she also knew he was trying to be supportive. "We'll just have to FaceTime loads," he continued, forcing a smile. "And I can irritate Dad from afar as much as I do when I'm at home. He won't feel like he's lost a son then!"

Aura chuckled, appreciating his attempt to lighten the mood. "I'll hold you to that," she said, nudging him playfully.

They sat in silence for a few more moments, soaking in the tranquillity of their surroundings. The bond they shared was unspoken but deeply felt, a connection that transcended words.

Finally, Tenney stood up and stretched. "We should head back. Don't want to keep the family waiting."

Aura nodded and stood up as well, brushing the moss from her jeans.

Just then, Bo stopped chewing his ball and looked into the dark woods, his ears raised and body tense. Tenney turned to see what the dog had heard and was dismayed to see a group of lads and girls, a couple of large dogs straining on their leads, interrupting their solitude. The tranquillity of the moment shattered like glass.

He recognised the group as former classmates from school. The leader, a thin lad with tattoos snaking up his neck, spotted the twins and smirked.

"Well, well," he declared to his followers, his voice dripping with mockery. "What do we have here then? If it isn't Mister Popular and his bitch of a sister." The group's leader laughed, a harsh, grating sound that echoed through the trees.

Tenney sighed, running a hand through his hair while the other one held on to Aura, his grip tightening protectively. "We're just leaving, Callum," he said, his voice steady but his eyes flashing with irritation. He turned Aura back to the path, only to find it blocked by two of the girls. They somehow managed to simultaneously eye Tenney up and down while shooting dirty, jealous looks at Aura.

"Hi Tenney," one of them said, her voice a poor attempt at being flirty as she twirled a strand of overly dyed hair around her manicured finger. She licked her glossy lips, her eyes gleaming with mischief. "Remember that time behind the art studio at school? Wanna relive that with me? I know a nice quiet spot where your dirty sister can't find us." The gang laughed again, the sound cruel and mocking, as the girl tried to hide behind a stuttering laugh the fact that she had meant every word.

Aura felt a surge of anger and humiliation. She could feel Tenney's muscles tense beside her, his jaw clenching and unclenching as he struggled to keep his composure. The air was thick with tension, the peacefulness of their favourite spot now a distant memory.

Tenney took a deep breath, his eyes locking onto Callum's with a steely determination. "We're not looking for trouble," he said, his voice low and controlled. "Just let us pass."

Callum's smirk widened, but before he could respond, Bo let out a low growl, his hackles raised. The large dogs on their leads barked in response, pulling at their restraints. The sudden noise startled the group, and for a moment, the balance of power shifted.

Seizing the opportunity, Tenney tightened his grip on Aura's hand and began to move forward, his eyes never leaving Callum's. The girls reluctantly stepped aside, their expressions a mix of disappointment and resentment.

As they walked past, Aura could feel the weight of the group's stares on her back. She held her head high, refusing to let them see how much their words had hurt. Beside her, Tenney's presence was a comforting anchor, grounding her in the midst of the turmoil.

"Oi, Cal," shouted the girl Tenney had spurned, her voice tinged with hurt from being spurned. "Wotcha gonna do about him! The cheeky bugger!"

Callum knew that he wouldn't last a round with Tenney; he had been on the receiving end of one of his blows before, and he didn't want to look like an idiot in front of his mates and the girls. His eyes cast down to the small dog standing between his dogs and the Wiseman twins. He smiled wickedly.

"Looks like we have a bit of a mutt problem that needs sorting out." He unclipped the larger dogs from their leads. "Go get it!" he shouted gleefully.

The dogs barked once before setting their sights on the terrier. Time seemed to slow down as Tenney watched the two big dogs bearing down on Bo. He felt Aura behind him, quaking. He heard his voice call his dog as though he were shouting through water, watching as Bo barked back at his assailants, unaware of the vast size difference. The gang's laughter echoed around them, cruel and mocking. The bomb began to tick in his head as he saw red…

Suddenly, with a rush, time sped up as another massive creature effortlessly knocked the dogs away. A maelstrom of brown fur erupted as the new dog, as big and as vicious as a wolf, wrestled with the attacking dogs. The air was filled with growls and yelps, the scene a blur of fur and fury.

A man emerged from the woods behind this beast, moving with swift precision. He scooped Bo up without stopping, his movements fluid and practiced. He carefully handed the trembling terrier over to Aura. Tenney heard her gasp and turned to see the young man, a stranger with long black hair scraped back into a messy ponytail, staring deeply into Aura's eyes.

"Stay there," he instructed her, his hoarse, deep voice carrying a Welsh lilt. His eyes, intense and unwavering, conveyed a sense of urgency and command.

Aura clutched Bo to her chest, her heart pounding. The stranger's presence was both reassuring and unsettling. Tenney, still seething with anger, felt a strange mix of gratitude and suspicion towards the newcomer.

Fearlessly, he entered the fray of fighting canines, pulling Callum's dogs away from the brown wolfdog. One of the dogs bit his arm, but he didn't appear to feel it, shaking the animal off as if it were a rag. He bent down next to the wolfdog, their eyes never leaving those of the attacking dogs, and growled low in his throat as they stared them down. The whole clearing stilled as the seconds dragged on, the tension palpable.

The stranger and the brown wolfdog exuded the sensation of dominance, their combined presence a force of nature. The violent dogs, once aggressive and unyielding, began to falter under the intense gaze of the man and his companion. With their tails between their legs, they whimpered and retreated, running into the woodland, their spirits broken.

The clearing remained silent, the echoes of the confrontation lingering in the air. The stranger stood tall, his eyes still fixed on the spot where the dogs had disappeared, his breathing steady and controlled. The brown wolfdog, equally composed, stayed by his side, its eyes gleaming with a fierce loyalty.

Tenney and Aura watched in awe, their hearts pounding. The man's display of strength and control was both impressive and unsettling. As the adrenaline began to fade, they felt a renewed sense of gratitude and curiosity towards the enigmatic stranger who had come to their aid.

"My dogs!" cried Callum. "What did you do?"

The man turned to Callum, seeming in disbelief that he had spoken to him, a look of utter contempt on his face. He pulled the same trick on Callum as he had done on the dogs. The acrid scent of urine wafted on the breeze as Callum wet himself. Gulping, dominated by a person of greater will and power, he turned on his heel, racing back into the woods, his gang hot on his heels.

Tenney was equal parts impressed and perturbed by this strange man and his wolfdog. While he was grateful that Bo had been saved from danger, he hadn't liked the way the man had stared at Aura, his green eyes flashing as though he had recognised her. He also hadn't appreciated her reaction to him, as though on some level she knew him as well.

Standing at his full height, Tenney forced Aura, with Bo in her arms, behind him. He stood a few inches above the man, unsure for the first time in his life if he would win if this man decided to fight him. This person exuded a feral, untamed strength and power from every pore.

"Thanks, mate," Tenney began, his voice steady but cautious.

The man just smiled. His wolfdog, one of the biggest dogs Tenney had ever seen, its powerful shoulders reaching the same height as the man's waist, licked the bite wound on his arm. After sizing Tenney up, he again turned his focus on Aura. He smiled a closed-lip smile, his green eyes sparkling with an unsettling familiarity.

"*Fy nghariad*," he said. Then in English, "Take care of that dog." He smiled one last time, looking at Aura as though he wanted to memorise her face. Then he turned back, disappearing into the shadows of the trees, his wolfdog scouting ahead.

Tenney let out a breath he hadn't realised he had been holding. He turned to Aura and checked her over, pulling her into his arms as he asked over and over if she was okay.

Aura nodded, her eyes wide and still fixed on the spot where the man had disappeared. "I'm fine," she whispered, her voice trembling slightly. "But who was that?"

"I don't know," Tenney replied, his voice filled with a mix of confusion and concern. "But I don't think this is the last we'll see of him."

They stood there for a moment, holding each other tightly, the weight of the encounter settling over them. The forest, once a place of solace and peace, now felt charged with an unfamiliar tension. As they made their way back home, the shadows seemed to stretch longer, and the rustling leaves whispered secrets they couldn't quite hear.

**

The stranger watched them as they made their way home, he and his companion staying in the shadows to avoid being seen. As the twins left the shelter of the woods and walked along the path behind the barracks, he pulled an old Nokia from his back pocket and sent a message.

I've found them.

His fingers moved swiftly over the keys, the message brief but loaded with significance. He glanced up, his eyes narrowing as he tracked the twins' progress. The wolfdog at his side remained alert, its ears twitching at every sound.

The stranger's face was a mask of determination and resolve. He had been searching for a long time, and now that he had found them, he knew the next steps would be crucial. The shadows seemed to cling to him, as if the darkness itself was his ally.

As the twins disappeared from view, he slipped the phone back into his pocket and melted deeper into the forest, his presence as fleeting as a whisper in the wind. The hunt was far from over, but for now, he had the advantage.

**

The old man watched from the conservatory, his grin stretching so wide it seemed too big for his face. His eyes gleamed with a mix of satisfaction and anticipation as he saw the dark-haired man and the brown wolf. He was finally close to getting what he wanted.

The conservatory, filled with the scent of mildew and the faint aroma of tea, seemed to darken as his thoughts turned to his plans. These two arriving now were the major pieces of his puzzle. Their presence signalled the beginning of the endgame.

He leaned back in his chair, the leather creaking under his weight, and steepled his fingers. The grin never left his face as he contemplated the next steps. Now that the wolves had made their appearance, the die had been cast, and finally, after waiting for such a long time, things were falling into place.

The old man's heart raced with a mix of excitement and impatience. He had waited so long, and now, the culmination of his efforts was within reach. The shadows in the room seemed to dance with his dark thoughts, and he revelled in the feeling of power and control.

Chapter 3

When they arrived back home, they were met with a hive of activity. Their dad had brought down Tenney's large travel rucksack, a smaller backpack, and his laptop bag, bulging with books and his computer. Their mum was fussing, adding a packet of pasta to the larger bag.

"Have you packed enough of everything?" she asked, all thought of a greeting gone from her mind. "Socks? Pants? Tops? At least to last the first week until you figure out the laundry system."

Tenney replied yes to each question, his voice steady. Silently, he shared a look with Aura.

Don't tell them about what happened at the fort, he willed her. As though hearing him, Aura nodded once. She would keep it, as she kept all of the things he hid from their family, secret. Their mother continued.

"Is your phone charged? Have you got your wallet? Dad wants to put a little something in there to tide you over for the first week." Tenney replied yes, it was in his backpack, along with his train tickets and documents to show the university.

Tenney moved over to the bookshelf and retrieved the book Aura had given him, her picture still acting as a bookmark. He carefully added it to his backpack and put his now slightly fuller wallet in his back pocket.

Their mum's fussing continued, her worry manifesting in a flurry of questions and last-minute additions to the bags. "Do you have your charger? What about your toiletries? And don't forget your jacket, it might get cold."

Tenney nodded, his patience unwavering. "Yes, Ma, I've got everything."

Aura watched the scene unfold, a small smile playing on her lips. Despite the chaos, there was a comforting familiarity to it all. She knew Tenney was ready for this new chapter, even if their parents – and she - were struggling to let go.

As Tenney zipped up his bags, he turned to Aura and gave her a reassuring nod. They both knew that no matter what challenges lay ahead, they would face them together, just as they always had.

And then, just like that, it was time for them to leave. Tenney bent down to say goodbye to the two dogs. Jess gave a solitary wag of her tail. They all squeezed into the car, with Aura in the middle and Sam snagging the space behind the passenger seat, forcing Tenney to fold his long legs behind his father.

"Ow! Watch those knees, Son!" Samuel exclaimed.

They drove down the lane and through the village, passing the pub, village stores, primary school, and church. Aura pointed out the gates to the Manor house. They continued down the main road out of Denebury, with houses on either side spaced out and clinging precariously to the sides of the hill. They caught another glimpse of the Severn Valley before rounding another corner. All too soon, they were on the A48, driving to the city.

**

The old Land Rover pulled in behind the family's estate car at the train station. He watched them. The tall boy pulled a variety of bags from the boot, his sister helping as he struggled with the countless straps. He observed the way they interacted, how they subconsciously sought each other out, communicating without words. He felt the spark between them—untrained and dangerous.

If the boy was leaving and she stayed… he couldn't bear to think about the consequences of losing her again so soon after finding her.

When the family walked onto the station platform, he left his vehicle and followed them.

**

The train pulled slowly into the station. The time had come, and suddenly Tenney felt scared. He wished Aura would ask him to stay, even though he knew she wouldn't. She understood that this was something he needed and wanted to do. Her eyes, now a softer, sadder blue, looked up at him as he embraced each of his family members. When he reached her, he whispered that he would be back soon. Their birthday wasn't far away. He felt her small hands ball up the back of his hoodie, her tears staining his front.

Painfully, he pulled away. An invisible thread between them stretched taut. As the doors opened, he forced his suddenly heavy feet to step into the carriage. Finding his seat, grateful it was by the window on the platform side, he felt as though more than a pane of glass separated them. Tenney placed his hand on the glass, Aura mirroring it on the other side until their father gently pulled her away as the train began to move.

Tenney strained to see her before she disappeared around the bend. The thread snapped. As he stared at the ghostly print of her hand, the bomb began to tick in his head as he saw red…

**

Aura felt weightless, supported only by her father's hands. As the train disappeared, it seemed to take her breath with it. Through a thick fog, as the world began to darken, she heard her mother scream. She fell backward and was caught by powerful hands.

"Tenney?" she murmured. The last thing she saw were emerald, green eyes. The last thing she heard before the darkness took her was a strong, deep Welsh voice shouting, "Get him back!"

**

Tenney sat still on the train, oblivious to the other passengers. He couldn't think beyond the ticking in his head. A vice squeezed his brain, heart, and lungs. His fists balled up in his lap. The passenger beside him, sensing the waves of fury emanating from him, moved to sit elsewhere.

Running on autopilot, he changed trains at Birmingham. As he approached the next leg of his journey away from her, he was jostled by three men pushing past him. The ticking inside him sped up as he followed them onto the train which would take him one step closer to Lincoln.

Chapter 4

Jude Marcello stretched her aching limbs. As summer had passed and the days became more autumnal, she could feel the effects of the weather on her body. Today would be her last day treading the streets of Lincoln. As she pulled on her regulation boots, strapped the tool belt around her waist, slipped the hi-vis over her jacket, and placed the round bowler hat over her curls, now tamed into a tight bun, a part of her felt relief. Tomorrow, she would take the month off as planned, spend some time with her mother, who had been quieter than usual, and prepare herself for her new role as a desk sergeant.

She stared at herself in the mirror. Constable Marcello stared back. Behind her, smiling broadly so that the freckles stretched over her nose, was her best friend and beat partner, Ellie Brown.

"No arguments, I am taking you out tonight to celebrate!" Ellie declared. "You can continue to convince me that my new partner will be half as good as you, and I will lament that we won't be hiking up and down Steep Hill together anymore, wrestling drunks and helping people find lost keys."

Jude couldn't help but smile. Ellie always knew how to cheer her up, her full brown lips spreading over her teeth, and her dark honey-coloured eyes smiling back at her friend.

"Ready?"

"Ready," Jude replied.

Together, they stepped out into the morning sunshine and faced the city of Lincoln.

**

His gaze was hyper-focused on the men who had pushed past him. He couldn't think straight. He needed to act. His mind ticked faster, his hands clenched tighter, the knuckles turning white. He followed them as they made their final change onto the train to Nottingham. One of the men noticed him staring and confronted him.

**

The day had been slow so far, their shift nearly over, when their radios crackled to life. A fight had broken out on one of the trains coming into Lincoln. The perpetrators were being held at the train station. Ellie and Jude, finishing their walk down High Street, turned right and made their way to the station.

**

Tenney sat in a room, alone for the first time since he had left. His knuckles were cracked and bleeding, his eye throbbed where a fist had made contact, and his chest felt bruised. But the physical pain was nothing compared to the inner torment his soul was experiencing. He felt fractured, split in two.

She called to him in the darkness, but he couldn't find her. The momentary reprieve of solitude failed to stop the returning waves of rage and unadulterated pain that tore through him, leaving him powerless to stop them.

**

"Fight on a train from Nottingham. Three young lads got a beating from a single man. It took most of us to bring the guy down." The guard paused, panting as he moved the cool pack from his bruised eye. "Guy must be high on something… His strength… and his eyes… my God!" He shook his head in disbelief.

Jude gently touched his arm, forcing him to stop as he began to ramble. "Where is he now?" she asked calmly.

"We've got him in the guard room." The cops looked at each other.

"Lead the way," said Jude.

Paramedics were nursing the three men from the train. They were badly bruised, with gashes on their heads. A couple of them looked dazed. As she passed them, she overheard one of the men talking to a medic as she strapped a piece of gauze to his forehead. He said he had noticed the man watching them, and when he wandered over to ask what his problem was, the man just went crazy. The paramedic put a comforting arm over his shoulders. She looked up at the PCs and sombrely shook her head.

Jude and Amelia were led to the guard's office. Through the window of the locked door, she saw another young man, head bowed, brown hair obscuring his face. His hands, cable-tied at the wrists, were clenched together. Fists that were bruised and torn from the power of his punches.

"What's his name?" Jude asked the guard.

"His ticket said Tennyson Wiseman, originated in Gloucester, boarded the train to Lincoln, changed first at Birmingham, then Nottingham. That's when the fight broke out, but from other witnesses making the same journey, he had been bubbling for the past few hours. Muttering to himself, agitated, you know? Some claim they saw him crack a window, but we're still waiting on the report about that. He's not saying much now though. I mean, he's more animal. Savage. And strong!" He handed the keys to the office to Jude, grateful that this problem would no longer be his to bear.

Unlocking the door, Jude quietly slipped in, trying not to appear as a threat. His whole body screamed of tension and stress. She could see the curve of his spine, the shape of his muscles through his hoodie. Even seated, he appeared tall; she estimated that when he stood up, he would be well over six feet. Carefully, feeling her joints crackle in her knees, she hunkered down in front of him. She saw his eyes flicker beneath long, dark eyelashes. His mouth was moving, cupid bow lips muttering what sounded like the same line over and over – "I am here at the gate alone, I am here at the gate alone, I am here…"

"Tennyson?" she whispered.

He paused. She tried again.

"Tennyson, my name is Jude, and I want to help you."

He looked up at her. She felt taken aback, knocked off course. She was right; cupid bow lips in a face that would make any talent scout look up. One of his eyes was starting to swell shut, but she could see the fire burning hot behind his hazel eyes. Around the pupils, separating them from the irises, were thin red lines. She could feel the waves of anger and volatility rolling off him, and yet she couldn't look away. She took a deep breath, gave herself a talking-to, and tried again.

"Tennyson, will you let me help you?"

**

He tried to remember the lines, the words they had learned by heart, hoping they might help him connect to her. But all he felt was the terrifying void of nothingness. She wasn't there. She wasn't listening. Her voice in his mind had silenced for the first time since they were children.

Tennyson? He heard her, finally she called him. But something was wrong. Her cadence was off, her accent different. She never called him by his birth name.

"Tennyson? My name is Jude…" This time he heard her, and he looked up. Eyes like honeyed chocolate sparkled. The golden dagger of his nightmare flew into his heart.

**

Ellie stood outside the room, watching Jude through the door.

"Has he been drinking?"

The guard shook his head. "We don't think so. We couldn't smell any on his breath."

"Drugs?"

"Possibly. That's what we think, but there are no track marks on his arms and nothing in his bags or pockets. Not even cigarettes or vapes."

"Where are his belongings?"

The guard directed Ellie to another table. On it was a large rucksack, the kind backpackers take on their adventures. The top of the bag held a textbook titled *An Introduction to Animal Behaviour*, with a cover image of a pack of wolves. She flicked through it; the guy had obviously been reading it.

The rest of the bag was filled with enough t-shirts, jeans, jumpers, and pants to last a couple of weeks, along with some basic food provisions—pasta and suchlike. The second bag contained his laptop, more books, and an iPad. In his smaller backpack were his iPhone, headphones, wallet, and more books. The wallet held his train tickets—just as the guard said, Gloucester to Lincoln, with changes at Birmingham and Nottingham. There was about £100 in cash, a bank card, student ID (confirming her suspicions), and a driver's licence. Tucked down the side of the bag was a thin blue book. It looked old, its hard cover stained and mottled from use, its spine cracked from reading. Embossed in gold letters on the front was the title: *Maud* by Alfred, Lord Tennyson.

Carefully, intrigued, she opened the book. The pages were yellowed, the publication date read 1921. Lines and verse had been annotated, underlined. Something fluttered from within its pages. Leaning down, Ellie scooped up a photo of a young blond girl, a squirming puppy in her hands. Happiness radiated out of the image. Ellie approached Jude and the man.

"I think he's a new student, headed for the Uni. Bad way to start." Jude shook her head. Ellie had broken some sort of trance she had slipped into. She gingerly stood up and went to her friend. "He had this picture inside a book of poetry," Ellie said, handing the photo to Jude. "It might be his girlfriend or something." Acting instinctively, Jude took the photo and returned to her charge. She held the photo of the blonde up so he could see it.

Tenney sat bolt upright, the movement so sudden, so unexpected Jude almost fell back. He stared at the picture, hungrily. "Who's this?" she asked; "your girlfriend?"

Tenney smiled, and then laughed cruelly. "Stupid bitch," he spat. In one move he jumped up, thrust his hands out as far as the makeshift cuffs would allow him, grasping for the picture.

Thinking back to that moment, Jude still wasn't sure how it had happened. The change in him was as marked as the change from day to night. The waves of anger left him. He seemed defeated, hollowed out, exhausted. As his finger had touched the image, a bloodied print left in its wake, he became more lucid. He apologised for his behaviour, saying he did not know what had come over him. Promising that it wouldn't happen again. His eyes began to clear, the pupils becoming a normal size, the red around the iris diminishing as the hazel reappeared. He answered their questions, begged the officers to let him go. They discussed their options. He had no priors, but he was obviously mentally unstable.

After calling in to their Commanding Officer, Jude was a little surprised to hear that they were to release Tennyson. She relayed her conversation to Ellie, and together they decided to hold him in the guard's office for a few more hours. They watched him closely, ensuring he remained calm. Before releasing him, they issued a warning and asked him to report to the police station tomorrow at 9 a.m. sharp. They also informed him that he was banned from using trains in and out of Lincoln and would need to find another form of transport.

Tennyson thanked them, washed the blood off his hands, the shake associated with shock finally kicking in. He collected his belongings and meekly left. Jude watched him go, her brown eyes reflecting the puzzlement she felt at the events of the afternoon.

He is quite handsome, she caught herself thinking, as she watched him walk towards the University. *When he isn't frowning…*

"Ready to go, Jude?" Ellie asked. Jude nodded, before following her partner out of the station. It was sometime later that she found she still had the photo of the blonde in her pocket.

**

Chief Superintendent Mikkelson replaced the handset after speaking to Officer Marcello and leaned back in his chair, stretching his long, lithe legs under his antique desk. He Pressed his fingertips together and tapped them lightly on his bottom lip, his light, golden eyes crinkling as he gave a small smile.

Things were in motion. His vow not to interfere was one he was willing to break to ensure the future unfolded as it must. He had invested too much to ensure these people were in the right place at the right times, and now he couldn't simply spectate anymore. To achieve the end game, the boy had to be free before it was too late, and Jude Marcello was the key to that success.

He rolled his powerful shoulders back, revelling in the familiar itch between his shoulder blades. The next phase was about to begin. Quickly, he made a decision and leaned forward across the desk, pressing the intercom button to his PA.

"Asima, connect me to Gloucester City Police Department…"

Chapter 5

Tenney arrived at the campus and his halls of residence, feeling confused and unfocused. He stumbled, his heart clenching painfully in his chest.

A girl. He had nearly knocked her down. He apologised, and she smiled flirtatiously. Something stirred inside him, toying with the strands of the thread that had been torn away from him. She moved on, casting a cute glance back over her shoulder.

Tenney smiled darkly.

After signing in at the main office, Tenney received the key to his room. The weight of the metal felt oddly significant in his hand, a tangible symbol of his new, solitary life. He showered quickly, the hot water doing little to wash away the anxiety clinging to him. Dressed in fresh clothes, he made his way down to the student bar, hoping to drown his homesickness in the familiar burn of alcohol.

Finding a perch on a bar stool, he ordered a whisky chaser. The warm, rich liquid shot down, burning his mouth and throat in a way that was both painful and oddly comforting. He quickly soothed the fire with a pint of lager, the coolness a stark contrast to the whisky's heat. The bartender watched him with a knowing look, recognising the signs of a homesick fresher trying to find his footing in an unfamiliar world.

"Another," Tenney said, pulling out his wallet with a hand that trembled slightly. He wasn't sure if it was from the alcohol or the overwhelming sense of displacement.

As he turned away from his fifth chaser, a girl walked up behind him and tapped him on the shoulder. "Hi again," she said, smiling suggestively. Tenney looked her up and down, taking in her long hair, dyed a vibrant red and straightened to perfection. She looked about eighteen, a fresher like him, but a couple of years younger. Her short skirt and low-cut top signalled her desperate desire to be noticed. Well, he noticed her.

He didn't say anything, only held out his hand to her. She took it, her touch a brief anchor in the storm of his emotions and allowed herself to be helped onto the barstool beside him. As they drank together, she began to whisper in his ear, her words a soothing balm to his troubled mind. Whispers turned to kisses, and his mind, addled by more than the strong drinks he had downed, let her lead him out of the bar.

Inside, Tenney's thoughts were a chaotic swirl. He missed Aura with an intensity that bordered on physical pain. The bond they shared was more than just familial; it was a lifeline, and without her, he felt adrift. The girl beside him was a temporary distraction, a way to numb the ache of separation. But even as he followed her, a part of him remained distant, locked in a silent scream for the twin who was his other half.

They found a secluded spot, away from prying eyes. The moonlight filtered through the trees, casting a silvery glow on their surroundings. He pushed her against a rough, bark-covered tree, and they kissed again, desperately. Their hands roamed each other's bodies, exploring with a feverish intensity as their ardour rose.

Tenney gasped and fell backward, his breath coming in ragged bursts. What was happening to him? His mind was a chaotic storm, the rational part of his brain screaming at him to stop as the invisible ends of the thread frayed further, breaking down his sanity.

The girl grabbed his hoodie and pulled him back to her, her eyes glinting with a mix of desire and curiosity. Under the light of the full moon, Tenney responded to her touch, his movements driven by an uncontrollable force. She smiled, her lips parting in a gasp of pleasure as they continued their frantic embrace.

**

The next morning. The second day of the full moon.

Sunlight broke through the clouds of acrid smoke, casting dappled shadows on the ground. Tenney found himself back at the fort, lying amidst a field of bodies. The once serene woodland was now a scene of chaos. Flames licked hungrily at the trees, their fiery tongues consuming leaves and branches with a crackling roar. The scent of burning wood and foliage was overpowering, a mix of pine, oak, and the unmistakable tang of scorched earth.

The fire cast an eerie, flickering light, turning the forest into a landscape of shadows and glowing embers. Trees, once towering and majestic, now stood as blackened skeletons, their branches reaching out like twisted, charred fingers. The ground was a carpet of ash and smouldering debris, each step releasing a puff of grey dust into the air.

In the distance, the haunting screams of the dying echoed, a chilling reminder of the devastation. Tenney's eyes flashed over the part of his soul he had lost as she lay lifeless before him. A black form crept up his body, the stench of sulphur turning his blood to ice.

Tenney woke up screaming, the morning dew clinging to his skin. His body throbbed with pain, each ache a reminder of the previous night's excesses. The girl's hand was splayed over his chest, her garish pink nails leaving angry red marks on his skin. He turned to look at her, their clothes strewn haphazardly around them. A wave of nausea hit him, and he quickly sat up, running a hand through his dishevelled hair, disturbing the girl beside him.

"Morning…" she purred, moving closer to him, her voice a seductive whisper.

Tenney glowered at her, pulling away from her grasp as he reached for his jeans. The girl's attempts to tempt him back only fuelled his repulsion. In the cold light of day, the previous night's allure had vanished, replaced by a gnawing sense of regret. He turned away from her and continued to dress, pulling his hoodie over his head. He hunkered down to pull on his trainers, and in one fluid motion, stood back up again.

"Oi!" she yelled, realisation dawning on her that he wasn't going to stay, shattering her naive dreams of a romantic day. "Don't you even want to know my name?"

"No," Tenney said, his voice cold and detached as he walked away, never looking back. His eyes were bloodshot, a halo of red around his irises, his soul in turmoil.

He wandered through the streets as businesses opened, people rushing past him to open shops or attend early morning meetings. The River Witham flowed serenely to the Brayford Pool; narrow boats moored behind the small island. The restaurants on the wharf stood silent after another busy night of business. Tenney took none of it in, his mind slipping further into the darkness with each step. Finally, he found himself on The Strait, where the pavements turned to cobbles and medieval buildings hung over the street like the branches of trees, laden with spring growth over the lanes around his home. The air was thick with history, but Tenney felt only the weight of his own despair.

A laugh, youthful and happy, pierced the gloom. He saw the ghosts of two young girls, no more than nine or ten years old, their blonde hair streaming behind them as they moved together. He knew their faces—identical in every way except for their eyes. Blue eyes beamed at him from the face of one, while her sister, with eyes of a different hue, pulled her away as they skipped up the hill.

"Aura?" he whispered, his voice trembling. The ghost turned and smiled at him, beckoning him forward, speaking a language he did not understand but felt deep in his soul. Lost and desperate, he followed the spirits as they guided him from The Strait to the base of Steep Hill, each step echoing with the memories of a bond that transcended time and space. The cobblestones beneath his feet seemed to pulse with the energy of the past, and for a moment, he felt a flicker of hope amidst the encroaching darkness.

**

Jude had just sat down at a table on the veranda to enjoy a morning coffee at her favourite café. Despite the late night out with Ellie, she was so accustomed to getting up early for work that she couldn't sleep in. She decided to treat herself on her first day of leave. The café, nestled in an old church halfway up Steep Hill, was a sanctuary. Jude lived a few streets over, and the walk up the hill was worth it for the frothy coffee and toasted tea cake that awaited her.

Pulling out her phone, she checked again. Still no message from her mum, her location still turned off. A knot of worry formed in her belly. Her mother had always been flighty, disappearing for days or weeks at a time, chasing down some story. But since her dad had passed ten years before, she had withdrawn from the world, from her only child. Jude felt the distance between them growing every day, wishing that she was enough to pull her mum back into the world. She was used to not getting a reply immediately, sometimes for several days. But this was the longest time she had been gone with no word…

Jude's thoughts drifted back to her childhood, to the days when her mother was her hero. She remembered the bedtime stories, the spontaneous adventures, and the way her mother could make the mundane seem magical. But those memories were tainted by the years of absence, the missed birthdays, and the countless times she had waited by the phone, hoping for a call that never came. The grief of losing her father had only deepened the chasm between them. Jude had tried to be strong, to be the anchor her mother needed, but it never seemed to be enough.

She sighed, feeling the familiar ache of longing and frustration. Why couldn't her mother see how much she needed her? Why did she always have to chase after something that seemed more important than her own daughter? Jude's eyes stung with unshed tears as she stared at her phone, willing it to light up with a message, a sign that her mother was safe and thinking of her.

Then there was the mystery of Tennyson Wiseman. She looked at the picture of the girl, intending to return it to the police station so he could claim it when he reported there in an hour's time. His bloodied fingerprint was still visible over the girl's face. Jude resigned herself to never knowing more than the few scant details she had of this strange man who had haunted her dreams the night before.

Rolling her stiff shoulders, she leaned down to take a sip of her drink and spotted a figure moving slowly up the hill. Hood pulled over his head and hands firmly inside the pocket at the front, there was something familiar about him.

As he passed, he turned to look at her, hazel eyes meeting brown. She gasped, spilling some coffee on her top. He gave a small, crooked smile, as though he and she shared a secret, before turning away again and continuing his way up the hill.

Leaving a tip under the mug, Jude left her half-finished coffee, her mind a whirl of questions and emotions. The worry for her mother, the mystery of Tenney, and the weight of her own loneliness pressed heavily on her heart as she walked away from the café.

**

The girls were moving faster, their ghostly forms slipping through the morning mist. Tenney found it harder to keep up with them, his breath coming in ragged gasps. When he reached Castle Hill, they had disappeared completely, their laughter echoing eerily around the ancient buildings.

To his right, the mighty wall of Lincoln Castle loomed, a testament to centuries of history and power. To his left, the cathedral stood majestic, its three towers reigning over the city below as they touched the sky. Scaffolding surrounded the towers, a team of renovators about to start their day cleaning and repairing the weathered masonry.

Tenney felt the walls of the city closing in on him, the weight of his thoughts pressing down like a physical force. He needed air, he needed to escape the claustrophobia of the narrow streets and the oppressive memories they held.

He turned left and crept past the workmen, their voices a distant murmur. By the time they realised they had an intruder, he had already scaled the scaffolding to the highest point. The wind whipped around him, and for a moment, he felt a fleeting sense of freedom, standing above the city, looking down on the world that seemed so far removed from his inner turmoil.

**

At Castle Hill, Jude turned on the spot, frantically trying to spot him. She spun around, her eyes darting over the walls of the castle, the fudge shop, the closed bars, and tourist shops. Where could he be?

A commotion at the cathedral caught her attention. Workmen were yelling and pointing upwards. Following their gazes, she looked up and saw a solitary figure standing on the edge of the scaffolding, his arms open as though he might fly.

She rushed over and asked a mason what had happened. He told her that the man had vaulted a fence and climbed to the highest platform. If any of the renovation workers or cathedral security guards tried to get close enough to pull him back, they were thrown violently back onto the scaffold platform.

"He is strong," the man said, "and he growled at them inarticulately. His eyes… well, his eyes were red like he was on drugs."

"He was crazy," one onlooker said.

"Not 'all there' in the head," said another, tapping the side of his head.

Jude asked what the fastest way to reach the man was. The renovation worker pointed to a tall ladder that led up to a series of platforms and more ladders until they reached the highest point. Jude knew that the best way to approach him would be alone and quickly. She could see his shape clearly as he looked out over the city.

"I'll go up," Jude said, determination in her voice.

She stood at the base of the ladder and took a deep breath. Heights had always unnerved her. Closing her eyes, she remembered what her dad had always told her.

"Take a deep breath and try. If you fail, at least you tried, but if you don't try, you've failed already. Mind over matter, Judy. You can do anything if you just try."

Thoughts of her dad calmed her racing heartbeat. She took a deep breath and gripped the ladder.

"Hold on, love!" one of the workers rushed up to her, hard hat in hand.

"Thanks," she replied, placing it over her loose black curls. Damping down the last of her fear, she began the ascent, each step a testament to her resolve.

**

Tenney looked out over the city. His hair blew across his face as he felt the wind embrace him. He could see the castle, the higgledy piggledy streets below; in the distance the river Witham flowed through the town and past the campus where he should have been. He saw the people gathering in the Minster Yard and on Castle Hill below, saw the lights and heard the sirens of the police cars and ambulance as they pulled up to the cathedral. He was detached from it. His mind was consumed by one thing, and one thing only: Aura.

He stared out, his vision blurring as memories and hallucinations intertwined. Through the mists of the present, he believed he saw various incarnations of his sister, different people with the same soul, the same wild blue eyes. Images flashed through his mind like a slide show, each one more vivid than the last. He could hear her laugh, a sound that had always calmed him, and see her smile, a beacon of support in his darkest moments. He saw her heart break as he left the station, her silent scream reverberating through him, a haunting echo of his own pain.

Then, the visions darkened. He saw black ghouls, their long, skeletal fingers grasping at her, pulling the very air from her lungs, making her vanish into the void. The sight filled him with a cold, paralyzing dread. He felt powerless, a mere spectator to his sister's torment.

He repeated the verse he hadn't known he had been mumbling as he journeyed to this point. *"Come into the garden, Maud, for the black bat, night, has flown, I am here at the gate alone."*

As the madness finally fully engulfed him, he moved closer to the edge, waiting for the right time to jump.

**

Reaching the top, trying not to look down in case her bravery left her, Jude carefully approached him. The wind had picked up, whipping around them and making the platform quiver.

"Hello? Tennyson?" she called out tentatively, her voice barely carrying over the gusts.

"Aura…?" he said, almost too quietly for Jude to hear above the wind. Jude gasped in surprise. He had looked half-crazy yesterday. Today, she could see he had succumbed to the madness completely. His eyes were wild, unfocused, and he seemed to look right through her, his mouth set in a straight line, his jaw tense. She thought she saw disappointment in his eyes that she wasn't this Aura person.

"Tennyson," she called to him again, afraid to get too near when she saw how precariously close to the edge he stood. "It's Jude. Let me help you."

He smiled manically, a chilling sight. "I am here at the gate alone," he said, his voice eerily calm.

"What was that, Tennyson?" Jude felt sure she had misheard him.

"She is coming, my own my sweet; were it ever so airy a tread, my heart would hear her and beat, were it earth in an earthy bed…" He took another step towards the precipice. Jude's instincts screamed at her to rush forward and pull him back, but as the wind rose, the platform shook. If they were both going to survive this, she had to do this carefully, take her time, and then, hopefully, get close enough to pull him back.

"Tennyson?" she called to him, her voice steady despite the fear gripping her. "Who's coming?"

"My dove, my dear…" None of what he was saying made any sense. His words were a jumble of poetry and madness.

She tried again, remembering the girl in the photo which was in her pocket. "Who is she, Tennyson? Who is Aura?"

"She is mine: forever and ever mine…" His voice was filled with a desperate longing, and Jude could see the depth of his torment. She knew she had to reach him, to break through the madness that had consumed him.

Desperately buying time so she could reach him and pull him back, Jude stepped closer. The vertiginous drop sent her spinning, her stomach lurching with fear. Closing her eyes, she reached out and felt the rough texture of the cathedral under her hand. After taking a deep breath, she pulled out the image and refocused once more on Tennyson.

"Ok, Tennyson," she began, her voice steady despite the turmoil inside her. "Tell me about her…"

Tenney's eyes clouded over as he looked out into the abyss. Aura was calling him, beckoning him closer. But her hand was fading, slipping away like a wisp of smoke.

"She fits to me exactly; she can hide within me when she doesn't want to be seen or stand in front of me and shield me from myself. She is strong, I didn't know how strong. She let me go, even when I could see that it broke her heart. She is impulsive, passionate, adventurous, stubborn, intelligent, powerful… She is me, and I am her. I am not me without her."

The last few words were spoken with such passion, his reddened eyes now streaming with tears. His grip on the world and reality seemed to be slackening. Jude moved tentatively forward again, knocking something with her foot. It vibrated through her boot. Looking down, she saw the mobile phone rattling on the platform. Acting on her instincts, Jude bent down and picked it up, answering it before it disconnected.

A woman's voice, American, desperate with worry, spoke: "Tenney? Tenney, is that you?"

"Ma'am, this is Police Constable Jude Marcello," she answered, automatically using her former title. "May I ask who is calling?"

"The police? Where's Tenney? Where is my son? We need him! We need him to come home to us, we need him. NOW! It's his sister, she's…" The lady on the line stifled a sob. "Aura, she's dying…"

Jude gasped when she heard Aura's name. His sister? None of this was making any sense to her. The lady on the end of the phone was still talking, rapidly.

"I'm sorry, ma'am," said Jude. "Could you repeat that, please?" Jude listened intently as Tennyson's mother explained that his sister was close to death, comatose in the hospital. She asked Mrs. Wiseman to hold and turned back to Tenney.

"It's your mother, Tenney," she said, using his nickname, hoping to reach him. "Aura is ill. She's in the hospital. They want you to come home. Straight away. It sounds serious." Tenney's eyes began to clear slightly, the last strand of the thread holding tight. He began to turn around to face Jude again.

"What did you say?" he asked, his voice trembling.

"Your sister, Aura. This is her, isn't it?" she showed him the crumpled image in her shaky hand. "She's ill—very ill. Your family needs you to come home. Now. Come away from the edge, Tenney. Let's go home."

Tenney's eyes cleared further, the hazel colour she remembered from the day before pushing out the black of his pupils, the red halo diminishing. He moved to turn back from the edge, reaching out for the picture. As he twisted around, his foot slipped, and he cried out as he started to fall…

**

In his office, the Superintendent hung up his phone, a sense of urgency tightening his chest. Things were in motion. They weren't too late. Unlocking a drawer in his desk, he pulled out a private mobile phone and dialled the first number on it.

"You've been told where they are?" he said before the receiver had time to greet him. "When you have them, find Hedge."

He hung up and leaned back in his chair, the weight of responsibility pressing down on him. It would be up to them to see that these people were ready for what was to come. He had already interfered enough. His siblings would not be pleased.

The Superintendent's thoughts drifted to his siblings, each with their own agendas and powers. They had always been a formidable force, but their unity was fragile. He knew that his actions would be scrutinised, and any misstep could lead to dire consequences. Yet, he felt a deep conviction that what he was doing was necessary, even if it meant facing their wrath.

He had to ensure that Hedge and the others were prepared, that they understood the gravity of their roles. The future depended on it.

**

Jude darted forward. She didn't know how she did it; one minute he was falling, the next she had grabbed the material of his hoodie, clutching onto his arm. But he was slipping, her grip weakening. The rheumatic joints in her hands screamed in agony, each second feeling like an eternity. The hard hat slipped from her head, falling past him. The sickening thud it made at the base of the tower filled her with dread.

He looked at her, his hazel eyes now totally clear, filled with a new purpose. They stared right at her, into her, and she felt something give inside her, a surge of strength she didn't know she possessed. With every ounce of power left to her, she pulled him up and away from the abyss. They fell together onto the planks of the scaffolding, Tenney landing atop Jude, her arms tight around his shoulders. The 'thing' inside her amplified as she felt the weight of him, a strange energy coursing through her veins.

She held him tighter, his ear pressed against her rapidly beating heart. He started to speak, but his voice was muffled by her fleece.

"What did you say?" she asked, her voice trembling with relief and exhaustion.

He pulled back slightly from her, his eyes searching hers. "Take me home."

Chapter 6

What had she done? What had she committed herself to? It was totally out of character for her. As she watched him descend the final rungs of the ladder, his feet back on solid ground, she looped one arm through his, the other she wrapped around his waist, ushering him through the large crowd of onlookers. The murmurs and curious stares of the crowd faded into the background as she focused on getting him to safety.

She knew these streets, knew the quiet ones that would lead to her flat. The familiar paths offered a small comfort amidst the chaos. Settling him on the sofa, the photo gripped tightly between his fingers, she hastily packed her bag for a few nights away. As she packed, she phoned the police station, explaining what had happened, that she had been onsite and would take Tenney to the hospital.

She just failed to admit that the hospital they would be going to was in Gloucester, the other side of the country, 150 miles away. The lie of omission weighed heavily on her, but she pushed it aside, focusing on the immediate need to get Tenney to safety.

Walking back into her small sitting room, she sat beside Tenney, forcing him to look at her. "Tenney, we'll go to the halls to collect your belongings," she started. "Then I need to check in on someone, see if they're home, OK?" Her questions were rhetorical, an instruction masked by the illusion that he had a choice. Tenney knew, looking at her, that he had no choice.

As she stood up, he watched her walk into the kitchen. He wondered how old she was, convinced that she could not be more than 30 at the most. Her warm, brown skin was flawless, her eyes bewitching. He saw her move to a cupboard and remove what looked like an epi pen, along with several boxes of pills. She carefully stowed the medicine in a large handbag before returning to him.

Jude felt a mix of determination and anxiety. She had never done anything like this before, and the weight of her decision pressed down on her. But looking at Tenney, seeing the vulnerability in his eyes, she knew she had to help him. She had to see this through, no matter the cost.

Gripping the handle of a small suitcase, her hand hovered over two sets of keys before finally settling on one with a jaguar key ring. She opened the door and ushered him out, closing it firmly behind her.

Tenney, like an obedient dog, followed her down several flights of stairs to an underground garage. She led him to two vehicles, the smaller one covered in tarpaulin. She looked longingly at it before moving to a shiny red car. Tenney gawped, impressed by what he saw.

"1974 Jaguar E-Type V12 Roadster!" he exclaimed, regretting that he sounded like an overexcited kid. Jude was impressed.

"It was my dad's," she said. "We worked on it together before he died." Her eyes misted over as she thought about the past. She loved this car almost as much as she loved her other vehicle, loved putting the soft top down and feeling the purr of the engine as she sped down any road long enough and quiet enough to really let the beast go.

"Let's go," she said, unlocking the doors and placing her bags in the boot.

As promised, they stopped at the halls of residence. It took Tenney less than 10 minutes to gather his unpacked belongings before they set off to another part of the city. Pulling up in front of a small, terraced house, its curtains tightly drawn, Jude saw Tenney begin to tense again. She reassured him that she would not be long.

She unlocked the door, calling out to her mother as she entered.

Twenty minutes later, she exited the building, a satchel filled with papers and worry etched deeply across her face. The late morning sun cast short shadows on the pavement, highlighting the tension in her furrowed brow. Seeing the look in her eyes shook Tenney momentarily out of his stupor. He asked her if she was okay as she slid behind the wheel of the two-seater, igniting the engine once more. The car's low rumble seemed to echo the unease between them.

"She wasn't there," she explained, her voice tinged with frustration and fear. "It looks like she hasn't been home for a while." Tenney started aback as she hit the wheel in frustration, her eyes sparkling with unshed tears. The dashboard lights flickered, casting a soft glow on her determined expression.

"I should have called in on her sooner, forced her to talk to me," she muttered, her voice cracking slightly. The weight of regret hung heavy in the air.

Tenney did the only thing he could think to do. He took her hand in his, gripping it tightly. He felt electricity shoot up his arm, a small part of his deadened soul bursting back into life.

The warmth of her skin against his was a stark contrast to the cold dread that had settled in his chest.

"Take me home," he said softly, "And I will help you find her."

Jude felt the warmth spread through her, filling her from her head to her toes. She wiped away a tear, her resolve strengthening. "You've got a deal," she said, her voice steadier now.

He released her hand, his arm resting between their seats, applying a constant pressure to her side. As she changed gears, he moved his knee so her hand would brush it, a silent promise of support. Together, they left the city of her birth, the familiar streets fading into the distance as they drove across the country to Gloucestershire. The landscape changed from urban sprawl to rolling hills and lush greenery, the journey a quiet testament to their shared determination and the unspoken bond growing between them.

Chapter 7

When they arrived, Tenney jumped out of the car before Jude had fully stopped in the first space she could find. The tires screeched slightly as she hurriedly parked, her heart pounding in sync with the rain that hammered against the windshield. Tenney was already sprinting towards the hospital entrance, his movements driven by a desperate urgency. Jude followed, her breath coming in short gasps as she tried to keep up.

Inside, the sterile smell of antiseptic filled the air, mingling with the faint scent of rain-soaked earth that clung to their clothes. Jude went to the reception desk, her voice trembling as she asked for directions, but Tenney ran on, as though he had a homing beacon to follow. He knew exactly where his sister was.

Jude followed him as he bounded up the stairs to the ward, taking them two at a time. Her legs burned with the effort, but she pushed on, driven by the fear in Tenney's eyes. He went straight to the room, bursting through the door with a force that made it slam against the wall. Jude, a few steps behind and struggling to keep up, saw his family gathered around the bed.

The parents were clutching the hands of the slight figure in the bed, their faces etched with grief and exhaustion. The room was filled with the soft beeping of machines, but the girl was unconnected to any of them except the heart rate monitor. Jude felt a cold dread settle in her stomach; the heartbeat was so slow. In the corner, a teenage boy watched the scene silently, his hand clenched tightly around his mobile phone, his face ashen and his eyes brimming with unshed tears.

Suddenly, the machine monitoring her heart started to flatline. The piercing sound cut through the room, a harbinger of the inevitable. Tenney pushed forward, moving his family aside as he leaned over the girl in the bed. He held her to him, his voice breaking as he repeated her name over and over – "Aura, Aura, Aura, Aura…"

The continuous tone from the machine echoed around the room, alerting the medical staff to the patient's condition. Outside, Jude could hear the wind howl, the rain playing its heavy staccato beat on the window, mirroring the turmoil inside. Tenney's father stepped forward, placing a hand on his son's shoulder, his voice a broken whisper.

"She's gone, son," he whispered, his own grief barely contained. Tenney turned on him, his face contorted with pain and anger, pushing him off.

"No!" he shouted, spittle flying from his mouth. "Not yet."

Jude finally walked into the room fully, closing the door behind her to give the family some privacy before the doctor arrived to pronounce the time of death. Tenney was shaking the girl in the bed, intermittently stroking her hair and face, telling her he was there, calling to her, and begging her to come back. His breath moved her hair, giving her a halo-like effect.

His family stood back in shock and grief, their faces pale and eyes wide. The wind howled again outside, a mournful sound that seemed to echo their despair. Jude closed her eyes and said a small prayer, feeling a warm breeze pass over her. Opening her eyes again, she turned to check the door. It and the window were shut. The heaters were off. The breeze seemed to brush against her skin, then move on, past the family to Tenney. It looked like it caressed him, almost playing with the locks of his brown hair.

And then the body on the bed took a breath.

Where Tenney touched her, colour began to return. She breathed again. And again. A single tear from his eye fell on her skin and disappeared into her. As the body on the bed grew more substantial, Tenney changed also. The tension left his body in waves. When he moved back slightly to look down at his sister, Jude saw him as he really was – a healthy, handsome man in his prime, not the haggard, lost soul she had saved in Lincoln.

"Aura…?" he asked tentatively.

Outside, the storm rapidly calmed, and the sky cleared to show the midday sun, its rays of light bursting through the clouds like fingers from heaven. Finally, Aura opened her eyes and smiled up at Tenney, locking her gaze with his.

"I wait…" she whispered; her voice still rough from where the tube had been.

The family ran to her as Tenney held her hand, like he would never let it go again. He was radiant, relaxed, healthy, and whole. Jude's heart skipped a beat when he turned away from Aura, his eyes clear and sparkling with happiness, and looked directly at her.

"Thank you," he mouthed to Jude.

**

A figure stood up from a chair in the waiting room, his presence almost ethereal in the harsh fluorescent light. He smiled, a bittersweet expression that hinted at the knowledge he carried. His senses heightened the closer it came to the time when he would be forced to leave again. He had never seen a bond as strong as the one he sensed flowing between the twins in the closed-off room. His extra sight revealed the solid tendrils of light that connected them, so cruelly severed when the train had left the station.

He felt his body shiver, a sign that he needed to return to the woods. The pull of the forest was strong, a sanctuary where he could wait for her and hope she would understand why he could not stay. The hospital's sterile environment felt suffocating compared to the freedom of the wild.

He walked out of the hospital, the automatic doors sliding open with a soft whoosh. The rain had stopped, leaving the air crisp and cool. He crossed the car park to his Land Rover, the vehicle a stark contrast to the modern cars surrounding it. Checking his old phone, he saw that the man had replied.

I am on my way.

The message was brief but filled him with a sense of urgency. He climbed into the Land Rover, the familiar creak of the seat and the smell of worn leather grounding him. As he started the engine, he cast one last glance at the hospital, a silent promise lingering in the air.

Chapter 8

Tenney watched as his parents left to get their coffees, the soft murmur of their voices fading down the hallway. Aura slept peacefully beside him, her chest rising and falling in a steady rhythm. The nightmare hung heavily on his shoulders, the memory of honeyed eyes tormenting him. He regretted not getting Jude's number, wishing again to thank her, wishing just to see her one more time.

He felt Aura stir and open her eyes. For a moment, they were unfocused, the blues and greys swirling like a storm. He gently stroked her head, reminding her that he was with her. As her eyes settled on a soft grey, he stood up.

"Shove over," he said, echoing their last morning together.

Tenney wrapped one long arm around her shoulders, pulling her in close as her head found its natural resting spot on his shoulder. They felt their heartbeats find the same rhythm, their breathing the same pattern, and sat in silence, happy to be together.

"I had the most awful nightmare," she whispered. "After you left, and I fell asleep." Aura wasn't ready yet to admit how close to death she had been, instead choosing to refer to her comatose state as being 'deeply asleep.'

"What did you dream?" Tenney asked softly, his voice calming her frayed nerves.

The black mud covered her feet, its cold grip tightening with every passing second. She could not walk away. She could not free herself. All around her, the trees moved as one, their branches swaying ominously, the shadows under their boughs blacker than the deepest hole. The moon, waning after its fullness, still shone brightly down, but clouds were moving over it, blocking its face, and making the darkness darker still.

Trapped, held in place by the thick mud as it slowly sucked her down, she screamed, her voice echoing through the silent forest. From the shadows, she heard voices, a language harsh and jagged, scarring the air around her. She screamed again, as a flash of blue light weakly ballooned around her. Sinking still, the mud was up to her waist. She was lost.

The shadows moved. Creatures, skeletal and ominous, their skin hanging from their bones like rags. Their mouths open, their eyes fixed on her, their prey. The smell of blood, death, and sulphur filled the air – the acrid stench of rotten eggs and burning flesh moved like a green gas across the ground towards her. Behind the ghouls stood a scarred giant, their leader.

His head was bare, tattoos covering his chest and neck. No, not tattoos – scorch marks. The massive eagle, wings outstretched, perched over SPQR IX was branded into him, the skin puckered and scarred around the horrific image.

His hand held the leashes of four enormous dogs, each powerful and straining at their bindings as they tried to get to their prey in the centre of the clearing. He laughed as the dogs and the ghouls howled, their red eyes burning with hunger. His teeth were sharp like a shark's, his tongue licking the air, tasting her fear.

As he roared with his army of creatures, another shape broke free from the shadows and raced unhindered towards her. She screamed again, the mud now at her chest, her hands scrabbling for any handhold, as the beast charged. She faced the inevitable, thinking only of him and wishing he were here with her. She would be safe on solid ground if he had been here.

The mud continued to pull her down, now reaching her shoulders. Her fingers clawed at the slick surface, but it was no use. The skeletal creatures drew closer, their bony fingers outstretched, ready to grasp her. The giant's laughter echoed through the clearing, a chilling sound that sent shivers down her spine.

The beast from the shadows moved with incredible speed, its form a blur against the dark backdrop of the forest. As it neared, she could see its eyes, glowing with an intense, otherworldly light. It leaped over the mud, landing gracefully beside her. She felt a surge of hope, but it was quickly dashed as the beast turned its gaze towards the giant, a low growl rumbling from its throat.

The giant's dogs strained harder against their leashes, their snarls filling the air. The ghouls hesitated, their eyes flicking between the beast and their master. The giant's smile faltered for a moment, but then he yanked on the leashes, pulling the dogs back to his side. The giant took a step forward, his eyes narrowing as he assessed the new threat.

A brush of fur as the creature leapt over her. She tentatively opened an eye, and she saw a thick, black pelt that shone in the last rays of moonlight. Green eyes stared at her from his lupine face. He, for she knew instinctively that that was what this creature was, moved closer towards her, positioning himself between her and the demonic army. With the last of her strength, she grabbed hold of his fur and felt him begin to pull her out of the hole.

The giant roared again, and the army charged at them. The wolf bared his teeth at the enemies, a low growl rumbling from his throat as he tried desperately to pull her free from the hole. But the pit's dark grip had its insidious hold on her again and began to suck her down, down, down.

She lost her grip as the earth swallowed her, and she felt the last of her blue light die. The air was gone. Only the suffocating stillness, her senses deprived of everything. Time stopped. She waited for a sign – any sign – that this was the end of her life. That this would be it.

As she resigned herself to her fate, she heard his voice, as though through syrup. Quiet at first, but it was getting stronger. The familiar lines of the poem floated around her, and then he said her name. Light burst forth. Rich and warm, it held her in the dark. Her blue glow merged with the gold that surrounded her.

She opened her eyes and saw his hazel ones smiling down at her. The warmth of his presence enveloped her, a stark contrast to the cold, suffocating darkness she had just escaped. His hand reached out, gently brushing a strand of hair from her face.

"You're safe now," he whispered, his words spinning around her like a spell, tethering her back to the world.

**

Jude finished booking her room at the hotel. She decided to give it a few days, treat it as a holiday, and read her mother's journals and letters before deciding what to do next. The thought of delving into her mother's past filled her with a mix of anticipation and trepidation. She walked down the corridor, back to the room where he was, wanting to say goodbye.

She knocked softly and waited, her heart pounding in her chest. "Come in," said a young woman's voice. Jude, nervous now as she realised that this was probably his sister who answered her, cracked open the door. She saw Aura sitting up in bed, propped up by pillows. The change in her in only a few hours was remarkable. She thrummed with energy, her skin glowing with health. Her smile was wide and welcoming.

"You must be Jude!" she declared, her voice filled with warmth and gratitude.

Jude nodded, suddenly lost for words. Aura beckoned her into the room. "He's in the loo, having a shower," she said, nodding towards the closed door of the en suite. "He won't be long. I told him he stank." Her infectious humour worked its magic on Jude, who smiled back at her, beginning to feel at ease.

"I just wanted to say that I'm heading off, and, you know, say goodbye," Jude said, her voice tinged with reluctance.

Aura gestured to the empty chair beside her bed. "Stay a while, won't you? I know he'll want to see you. And I want to thank you."

"Thank me?" Jude felt perplexed.

"Yes, for bringing him back to me, for pulling him back from the edge and giving him a reason to want to be in the world again." Aura's words struck her deeply, a ball of emotion rising from her chest. Aura reached out, placing her hand on Jude's arm. "You trusted your instincts, and you saved us both."

Just then, the door to the en suite opened, and Tenney emerged, clad in loose jogging bottoms. His hair, still wet from the shower, dripped down his face. He lifted the hem of his t-shirt to wipe the moisture away, revealing a tanned and toned torso. A bruise and scratches marred his belly. Under his left arm, Jude noticed an intricate, indecipherable script tattoo following the line of his bicep. Embarrassed to be gawping like a teenager, she turned away, her cheeks flushing.

Tenney noticed her and smiled, a warmth in his eyes that made her heart skip a beat. "Jude," he said, his voice soft and filled with gratitude. "I'm so glad you're here."

Jude turned back to face him, her embarrassment fading as she saw the genuine appreciation in his eyes. "I just wanted to say goodbye," she said, her voice steady now.

"Where are you going?" Tenney asked, recalling that she had packed for more than one night away.

Jude explained that she had decided to stay at a hotel in a place called The Forest of Dean. She failed to see the smiles the twins shared when she mentioned their homeland.

"Whereabouts?" Tenney asked, his curiosity piqued and a plan forming in his mind. He was determined to find her and show her the sights.

"A small village, somewhere called Dennybury?" Her mispronunciation of their home village made him whoop with glee.

"Dennybury!" he exclaimed, laughter bubbling up. "You mean *Dene*bury! That's our home village!"

Aura joined in the laughter, her eyes sparkling with amusement. "You're staying in our neck of the woods, Jude. You'll love it there."

Jude felt a wave of relief and excitement wash over her. "Really? That's amazing! I had no idea."

Tenney's eyes twinkled with mischief. "Well, now you have two local guides. We'll show you all the best spots."

Aura nodded enthusiastically. "The forest– it's magical."

Jude's heart swelled with gratitude and anticipation. "I'd love that. Thank you both."

Tenney's expression softened, a hint of something deeper in his gaze. "It's the least we can do. You've done so much for us."

As they chatted about the Forest of Dean and all its hidden gems, Jude felt a sense of belonging she hadn't experienced in a long time. The twins' warmth and hospitality made her feel welcome, and she looked forward to exploring their home with them.

Chapter 9

The Forest of Dean rose up before her, a vast expanse of ancient woodland that seemed to stretch endlessly into the horizon. Born and raised in Lincolnshire, Jude was accustomed to the flat, open landscapes where the only real hill was the one upon which the city stood. Her childhood had been spent exploring with her parents the fens towards Boston, where the land was so flat you could see for miles. Landmarks like The Stump, Crowland Abbey, and the towers of the cathedral were visible from great distances, standing as solitary sentinels in the vast, open sky.

Her canopy had always been an unending expanse of blue, occasionally dotted with clouds, not the dense, overhanging trees of the Forest of Dean. The transition was stark and almost overwhelming. "This is going to take a bit of getting used to," Jude thought to herself as she followed the Wisemans up the winding roads that led to their village.

The scenery was breathtaking. Houses clung precariously to cliff sides, their artful shabbiness adding to the charm of the small towns and villages that seemed to meld seamlessly into the surrounding trees. Jude gasped in delight as she spotted a deer running gracefully beside the road, its movements fluid and elegant. She squealed in surprise when a flock of sheep ambled casually out in front of her car, forcing her to slow down and navigate carefully around them.

As the car in front indicated left, turning down a narrow lane towards The Barracks, Jude continued through the village, eventually pulling into the hotel car park. The journey had been long, and she felt a wave of weariness wash over her. Aware that she needed to take her medication, she pulled her suitcase and bags from the boot of the car and made her way to the reception desk to sign in.

The hotel was quaint, with a cozy, welcoming atmosphere. The receptionist greeted her with a warm smile, and after a brief check-in process, handed her the key to her room. Jude made her way up the narrow staircase, the wooden steps creaking softly under her feet. Her room was small but comfortable, with a window that offered a stunning view of the forest beyond.

A large, comfortable bed dominated the space. In one corner stood a tall Victorian mirror, its ornate frame adding a touch of elegance. A rattan chair occupied another corner, inviting in its simplicity. A dressing table held the customary kettle and assortment of tea bags, coffees, and biscuits found in all hotels. A wardrobe stood along the side of the room between the doorway and the en suite.

The small bathroom featured a shell-shaped sink, an old-style toilet, and, thankfully, a modernised shower cubicle. Jude unpacked her few belongings, placing the bag that held her mother's journals on the chair and her toiletries on the dressing table. Moving to the bathroom, she removed one of the luxuriously soft towels and draped it over the tall mirror in her room.

She sat on the bed, opened her bag, and pulled out the medipen, an alcohol wipe, and a small round plaster. Removing the lid of the pen, she pinched the skin on her stomach and injected the methotrexate into her system. The day she had received her diagnosis of rheumatoid arthritis six months earlier had been the day she decided not to pursue relationships. The medication the consultant wanted to start her on would give her the best chance to remain as active as possible, but it came with a major side effect. If she were to fall pregnant, the foetus would be at risk of severe damage, potentially causing death or long-term brain and physical defects.

Her thirtieth birthday was approaching, and she felt her life ebbing away as she considered her options. She was still young enough to live a good life, but her condition made her feel as though she had the body of an elderly woman. That night after her diagnosis, she had broken up with her boyfriend of two months, phoned Ellie, and together they had drunk cocktails and watched soppy movies. It was then she decided to close her heart off from love and abandon the dream of having a family.

The attraction she felt for Tenney, so sudden and unexpected, had to be quashed. There was no way he would want to be with her. She was too old, too broken for someone like him to even really look at. And if he did think of her that way, he would soon come to regret it. She had promised to see him and Aura again, but after that, she would move on, find another place to stay, or head home to continue her search for her mother.

Automatically, thoughts of her mum made her check her phone. She scrolled through her messages, hoping for some sign, some clue that would lead her to the woman who had disappeared from her life so abruptly. The search for her mother was becoming a consuming quest, one that she hoped would bring some sense of closure or understanding.

She read a text from Tenney, saying that Aura would be released from the hospital tomorrow. They wanted to take her out for fish and chips. She couldn't help but smile when she saw the single "x" at the end. A small kiss. It was a simple gesture, but it warmed her heart in a way she hadn't felt in a long time.

There was also an answerphone message from an unknown number. Still smiling as she inadvertently let herself feel warmth, she listened to the message.

"Jude? Jude? It's your mum. I'm okay, darling. I'm safe. I must make something right before I can come home. Jude, Glendower has something… I lo…"

The message cut off abruptly, leaving Jude staring at her phone in shock. Her heart raced as she replayed the message, trying to decipher the cryptic words. Her mother was alive and safe, but what did she mean by "Glendower has something"? And what was she trying to say at the end?

Jude's mind whirled with questions and emotions. Relief that her mother was safe, frustration at the lack of information, and a renewed sense of urgency to find her. She felt a mix of hope and dread, wondering what her mother was involved in and why she couldn't come home yet.

She sat on the bed, her thoughts racing. The attraction she was fighting for Tenney, the warmth of his text, and the mystery of her mother's message all swirled together, leaving her feeling overwhelmed. She knew she had to stay focused, to keep searching for answers, but the emotional toll was heavy.

Taking a deep breath, she decided to text Tenney back, agreeing to the fish and chips outing. She needed a distraction, something to look forward to, even if just for a little while. As she typed out her response, she couldn't help but feel a glimmer of hope. Maybe, just maybe, things would start to make sense soon.

**

The following day. The first day after the full moon cycle.

They had returned from the hospital earlier that morning, the doctors still baffled by how the girl had been so close to death only 24 hours earlier.

Tenney reclined on the sofa in the kitchen next to his sister, Aura. Her small body, nestled under the covers of a blanket, instinctively rolled into his side, seeking comfort as she slept. He looked down at his socked feet, then at his hands, which still bore the marks of the fight. The bruises on his knuckles were a stark reminder of the violence he had unleashed. He had been shocked when he first looked in the mirror, seeing the bruise under his eye and the larger one on his torso. He still didn't know how it had happened or what had come over him.

He was pretty sure he had ruined any chance of returning to Lincoln. He would have a black mark against his name in the city, he was certain. The thought of it filled him with a mix of regret and resignation. He also felt a twinge of guilt at leaving the girl as he had. It wasn't really his style to do anything so cruel. He must have been in a fit of madness, the cause of which baffled him. How could being away from home cause such an extreme reaction in him?

His mind flashed back to the tower of the cathedral. He remembered the brown eyes that had urged him back from the brink, eyes he looked forward to seeing again. He checked his phone once more, pleased to see her reply, happy that she had returned the innocuous "x" at the end. It was a small gesture, but it meant a lot to him.

Aura murmured in her sleep, her brow furrowing. Placing his phone down, he held her close, whispering the lines from "Maud" that they loved. The familiar words seemed to soothe her, and she relaxed against him. He felt a surge of protectiveness and love for his sister, vowing silently to keep her safe no matter what.

As he rested there, his thoughts drifted back to Jude. The attraction he felt for her was undeniable, but he knew he had to tread carefully. His life was complicated enough without adding more uncertainty. Yet, he couldn't help but hope that maybe, just maybe, there was a chance for something more.

**

"Tenney, love," Martha said, eyeing the sleeping dogs in their bed. "I think they need to go for their walk."

Tenney looked up. Aura, now awake, leaned against him, the glow of daytime TV casting a soft light on them. She noticed his jaw tense and his eyes flicker to his sister. When he looked back at her, his gaze had turned steely, preparing to defy her.

"Good idea, Ma!" Aura chirped. "I could do with some fresh air." She stood up, her legs wavering slightly under her.

Samuel, alerted to his daughter's movement, looked away from the computer screen. "I don't think that's a good idea, love," he said softly. "You need your rest."

Aura walked over to him, placing a loving kiss atop his balding head. "Honestly, the fresh air will help me more than staying on the sofa," she reassured him. "And if we take Jess as well, we can't go far."

Hearing her name, Jess looked up through clouded eyes and wagged her tail once. Samuel turned his attention to Tenney. "When you get back, you and I need to have a chat about what happened while you were in Lincoln." Tenney squirmed, using the act of leashing the dogs to hide his face. He nodded once, his mind already thinking of the half-truth he would share.

Martha watched as Tenney helped Aura with her jacket and prepared to leave the house. As Tenney passed her, he dropped a kiss on her head and told her not to worry. When Aura walked by, Martha put a hand on her daughter's arm, detaining her for a moment. "Should you go out, Aura? Are you well enough?" she couldn't hide her concern.

"I'm fine, Ma, honest." And like her brother, she kissed Martha, then walked out and closed the door behind her.

And she did look fine. In fact, she looked radiant. Martha stood for a long while in the quiet house, twisting a cloth in her hands. Samuel walked up behind her as she looked down the empty path where they had trod, and pulled his wife in close, her hand resting in his as he hugged her shoulder. She still felt like the luckiest woman in the world, meeting and marrying Samuel. His understanding and love for her still had the capacity to render her speechless.

The closeness of the twins had at first charmed and then puzzled her. It had been this way all their lives. Martha had watched their strange dependency on each other grow and change over the years, and she had worried. She was thrilled when Tenney announced that he would finally take his place at university. And now it seemed that her worry had been justified.

"We will have to tell them," she stated matter-of-factly to her husband. They were words he knew would come but ones he had dreaded.

"I know," he said, swallowing the hard emotions that welled up from their hidden spaces deep inside him. He tightened his grip on her shoulder, offering silent support as they both faced the inevitable.

Martha sighed, leaning into Samuel's embrace. "I just hope they understand," she whispered, her voice tinged with anxiety. "It's not going to be easy for them."

Samuel nodded; his own heart heavy with the weight of what they had to reveal. "We'll get through this together," he reassured her. "We always do."

They stood there for a moment longer, drawing strength from each other. The house was quiet, but the air was thick with unspoken fears and hopes. Martha knew that whatever happened, they would face it as a family. And that, at least, was a comfort.

**

Stace Caedmon sat in the shadows of an awning outside the pub, his beer untouched in front of him. He waited. He was used to waiting.

He heard them before he saw them. They were talking about everything and nothing, for all intents and purposes, a regular brother and sister out for a dog walk. They were a striking pair. No one could fail to notice the boy, his height alone meant he stood out in a crowd. But Stace also sensed a power within him, a charisma which attracted people to him.

But the girl… he gasped when he saw her. She did not look like her brother at all. Where he was dark, she was light. Where he saw only her, her bright eyes seemed to take in anything. *She had not looked this way for a long time*, he thought.

Finally, his partner returned, having flirted with the female bar worker. In her one hand she carried a napkin around a fork and steak knife. In the other, a cold bottle of cider, the condensation dripping down the sides, leaving wet marks on her tight, black jeans. He could hear her stomach rumble as she sat across from him is broad sunlight.

"Did you see them?" she asked. Her yellow eyes sparked with intelligence beneath the choppy fringe of her short brown hair.

Stace nodded once. "We have to go carefully with them, Meg," he said. "They are raw power, untapped energy. If they become separated again, I cannot say what the consequences will be."

Meg raised the bottle to her lips and took a long drink, considering what to say. "We need to find Hedge first," she said. "Then we can approach them."

Stace leaned forward, just out of reach of the sun's rays. His light brown hair hung around his face. His eyes glowed amber, reds shining through ochre. His powerful upper body made the table creak and tip as he rested his elbows on its tabletop.

"I will find us a base," he said, his voice and his countenance was used to giving commands and having them obeyed without question. "You find Hedge."

Meg leaned back and smiled as the waitress brought her bloodied, rare steak, winking at the girl, pleased when she saw her blush. She nodded once before attacking the almost raw chunk of meat.

Chapter 10

Jude listened again to her mother's answerphone message, the knot of worry tightening inside her as she replayed the ending, the way the message just cut off mid-word. Pulling out her laptop, she Googled the name 'Glendower.'

The search engine didn't disappoint. Straight away, she was bombarded with a lengthy list of websites and pictures for Glendower Springs, a hugely popular brand of Highland Spring water. They had offices in Scotland, Singapore, and LA. Seeing the images of the bottles and their distinctive logo – a Highland Stag over a bubbling brook, with a strange eel in its waters – made her recall her last visit to her mother, a month ago. She had seen several bottles of the water on the work surfaces of her small kitchen in her flat. Her mother had been furiously making notes in one of her journals. When Jude looked over her shoulder, she had hastily closed the book, but not quickly enough for Jude to notice the incomprehensible, made-up language her mother had been using.

For a long time, Jude had realised that her mother was a bit of a conspiracy theory nut, her often groundless suspicions about people and companies frequently coming to nothing. Jude had simply chalked her mother's behaviour up to more evidence of her growing eccentricity after the loss of her husband.

Jude continued to scroll through the list, before clicking on the news tab at the top of the page. The headline read: **GLENDOWER TO MAKE A SPLASH AT BRISTOL DRINKS CON.!**

The story detailed that the CEO of the company, Humphrey Glendower, was set to launch a new line of flavoured drinks at the upcoming Drinks Convention, held at the Avon Gorge Hotel in Clifton, Bristol, at the end of October, just over a month away. What her mother had – or thought she had – over this man and his company, Jude could not fathom. If anything, he seemed too good to be true, fronting and supporting a number of charities both in Great Britain and abroad. His philanthropic and humanitarian works were impressive. He had even adopted two children – one now a teenager, the other found abandoned beside a gem mine in Botswana and still a baby.

Jude's mind raced as she tried to piece together the puzzle. What could her mother possibly have on Humphrey Glendower? And why was she so secretive about it? The more Jude thought about it, the more she realised she needed to dig deeper. Her mother's cryptic message and the strange symbols in her journal hinted at something much larger than a simple conspiracy theory.

Determined to uncover the truth, Jude decided to attend the Drinks Convention. It was a long shot, but it was the only lead she had. She hoped that by being there, she might find some answers or at least get closer to understanding what her mother was involved in. With a renewed sense of purpose, she began to make plans for her trip to Bristol, her mind filled with questions and a growing sense of urgency.

What to do in the weeks between went unanswered. If she wanted to stay in the Forest, she would need to book a holiday cottage; her funds wouldn't stretch to a month of hotel fees. Or she could travel, visit South Wales or Somerset. Maybe camp out. As she considered her choices, she heard a tap on her door.

**

Tenney looked back at Jude as she walked with Aura down the road towards the park and the chip shop. His smile beamed from his face, once again transforming his features into something new. His hands were full with the leads he held, both dogs walking obediently beside him. Jude felt sure that Aura, her arm slung companionably through Jude's arm, could feel the heat as it rose unbidden and unwanted through her body.

Instead, Aura began to tell Jude about the history of the village. She started with its Celtic roots, pointing up a hill that the village skirted around, explaining that at the summit were the ruins of a hill fort believed to have been inhabited by members of the Dobunni tribe. She mentioned that their home was at the foot of the hill, and it was one of their favourite places to visit.

Then she pointed out the high wall surrounding the Manor. It held the Guinness record for being the oldest inhabited house in Britain, its cellar having once been a Saxon Hall. She shared stories about its role in the Civil War, how it had been a bastion for Cavaliers, with hidden passages purportedly leading to the Abbey at Flaxley, some three miles away. She painted a vivid picture for Jude of a stately home guarded by gargoyles, haunted by ghosts, and a blood stain in the hall that would not wash away.

Aura continued, "Dad's been asked to lead a dig there by the University. When the owners dredged the pond, they found evidence of a structure, possibly a temple of some kind. If Dad can do so, he hopes to prove that people have been using the Manor a long time before the

Saxons came." Jude was impressed by Aura's knowledge. "He has asked me to be a part of his team. It was what I was going to do while Tenney was," she paused, looking at her brother's back, "away."

Tenney seemed to sense his sister's change of mood. He stopped and turned back to her. Awkwardly, the leads still in his hand, he hugged her tight, swearing that he wouldn't leave her again.

Rather than placating her, Jude saw that Aura only grew sadder. She gripped his top in her hand, thumping his chest lightly. "I'm sorry, Ten," she murmured.

"What do you have to be sorry for?" he asked her quietly. "I made the choice to come home when I heard you were ill. It may have been the only choice, but it was mine to make."

He kissed the top of her head, releasing himself from her grip. Turning to Jude, he forced a smile onto his face and, with his free hand, pointed to the chip shop. "Now, tell me, Officer Marcello, are you ready for possibly the best fish and chips you have ever tasted?"

And they were good fish and chips. Growing up relatively close to the sea, fresh fish was in abundance, and she thought nothing could come close to the chip meals she had enjoyed at Chapel St. Leonards. But these were exceptional, crispy and golden, with the perfect balance of salt and vinegar.

As they ate, Jude shared a little of her story, telling them about her missing mother and her plan to go to Clifton on the night of the convention to look for her. Aura asked her what her plans were before that date. Jude shrugged, outlining her options.

Tenney, now lying on his back, one arm across his face, spoke. "We think you should stay." Jude looked at them, no words had been shared between them, but Aura seemed not to mind that Tenney had included her in his statement. "Mum knows the owners of the hotel; she can probably get mate's rates for you."

"I don't know…" she said, uncertainly.

"We are," said Aura. "You should definitely stay. It'll be our 21st birthday soon, and we both want you to be there to help us celebrate. Think of it as our way of thanking you again for everything."

Jude felt her defences weaken. "I'll have to go home, get more clothes. And collect something I need…"

"Decision made!" Tenney suddenly sat up and leaned across them, enveloping them both in a massive bear hug.

Under the trees, Stace watched them. He looked at the third person. She reminded him of someone, but who he couldn't recall. Mikkelson had alluded to her presence being significant, that she would play a crucial role in the lives of these young adults. What that role was, he would have to wait to find out.

Jude felt a mix of emotions as she considered their offer. The warmth and camaraderie she felt with Tenney and Aura were undeniable. She had been on her own for so long, the idea of staying and being part of their lives, even temporarily, was incredibly appealing. She looked at Tenney, his earnest expression, and Aura, who was watching her with hopeful eyes.

"Alright," she said finally, a smile spreading across her face. "I'll stay. But I really do need to go back and get some things."

Tenney grinned, his relief palpable. "We'll help you with whatever you need," he said. "And we'll make sure you have the best time while you're here."

Aura nodded enthusiastically. "It's settled then. You're staying with us."

As they finished their meal, the bond between them grew stronger. Jude felt a sense of belonging she hadn't experienced in a long time. She knew there were challenges ahead, but for now, she was content to be part of this newfound family.

Chapter 11

The old man watched the moon hanging in the sky as it started to wane. He had heard the wolf howl at the fullness as it hung, suspended in the sky only a couple of nights ago. He shifted the body which clothed him.

Trapped in the frail body of his elderly host, he seethed with frustration. How could he have been so blind? The twins had been right under his nose, their presence masked by the only force in the universe capable of making his black soul shiver. He berated himself, replaying the moments in his mind, searching for the signs he had missed. Their proximity to the house had been cleverly concealed, a testament to the power shielding them. It was a power he both feared and loathed, one that could pierce through his malevolent essence and leave him trembling.

His bones cracked as he shifted in the chair to which he was confined, he would need a new, younger host. His black eyes piercing the darkness. A noise. Voices behind the houses. Dogs yipping on their leashes. Carefully, using a cane for support, he stood and walked to the window, watching the group of boys as they passed. The leader stopped, spying the old man in his house. Tattoos snaked up his neck, his hair cut short like a soldier's.

The old man smiled. He'll do, he thought.

With a scream, his head flopped backward. As clouds scudded over the moon, obscuring its dim light, a darkness left the man. Like smoke, it threaded through the grass.

The boy didn't stand a chance. His friends disappeared down the track, leaving him defenceless as the smoke moved up his body and forced its way into his screaming mouth. The boy who was no longer a boy walked to the conservatory and looked out of his new eyes at the crumpled sack of the body which had hosted him these past years. He opened the door, stepped over the husk, and went to the kitchen.

Tearing his shirt from his thin, strong, young body, he took a knife and began to carve into his new flesh. The pain was intense, but he welcomed it, feeling the power surge through him as he etched ancient symbols into his skin. Each cut was precise, each mark deliberate, as he prepared himself for what was to come.

The demon, now housed in this youthful body, felt a renewed sense of purpose. He had waited so long for this moment, and now it was finally within reach. The reckoning was near, and he would be ready. He would lead his brethren, and together they would fulfil the prophecy that had been foretold.

As he finished the last symbol, he looked at his reflection in the kitchen window. The boy's face stared back at him, but the eyes were his own – dark, ancient, and filled with malevolent determination. He smiled, a cold, cruel smile, and whispered to himself, "Let the reckoning begin."

**

Lying in his bed, Tenney stared at the ceiling and drummed a rhythm on his chest. Next to him, on the bedside table, lay the blue book containing the poem "Maud." His mind turned to death; both he and Aura had come within a breath of touching it, of welcoming it. The opening lines of the poem came to his mind:

She is coming, my dove, my dear,
Its lips in the field above are dabbled with blood-red heath,
The red-ribb'd ledges drip with a silent horror of blood,
And Echo there, whatever is ask'd her, answers 'Death.'

He felt the stain of death on him, it reverberated through him like the Echo of the poem. His hand stopped its rhythm, his fingers beginning to shake as he thought about what they had come so close to losing.

A grip tightened over his quavering fingers. Aura had tiptoed in, sensitive as always to his moods. Her eyes held his until they both felt their pulses slow. Pulling back the cover, he made room for her. Within moments, shoulder to shoulder, she fell into a deep sleep.

In the quiet of the night, Tenney's mind drifted back to the events that had brought them so close to the edge. The fear, the pain, and the overwhelming sense of helplessness. He had never felt so vulnerable, so exposed. But now, with Aura beside him, he felt a glimmer of hope. They had survived, and they would continue to fight, together.

Aura's presence was a balm to his troubled soul. Her steady breathing, the warmth of her body next to his, all served to ground him, to remind him that they were still here, still alive. He knew that the road ahead would not be easy, but as long as they had each other, they could face whatever came their way.

As he joined her in sleep, the moonlight filtered through the curtains, casting a soft glow over the room. The shadows danced on the walls, creating a serene and almost magical atmosphere. In that moment, everything felt right. The world outside could wait; for now, they had each other, and that should have been enough.

**

As the blade embedded itself deep within him, he felt something new. A cold breeze moved over him. In his death state, he wished it would go, let him die in peace. But the wind grew stronger, the curtains rattled on their hooks, a dog barked...

Tenney sat up with a start. His window was wide open, a figure perched on the sill looking out. He looked beside him. Aura was gone. Slowly, he pulled back the cover and placed his bare feet on the floorboards.

The figure turned to him. Her eyes were fathomless and wide. She smiled. And jumped.

"AURA!" Tenney screamed, rushing to the window. He couldn't see anything below, the garden in darkness. Heedless now of the noise he was making, he raced from his room, down the stairs, through the kitchen, and out onto the lawn.

She wasn't there. Her pyjamas lay torn and scattered across the grass, heading towards the gate and the hill. The bomb in his head began to tick loudly again.

Behind him, someone switched on the light, calling his name, shouting it – but he was deaf to all but his loss. He raced down the path, jumped the gate, and disappeared.

Samuel stood helplessly at the back door, Martha's old baseball bat hanging limply by his side. The dogs barked furiously behind him, their growls echoing through the night. Martha rushed to his side, her eyes wide with fear, frantically tugging at his arm. "Samuel, Aura's missing – she's not in her room!"

Samuel, panting slightly from the shock of waking to his son's screams, made a decision. He tightened his grip on the bat, his knuckles turning white. "Find Tenney's phone, and call that police lady - Jude," he said, his voice steady despite the chaos around them.

Martha nodded and ran up to Tenney's room. She found his phone, mercifully unlocked for once, on his bedside table. With trembling fingers, she dialled Jude's number, praying she would answer quickly.

Meanwhile, Tenney ran through the darkness, his heart pounding in his chest. The night air was cold against his skin, but he barely felt it. His mind was consumed with fear and desperation. He had to find Aura. He couldn't lose her.

**

Blood dripped down his chest from the crude sigil he had carved into his new body. He laughed as the protection cast on the twins began to clear, allowing him to finally see them for who they truly were. He had heard the boy's screams and seen the shadow fly across the trees. He breathed out, thinking of all the ways he would hurt them for being so close yet out of his sight for so long. As he roared, the pain from the cuts was sharp, but it fuelled his determination. He pulled his shoulders back, making the eagle on his chest spread its wings, the blood tracing the intricate lines of the symbol, and screamed his battle cry.

The night air was cold against his skin, but he welcomed it. The sigil was a mark of power, a connection to the ancient forces he sought to control. He could feel the energy coursing through him, a dark and potent force that made him feel invincible. The reckoning was almost upon them, and he was ready.

He turned his gaze towards the hill, where the ruins of the old fort stood silhouetted against the moonlit sky. He could still see the faint figure of the boy, his form illuminated by the pale light as he rushed into the trees. He and the girl were his targets, the key to fulfilling the destiny his kind had longed for since they Fell.

**

Tenney kept running, the soles of his bare feet becoming blistered and torn as he thundered up through the woods. Images kept flashing before his eyes: treetops, the view as she soared above the river. He saw Samuel's dig at the water temple and then he saw the people with the wolf in the clearing of the fort.

The pictures kept assaulting him. The ground below him was not the ground he ran on; instead, it was the basin of the valley below, undulating fields giving way to smaller woodlands, villages, towns, and a city. He was following the Sabrina as she snaked beneath him. Then he was over the Malvern Hills, tracing its spine with his hand.

The images kept coming. Faster and faster and faster. Soon he was relying purely on instinct to take him where he needed to go, his other senses lost in another place, in another body.

The mended thread stretched, pulling him towards an unknown destination. His mind was a whirlwind of visions, each one more vivid than the last. He saw the ancient fort, its stones weathered by time, and the figures gathered there, their faces obscured by shadows. He felt the weight of history pressing down on him, the echoes of past lives intertwining with his own.

As he ran, the landscape around him seemed to blur and shift. He was no longer in the present but caught in a liminal space where time and place converged. The air was thick with the scent of earth and foliage, the sounds of the night blending into a symphony of whispers.

He could feel the presence of others, their energy mingling with his own. They were close, closer than he had ever realised. The path he was on was not just a physical one but a journey through the layers of reality, each step bringing him closer to the truth.

The thread that connected him to Aura was taut, vibrating with a sense of urgency. He knew he had to reach her, to save her from whatever darkness threatened to consume them both. The bond they shared was his guiding light, a beacon in the chaos that surrounded him.

With every stride, he felt the power of unknown ancient forces that had been awakened. The weight of an unknown destiny pressed upon him, but he refused to falter. He would find Aura.

**

"Mr and Mrs Wiseman, tell me what happened. Exactly."

Jude had come as soon as she got the phone call from Martha. The three of them sat across the table in the kitchen, the middle of the night adding a stillness to a house that Jude assumed was normally so full of life and love. Sam had gone back to bed, mumbling something about not being able to take much more of their drama.

"The house was quiet, we assumed everyone was asleep." Samuel drew in a sharp breath and sat up straighter as his wife gripped his clenched hands.

"The next thing we know, we are woken be a loud noise, and Tenney's running past our bedroom, calling for his sister. I followed him out, sure that we were being burgled or something." His eyes drifted down to the baseball bat at his feet. "But I was too slow, too clumsy, and couldn't stop him. He's always been athletic, fast, but I have never seen him move so quickly! I lost sight of him on the track at the back of the houses. Martha went to check on Aura. She wasn't in her brother's room, or her own. Her bed looked unslept in."

Jude sat back, puzzled by this revelation about the twins. Martha caught her expression. "They're very close," she explained. "We will quite often find them in the same bed. They've been doing it since their rooms were first separated as kids."

"Okay…" said Jude, deciding to tackle that revelation at some later point. "Then what happened, after you found Aura was also missing?"

Samuel continued. "Tenney was in the garden. Spinning around, looking up at the sky. My god, his eyes, he looked half mad…" he trailed off.

Jude could picture that look well. It haunted her dreams, the young man in the guard's office. His face on the tower. The ferocity and then the desperation that rolled off him in waves. She shook herself slightly, trying to dislodge the memory. He wasn't that person, not anymore. She was getting to see him as he must normally be. And she found that she cherished those moments.

"Then what?" she asked as gently as she could.

"He just ran off. No shoes on, no jacket. He's only wearing the clothes he sleeps in."

Samuel, his visage dropping, raised a hand to his face, his beard wrapping around his fingers as they struggled to stifle the emotion which bubbled just below the surface. Jude realised that in the last few days these parents had experienced so much grief and heart ache at the hands of their two children, she didn't know how much more they could take. She mentally readied herself to ask a difficult question, one she knew which could alter her perception of these people.

"Is there any history of mental illness or psychosis in either of your families?"

The parents looked up and began to fidget nervously. Martha turned to her husband and gave him silent permission to tell Jude the truth.

"Ok, Love." he said, raising her hand to his lips. Turning back to Jude he announced: "I love my children, Miss Marcello, all three of them. Very, very much."

Jude wondered why he felt the need to clarify that. It was obvious that this was a loving family. It had never occurred to her that these people hadn't ever done anything but their best for their children. Her unspoken question was answered as Samuel continued to explain:

"I am not the twin's biological father."

**

Sam, forgotten and alone, sat in the shadows of the stairs, listening to the conversation. His father's words cut him to the quick.

"Martha was seduced by a much older man, a professor at our college in the States. He was my boss. I was there for a year's placement, assisting this reclusive, but brilliant, Brit in his lectures. I learned a lot from him about the intricacies and the subtleties, as well as the detective work that is required to be a successful archaeologist. I met Martha fairly early on in my stay. I fell for her, hook, line, and sinker, but she only had eyes for the Prof.

"One night, she succumbed to him, and the next day he was gone. No goodbye, nothing. Vanished, like he had never been there. A month or so later, she discovered she was pregnant. Her parents, devout people, wanted to disown her; the shame for them was too great. So, I supported her and did the only thing I could think of to protect her. I asked her to marry me. I know it's old-fashioned, but I wanted her to know that she didn't have to worry or be alone.

"She agreed, and we got to know each other better over the short engagement. Martha tells me that that was when she realised, she had fallen deeply in love with me."

Martha cut in at that point. "Without the Professor there, blurring my vision as it were, I finally truly saw Samuel as more than just a friend. I saw his kind heart, and I knew I could be happy with him. That he would make a good father to my children. Soon I realised that I couldn't be happy without him."

There was a slight pause before Samuel picked the story back up.

"We married a month before the twins were born. In fact, they were born a month early. Throughout the eight months of Martha's pregnancy, we were told 'one baby, one baby.' Imagine our shock when Aura was born! This all happened nearly 21 years ago. Their birthday is in a few weeks' time."

Sam heard his father draw in a deep breath, aware that he was beginning to ramble.

"We moved back to the UK in January, when the babies were three months old. It was the end of my permit to work in America. From the moment I first held them in my arms, I have loved them as though they were my own. As far as they and their brother are concerned, I am their only father." Samuel took another deep breath and let it out slowly. Sam envisioned him running his hand down his face as he said, "So, in answer to your question, Jude, there is no history of mental illness from Martha's side of the family. On their father's side, who knows? Possibly."

Sam had heard enough. Things began to click into place in his mind's eye. He had always felt the outcast in the family; Tenney and Aura were so close, and Samuel always seemed to be trying to compensate for something with them. Now, even though he knew that he was his father's one true son, his brother and sister – no! He corrected himself – his *half*-brother and sister, were favoured by Dad because they weren't really his. That was why he made more of an effort with them, probably to try to make up for the fact their real Dad didn't want to know.

Sam stood back up and climbed the stairs silently to his bedroom. He shut the door and walked over to his computer monitor. Typing in his password, he accessed the online fantasy world game and entered the chat room.

Sam: *Theo?*

Sam stared at the screen, his mind racing with the revelations he had just heard. He felt a mix of anger, confusion, and a strange sense of relief. At least now he understood why things had always felt different, why he had always felt like an outsider in his own family.

Sam: *Theo, you there?*
Theo: *Yeah, I'm here. What's up?*

Sam hesitated for a moment, then began to type.

Sam: *Just found out some stuff about my family. It's… a lot to process.*
Theo: *Want to talk about it?*

Sam took a deep breath, feeling the weight of the night's events pressing down on him.

Sam: *Yeah, I think I do.*

As he started to share his story with Theo, he felt a small measure of comfort. Even in the virtual world, he wasn't completely alone. And maybe, just maybe, he could find a way to navigate the complicated reality of his family.

**

Jude asked if she could go and see their rooms. Samuel showed her to the two doors. He opened the door on the right first, Aura's bedroom. Jude entered; all her cop instincts ramped up as she cast her eyes over the room.

The single bed was pushed right up against the wall, directly opposite the door. As Samuel had said, the sheets were still neat, the bed unslept in. It looked like a typical girl's bedroom, with old posters of film stars on the walls, a pinkish duvet, and a well-loved teddy bear. Under the window, which looked out across the garden to the hill beyond, was a desk with a laptop, an overfilled bookshelf beside it. Jude noticed well-thumbed books like *Anne of Green Gables* and *Little Women*, novels by Deborah Harkness, and books charting the local history of The Forest and Gloucestershire. A chest of drawers stood beside the wardrobe in the corner opposite the window. On top of the chest of drawers were a mirror and a hairbrush.

Photos of her family adorned all the free spaces on the furniture tops. Next to her mirror was a photo of two children grinning gap-toothed gummy smiles up at the camera. Jude picked it up, smiling at the image of Aura and Tenney as children.

All perfectly normal.

Putting the picture back where she had found it, she turned around and nodded to Samuel. He stood aside as she left Aura's room, turning to the next door. Jude pushed down the handle and entered Tenney's room.

The first thing she noticed was that Tenney's bedroom was almost a mirror image of his sister's, but the colours were darker, more boyish than his sister's light and airy room had been. On the walls were pictures of classic sports cars, among them a Jaguar like hers. His bookshelf held countless comics and graphic novels of superheroes and antiheroes. Another shelf was filled with books about animals – their care and anatomy, how to train them. A frame held a picture of a dog like the spaniel she had seen downstairs. Under the image was the name 'Frodo' and two dates. She realised it was a memento of a pet who had passed away.

The chest of drawers, wardrobe, and the desk all reflected the pieces in Aura's room. His single bed was pushed against the wall, mirroring where his sister slept like a butterfly's wings. It was as though even a thin wall was too much of a separation for them. Her fingers alighted softly on the embossed letters in the blue cover of the book beside his bed. Absently, she made a mental note to ask him why that poem was so special to him.

Like his sister's room, his desk was beneath the window overlooking the garden. The chill she felt coursed down her spine was added to by a sudden gust of air from the open window. Jude leaned over the desk and peered out. The familiar feeling of vertigo hit her. To steady herself, she breathed in the night air and placed her hands on the windowsill. Pulling back slightly, she looked under her hands and saw what her fingers had felt. On the very edge of the sill were four deep marks gouged into the wood. It was like a mighty eagle had launched itself from its perch.

She turned back to the room. This bed had definitely been slept in. She could just about discern the depression of two heads on the pillow. The duvet had been flung back carelessly. Jude shut her eyes and took a deep breath as she tried to make a deduction from all the evidence that was around her. Breathing in caused her to smell the room. A rich scent of spice assaulted her. Threaded through it, she thought she could discern the clean smell of fresh, mountain air, wild and untamed. Yet it filled her with the feeling of warmth and safety. It smelled like him, she realised. She shook her head. "Focus!" she told herself internally.

"This was once one room." Martha's tired voice startled Jude. "We had to put a dividing wall up when we felt that they were getting too old to share a room. For days, Tenney screamed the house down, Aura retreated into herself. It was then that we pushed the beds together, the wall separating them. Tenney calmed down, and Aura was Aura again."

"You said they have always been close…" Jude's unvoiced concern hung in the space between the two women. Martha smiled sadly as she sat on the edge of his bed, stroking the empty sheets.

"Yes, but perhaps not in the way you are thinking. From the moment they were born, Tenney has struggled to be parted from Aura. If they were, Aura diminished, and I confess, sometimes I had to remind myself that I had a daughter as well as sons." Martha paused, raising a hand to her face as a single tear rolled down her cheek. "In the years between school and now, they have worked the same shifts at the pub, walked the same walks together. No one could come between them. When Tenney told me that he had finally agreed to accept his university placement, I felt such relief. He could live a life without worrying about his sister. And she may finally begin to see her own great worth as she stepped out of his shadow. I didn't know that…"

Jude went to her, wrapping an arm around her shoulders as the older lady sobbed. "How were we to know that their dependence on each other wasn't just because they were twins? They need each other. Tenney is not Tenney without Aura. Aura disappears without Tenney."

"Come on," Jude said softly, helping the heartsick woman up. Together, they left his room and walked down the stairs.

Passing Samuel in the kitchen, Jude stopped and asked him, "Do the twins have a special place? Somewhere they like to go together?"

Samuel hesitated for a moment, then nodded. "There's a spot they always go to. It's an old fort on the hill, just beyond the woods. They call it their 'hideaway.' They've been going there since they were kids. It's a bit of a trek, but they love it up there."

Jude felt a surge of hope. "Thank you, Samuel. I'll head there right away."

**

He couldn't see or feel anything apart from the splintering of his soul and the rapid images being forced into his consciousness. Pure, animalistic instinct was driving him completely as he crawled on bloodied, raw, and torn hands, knees, and feet to the flat stones.

Suddenly, strong hands grabbed him. He felt the weightlessness as he was carried through the air.

"He's too far gone," said a man's voice.

"What do we do?" a woman replied.

Somewhere nearby, a large animal moved and growled deeply in its throat.

"There is nothing we can do. Not until she returns. I am not convinced that she knows what she's doing." A sigh. "All we can do is wait."

"Have you ever seen a Tethering as strong as this before?"

"No, never. I thought her last life held a strong connection, but we were with her, we taught her how to control it, how to live happily with her sister and still have healthy relationships with other people. This time, she has no understanding. We may be too late to help her. We may have already lost her."

The noise of the people talking was drowned out as a new image came to Tenney. He was looking down on the clearing through a break in the clouds. In the distance, the light of a powerful torch threaded its way through the trees. A fire had been built between the stones. A black wolf sat near a woman whilst a man was putting coats and blankets over the body of a young man. Recognition hit him.

He was looking down at himself. Suddenly, the version of himself which lay on the ground sat bolt upright, his head tipped to the sky.

"Aura…" his other self called out.

A bright light erupted behind his eyes as his world imploded with a bang.

Stace looked up to the sky as soon as Tenney did. He saw a shape blot out the rising sun's rays. "She's here," he said.

Chapter 12

Jude trekked up the hill, the light of the torch Samuel had loaned her creating shadows where there were none. As she crested the hill, the dawn sun rose between a break in the trees. For a moment, the sheer wonder of the view, the sun's new rays adding a glow to everything it touched, mesmerised her. She dragged her eyes away from the sight below and looked around the summit of the hill. Flat rocks lay at its centre, and huddled around the fire, two people and a very large dog kept vigil over the sleeping forms beneath coats and blankets.

The man spotted her. As he rose up, his bulk pure muscle, his height would rival that of Tenney's. He should have been intimidating, except Jude's gut told her that here was someone she might be able to trust, if that trust was earned.

He beckoned her over.

"Hello, Miss Marcello," he said. His voice sounded northern, the bass of it echoing around the clearing.

Jude stepped closer, her eyes darting down to the sleeping pair. She saw the steady rise and fall of their chests as they breathed together. She felt her heart hitch to see them look so vulnerable.

"They're fine," he said, having seen her eyes flicker down. "Though we will have a lot of work to do with them if they are to survive."

"Survive?" asked Jude, incredulous now. Nothing was fine about what she was witnessing.

The man gestured for her to sit. She obliged, sitting as close to the twins as she dared, never taking her eyes off the people sitting across from her. The man placed a wide-brimmed hat over his head. The sunlight slowly filled the clearing.

"My name," he began, "is Stace Caedmon, and this is my associate, Meg." The woman looked at her, her gaze disconcerting as her yellow eyes took everything in. Deftly, she reached inside her jacket and with a small flourish presented a business card to Jude.

It read, 'Caedmon and Smith'. Underneath the names were two mobile numbers. Above the two names, an outline of a blue dragon shimmered.

Jude sat back, fingering the card and waited for an explanation.

"We have searched for them for many years," he began. Jude stiffened, thinking of the stalkers she had arrested over the years. She moved closer to the twins, getting ready to wake them and make them run if her gut was wrong.

"You must believe me, Miss Marcello. All we want is their safety and happiness. We want to teach them to be able to live separately for periods of time, to enjoy this short, fragile, human gift of life. We are sorry that we hadn't found them sooner, we could have given them the tools to manage their lives. Instead, we may be too late. Their bond is strong, powerful, and dangerous."

He let the last word hang in the air. Dangerous. Dangerous to them, or to the people around them?

Jude felt the bodies stir at her feet. Tenney groaned softly as he began to wake up. "When you bring them back here," Stace continued, "and you are ready to hear it, I will tell some of their story."

Tenney and Aura opened their eyes together; they seemed to stare deeply into each other's souls. Aura smiled.

"Did I sleepwalk again, Ten? I had the most vivid dream…"

**

Tenney and Aura sat together on the sofa of the family room, their father pacing the floor in front of them whilst their mother hovered near the door, a steaming mug of black coffee in her hands. The tension in the room was palpable, each tick of the clock amplifying the silence that hung heavily between them. They did not understand how Aura had arrived at the fort unscathed, or why Tenney had relapsed again.

Earlier that night, Meg and the wolf had taken them to an old Land Rover, parked off the lane. Inside, Aura had found several items of men's clothing, including a t-shirt and a pair of shorts with a belt. Now, she twisted the material between her finger and thumb, anxiety about their parents' reaction mixing with the questions she knew they both had about the night's events. The fabric felt rough and unfamiliar, much like the situation they found themselves in.

Tenney had also made use of the clothing in the back of the vehicle. He wore the coat which had covered him as he slept on the hill, and he had torn up one of the older-looking t-shirts to use as makeshift bandages, wrapping them around his hands and feet. They were a stark reminder of the ordeal they had just endured.

The wolf had started pawing at a rock under a bush at the side of the forest road. Hidden under it were the keys to the vehicle. "Good wolf," said Tenney, his voice a mix of relief and gratitude. The wolf sat on his haunches and let his tongue loll out, a picture of canine contentment. As Aura changed out of Jude's jacket, which she had borrowed for the walk down the hill, and into the t-shirt and shorts, belted up tightly around her waist, the wolf respectfully turned his head away.

"You're an odd one, Wolf," Tenney remarked when he saw the animal's courtesy to his sister's modesty. Jude had driven them home in the Land Rover, leaving them at their door before returning to her hotel. Every inch of her body was in agony, and she longed for the pain relief only a hot shower and rest could give her.

Now they were back at the house, they prepared to say what they had rehearsed in the car. They began by apologising to their parents for the concern they had caused. Their mother was too upset to say much, instead nursing her coffee, her face ashen with worry. Her eyes, usually so full of warmth, were now clouded with fear and exhaustion. Their father just paced the floor, his footsteps a steady rhythm of worry and frustration, as they gave their feeble excuses.

Finally, Samuel stopped them. His face was a mask of barely contained fury. "Bullshit," he said simply, his voice cutting through the room like a knife. He pointed a warning finger at the twins. "You two are grounded." They had never seen their father so angry, his usual calm demeanour shattered.

"But Dad," Tenney protested, his voice rising in outrage. "You can't ground us. We're nearly 21 - adults!"

Their father turned back to them, his eyes blazing. He spoke quietly, but each word was laced with a quiet intensity that made them shiver. "I have stood up for you both countless times, placating your mother when she is half out of her mind with worry. But this is too much." He stood up and turned away from them, his face grey, the tiredness from the broken night of worry weeping from his pores. When he reached the door, he stopped and turned back to them slightly. "While you are under my roof, you will abide by my rules. You have caused your mother enough worry these last few days. If you had any compassion for anybody beside yourselves, you would do what I ask." He emphasised the next two words as his fist pounded gently but firmly on the door frame. "Stay. Put."

He turned to Martha, his voice softening slightly. "Get dressed, love. We'll drop Sam off at school, and then I am going to take you out for the day. Somewhere nice, somewhere away from here." He waved his hands, encompassing the house and the twins. "We'll take the dogs too, seeing as though these two are not to even contemplate stepping one foot out of the door."

Martha gave him a small smile as he passed her, squeezing his arm gently. She walked over to her children and kissed them each on the cheek. "Dad and I worry about you, is all. You may be all grown up, but you will always be our kids. Do what he says and get cleaned and patched up." Martha stopped at the doorway and looked back over her shoulder. "And Ten?"

"Yeah, Ma?" Tenney's voice was subdued, the fight gone out of him.

"Take care of your sister." She walked away, leaving the twins, bloodied and torn, alone in the house.

The silence that followed was heavy, each of them lost in their own thoughts. Aura glanced at Tenney, her eyes filled with a mixture of guilt and relief. "We really messed up this time, didn't we?"

Tenney nodded, his expression grim. "Yeah, we did. But we'll make it right. We have to."

**

Aura led Tenney upstairs to the bathroom. She pushed down the loo seat lid, turned back to him, and instructed him to strip. He removed his shredded t-shirt. She barely glanced at him as he undressed; they were unembarrassed in front of each other. She turned to the cupboard that contained the first aid kit.

When Aura turned back to him, she shook her head in despair and tutted. Tenney gave a small, cheeky smile.

"Look at the state of you!" she exclaimed. His bared torso showed the extent of the injuries caused by his crawl to the Fort. Not only were his hands, knees, and feet bloodied and bruised, but his torso and arms were also covered with vicious scratches from brambles. The large bruise on his ribs caused by the fights Tenney had been in had faded, only to be replaced by a multitude of smaller ones where he had fallen or walked blindly into obstacles.

"And don't smile like that. I know you're hurting, you idiot." Her words were softened with a small, tired smile. She nodded to the loo. "Sit," she commanded.

He quickly obeyed, wincing as he felt the stiffness in his body. She tossed a towel into his lap as he pulled down his ruined pyjama bottoms. Kneeling in front of him, TCP and cotton wool at the ready, she began to clean his wounds.

"Ouch!" he yelped as the antiseptic touched his knees.

"Baby," she joked. Carefully, she lifted one of his feet and rested it on her knee. This time she winced.

"Oh, Ten. They're torn up so badly. How could you not realise what you were doing to yourself?" She looked up at him, her eyes beginning to tear up. He smiled grimly.

"I don't know." Carefully, he caught a tear from her eye. They watched as his skin absorbed it. She took a deep breath, wiped her eyes on the sleeve of her jumper, and returned to the task at hand.

As gently as she could, she cleaned his feet and then went to work on his hands. They weren't much better than his feet and knees, the heels of his hands bruised and grazed deeply. His fingernails were broken and blackened from clawing through the mud.

When she was satisfied that she had removed as much of the grit and dirt as she could, she pushed herself up. "I'll run you a bath," she said.

"Fine. Just don't use any of that froo froo girly smelly stuff," he joked, turning his nose up.

When the bath was nearly full of hot water, Aura helped Tenney up and left the bathroom as he slipped into the warm water. He sank down into the warmth, feeling some of his muscles begin to unwind, and listened to her pace between their rooms and along the corridor.

When he had finished, it was Aura's turn to shower. She stood under the hot spray of the cascading water, relishing the feel of it as it washed the night from her skin. When they were finally clean and dressed, Aura carefully bandaged his hands and feet. As if she were a magician, she produced a pair of garish, fluffy, pink bed socks.

"NO WAY!" Tenney declared.

"Yes way. They're soft and they will make walking easier." With no further preamble, she lifted his feet up and adorned them in their mother's socks. Aura supported Tenney towards his room, his arm draped around her shoulder, as she walked with her head by his armpit, both arms circling his waist.

They slumped onto his bed, holding each other close, her head on his heart.

"Ten?" Aura's voice was soft, almost a whisper.

"Yeah?" he replied, his voice equally quiet.

"Who are these people who claim to know more about us than we do?"

Tenney stroked her head, feeling her warm tears under his hand and soaking through his sweatshirt. He kissed the top of her head. There were no words he could use to answer the same question that plagued him.

**

They were woken by their mother bringing them steaming cups of tea. The comforting aroma filled the room as she gently nudged them awake. "Come downstairs soon for dinner," she said softly. As they descended behind her, Martha told them that their father had calmed down, but his words still stuck. If they wanted to stay here, they were to abide by his rules, at least until their birthday. That meant staying close to home or helping him out at the dig.

They consented to his wishes, both thinking of ways they could sneak out that night and maybe, just maybe, finally get some answers that didn't raise more questions.

They ate their meal together around the kitchen table. The conversation was still awkward, each one avoiding anything related to the occurrences of the last couple of days. The clinking of cutlery and the occasional murmur of small talk filled the silence. Afterwards, in a show of familial solidarity, they settled in the family room, the five of them together, and watched a new murder mystery on ITV1. The flickering light of the television cast a warm glow over their faces, momentarily masking the tension that lingered in the air.

At 10pm, they all retired upstairs, their father making a point of watching the twins go into their own rooms. His stern gaze followed them until their doors clicked shut. By midnight, when they were sure their family was asleep, Tenney messaged Jude. Silently, grabbing the younger dog on the way to stop him barking, they sneaked out of the house and met her at the

Land Rover parked up the road. The night air was cool and crisp, a stark contrast to the warmth of their home.

They jumped in and followed the directions Meg had sent Jude. It wasn't far from the village, but the drive was tense, the silence only broken by the occasional rustle of the dog shifting in the back seat. None of them spoke. They didn't know what they were letting themselves in for, but each of them knew that they would get answers tonight. One way or the other.

As they drove deeper into the night, the landscape around them pulsed with history; ancient and powerful. They were venturing into one of the oldest parts of the forest, where the trees grew as they pleased, not in the straight, regimented lines created by generations of foresters. The air seemed thicker here, laden with the whispers of centuries past. The trees seemed to close in, their branches casting eerie shadows on the road, creating a tunnel of darkness that their headlights barely penetrated.

The anticipation was palpable, each of them lost in their thoughts, wondering what awaited them at their destination. The silence in the Land Rover was heavy, broken only by the occasional rustle of leaves against the windows and the soft hum of the engine. Jude's hands gripped the steering wheel tightly, her knuckles white in the dim light. Tenney stared out the window, his mind racing with questions and possibilities, while Aura sat quietly, her eyes fixed on the road ahead, trying to steady her breathing.

The deeper they went, the more the forest seemed to come alive around them. The rustling of leaves sounded like whispers, and the occasional snap of a twig echoed like a distant footstep. It was as if the forest itself was aware of their presence, watching and waiting.

Chapter 13

"I know where we are!" Aura exclaimed from the back of the car, her voice filled with a mix of surprise and recognition.

Jude had turned off the lane and followed a forestry track deeper into the woods. The path was narrow and winding, flanked by ancient trees whose branches seemed to reach out like skeletal fingers. The track ended in a wide, gravelled driveway, leading up to a large house that had clearly seen better days. Its once grand facade was now weathered and overgrown with ivy, giving it an eerie, abandoned look.

"It's the old Verderer's Lodge!" Aura continued, her eyes wide with a mix of awe and apprehension.

The wolf paced backwards and forwards, his green eyes flashing in the car's headlights. His movements were restless, as if he sensed the significance of this place. Stace stood in the doorway, his hands behind his back, as still as if he were a soldier presenting himself on parade. His posture was rigid, his expression unreadable.

Meg loped out of the trees; a brace of rabbits flung over her shoulder. Casually, she tossed one at the wolf, watching as he caught it mid-air before carrying it into the shadows of the house to eat in solitude. The ease with which she moved, and the casual nature of her actions contrasted sharply with the tension that hung in the air.

After Jude pulled up, they looked at each other, the three of them bracing themselves for what was to come. The silence in the car was thick with unspoken fears and questions. They knew that whatever awaited them inside the lodge would change everything.

Stace stepped to the side, ushering them in with a formal nod. "Welcome to Denebury Lodge," he said, his voice calm and measured.

As they stepped out of the car, the gravel crunched under their feet, the sound echoing in the stillness of the night. They followed Stace into the lodge, the heavy wooden door creaking as it swung open. Inside, the air was cool and musty, filled with the scent of old wood and forgotten memories. The dim light from a single chandelier cast long shadows on the walls, adding to the sense of foreboding.

They exchanged nervous glances, each of them steeling themselves for the revelations that lay ahead. The lodge, with its history and secrets, seemed to watch them as they entered, its walls whispering tales of the past.

**

Meg paced around outside, feeding another rabbit to the wolf. A canopy of stars hung over her head, twinkling like a thousand tiny lanterns. It was only a few nights since the moon had been at its fullness, and she could still feel the pull of the heavenly body that exerted such control over her life, and that of the one she loved best. She clutched her arms to her sides more firmly, reassuring herself of the shape of her body, and resumed her pacing.

The wolf still seemed a little nervous about being around human beings and their belongings. She could understand that. He was a wild animal, his instincts told him to avoid mankind. But something else overrode his natural inclinations, something far more powerful, and so he made himself stay and suffer the torment of being amongst them. His eyes glinted in the moonlight, reflecting a mixture of wariness and determination.

When the trio had arrived, she watched them closely. The woman smelled as though she was in her late twenties or early thirties, but she looked younger. Meg sniffed the air again and detected the strong medication that flowed through her body, fighting the arthritis that had begun to riddle her joints. She may look young, but her body was failing her. The scent of the medication was sharp and medicinal, a stark contrast to the natural aromas of the forest.

As they passed her, she sniffed again. This time, she caught the distinctive whiff of the pheromone for attraction. She marvelled that no one else could smell it; it came off her and the boy in such a strong wave, she almost gagged. The intensity of their mutual attraction was almost palpable, a silent undercurrent that seemed to hum in the air around them.

In the shadows, she heard the wolf make a sound that could have been a laugh had he been human. It was a low, rumbling noise, filled with a kind of knowing amusement.

"Oh, shut up, Hedge," she said, tossing him the last rabbit. The wolf caught it effortlessly, his movements fluid and graceful. He retreated into the shadows to eat in solitude, his eyes never leaving the humans for long.

Meg continued to pace, her thoughts a whirlwind of emotions and concerns. The presence of the trio had stirred something deep within her, a sense of anticipation mixed with dread. She knew that tonight would bring some answers, but she also knew that those answers might come at a cost.

The night was alive with the sounds of the forest, the rustling of leaves, the distant hoot of an owl, and the soft murmur of the wind through the trees. It was a night filled with possibilities, and Meg could feel the weight of it pressing down on her. She took a deep breath, steeling herself for whatever was to come.

**

Jude wrapped her arms around her body. The house was large, the rooms sparsely furnished. Jude looked all around her as she followed Tenney and Aura in. Aura, the little dog in her arms, peeked over her shoulder and nudged her brother. He looked where she directed and noticed Jude shiver. He stepped back, and wrapped an arm around her shoulders, rubbing her arm. His proximity warmed her. The scent that was purely him, assaulted her nose again. She really had to get a grip, or she was going to do something foolish.

Like admit she had feelings for someone nearly a decade younger than her.

They were shown into a large room, tatty armchairs and a worn sofa were placed around the roaring fireplace.

"We thought we should talk here," said Stace. "I have only just moved in, and as you can see, the old place needs some work doing to it. But it has running water, and the means to boil it," Jude's eyes looked to the fire, where an iron stove hung over the flames. "This is by far the warmest room."

Tenney nodded, and lead the girls over to the sofa, as Stace folded his body into one of the armchairs. He sat back, his legs crossed and his fingers steepled, as though he was a professor, waiting for his students to ask questions, and deduce answers.

"So, what's with the wolf?" Tenney asked, his question taking Jude of guard, but Aura simply smiled. "I mean, it is a wolf, isn't it? Not some wolfdog hybrid?"

Stace nodded, "Yes," he answered patiently, aware that the boy needed to get an inane question out before he could ask the deeper ones. "Hedge is a wolf. He has adopted us into his pack, as it were." Tenney looked troubled. "What is it?" Stace asked opening the floor up to him once more.

"Just before I left, we were at the hill fort. A moron set his dogs on Bo," The little dog, curled up in front of the fire, opened on eye at the sound of his name. "He would have been killed, if the brown wolfdog hadn't saved him. I'm thinking now that maybe that wasn't a dog, but a wolf as well? Where has it gone?"

Stace smiled mysteriously.

"She will appear again soon, when she is ready." he answered cryptically.

"And the man who was with her? He received a nasty bitemark on his arm. Where is he?"

Stace looked up as Meg entered.

"So that was how he got his injury... *Fili mi*..." she said, disappearing once more to the driveway.

"He will be back as well, but not yet. Now ask me the real question you have."

This time Jude pushed herself forwards, conscious of the pressure of Tenney's thigh against hers.

"Just what the hell is going on?"

Stace eyed her over his fingers. She blinked and he was no longer seated in his chair, benign and harmless. He towered over them, blocking the light from the fire.

"I think maybe it is better that I show you." In a flash, he grabbed Tenney by his jumper, effortlessly lifting him off his feet. A blur of movement, too fast for the eye to see, and they were gone, the front door swinging on its hinges.

Aura, shrieking, moved forward off the couch. The wolf, a low growl rumbling in its throat, stood in the doorway, warding her off. Bo had no such qualms and darted between the wolf's legs, running as fast as his short legs would take him in the direction Tenney and Stace had gone.

"NO!" screamed Aura. She started to vibrate and glow, a beacon in the night. Again, she made to get past the black wolf. He growled once more, baring his teeth. Meg came up behind her, grabbing her by her shoulders, grounding her to the spot, preventing her from transforming. Struggling to hold the unstable Aura, she turned and looked straight at Jude.

Jude didn't know what to do. Her heart screamed to chase after Tenney, but her head said to stay with Aura. The conflict tore at her, each second feeling like an eternity.

"Make your choice," Meg said, her voice firm but understanding.

With an apologetic shake of her head, Jude followed her heart. She bolted out the door, the cool night air hitting her face as she ran. The forest loomed ahead, dark and foreboding, but she didn't hesitate. She could hear Bo's frantic barks in the distance, guiding her through the maze of trees.

Back in the house, Aura's glow intensified, casting eerie shadows on the walls. Meg tightened her grip, whispering soothing words to calm her. "Stay with me, Aura. We need to stay grounded."

Aura's breathing was ragged, her eyes wild with fear and frustration. Her mouth gaped as she struggled to breathe, her chest heaving with the effort. The room seemed to spin around her, the edges of her vision darkening. She felt the blessed oblivion sweeping over her, a merciful escape from the chaos and fear that gripped her.

Meg tightened her hold, her voice urgent but soothing. "Stay with me, Aura. Breathe. Focus on my voice."

But Aura's body was betraying her, the glow around her intensifying as she teetered on the edge of consciousness. Her legs gave way, and she collapsed into Meg's arms, her mind slipping into darkness.

Chapter 14

The suddenness of the movement made Tenney's head spin. Strong arms had rugby tackled him and carried him away, the scenery moving by so fast he felt completely lost. The world around him blurred into a dizzying whirl of trees and shadows. Finally, his assailant stopped and flung him against a tree, causing the ancient, gnarled oak to splinter under the impact.

Tenney let out a breath as the force shook him. The rough bark bit into his back, and he winced at the pain. Ropes were bound to the tree, and Stace began to tie him up, securing the knots with practiced precision. Tenney fought against his bonds, straining to get free, but the ropes held firm, digging into his skin.

When Stace was satisfied the bonds would hold, he stepped in front of Tenney, crossing his arms and calmly watching his reaction. The boy was panting hard, his chest heaving with exertion. He could feel his anger rising, boiling uncontrollably from deep within. His vision tinged with red as his eyes changed, a sign of the fury that threatened to consume him. Stace, on the other hand, was unruffled, as though he had just taken a leisurely stroll and not run at high speed through the woods.

Tenney looked around him, trying to get his bearings. In the dark, the woodland was unfamiliar, the trees towering above him like silent watchmen, guarding a secret at its heart. He was in a completely different part of the hill, maybe even a different part of the forest. He didn't know how far they had travelled, but it felt like miles. Jude was no longer in front of him, and Aura wasn't beside him. The realisation hit him like a punch to the gut, and he struggled even harder against his bonds.

"Where are they?" he demanded; his voice hoarse with desperation. "What have you done with them?"

Stace remained silent, his expression unreadable. He watched Tenney with a detached curiosity, as if observing a specimen under a microscope. The silence stretched on, each second feeling like an eternity.

Tenney's mind raced, a thousand thoughts and fears swirling in his head. He had to get free, had to find Jude and Aura. The ropes cut into his wrists, but he ignored the pain, focusing all his energy on breaking free. His muscles strained, his breath coming in ragged gasps.

Stace finally spoke, his voice calm and measured. "They are safe, for now. But you need to understand something, Tenney. This is bigger than you, bigger than all of us. There are forces at play here that you can't even begin to comprehend."

Tenney glared at him, his anger flaring even hotter. "I don't care about your cryptic nonsense. Let me go!"

The tension in the clearing was palpable, the air charged with unspoken threats. Tenney's heart pounded in his chest, a mixture of hope and dread. He knew that whatever happened next would change everything.

**

Aura turned on Meg and hit her chest weakly. "What have you done?" she railed against her. "Do you know what will happen? Where has he taken him? Where is he? Where is my brother?" Each statement, punctuated by a fisted hand, became weaker as Aura felt her throat begin to close up.

"Where. Is. Tenney?" she asked, her voice barely a whisper before fainting into Meg's arms.

Meg caught her, lowering her gently to the floor. "It's okay, Aura. I've got you," she murmured, her own heart pounding loudly in her chest.

**

Tenney slumped back against the tree, his breath coming in ragged gasps. He waited, watching to see if Stace would move closer. The older man stayed perfectly still; his eyes locked onto Tenney's with an unsettling calmness. The silence between them was thick, charged with unspoken tension.

Suddenly, Tenney exploded forward as far as he could reach with his hands tied. The muscles in his arms, chest, and neck bulged as he used all his strength to get free, his body straining against the ropes. His eyes burned with fury; his mind consumed with the desire to kill the man who had separated him from his sister. But no matter how hard he tried, Stace was always just out of reach.

Tenney's blood began to boil, a primal rage surging through his veins. His vision blurred with red, and he let out a guttural roar of frustration. The ropes cut into his wrists, but he barely felt the pain, his focus entirely on Stace.

Stace remained unruffled, his expression almost serene. "You're wasting your energy, Tenney," he said calmly. "This anger will get you nowhere."

Tenney snarled, his teeth bared in a feral grimace. "I'll kill you," he spat, his voice raw with hatred. "I'll tear you apart."

Stace shook his head slowly, a hint of sadness in his eyes. "You don't understand, do you? This isn't about you or me. It's about something much bigger."

Tenney's struggles intensified, his body trembling with the effort. "I don't care about your cryptic nonsense!" he shouted. "Let me go!"

Stace sighed, stepping closer but still out of reach. "You need to see the bigger picture, Tenney. Only then will you understand why this is happening."

Before Tenney could respond, a rustling sound came from the edge of the clearing. He turned his head, straining to see through the darkness. A figure emerged from the shadows. It was Jude, her eyes wide with determination and fear.

**

Cool drops splashed down on Aura's face. Under her head, she felt the warm pelt of the wolf's body acting as a pillow. She felt strangely comforted by the sound of his heartbeat, a steady rhythm that grounded her in the present moment. Opening her eyes gingerly, she saw Meg standing over her, dripping water from a soaked cloth onto her face, slowly reviving her.

"We thought we were going to lose you," Meg said, her voice filled with relief.

"What do you mean 'we'?" Aura asked, her voice weak but curious.

Meg just smiled magnanimously down at her. Aura shifted up to sit more upright, but still leaned against the body of the wolf. The wolf's presence was oddly reassuring, his steady breathing a reminder that she was not alone.

"What's going on?" she finally asked, feeling exhausted and breathless. Meg sat back on her haunches, her unusual eyes taking stock of the girl in front of her.

"You know, I came here from Turkey?" The sudden change in topic caused Aura to look at Meg in amazement. Her head was so full of Tenney, of finding him, that she wasn't sure what Meg's life story had to do with getting her brother back. But Meg held all the cards, and if she wanted to get Tenney back, she would have to play along for a little while longer. Meg continued when she saw that Aura wasn't going to stop her.

"But I was married here. My son, Wilfrid, was born in these woods. Very close to this spot, in fact. I had to give him up when he was still a baby, through no fault of my own." Aura felt the wolf stir, his head turning to look at Meg, his eyes reflecting a deep understanding.

"Why are you telling me this?" Aura asked her, confusion and frustration mingling in her voice.

"Because I need you to understand the sacrifices that have been made to keep you safe, and to keep you fixed to the world." Meg quickly changed the subject again. "Describe to me all you felt when you saw your brother being pulled away?"

Aura drew in a breath. What choice did she have but to answer her? She was too weak to fight, too weak even to stand. All she could do was talk, so she did, recounting all the times she had suffered from his absence, and how she felt hollow, insubstantial, flimsy, and breakable.

"I felt like I would shatter into a thousand pieces and be carried away in the wind, forgotten by everyone I loved," she said, her voice trembling with emotion.

Meg listened closely, her eyes never leaving Aura's face. "I understand," she said softly. "That's why it's so important for you to stay strong. Your bond with Tenney is powerful, but it can also be your greatest weakness if you let it consume you."

Aura nodded slowly, the weight of Meg's words sinking in. She felt a renewed sense of determination, a flicker of hope that she could hold onto. "I just want him back," she whispered.

The wolf nuzzled Aura gently, his warm breath a comforting presence. She leaned into him, drawing strength from his solid form. For the first time since Tenney had been taken, she felt a glimmer of hope.

**

Jude could hear the rage in Tenney's voice long before she had found him, tied to the tree, Stace standing perfectly still and simply watching him. She ran forwards, heedless of the branches that struck her face or the roots that threatened to trip her. The forest seemed to close in around her, the darkness pressing in as she pushed through the underbrush.

As she drew closer, she saw the dog cowering behind Stace, seemingly afraid of the person Tenney had become. His face was bright red, his veins standing out, and his eyes had become severely bloodshot, like they had been at the train station. He was straining against his imprisonment, the ropes cutting into his skin.

She gasped and ran forward. "Let him GO!" she shouted at Stace. "This is kidnapping! And wrongful imprisonment! I'm arresting you, Eustace Whatever-your-surname-is…"

Stace held up a hand in her direction. That one simple movement brought her up short. He never took his eyes off Tenney. "Officer Marcello," he said, using her professional title, as calmly as though they were two friends chatting over a coffee. "If I release Tenney now, he will try to kill us both. This has been allowed to go on for too long. We should have found them sooner, taught them how to control the separation. And this is the result of it."

Tenney screamed again, a sound filled with raw, unbridled fury. His muscles strained against the ropes, his body trembling with the effort. Jude could see the desperation in his eyes, the wild, uncontrollable anger that threatened to consume him.

"Tenney, please!" she cried, her voice breaking. "Calm down! We'll figure this out, I promise!"

Stace remained unruffled, his gaze steady. "He can't hear you right now," he said softly. "The rage has taken over. It's a side effect of the separation. Without proper training, it's nearly impossible to control."

Jude's heart ached at the sight of Tenney's suffering. She took a step closer, her hands outstretched in a gesture of peace. "There has to be another way," she pleaded. "We can help him. Just let him go."

Stace shook his head slowly. "Not until he calms down. If I let him go now, he'll destroy everything in his path, including you."

Jude's mind raced, searching for a solution. She knew she had to do something, anything, to reach Tenney. Taking a deep breath, she stepped even closer, her voice gentle but firm. "Tenney, listen to me. I'm here. We're going to get through this together. Just breathe, okay? Focus on my voice."

For a moment, it seemed as though Tenney's eyes flickered with recognition. The tension in his body eased slightly, and his breathing became less ragged. Jude continued to speak softly, her words a lifeline in the storm of his emotions.

Stace watched them, his expression unreadable. "You're stronger than I thought," he said quietly. "But this is far from over."

**

Everything was foggy. Tenney's head was thumping behind his eyes, each pulse sending waves of pain through his skull. He could only see in tunnel vision, and everything in that red tunnel was his enemy. The world around him was a blur of shadows and threats. He had to fight through these monsters; he had to get back to himself.

He pulled on the ropes again, feeling them give and fray under the strain. His muscles burned with the effort, but he didn't care. The need to break free, to escape this nightmare, consumed him entirely. The rough fibres of the ropes bit into his skin, but the pain only fuelled his determination.

In the distance, he could hear Jude's voice, a faint beacon of hope cutting through the fog. Her words were muffled, but the tone was unmistakable—calm, soothing, and filled with concern. He tried to focus on her voice, to let it guide him back to reality, but the rage was too strong, drowning out everything else.

He pulled harder, the ropes creaking ominously. The red tunnel seemed to close in around him, the edges darkening as his vision narrowed further. He could feel the ropes starting to give way, the fibres snapping one by one. Just a little more, he thought, just a little more and I'll be free.

**

Tenney seemed to calm, his breathing gradually steadying. Jude watched him closely, relief washing over her as he closed his eyes, appearing defeated. Satisfied that Tenney was no longer a threat to himself or others, she turned away from him to look at Stace.

"Okay," said Jude, trying to adopt the calm, nonthreatening voice she used when dealing with drunks or the drug-addled people on the streets. "But he was fine before you took him." She was obviously in the presence of a madman, and she needed to tread carefully.

Stace's gaze remained steady, his expression calm. "He wasn't fine, Officer Marcello. Neither of them have been fine for a very long time." He finally turned to look at her, his eyes piercing. "Tell me how you met? I mean, you are obviously older than him. I would guess," he narrowed his eyes and looked at her, thinking, "28? 29?"

Jude was flabbergasted. People often mistook her for younger. "How did you know…?" she began, but Stace silenced her with a single look.

"I've been around a long time, Officer Marcello. I've seen your kind before." His words were cryptic, filled with an unsettling certainty.

Before she could ask him exactly what he meant, Tenney broke free from the tree. The ropes snapped under the strain, and he stumbled forward, his eyes blazing with a mixture of anger and confusion.

**

The ropes came away from the tree, snapping in two. Tenney used the momentum to propel himself forward. Before Jude could react, a force knocked her away. She fell in a heap of dried leaves several feet from the tree. The dog ran to her, hiding under her arm. She gathered the quivering body close to her as she looked back to where she had been standing and saw Stace pinning Tenney to the ground.

Tenney lunged forward towards the man, his fingers outstretched like claws. He went to grab him, to kill him, but his prey had moved. One second, he was there looking over his shoulder at the woman, and the next moment he was gone. Tenney howled in frustration and spun around. He was roughly tackled to the ground, the two of them sliding for several feet before coming to a stop. The man was much stronger than him, and he exerted that strength over Tenney. He punched Tenney in the jaw, rendering him semi-conscious.

Then he reared back, still straddling the temporarily stunned boy, and looked at the sky. Long, sharp teeth protruded from his mouth. His eyes turned red, his pupil's dark pinpricks in the crimson orbs. The night was filled with the sound of blood coursing through all the mammals in the area, the strongest coming from the body beneath him. He lunged forward towards Tenney's neck.

Jude scrambled back up and screamed at Stace to get off Tenney. She put the dog on the ground and fumbled around for a weapon. Finding a sturdy branch, she braced it above her head and ran towards the men. Sensing her movement, Stace stopped his descent. Something about this woman reminded him… His teeth retracted back into his mouth and his eyes once more became hazel. He raised a hand and stopped the momentum of the makeshift club aimed for his skull, smashing the wood as though it was kindling.

He looked down at Tenney, still stunned beneath him, and then back at Jude. "I'm sorry…" he started to say, "I had to do it this way. It was the only way we could assess how strong their connection was, how far it had gone."

Jude breathed heavily, fear stopping her from getting too close to either man. Then a thought occurred to her. The last time Tenney was this bad, his sister had nearly died. "Aura…" she whispered. "We need to get him back to Aura."

Stace stood back up and scooped Tenney up like he was a baby. He ran back to the lodge at a speed Jude could just about keep up with, Bo hard on her heels. The forest blurred around them, the trees whipping past as they raced through the night. Jude's heart pounded in her chest, a mixture of fear and determination driving her forward.

When they reached the lodge, Meg was waiting at the door. "What happened?" she asked, her voice trembling.

"No time to explain," Jude panted. "We need to get him to Aura, now."

They hurried inside, the warmth of the lodge a stark contrast to the cold night air. Aura lay on the floor, her face pale and her breathing shallow. The wolf was curled around her protectively, its eyes watching them with a mix of curiosity and caution.

Stace gently laid Tenney down beside his sister, his movements careful and deliberate. "They need each other," he said softly. "Their bond is what keeps them grounded."

Jude knelt beside them, her heart aching as she watched the twins. "Please," she whispered, "let them be okay."

Chapter 15

Aura felt so tired, all the fight had left her body. She knew she was slipping into the abyss, and there was nothing to stop her. She saw a blue cord leading her down, down into the dark, but it was fraying. If she didn't follow it soon, it would snap, and she would have nothing keeping her in the world. The wolf curled himself around her body as she began to drift away.

Through the dark, she felt a thick, warm tongue lick her face. "Urrgh…" she moaned. Why wouldn't Tenney come and get his dog? Couldn't he see she was trying to sleep?

"Ten?" she called out, still half asleep.

"I'm right here, sis."

"Tenney, get Bo off my face…"

"Uh, Aura… it's not Bo… and he's not letting me get any closer to you…"

"What?" Aura opened her eyes. Emerald, green eyes burned down at her. She smiled as she recognised the light in them. They pierced through the last of her haze, bringing her back from the abyss. She saw a black, moist nose at the end of a long, lupine face. His ears twitched as the long tongue shot out to lick her face once more.

She shifted back a bit and looked around. The wolf was sitting beside her, watching her. She remembered the feel of his strong body supporting her after Tenney had been taken…

TENNEY! Aura quickly sat up; the world spun a bit as she got her bearings.

"TENNEY!" she cried out again. Where was he? Frantically, she looked around the fireplace. Jude was sitting close by, Bo by her side. Meg and Stace sat on the other side of her. But where was Tenney?

"Ten?" she called out again. The fire roared in front of her, sparks flying in the air as a gust of wind blew down the grate.

"TEN?" she screamed his name, the panic rising inside her.

From the other side of the room, a shape rose up. The wolf growled. The dark figure walked closer to her. She thought he walked oddly, and as he came closer, she saw that his hands were tied together behind his back. The wolf's growl became a snarl as the figure came closer. For a moment, she thought it was the ghoul from her nightmare returning for her. She shrunk back until she felt the cord between her and Tenney snap back into life, and she recognised the man in front of her.

Aura shifted up to her knees, putting a restraining hand on the neck of her protector wolf. "It's okay," she said to him, willing him to understand. "He won't hurt me." She wasn't sure that the wolf did understand, and for a few tense moments, she felt sure he was going to tear Tenney's throat out. Subtly, Meg nodded to the wolf. With a sound that could have been a 'huff,' the wolf reluctantly backed down.

Aura leapt up and ran to meet her brother. They collapsed to their knees, Aura embracing him tightly to her. He cried desperate tears into her shoulder, his body shaking with the force of his sobs. She pulled back slightly and held his face in both her hands. That was when she noticed the large, ugly bruises beginning to form on his jaw. He looked wretched, broken.

In her mind's eye, she pictured hundreds more of the bright blue threads coming from her soul and attaching them to his. She pictured them repairing the fractured spirit that was forced to exist in two separate bodies. The threads glowed with a soft, ethereal light, weaving themselves into the fabric of his being, mending the rifts and soothing the pain.

"Stace…" whispered Meg, her voice filled with awe.

"I know… I can see it," he replied quietly, his eyes fixed on the twins.

Slowly, the twins became whole again. The blue threads pulsed with energy, binding their souls together in a way that transcended the physical. Aura could feel the strength returning to Tenney, his spirit lifting as the connection between them grew stronger. The bruises on his face seemed to fade slightly, the pain easing as their bond healed him from within.

Jude watched in amazement, her heart swelling with hope. She had never seen anything like this before, but she knew that whatever was happening, it was a miracle. The wolf, sensing the change, relaxed its stance, its eyes softening as it watched over the twins.

Aura and Tenney clung to each other, their breaths synchronising, their hearts beating as one. The world around them seemed to fade away, leaving only the two of them, united in their shared strength and love.

Meg and Stace stood back, giving them space. "They're stronger together," Meg said softly, her eyes glistening with unshed tears.

Stace nodded, a small smile playing at the corners of his mouth. "Yes, they are. And they'll need that strength for what's to come."

As the night deepened, the fire crackled warmly, casting a comforting glow over the reunited siblings. They knew that their journey was far from over, but for now, they had each other. And that was enough.

**

They were all sitting around the fire, watching the flames burn. Tenney leaned heavily on Aura, his exhaustion evident in the way he slumped against her. Jude sat close enough to touch him if she had wanted to, but she used Bo as a barrier, focusing on comforting the dog who was already calm and snoring peacefully. Stace could see the small spark of fear in her eyes as she remembered the crazed man Tenney had become.

By the time Stace had carried Tenney back to the fire, Aura was fading fast. She looked ethereal, insubstantial, as if she might disappear at any moment. Tenney, regaining his consciousness but still caught up in the madness, struck out at Stace and tried to get to his sister. The wolf leapt on Tenney, helping to pin him down as Stace was forced to tie his hands together behind his back. He struck him another blow, rendering him unconscious but not permanently hurt. Stace, a symptom of his very nature, knew the anatomy of the human body better than anything on earth. He knew how to knock someone out without causing permanent damage. Jude had visibly winced at the sight.

But Tenney's proximity to Aura had slowly begun to revive her and return his sanity. If the wolf had let him get closer to his twin, they would have come around faster. Meg glanced at Stace, her concern evident. She was worried about the strong protective instincts of the wolf towards the girl. "Things could get complicated," she would later say to Stace after the trio had left the lodge. But for now, the three of them—Tenney, Aura, and Jude—wanted answers. The night was passing, and soon they would need to leave to get home before their family woke up. Time was of the essence.

The fire crackled, casting flickering shadows on their faces. Tenney's breathing had steadied, and he leaned into Aura, drawing strength from her presence. Jude watched them, her mind racing with questions. She knew they needed to understand what was happening to them, and they needed to understand it now.

Stace broke the silence, his voice calm and measured. "You have questions, and I will do my best to answer them. But you must understand, this is not something that can be easily explained."

Jude nodded; her eyes fixed on him. "We need to know what's happening to them. Why are they like this?"

Stace took a deep breath, his gaze shifting to the twins. "Tenney and Aura share a unique bond, one that goes beyond the physical. It's a connection that ties their very souls together. When they are separated, it causes a rift, a fracture in their spirits. This bond is both their greatest strength and their greatest vulnerability.

"The twins are made up of one immortal being and one human," he continued. "The immortal twin, at the time of the Fade, which happens after their human twin dies and their body is cut off from their element—in this case, Aura, you will learn to control the air. You will be able to change at whim into any creature of the air, from the smallest fly to a mighty dragon." Tenney and Aura moved closer together vague memories of the strange dream they had shared the night before.

"When the Tether has died, the spirit of the immortal seeks out the nearest pregnant woman carrying a child whose gender the being most associates itself with. They attach themselves to the placenta of the baby already in the womb. The woman then gives birth, and they experience what scientists call Hidden Twin Syndrome. The twins are two souls, but their souls become so tightly entwined they are like one soul. Effectively, one person in two bodies. The immortal twin is one of an ancient race of beings called στοιχεῖα* - the Elementals. The Human twin is called δεσμός* - the Tether. They are the only ones who can keep the Elemental truly grounded, tethered to the world—no matter who else they may love or give their hearts to."

With the last remark, he looked straight at the wolf, who gave a strange harumph noise and settled his long nose on his paws, feigning sleep. Bo jumped down from Jude's arms and curled up beside the larger body of the wolf.

***στοιχεῖα** (stoicheia) ** **δεσμός** (desmos)

"We," he looked at Meg, "are part of a brethren of beings who have dedicated their immortal lives to protecting and teaching these children."

During the story, Jude had subconsciously moved closer to Tenney. She shuddered at Stace's explanation of the protectors. What she had seen in the woods, the creature this placid man had become, was an awful lot like the stories of vampires she had grown up reading about and watching in films. Her mother, when she was a child, spun the most fantastic stories about creatures such as he. Tenney, feeling the shudder down his side, wrapped his free arm around her shoulders and pulled her closer. Bo began to snore as he nestled into the body of the wolf, totally oblivious to the revelations going on around him.

The fire crackled, casting flickering shadows on their faces. The night was passing, and soon they would need to leave to get home before their family woke up. Time was of the essence.

"But these protectors are powerless if the twins are separated for too long. The Tether becomes unstable, their souls torn apart. It's as if a vital piece of their essence is missing, like a body without a heart. Such a soul cannot survive for long."

Tenney recalled the excruciating sensation of a vital part of himself being severed. He clenched his teeth, struggling to concentrate on Stace's words.

"The Elemental's presence gradually wanes as the cord binding them to the world frays. Eventually, they fade from existence, their connection to the human realm severed until they find a new host."

Aura and Tenney felt a heavy despair settle upon them as the truth was confirmed. The prospect of a 'normal' life, of forming healthy relationships, and living independently now seemed impossible.

Tenney glanced at Jude from the corner of his eye. Her head hung low, deep in thought over Stace's revelations. The trio on the sofa huddled closer together, Jude's hand subconsciously threading with Tenney's.

"But there is hope," Stace continued. "The twins share powerful telepathic and empathic bonds. With training, they can communicate from a distance, remaining connected even when apart. This means they could potentially lead semi-separate lives."

He paused, ensuring they grasped the gravity of his next words. "However, when the Tether dies, the Elemental will always move on. That is inevitable."

"And where there is a tethered pair," Meg interjected, "you will find those who wish to exploit the Elementals' powers for ill. Creatures from hell itself, made of sulphur, blood, and darkness, invade your dreams. Some can manifest in the bodies of the weak-willed." She paused, considering her next words.

"Their goal is simple: to disrupt humanity, to reshape the world as they see fit. Some of the ancient ones, driven mad by their incorporeal form and reliance on possessing a host to walk this plane of existence, seek answers about their condition, wanting to be what they once were while searching for tools that would make them truly terrifying."

"They have come close to harnessing an Elemental, forcing them to use their powers not for the benefit of mankind, but for its detriment. You may have heard about the tsunami that nearly wiped-out Lisbon in 1755? Or the massive eruption of Vesuvius in 79 AD? Or more recently, the wars of the past hundred and fifty years, the earthquakes, and hurricanes. All these events show that the Legion has grown in number again, and the world is out of balance."

"How do we stop them?" Aura whispered.

"There is a weapon that has harmed them in the past, but it was lost a long, long time ago and has not been seen since," answered Stace.

Bo squirmed as the wolf lifted his head to look at Meg. Tenney froze, momentarily transported back to his nightmare. In it he saw the golden dagger with burning rubies flying towards his heart.

Jude, listening intently, had picked up on an obvious irregularity. She looked up at Stace. "You kept referring to Aura being a twin to sisters," she said. "You never mentioned a brother and a sister."

Stace shifted, suddenly unsure of himself. "Yes," he admitted. "We have never heard of or experienced a fraternal pairing. The Elementals have very specific genders they identify with and have always chosen children of the same gender. It is easier for them to be accepted into the host family if they have a face and a body to clone their own on. This may be the first brother-sister pairing we have witnessed, but by all accounts, it is one of the strongest, maybe even the strongest."

"Hold on," Jude held up her hand to stop Stace. "You also referred to The Elementals, inferring that Aura isn't the only one?" The twins hadn't picked up on this, but thinking back, several times Stace seemed to refer to them in the plural form. They had assumed that he meant all the different versions of Aura, but now they were not so sure.

"Just how many Elementals are there?" Tenney asked, the vein in his forehead pulsing as he struggled to rein in his temper at the omission of an important piece of their history.

Stace looked at Meg before turning back to the trio. "There are five," he admitted.

Chapter 16

Silently and wearily, they crept into the house before their family woke up. They climbed into their beds, knowing the other was awake through the thin partitioned wall, until they heard movement coming from their parents' room. Neither had spoken, but they were thinking the same thing.

What happens next?

They explained Tenney's battered jaw as delayed bruising from the night before when he had run blindly out into the night. Their parents seemed unconvinced, but there was no other explanation as to how they got there. After all, the twins had been grounded. They had never left the house.

It felt too oppressive indoors. They needed to get out, but Samuel was watching them, ensuring they held their side of the bargain and stayed home. So, they decided to go into the back garden. They lay on their backs on a rug and watched the clouds roll over them.

Autumn was making itself known in the chill winds that were the first herald of the winter to come, and so they had put on their warmest jumpers and pulled beanies down over their heads. They lay side by side, but neither touched the other as they both tried to make sense of everything they had learned.

Aura turned her head to Tenney. "I'm sorry, Ten," she said softly, her voice barely audible over the rustling leaves.

"What for?" Tenney was genuinely confused, his brow furrowing as he looked at her.

"I'm sorry that I am holding you back. You could have been normal!" Tenney turned to look at her and saw her wipe an angry tear from her face. "You could have gone to uni, had a normal life—kids, a career… dammit! You could have had so much… more! Instead, I'm holding you back, all because some 'past-me' decided that Ma's womb was the easiest place to start from."

He didn't know what to say, and before he could utter a single syllable, she continued.

"I'm not even properly related to you or Ma, Dad, and Sam. I'm not a proper sister or daughter. I'm a parasite…" Aura wrapped her arms around her chest and sobbed. Her words cut Tenney to the quick. He closed his eyes, pushed his beanie off, and ran his hand through his hair, his tell when he was thinking deeply.

He couldn't help it; she had put the imagery in his mind, and he thought about what his life would've been like without her. He saw himself growing up in England, an only child until Sam came along. He saw how different his relationship with his brother could've been without the distraction of his sister. He saw his parents, never having to worry about a child of theirs suffering unduly, them not being brought before the head teacher every time he got into fights because his rage boiled up when the school separated them. He could have had healthy relationships with girls, choosing someone who he actually wanted to be with.

Then he saw himself travelling to Lincoln, in his right mind, arriving at the station, happy and excited. Maybe being less of a dick to that girl at the bar. He would have completed his studies, hopefully doing his dream job of working with and studying the wolf packs in their natural habitat. He would have been happy with that. Contented even.

And then he thought about his life with Aura, all the times he had lost his mind, his grasp on reality. He thought of the intense, momentary relationships with random girls, the way he could never form a proper, healthy relationship with anyone else. The people who had commented on their close bond, which nobody else had a hope in hell of breaking.

He thought of the times he had nearly lost her to an 'asthma' attack. All the fights he had had to protect her. Then he thought uncomfortably of the times he had seen no other way to keep the girls who bullied her off her back, other than to give them what they wanted.

Then he remembered when they laughed together, cried together. The peace they felt being in each other's company. She was his confidante, his best friend. In his eyes, she was a true sister; it didn't matter to him what her beginnings were.

He recalled the revelation that he had had in Lincoln, just before he fell. There was no Tenney without Aura. That if she hadn't chosen him, he wouldn't be the man he was now. He knew in his heart that he would've still had anger issues. He would probably have been in very serious trouble if she hadn't calmed him. Her calm balanced his passion perfectly.

And, if he hadn't gone to Lincoln that fateful weekend, he would never have met Jude.

Tenney sat up and positioned himself so that when she looked up, she had no choice but to see his face, see that he meant every word he uttered. Aura sat up and faced him, her face red from the tears as much as from the cold. He smiled at her and gently lifted her chin, forcing her to look him deep in his eyes. When he felt the connection between them spark, he spoke quietly but emphatically.

"I love you, Aura."

He didn't need to say any more than that. There was nothing for him to forgive. He knew now that she could feel all the things he felt. So, he made sure she felt his overwhelming gratitude that she was in his life.

It was nearly their birthday. The twins felt a sense of urgency, a need to learn as much as they could before they turned 21. The weight of the approaching milestone pressed on them, making every moment feel precious. Tenney pulled his phone out of his pocket, his fingers trembling slightly as he dialled the first of two numbers.

**

That night, having successfully crept out of the house again, they walked up to the fort. Stace was standing with his feet spread wide and his arms crossed. At his hips, hung two short swords from his belt. Tenney, Aura and Jude approached him as Meg and the wolf emerged from the shadows of the tree line. They congregated at the centre most point of the summit, the site of the ancient fort.

Stace pointed to Tenney. "You. Come with me." Tenney looked at his sister, nodded once, and then followed Stace out of the clearing.

Meg walked up to Aura, "How do you feel Aura?" she asked. Aura was lightheaded, and it was getting worse the further her brother walked away from her.

"Breathe, Aura," said Meg. The wolf instinctively moved to Aura's side. His weight at her hip was comforting and she felt herself relax into him. Jude squeezed Aura's arm.

"I'll be right over there," she said, nodding at a fallen tree. Stace had warned her that she might witness things she didn't agree with. He told her not to interfere, unless he or Meg asked her to help. All she had to do was watch and learn. These lessons were as much for her benefit as they were for the twins. Aura nodded again and tried to smile at Jude, but the pressure on her chest was too great.

Suddenly they heard a fight coming from the direction where Tenney and Stace had walked. Tenney's voice begging Stace to let him go back. It was then that they heard the clash of steel. Aura suddenly perked up. She saw the world slow down, the particles of air move towards her. She clenched her fists, closed her eyes and saw Stace standing over them, the point of his sword about to be thrust down towards their throat.

Aura felt the air surround her, "*up!*" She thought. The air lifted her. "*Tenney,*" she thought again. Jude gasped as Aura flew across the clearing towards her brother.

Meg and the wolf ran after her, Jude trying in vain to keep up with them. When she reached them, she saw Aura lying across Tenney's body, one hand raised towards Stace, who was frozen mid strike of the sword. Her eyes were like two orbs of burning blue fire.

Tenney reached up and forced Aura to look at him. "It's okay, it's okay!" he repeated to her. He looked as shocked as Jude felt. Aura dropped her hand as Tenney managed to penetrate through her defences. Stace was able to move again. He turned and smiled broadly at Meg.

"Well, we've established that Aura can fly in her human form and that she sees and feels things through Tenney's eyes and senses. Now let's see if he can return the favour."

"You are fucking lunatics!" cried Jude. When Stace had said she might not agree with his techniques, she had never imagined that included near death experiences! The stresses of the last few days since meeting Tenney; of being forced to take a desk job and not do the work she loved; and then, before any of that, the worry of her mother going missing, she felt herself finally explode in an impassioned tirade. "How the fuck do we even know that you're not getting your kicks through terrifying kids?!"

Tenney felt a part of him break when he saw Jude's tears, her concern; and then she had referred to them as kids. He sat up, holding Aura to him as he looked steely eyed at Jude. He had believed that she saw them as equals, friends, and not just some kids to look after. This revelation hurt him. Deeply. He helped Aura up and pushed past Jude.

"We're going home." he said. His voice brokered no argument.

"Shit." whispered Jude, at a loss for what to do.

**

The next morning, the twins were in Tenney's room, watching a film on his laptop, trying to act 'normally'. They needed to feel human again, making a pact not to talk about anything supernatural or unexplainable. Tenney didn't want to talk about Jude.

They heard the doorbell ring and their mother opening it. They heard her talk to someone in muffled, inaudible tones, thinking nothing of it, until they heard a tap on his door. Their mother poked her head around it.

"Tenney, Aura, there's a lady here to see you, from Lincoln University. She wants to talk to both of you." When the pair made no attempts to move, Martha walked into the room and pushed the laptop's lid down. "Come on, you two. This could be important! Shift!" She pointed to the door. It was the most excited they had seen their mother in a while.

Grudgingly, they got up and went down the stairs and into the living room, which the family hardly used except when they had guests. Dust motes floated in the rays of sunlight that broke through the cracks in the curtains.

A woman in a smart suit sat on the couch, a briefcase at her feet, and a phone on the coffee table. Her short brown hair was brushed neatly from her face, and black-rimmed glasses perched on her nose. She exuded an air of professionalism and confidence.

She stood up to shake their hands. "Tennyson and Aura Wiseman? My name is Margaret Smith." Her yellow eyes shone with mirth through the frames of her glasses.

**

When their mother had left the room to make coffees, Meg relaxed into the couch. She let out a contented purr. "Oh boy, I haven't sat on a couch like this in forever!"

"Meg!" hissed Tenney. "What are you doing here?" The twins were flummoxed at her audacity as they sat together on the couch opposite hers.

"Ok," she said, sitting back upright. "Straight to it then! Aura, you are the ancient Elemental of Air. This means you can control the very air around you – hence the spontaneous flight last night. You literally have at your fingertips the power to give air or take it away. You can summon gales and create blasts of pure energy."

She saw them share a glance.

"Ah," she said, smiling, "You've already worked that one out, right? Let me guess, Tenney was in danger, and your instincts kicked in? Time slowed, particles moved to you, and then you released them?"

"Yes," Aura said, nodding. Tenney nodded for her to continue.

"A year or so ago, at the pub, we were in the beer garden collecting glasses and suchlike. Some girls we knew from school were annoying Ten, wanting to get his attention. I felt him stiffen when one of them grabbed his arm, trying to pull him down. Fawning all over him."

Tenney turned his face away, either from embarrassment or shame, Meg wasn't sure. "I didn't know how it happened, but I kind of wished that the air would blow them away from him. It was like the garden slowed down and I could see every dust particle, every strand of air moving around me. I willed it to separate Tenney from the unwanted attention, and I saw a mini tornado blow around the girls, lifting their hair, pushing them back off the bench. Tenney was free."

Meg nodded; her expression serious. "That's exactly what I'm talking about. Your powers are tied to your emotions and instincts. The more you understand and control them, the more powerful you'll become. You need to learn how to use it wisely, so that it doesn't use you."

Tenney looked at Meg, his eyes filled with a mix of awe and fear. "What about me? Do I have powers too?"

Meg smiled gently. "In a way, Tenney. You and Aura are connected in ways that go beyond the physical. Your bond amplifies her abilities, and in turn, she stabilises your emotions. Together, you're stronger than you could ever be apart. But you also have your own unique strengths. We'll explore those in time."

Meg thought for a moment. "Aura," she asked, "Do you have any recurring dreams?"

Aura nodded. "We both do."

"Tell me."

"Ten dreams about a dagger, golden with red rubies. He dreams that it flies towards him." Tenney twitched, scratching an itch under one of the plasters on his hand. Neither of them noticed the briefest look of alarm that flitted across Meg's face. "My dream is different. I dream that I go to Tenney, I whisper in his ear and tell him to sleep. I'm safe. Then I am free, I am flying over the valley."

Meg considered this. "When you fly, are you you, or are you something else?"

"She's always a dragon," Tenney whispered the answer for her. "Always." Meg smiled mysteriously. Another secret.

Aura took a deep breath, trying to process everything. "So, what do we do now?"

Meg leaned forward, her eyes shining with determination. "Now, we train. We learn. We prepare for whatever comes next. You're not alone in this. We're here to help you every step of the way."

The twins exchanged a look, a silent agreement passing between them. They were ready to face whatever challenges lay ahead, together.

Meg sat up straighter, looking away in thought. Finally, after what felt like an indeterminable age, she spoke again. "Can you come up to the Fort again tonight?"

As Meg rose to leave, Aura placed a hand on her arm, preventing her from going. Something Meg had said, a look on her face at the lodge, had sparked a question.

"Meg, the young man we met on the hill," Aura began. Something passed across Meg's eyes, a fleeting look of longing and loss. "You talked about the wound he had received—from the dogs?" Meg nodded slightly and tried to look away. Aura persisted, needing to know.

"Meg, do you know that man? The man with emerald, green eyes?"

Meg took a deep breath and seemed to deflate a little.

"Yes," she answered. "He is my son."

**

"So, she hasn't accepted yet that the dragon dreams are real?" Stace asked Meg when she returned to the Fort, recounting her conversation with the twins.

"No, not yet. And they are already communicating telepathically and empathically. But again, they don't seem to know they're doing it, or how they do it."

"Are they coming here tonight?"

"Yes, just before midnight when they can get away unseen."

Stace sat back against a tree. The light was changing as dusk settled across the land. He could already feel himself rejuvenating as the sun dipped. In the distance, he heard a noise.

"Stace," Meg began, "Stace, they've met him. I had forgotten in my confusion. But she has seen him, spoken to him. I told you things might get complicated." Stace, knowing how her heart ached for the son she would never see, never hold, understood how it would break for him as he came back into Aura's life. They had time, a couple of weeks still before they needed to worry about what may or may not happen should they spend any length of time together, how he might tip the delicate scales that they had worked so hard these past days to steady. He embraced her to him.

She had heard the noise in the woods as well, her senses still sharp.

"Go," she said, patting her oldest friend on his back. "Go."

In one fluid motion, he moved out of the embrace. He could sense the buck nearby, naively believing that because the wolf was elsewhere in the woods, it was safe. The young male deer had no idea that a far greater danger was closer to hand.

"I'm going to catch something to eat," he said. "And then I'll make a visit to Officer Marcello." Meg watched him as he strode away, turning to approach the oblivious animal from downwind.

"Stace," she called after him, "maybe less swords and more talk, ok?"

He smiled back at her, red eyes glowing in the rising moonlight. Letting out a short bark of a laugh, Meg saw his long, deadly teeth pushing through his gums in anticipation of the meal to come. Then, in the blink of an eye, he disappeared into the lengthening shadows.

Chapter 17

Jude paced the room of the hotel, thinking about what to do. On her dressing table lay the pile of files she had gathered relating to her mother. Somewhere, amongst the pile of correspondence and diary entries, was the clue she needed to get her answers. It was just, with everything else that had gone on recently, she couldn't focus on any of it, and when she did look, her weariness meant none of it made any sense.

She was so tired. Tired of the violence she had witnessed, tired of the stress of watching out for Tenney, and subsequently Aura. She had seen him close down after she had referred to them as kids. Stupid, stupid mistake! Jude let out a groan of exasperation as she collapsed onto her bed, looking up at the ceiling.

It was times like this she wished her dad was still alive to give her his advice, his unflappable nature rubbing off on her as he sat quietly and listened to her, before he offered simple advice. She missed his voice, his soft American accent. She missed him.

Whilst her relationship with her mother had always been full of love, Jude often felt her mother lacked a capacity for understanding her daughter. Raechael Garbling-Marcello always seemed slightly remote, otherworldly, and fragile.

Rae had a wicked imagination though, and she enjoyed making up alternative fairy tales about monsters and heroes. But her favourite stories were the ones about The Councillors, a race of beings sent to watch the tumult on the earth. They were forbidden from interfering with mankind, and the penalty was high if they were discovered. "But sometimes the risk of discovery was worth it," she would say as she tucked Jude in. Jude often fell asleep, angels, monsters, and fallen heroes chasing through her nightmares.

Tony Marcello, lovingly watching his wife and child, would softly call to her mother as he rested casually against the door frame of Jude's room – "Rae, Darlin'," he'd say, "she's heard enough. Let Judy sleep." Her mother would stroke Jude's head, kiss her eyes as they began to close, and then walk into her husband's arms and let him lead her down the stairs.

When he had died of cancer when Jude was 18, the two of them felt their worlds crumble. There were no more family members to go to, unless they travelled to New York, which, with Rae's fear of flying, was never going to happen. They were cast adrift from each other.

Her mother had lost the love of her life, the heartbreak shutting her off from her daughter. Their relationship had been so strained over the last ten years, that it was almost a month before Jude knew her mother may be missing, and that was only because one day she realised that none of her messages had been answered. That that had been nearly three months ago.

Since the death of Tony, Rae had become virtually agoraphobic, barely stepping out of the house. When Jude had visited her small basement flat – was it really only a few days ago? - she saw no sign of struggle, no hint of desertion. All her clothes were in her drawers and wardrobes. The only thing missing was her rucksack and purse. It was as though she had simply decided to pop down to her local shop, the furthest place she felt safe enough to walk to. But she hadn't made it there or back home again.

She simply wasn't there anymore. Something had happened to her mother, and she was failing miserably in her duty to find her.

So, here in this small room, Jude had begun her own, unofficial investigation. Temporarily put on hold by one Mr. Tennyson Wiseman.

She groaned again and rubbed her face with her hands, when she was startled out of her reverie by a knock on the door. Jude sat bolt upright.

She put the chain on the door and carefully opened it, peering through the gap. Stace stood there, a long grey coat hanging from his shoulders and a soft scarf around his neck. Jude noticed a small spot of red at the corner of his mouth.

He was the last person she wanted to see at the moment, and she moved to close the door. His hand shot out, arresting the movement. Jude felt herself being pushed back into the room as he forced the door, ripping the chain from the door jamb. As Jude stumbled backwards against her dresser, he casually entered her room.

**

The demon rolled his shoulders in the body he had stolen. He looked up at the hotel through the eyes of the young man. For the last few weeks, he had been sitting in the conservatory, watching, waiting. Now in this new body, he was no less vigilant. It was because of his vigilance that he saw him, moving purposefully up the street.

Thinking back, he remembered with glee the look on the man's face as he banished his family and threw him into the bull. The ecstasy with every scream of the man dying torturously in the belly of the metal beast. As the music of his screams rolled over the writhing masses of the bodies around him, he had instructed the archers to take down the wife and children as they fled.

His triumph had been short-lived as he recalled the life being squeezed out of his host body as he was faced by the red-eyed monster the man became. Gingerly, he rubbed his new tattooed neck where he had felt the fangs pierce his artery. He had only just escaped in time. If he hadn't escaped the confines of that body, he would have been dragged down with the host as he died.

He had given up much that night, so many years ago, but still so fresh in his long memory. Anger coursed through his black veins as he saw him walk into the hotel to visit the police-bitch.

In a blur, he moved faster than a human body should have allowed and made preparations to muster his brethren. The time to act was nearly upon them.

**

Stace carefully closed the door behind him, letting the broken chain swing to and fro. He turned to face Jude. He blinked as she sprayed deodorant in his face. He barely felt the tingle of fragrant spray as it hit him in his eyes. She may as well have simply blown air at him; he was impervious to it. Wiping the moisture off his face, he looked at Jude. She held the useless improvised weapon in her hand and looked angry… and scared.

"I'm sorry to surprise you like this, Officer Marcello, but I didn't think you would see me otherwise."

Jude was shocked by the lack of effect the deodorant had had on Stace. She looked around for another weapon. Hairbrush? No. Her book beside her bed? It was too far away, and she doubted how much damage a paperback could do against him.

There was nothing else within reaching distance. Except the silver frame with her parents' picture in it. She swallowed as she thought about breaking it over Stace's head. Could she do it? As Stace walked nearer to her, she played for time as her hand felt along the surface behind her, feeling for the touch of silver… "Damn right I wouldn't!" she said, panting slightly.

"I felt we needed to talk, just the two of us. Set the record straight." He was close enough to her now.

She gripped the frame, and, with a silent apology to her parents, she swung it at Stace's temple.

She was fast, but he was faster. Stepping back, he blocked her arm and put her into an arm lock. She was forced to drop the picture. It fell to the floor, face down. Stace kicked it under the bed and walked her to the edge of her bed as he pulled the rattan chair over, sitting down to face her.

He released the arm lock. "Please, sit down," he asked, gentlemanly.

She had no other option. Rubbing her arm, she sat.

Stace took a deep breath, trying to calm the tension in the room. "I understand you're scared and angry, but I'm not here to hurt you. We need to talk about Tenney and Aura. There are things you need to know, things that can't wait."

Jude glared at him, still wary. "You could have just called."

Stace shook his head, his look suddenly like a parent or a teacher to a child. "Would you have answered?"

"Probably not." She replied, sullenly, still rubbing her arm.

Stace leaned in closer, his voice dropping to a whisper. "There are forces at play that you don't understand. Tenney and Aura are at the centre of it, but you're involved now too. We need to work together if we're going to protect them."

Jude's eyes narrowed. "Why should I trust you?"

Stace's expression softened. "Because I care about them too. And because, like it or not, we're all in this together."

Jude hesitated, then nodded slowly. "Fine. But next time, try knocking and waiting to be invited in."

Stace managed a small smile. "Deal."

**

"These twins are unlike other elemental-tether pairings. I sensed something in Tennyson that has perplexed me from the first. He is unstable; he would have been unstable whether he was tethered or not. I believe it is only the fact that he is tethered to an Elemental that he has not become completely unhinged."

Jude stared at him incredulously, her brown eyes burning into him. Her arms were crossed across her chest, a barrier against the 'man' sitting across from her. She was another one he couldn't totally figure out, but he was fairly certain he had correctly deduced her heritage, though she may have been second or third generation, the chances of another one happening within a relatively short period, seemed slim to him. He just couldn't quite see the part she had to play in this saga.

He couldn't shake the feeling that she was an important player in this game. There were aspects about her—the way she moved, though it sometimes pained her, her intelligence, and willingness to protect people she barely knew—that reminded him of someone who had crossed his path. But his life was very long, and he had seen and met countless beings, both human and supernatural, that he couldn't remember them all.

He relaxed his shoulders and tried to present himself as unthreateningly as he could. She shifted slightly on the edge of the bed, subconsciously beginning to mirror his relaxed pose.

"Not only are they brother and sister," he continued. "They are connected more deeply than any other I've seen. Tell me, Officer Marcello, did you see the blue lights coming from her body, attaching themselves to her brother after I separated them that night?"

Years of living with humans had given him the opportunity to study their body language. The way she shifted and averted her gaze told him that she had seen it.

"And you saw the way she only revived when he was near her, how he lost his madness when she lived again? That is why we need to teach them, to control their power. They need to be able to control their link so that they don't ultimately destroy each other.

"There is a very real chance that this may be her last life, our last opportunity to finally end the tethering and release them. All of them." He paused as he let his words sink in. "If we don't get it right, they may separate too soon. Tenney will go insane, and Aura will fade away into nothingness. The consequences for the world if that happened are dire."

"How do you know this?" Jude asked, curiosity winning out over the distress she had previously felt.

"In the first half of the last century, the elemental being of metal became untethered after being separated from his brother during an experiment. The brother went mad and killed himself and their captors. Untethered, Metal faded away. His guardian has scoured the whole earth, following every lead, for the last century. Metal hasn't been seen anywhere since.

"Even the Councillors have lost sight of him."

The Councillors? Jude thought her heart would stop as she remembered the stories her mother told her. She blinked away the memories. "When did this happen?" she asked Stace.

"1938," he said.

Jude was flabbergasted. "You mean they started the Second World War!?"

"No, not exactly. The men who experimented on them did that. Since the end of the war, the earth is losing its minerals and ore. Industry and pollution are rife, wars are worldwide and no longer just in pockets of the earth. With no Elemental to act as the balance, to encourage the world to replenish itself, I fear that the world is fast losing its valuable resources. And all because an elemental was separated forever from his Tether."

Stace could see that she still struggled to believe him.

"How did this tethering begin?" she asked.

"There are consciousnesses of the five core elements of the world: Metal, Fire, Earth, Water, and Air. They were used by the Creator at the dawn of time to build and maintain the world. They were beings of the very elements themselves, and their powers were exponential.

"As the world grew and changed, the Elementals began to use their powers to influence the Creator's children. They became false gods, relishing in the adoration of the people. And so, the Creator sent five of his most trusted soldiers to watch them and reign them in when necessary.

"But they had grown too used to the power they had over the world. They had children with humans, children who lived normal lives unless they were killed violently or martyred in defence of another. After this martyr's curse fell upon them, they would become demi-creatures, men and women ruled by the night and by their own violent instincts.

"One of the soldiers sent by the Creator saw the potential of the army of Demis and changed allegiances, falling completely to the earth.

"With them came their own band of acolytes, demons capable of possessing any soul weak enough to let them in. They walk the earth, blending in with man, their true selves only being shown when they are ready to fulfil their missions set by their leader."

Stace paused momentarily and rubbed his chin, considering where the story would go next. Jude saw his thumb linger on the burn scar, partly hidden under his hairline at the side of his face.

"The Elementals became legendary, their influence spreading across the globe. Until the Creator realised that if the world was to live in peace, he had to come to the earth himself. He witnessed the power of his fallen soldier on the earth, saw the hold they had over the Elementals. The only way he could prevent an apocalypse was to give the Elementals the opportunity to experience exactly what it means to be human.

"He returned to his throne and issued instructions to his last four soldiers, his Councillors. They rounded up the Demis and slaughtered them before moving on to their immortal parents.

"To teach them to respect the world and Man, he made them earthbound, tethering them to the souls of human children. They would grow in power until they were ready to find themselves again and restore the world to its natural rhythms. Mankind would no longer be enthralled to them."

"So," Jude asked, "what are you then?"

Stace knew this question would come. She had seen him for what he really is when he had wrestled Tenney to the floor.

"I am the son of the Element of Metal and Minerals. Conceived shortly before he became tethered. I was martyred to protect my family after I refused to renounce my mother's Celtic gods. The curse fell upon me, and I have walked this world for over 2000 years. I was met by a Councillor who gave me new purpose – to guard and teach the element of Air and her Tether."

"And Meg?"

"She was born a few centuries after the tethering, her mother living as a human. She was the first to be martyred since the tethering. Her birth proved that the power of conception and the curse of martyrdom had stayed with the Elementals."

Jude sat back. She didn't think he was crazy, but she couldn't be sure. She felt she knew what he was, as unreal as it seemed, but she needed him to confirm it.

"That night in the forest, when you separated Tenney and Aura. Your teeth, your eyes… you changed. And your strength and speed are unreal. I need to know… What are you?"

"I think you know what my kind are called. Although our beginnings are not the same as those that are glorified in films and novels."

"There's more of you?" she asked. "More than just you and Meg?"

"Yes, though not many, and I am the first since the Councillors crushed the original sons and daughters of the elements," he said. Feeling the need to explain one more salient point, he leaned forward slightly, his hazel eyes never leaving hers. She needed to know this if she was going to survive.

"Our own children carry the curse. Meg's son was martyred before his birth, and it is all he has ever known."

Jude analysed what she had heard. "What will happen now?" she asked him.

"We will train them. I think the Tether needs you to witness what is happening, to help talk him down when he loses control. He trusts you it would seem. Because he needs you, Aura will need you also." He let that sink in before pushing himself up on to his feet. As he approached the door, he turned once more to her. "You must do all that I ask of you. Do you understand? It could be dangerous for one such as you."

She nodded.

"The twins are coming tonight. Be at the clearing at the fort by Midnight."

She watched Stace as he slipped out of the door. She had never believed creatures like him existed outside of fantasy and horror. Jude couldn't help but feel sorry for Stace and Meg and the hand fate had dealt them. But the person she felt most sorry for Megs who had been child born into it, never knowing anything but his own vampirism.

Gingerly she stood up from the chair and locked the door. Walking over to her bed she reached under it. Her fingers felt for the silver edges of the frame. When she retrieved it, she was relieved to see that the frame and the precious picture of her parents was undamaged.

Chapter 18

The following morning, Jude got up early and waited for the taxi to take her to the station, a small rucksack over her shoulder. She glanced at her red Jaguar in the hotel car park, feeling a pang of attachment. She had lain awake thinking about everything she had experienced, especially the conversation with Stace.

As the dawn rays peeked under her curtain, she realised that with the mystery of the twins—one she felt compelled to unravel—and the hunt for her mother, she was probably going to be here longer than she had first thought. Her gut told her she would definitely need more than the two weeks she had left.

If she was going to stay, she needed to return to Lincoln, speak to the Chief back at work, and collect her mail from her neighbour at her flat. She also wanted to see her friend Ellie, maybe grab some lunch at the coffee shop halfway up Steep Hill. Jude felt a strong need to talk to someone untouched by anything supernatural.

But her main purpose for going home, and the reason she couldn't take her car, was that if she was going to stay longer, there was something she needed to have. Something that would help her think clearly and give her an escape if things got too overwhelming.

Subconsciously, as the taxi pulled up outside the hotel, her clenched fist rolled forwards and backwards, as though revving the throttle of a motorbike. A small smile ghosted her lips.

**

The training began that night and continued nightly over the following weeks. Jude watched from the sidelines as Tenney and Aura gradually learned to be separated and handle the new powers she had bestowed upon them. During the day, they caught up on sleep where they could, helped Samuel at the dig site, walked Bo, or simply sat together in seeming silence, strengthening their telepathic bond.

Each training session began with the separation of the twins, with either Stace or Meg teaching them to concentrate and fortify the thread between them. Initially, progress was slow. Tenney's rage became almost unmanageable, even for someone as strong as Stace, while Aura fainted from breathlessness. But they persevered, and soon the twins could be apart for longer periods with little distress.

At that point, Stace began training Tenney in combat, teaching him how to channel his excess energy and strength into self-defence. Jude would smile at Tenney when he walked to the fire, exhausted and battered, searching for a bottle of water. Initially, he still couldn't quite look at her without recalling her comment about them being kids. She waited patiently, following her father's example, knowing instinctively that he would talk to her when he was ready. If she pushed him too much, she would lose him, and she wasn't prepared to risk that.

Her patience and their training began to pay off, with Tenney choosing to spend more time with Jude. She found herself liking him more and more as they got to know each other. When they were apart, she would stand in front of the mirror, reminding her reflection that she was not there to start a relationship, that he saw her as a friend, and friendship was all she could offer him.

Sitting together by the campfire, she told him about her mother, her plans to go to Bristol before heading back to Lincoln, her arthritis and its impact on her daily life, her best friend Ellie, and the loss of her dad. He listened attentively, smiling when he mentioned they both shared something in common—an American parent. They laughed together, recounting funny tales of how his mother and her father tried to adjust to English life. His attention was fully on her as Aura practiced with Stace and Meg, and she basked in his glow.

In turn, he shared his dreams and frustrations, expressing that he could never be fully free but did not blame Aura. He explained how their relationship, while now more understood, was still ultimately that of a brother and sister, filled with teasing and occasional irritation. He wished he knew his younger brother Sam better and hoped that now, with a new way of living, it wasn't too late to build those bonds.

Things had finally settled into a happy rhythm. Then, the night before the first full moon of the month, the night before their 21st birthday, Stace kidnapped Aura.

**

Tenney, not expecting Stace to run off with Aura, was unprepared for her sudden absence. He forgot all his training and allowed the cord to become tight again. Rage swallowed him as he turned on Meg, attacking her for letting Aura go.

Before he could get a hold of Meg, Tenney was flat on his back, pinned down by the huge black wolf. The wolf's face was an inch away from Tenney's, its green eyes narrowed as its snarl sent drool landing on Tenney's face. If Tenney moved, the wolf snapped at him, its sharp claws digging painfully into his chest.

Meg calmly approached Tenney and knelt beside him, calling Jude over.

"Remember what I told you to do?" she said. Taking hold of his cheeks, Jude forced him to look away from the wolf's eyes and into her own. He saw into the eyes of someone he had grown close to, someone who had, he realised with a jolt, as much a hold on his heart as his sister did. Her soft brown eyes gazed down at him, bringing him back from his madness.

"Tenney!" Meg, kneeling beside Jude came into focus, her voice strangely calm said. "I want you to find your sister. Close your eyes, Tenney!" She slapped him lightly as he began to feel the rage again, the shock of the action helping to bring him back around. "Follow the cord, use your mind, and find Aura!"

Restricted by the huge beast on his chest and the strong, soft hands of the woman he was falling for, Tenney closed his eyes. He saw only darkness. He was alone, lost. Desperately, he called out to his sister.

It felt like forever before his mind quietened enough to hear her small voice, miles away, answer him.

-Ten…?

-Aura! Where are you? Has he hurt you?

-Ten, I'm okay, I'm okay! I don't know where I am, but we're definitely not in the Forest of Dean anymore…

-I'll find you.

-NO! Ten, it's too far. Stace told me I have to find my own way back. I will find you. Trust me, Ten. I love you…

She gently left his consciousness, but he could still feel her, pulling gently on the now stretchy cord that connected them. As he felt the rage subside, he blinked open his eyes. The wolf still lay atop him, staring menacingly down at him. Jude was still holding his face, Meg hovering next to her.

"Are you back?" the older woman asked, a little dubious.

116

He nodded. He was himself again.

Tenney looked up again and saw Jude, holding on to him tightly, tears in her eyes and on her cheeks.

His heart skipped a beat.

**

Stace stalked around Aura.

"Where are we?" she asked. He had carried her at such a fast speed for so long that when they finally stopped, she felt dizzy and was sick. She looked around and saw the treeless, green mountains. In the distance, faint lights of a small town flickered.

"Bannau Brycheiniog. Pen Y Fan to be precise." Aura gaped at him. Stace had just carried her 40 miles away at Superman-like speeds, and he didn't even look out of breath. Her head spun again.

Pen Y Fan, the highest peak in South Wales, stood majestically over its brothers and sisters. The mountain, part of the Bannau Brycheiniog National Park, its blanket of sweeping grassy moorlands lay below them. All around her, the panoramic view stretched for miles. A tapestry of natural beauty, with rolling hills, serene reservoirs, and ancient forests. The stars shone the brightest she had ever seen in the pitch-black sky. The moons shadow had retreated from its face; tomorrow it would be full once again.

"Where's Tenney?"

"Back at the hill fort. Ready yourself. Meg, Hedge, and Jude should have gained control of him by now."

"Oh no! Tenney!" she cried out, imagining him battling everyone just to get back to her. Then she felt it—a small tug. She closed her eyes.

"AURA?" Suddenly, as though he was standing beside her, she heard Tenney's voice desperately calling her over and over.

Opening her eyes, she looked at Stace. "What's happening?"

"Tenney is trying to reach you. Answer him, tell him you're okay. Do not tell him where we are. Tell him that it is up to you to get back to him. That he must wait for you. Can you do that, Aura?"

She nodded, breathed in deeply, and closed her eyes to talk to Tenney.

When she returned, she looked at Stace. "Okay, I've done that. You can take me back now."

Stace held his hands behind his back, smiled, and said, "I'm afraid you have to take yourself back to Tenney."

Aura had thought Stace was being stupid when he said she had to tell Tenney that she would make her own way back. She couldn't believe he meant it. It was the middle of the night, they were miles away from any town or village, with no transport or phones to call anyone. She didn't know how she was going to get back. Unless she walked. Determined to prove a point, angry at his stupidity, she started to stride out, following the thread that connected her to Tenney.

A blur moved in front of her, and she came face to face with the impenetrable chest of Stace Caedmon.

"Not like that," he stated.

Aura felt herself grow enraged. She hit his chest, doing very little damage other than bruising her own hands.

"How then?" she cried.

Stace gently took her hands. He guided her to a boulder and sat her down. He squatted in front of her and looked up at her tear-stained face.

"Meg told me you dream of being a dragon?"

"What?" she blurted.

"A dragon. We've seen you, in fact. I think it's only you and Tenney who don't believe it's real."

"Of course it's not real. How can it be real? Dragons don't exist." Why was he telling her these tales and not helping her get back?

"You are the Air Elemental, a being so powerful you can call air to you and use it to propel even the strongest of us away from you. I am an immortal who has walked this earth for 2000 years." He laughed softly. "Don't tell me that you still don't believe in what you have seen and witnessed? Why is becoming a dragon, the spirit of the sky, so hard to accept as true?"

"When you dream of the dragon, how do you feel?" Stace continued. He seemed genuinely interested. She wiped a tear from her face.

"Free, I guess. I know where Tenney is, and that he is safe. At least, most of the time. The last time I knew he would follow me. I dreamt that I had forgotten to tell him to stay."

"Don't you want to feel that freedom again?" He asked. "Don't you want to get back to him?"

"You know I do!"

"Then draw out the dragon!"

She knew he was purposefully being enigmatic, expecting her to understand what he was saying to her. She felt muddled. Despite the bright cord between her and Tenney, she couldn't think clearly without him. Anger and pain grew inside her. That passion brought her to her feet. She towered over Stace.

Literally towered over him.

Somehow Stace seemed smaller.

"That's it, Aura!" he cried out, looking up at her. "Think about Tenney! Think about the freedom! Follow the cord and fly to him!"

A tornado started at her feet and rose up around her. She felt her bones shift, her skin change. But it wasn't unpleasant. A lovely warm feeling spread over her, filling her with a sense of weightlessness and power. Her clothes began to rip as her body transformed. Her large eyes swirled, a miasma of different blues, swirling into the depths of her soul. Wings sprouted from her back, and finally, she took to the air.

She was an iridescent dragon, shimmering in different hues of blues, greys, and turquoises. Her scales caught the moonlight, reflecting a mesmerising array of colours that danced across her body.

Stace stood on the ground, looking up at her, smiling and laughing. She turned somersaults in the air, flew up through the clouds, and shot down to earth like an arrow. Blue smoke billowed from her nostrils as she thrilled at her newfound aerodynamics.

Then she saw the cord, leading her back to Tenney. With powerful beats of her wings, she flew back to her soul.

**

"Where is she?" Tenney was pacing the ground.

"Look up!" said Meg, pointing to the almost-full moon.

A shape, almost like a bat, flew past it. Then it flew down, getting bigger and bigger…

Jude took a step back as the great blue dragon flew directly towards them. Meg put a hand on her arm. "Don't scream. It's okay. Look."

Tenney began to run towards the monster. Jude wanted to cry out to him to come back. Meg shook her head vigorously and held a finger to her lips. The wolf wandered to the fire and picked up a blanket. He carried it to Meg.

"Thank you," she said quietly, stroking him between his ears, before draping it around Jude's shocked shoulders.

The dragon landed and bellowed at Tenney as it thundered towards him.

**

Tenney had never seen anything so beautiful. She glowed blue, her scales shimmering, the colours shifting continuously. The air around her vibrated with her power and majesty. He knew he had to get to her.

They met in a crash as he hit her square on the nose. She closed her eyes and made a purring noise in her throat. Her mind opened to him.

-Ten?

-Yes!

-I found you!

-You told me you would.

-Wanna fly?

He stepped back slightly. His smile said it all. She dipped her head and shoulder, and he vaulted onto her back. When he found their most comfortable spot, she concentrated and caused her scales to form a saddle-like seat to keep him safe and secure. She brought out two strong cords and wrapped them tightly around his waist, and then she leapt back into the sky.

The people on the ground heard Tenney's whoop of joy as she flew them away over the tops of the trees.

Part 2

X

There has fallen a splendid tear
From the passion-flower at the gate.
She is coming, my dove, my dear;
She is coming, my life, my fate;
The red rose cries, 'She is near, she is near;'
And the white rose weeps, 'She is late;'
The larkspur listens, 'I hear, I hear;'
And the lily whispers, 'I wait.'

XI.

She is coming, my own, my sweet;
Were it ever so airy a tread,
My heart would hear her and beat,
Were it earth in an earthy bed;
My dust would hear her and beat,
Had I lain for a century dead;
Would start and tremble under her feet,
And blossom in purple and red.

Maud: A Monodrama, Alfred, Lord Tennyson

Chapter 19

Aura flew with Tenney over vast swathes of land, past the moon. Tenney thought about how amazing it would be to fly in front of the moon as it reached its fullness over the coming nights. By the time the sun was rising, and they flew home, they had followed the mighty Severn past the tributaries of the Wye and Avon, down to the sea, and back again beyond Gloucester into the Cotswold Hills. Somehow, she was able to alter the air around her, distorting it so that the people below would not see the dragon—or its passenger—as it soared above them.

As she flew down towards their garden, she began to shrink. By the time their feet hit the ground, and Tenney had pulled a large towel left to dry overnight down from the line to cover her, she was herself again. The twins embraced. Tenney held his sister for the longest time, thanking her.

Tenney's house key was still in his pocket. After they let themselves in, they made their way silently to Tenney's room, a sleepy Jess and Bo, disturbed from their dog bed, plodding after them up the stairs.

Aura pulled on her pyjamas, discarding the towel on the floor which Jess curled herself onto, and they climbed into the bed, Bo jumping up and lying across them both. They quickly fell into a deep, dreamless sleep.

**

Tenney rubbed his eyes. Outside his room, he heard someone moving very quietly... No—more than one person! Paranoia made him sit upright, causing Bo to slip into the gap between him and his still sleeping sister. He shifted in his new position and quickly began to snore again.

Gently, he shook Aura's shoulder, waking her up.

"What is it?" she asked groggily.

He put a finger to his lips, instructing her to be quiet, then pointed to the shadows moving under the door. Aura's heart hammered in her chest, memories of the strange man on the hill and her dreams of the ghouls in the forest flooding back. She shrunk back against the headboard as Tenney silently slipped over her and the oblivious dog, positioning himself behind the door.

The door began to open, allowing the light from the landing to enter the room. They heard voices…

Singing "Happy Birthday."

The cake came first, followed by a smiling Martha, a still sleepy Sam, who was maybe a little grumpy to be woken up so early on a rare Friday when he was not expected at school. Following him, his hands on his shoulders as though the teenager needed the extra momentum just to get through the door, came a beaming Samuel, his deep voice reverberating around the room as he overdid the last 'you' in the birthday song.

Tenney's shoulders relaxed as he held the door open for his cake-laden mum, watching the slow smile spread across his sister's face.

It was the twins' 21st birthday.

**

The plan for the day was straightforward. With Sam's school closed for an inset day, the family had the entire day to enjoy together. The evening, however, was reserved for the twins, who were eager to meet up with friends and paint the town red.

Tonight, it didn't really matter to Samuel or Martha what they did. Their grounding was finally over, and they were determined to make the most of their newfound freedom. As long as they had fun, nothing else mattered.

The twins knew exactly what they wanted to do. After breakfast, Martha packed up a picnic and the whole family piled into the old estate car, Bo and Jess straddling the legs of the 'kids' squeezed in the back, and they set off for Caerleon, the ancient Roman town near Newport.

For a family of archaeologists, this was the perfect day out—an opportunity to experience living history. First, they visited the baths and walked around the raised wooden walkway, which allowed visitors to look down into it without damaging the ancient site. The baths, known as the *natatio*, were an immense open-air swimming pool that once held more than 80,000 gallons of water. Thanks to the wonders of film projection, they glimpsed a Roman soldier still diving the depths today. They had been a place of luxury and socialisation for Roman legionaries, a stark contrast to their otherwise harsh lives.

Tenney and Sam poked gentle fun at their dad as he got lost in the past, while Aura and Martha discussed the different archaeological finds that had been the norm for a Roman and his family to use—pots, utensils, and pieces of jewellery. There was even a strigil, a tool used to scrape the dirt and grime off a body.

This was Martha's area of interest, the everyday lives of people who lived millennia ago. Working part-time at the local high school teaching English Literature, she volunteered two days a week at a local heritage museum in the Forest, cataloguing artifacts and creating and maintaining the displays. The two women were discussing a large ring with a stone set in it. The stone was green, with white striations moving through it. It seemed to glow under the light of the display.

"Kind of looks like angel wings, don't you think?" Martha noted to her daughter.

Tenney and Sam's loud laughter coming from behind them ended their contemplation of the artifact. They turned around to see him and Sam pointing as their father argued with one of the museum curators.

-What's so funny, Ten?

The sudden, clear voice of Aura in his head made Tenney turn to look at her, his eyes dancing with mirth.

-Dad is telling that bloke that they've got the names wrong for some of the rooms! he told her.

"I think it's time to go, Mum," said Aura, aware that once her father started 'educating' someone without first giving his credentials, things could get messy. Martha agreed.

They collected the dogs, who were waiting patiently for them at the 'dog stop' outside the museum, tied loosely to a special ring in the shade next to a bowl of clean water. Sam held back as he watched his family walk away from the baths to the walls of the ancient amphitheatre. Built around AD 90, the amphitheatre was the Roman equivalent of today's multiplex cinema, seating up to 6,000 spectators who gathered to watch gladiatorial combat and exotic wild animals. Realising they were one member down, Tenney turned around and called over his shoulder, "You coming, Sammy?" Sam ran to catch up with his family.

A small, shy smile spread over his face as Tenney met him partway, encompassing him in a half hug. He finally realised that he was having fun! It was nice to have his brother's attention focused on him for a change.

He couldn't remember ever laughing so hard with Tenney. He was surprised to discover that they shared a similar sense of humour. Tenney, for the first time, seemed genuinely interested in Sam, asking him about his computer games, what school was like, and whether Mr. Bauer was still teaching art. It was like Tenney had finally cottoned onto the fact that he had a second sibling. And Sam was loving it. He felt a warmth and connection he hadn't experienced before, a sense of belonging and being seen.

Something had changed between Tenney and Aura, something was different. They weren't constantly next to each other or seeking the other out when they were apart. Tenney didn't fly into a rage, and Aura was breathing normally. In fact, Sam had never seen them so relaxed before.

Sam couldn't wait to tell his online friend, Theo, all about it when they finally got home. Theo had some ideas about Sam's half-siblings, and Sam wanted his take on this new development. He fingered his phone in his pocket in anticipation.

Under the early October sun, Sam, Tenney, and Samuel pretended to be Roman gladiators, running around the amphitheatre with imaginary swords in hand. Bo played the role of a ferocious lion, released into the ring. Aura and Martha, sitting on the bank wrapped up together in the picnic blanket, giving Jess a bit of a break, laughed when Tenney pretended to be taken down by the deadly beast, rolling on the ground with the young dog happily yipping and licking him. Sam, with a mighty battle cry, launched himself upon the writhing mass, as Bo nimbly sprang away to the relative safety of Samuel.

Her mum wrapped her arm around her and hugged her close.

"You seem happy, love," she said.

"I am," replied Aura, genuinely.

Sam, laughing so hard he could feel a stitch start in his side, rolled away and watched his sibling and father play, feeling a warmth he hadn't felt in a long time. The change in Tenney and Aura was palpable, and it made him hopeful. He felt a connection to his family that he hadn't experienced before. The attention Tenney was giving him was new and wonderful. For the first time, Sam felt truly seen by his older brother. He could begin to understand why Tenney was so popular without ever trying.

As the sun began to set, casting a golden glow over the ancient stones of the amphitheatre, Sam felt a sense of contentment. The day had been perfect, filled with laughter and bonding.

**

That evening, after they had arrived home, all of them happy, content, and agreeing that it had been a successful day, they heard the powerful engine of a bike as it pulled up outside the house, followed by a knock at the door.

Jude stood on the threshold in a bike jacket, her hair scraped back in a low bun. In one hand was a bottle of wine and in the other a bag which clinked promisingly. Tenney sidled up as his father called him to the door. Jude looked attractively uncertain as she stood on the doorstep. As a way of explanation, she offered him a small smile. "I heard it was your birthday…" she said, proffering the drinks towards him.

"Thanks…" said Tenney, opening the bag to see several bottles of fruity cider. Jude turned to go back down the path. Quickly, Tenney realised that he didn't want her to go. "Wait!" he called after her. "You look knackered…"

"Thanks a lot!" Jude replied, mock affront on her face.

"I mean, you look like you're about to drop. Come in, we're going to get some fish and chips. Birthday meal tradition." He was aware he was rambling; Aura was aware too. Gently, she nudged his mind, ensuring that he wouldn't take no for an answer from Jude. Tenney stood to one side, beckoning her in with his head. "Come on," he said, letting his megawatt smile appear as he saw Jude give in. "Aura says she'll kill me if I don't insist you stay."

Jude laughed and walked into the warmth of the house. The cozy interior, filled with the scent of home-cooked meals and the soft hum of family chatter, welcomed her. She shrugged off her jacket, revealing a casual yet stylish outfit underneath.

Martha was only too happy to welcome Jude in. She berated herself for not inviting her round sooner, to thank her for getting Tenney home when Aura had taken ill. She should have had her round weeks ago after she again managed to track their wayward children down that dreadful night.

Jude helped to lay the table as the family moved around her, each talking over the other. Jess slept in her dog bed, occasionally opening one eye to make sure they weren't already eating.

Tenney turned back to the door and grabbed his jacket and beanie, pulling it over his curls. "I'm off to get the food."

Martha felt a jolt of worry. Tenney was going out, leaving Aura. She looked at her daughter. Aura looked radiant, beautiful, none of the anxiety flowing across her eyes as so often happened when Tenney went out without her. Instead, she just turned and waved, told Tenney not to forget the curry sauce, and then carried on looking at the book of poetry by Maya Angelou that Sam had given her as a present.

Tenney looked at Jude. "Do you wanna come with me to get them?" Jude said yes and pulled her jacket back on.

**

Tenney and Jude walked down the street to the chippy. They shared anecdotes and when Jude laughed, Tenney felt a bit of his heart unravel.

"Tenney," she said, "I'm glad you're okay. It was amazing, seeing Aura like that, and then when you flew off together, well, I just couldn't believe it."

"It was amazing, Jude. Stace and Meg were right, our connection is stronger. Normally by now, I'd be getting angry just being a few doors away from her. But I can feel her with me, all the time. And I know she can feel me. We're never apart. Not really."

"That's great, Tenney." She smiled up at him.

"I'm sorry we worried you," he said sincerely.

"That's okay," she replied. Tenney gave her his megawatt smile again, as he instinctively held her hand.

**

When they returned to the house, Jude looked around the kitchen. She hadn't given it much more than an obligatory look when she was here to help find out what had happened to Tenney and Aura. It was very neat, well-ordered. The colour scheme encompassed varying shades of soothing blues and greens. A coffee pot was warming on the side; the smell had permeated into everything and reminded her of her father's habitual habit to keep the coffee on. She smiled at the memory.

A shelf of books lined one wall. When she looked closer, she saw a few cookery books, American and English, but the rest of the shelving unit was filled with books she hadn't expected to see in a kitchen.

Alongside some archaeology books, the shelves were crammed with books of poetry all squeezed together and well-thumbed, judging by the cracked spines. She saw Byron, Yeats, Cummings, Shakespeare's sonnets, Kipling, Plath, and Eugene Field. Books of poetry for children; compendiums, collections, and anthologies.

Walking closer to scan the titles, she quickly noticed that one name outnumbered the others. Tenney saw where she was looking, walked over, and gently bumped his shoulder against her. He smiled down at her, winking.

"Alright?" he asked.

"Yeah," she replied, happily.

"I guess you've worked out where Mum and Dad found the inspiration for my name?"

"They do seem to like Alfred, Lord Tennyson!" she joked.

Tenney laughed. "I had never understood why they didn't call Aura Guinevere, or Clare…"

He obviously knows the works of Tennyson well if he can spout off the names of some of the characters that featured in his works like that, Jude thought. She turned her face up to him when he paused. He had gone misty-eyed.

"…or Maud," he said almost too quietly for her to hear. He shook his head. "But they chose Aura. When we asked them, they could never give us a satisfactory answer." He smiled as he looked back at his sister, who was watching them. Again, Jude saw a minute darkening of his eyes. "I guess we know now though, don't we? The cosmos named her."

Jude felt a warmth spread through her as she looked up at him, and then back up to Aura. The bond between them was palpable, and she felt privileged to witness it. She glanced back at the shelf of poetry, feeling a deeper connection to the family and their history.

"Tenney!" called Samuel, "grab a beer for me, son, would you?" During the evening, Jude found that she was in awe of Samuel, and the secret he and Martha had carried for two decades. He had taken on another man's children, and he raised them and loved them as though they were his own flesh and blood.

That takes real strength, she thought. Tenney grabbed one of the ciders, using a novelty bottle opener which was, effectively, a dog's backside attached to the wall over a small basket, already filled with the caps of previous beers, lagers, and ciders. Together they walked over to join the family at the table.

"Tell us about your life, Jude," Martha began as she placed a homemade pecan pie on the table.

"MA!" Tenney exclaimed, embarrassed for Jude. She reached out and placed a hand on his arm. The action wasn't lost on anyone around the table, except for Tenney who remained oblivious to the looks his parents cast each other.

"It's okay, Tenney. I don't mind," Jude said. She removed her hand and drew in a deep breath. "As you know, I'm from Lincoln. Born and raised! I was lucky enough to be accepted for police training several years ago…" She took a breath. "I love my job; it seems to suit me. My dad died when I was 18. Cancer. Mum was never the same, and after his death, she became virtually housebound."

"Oh Jude," Martha sympathised towards their guest.

Jude felt Tenney press his thigh against hers as she forced out the sadness in her family history. Where his leg touched hers, she felt electricity travel through her, causing a shiver down her spine. Tenney, feeling the shiver, surreptitiously slipped his hand under the table and squeezed her leg, leaving his hand resting on her thigh.

"We were never that close after Dad died, but I made sure that I lived near to her, just so I could keep an eye on her." Turning to Martha, she continued, "You would have loved my dad. He was born in the Bronx to an Italian American family. I believe they still own the family business—a garage specialising in vintage cars." Martha gasped happily at this tenuous connection to her home country. "Though, I haven't seen them since Dad's funeral. We kinda lost touch as Mum's mental health declined." Again, she felt Tenney's hand on her thigh and drew comfort from his proximity.

"Mum was an investigative reporter—a conspiracy nut, really. I think she may be coming to Bristol at the end of the month." She didn't want to go into too much detail about her missing mother or the state of her personal health. She felt that she had already brought the group down with the story of her dad's passing.

"What are your plans while you are staying in this beautiful part of the world?" Martha quizzed, leaning forward slightly, resting her head on her hand, intrigue painted across her face.

"I went back to Lincoln earlier this month," Jude began, her eyes flickering towards Tenney. He hadn't known she had done that, and a pang of guilt struck him for not being there for her. "I collected more clothes and other things I need for a longer stay here. My boss called me in and offered a transfer to another constabulary, if I want it. It's all very sudden and unexpected. They've extended my leave so I can decide whether to take the job or not."

She hesitated, not yet ready to reveal that the transfer would be to Gloucestershire. She didn't want to see disappointed looks, as her decision was based on something so intangible, so delicate. Without realising it, Jude looked pointedly at Tenney, as though he held the power to sway her choice.

"Today, I rode down to Clifton and explored the sights. I wondered if my mother was already there, or if she was holed away somewhere, waiting for the convention. I left my details at the hotel, hopefully the man Mum wants to see will contact me. Until that time, I guess I'll keep exploring around here."

That's why she looked so tired when she came to the door! Tenney thought. She had travelled great distances alone, despite his promise to help her find her mum. Another wave of guilt washed over him. He had been so caught up in his own world, his own struggles, that he hadn't been there for her when she needed him most. The realisation hit him hard, filling him with a deep sense of responsibility. Aura looked at him, a frown creasing her nose. Gently, she piggybacked on his thoughts.

He remembered the promise he had made to her, the determination in her eyes when she spoke about finding her mother. He had vowed to stand by her side, to support her in every way possible, just as she was doing for them. Yet, here she was, exhausted from journeys she had undertaken alone. The thought of her navigating those miles, dealing with the emotional weight of her search without him, made his heart ache.

Tenney saw it all in her eyes—the fatigue, the resilience, the unspoken plea for support. Jude's hand slipped under the table and found Tenney's. They linked fingers, and he held her tight, silently vowing to be there for her from now on. Aura, feeling everything he felt, seeing his memories play out in her mind as though she were watching an old movie reel, beamed. She sensed the unspoken bond strengthening between them.

**

Martha stood at the window finishing her cup of coffee, and watched as the full moon began to rise over the trees on the hill. It had been a lovely day, one of the happiest.

She was startled out of her reverie when strong arms wrapped around her waist. She felt her husband's beard tickle her ear as he danced behind her. He began to whisper to her, his breath tinged with the smell of the beer he had consumed that evening. The children, the four of them huddled together over the table playing a board game, all stopped their happy chatter at their father's show of affection. Aware of the four pairs of eyes watching him, he began to speak louder to his audience, but it still felt intimately directed towards his wife.

"She came to the village church,
And sat by a pillar alone;
An angel watching an urn
Wept over her, carved in stone;
And once, but once, she lifted her eyes,
And suddenly, sweetly, strangely blush'd
To find they were met by my own;
And suddenly, sweetly, my heart beat stronger..."

Martha spun around in her husband's arms, laughing and clapping as he recited the verse. She kissed him deeply as Jude clapped and their children looked on, embarrassed.

"What was that?" Jude asked Tenney.

"A verse from Tennyson's poem, *Maud*. It's hugely long, swinging between grief for his father, who may have committed suicide, to his burgeoning feelings for Maud, a girl he played with as a kid. Tennyson used some of his most, er, flowery language to describe her. Associating her with lilies and roses and talking about her garden."

Tenney leant back in his chair watching his parents' performance, his sister coming to stand beside him. Sam mumbled an excuse and quickly disappeared up the stairs, his teenage nature finding such displays of affection between his parents—especially when they had a visitor—hugely uncomfortable.

"Ma loves Tennyson," Aura finished for him. "And Dad knows it!"

Their parents were spinning around the small kitchen, dancing to a tune all of their own. Tenney shifted away from the table, Aura swiftly joining him and grabbing her coat.

"And with that, I think it's time we went," he smiled at Jude.

Martha leant her back into Samuel as he wrapped his hands around her waist, happiness making her glow as she watched them walk up the road.

Chapter 20

"I'll meet you at the hotel," Jude said, zipping up her jacket. Tenney looked confused. "You are coming, aren't you?" He felt the worry hitting him in the stomach as he thought that she might be leaving them.

Jude laughed, winking at him mischievously. "I'll see you there!" she said as she walked away.

As the twins made their way down the lane, they were overtaken by a fast sports motorbike. They saw its indicator flash right as it approached the junction in the village, turning up the road that led to the hotel. As the building came into view, they saw the gleam of her red Jag in the car park. Next to it, helmet in hand, leaning against the bike, smiling broadly, was Jude.

Aura laughed when Tenney's jaw dropped. He walked around the blue and silver Yamaha YZF-R1 Superbike. "You'll have to forgive him, Jude, he's a bit of a sucker for fast bikes!" Jude raised her eyebrows as Tenney stopped in front of her.

"I'll have to give you a ride then," she said. Aura detected the hint of flirtatiousness in her voice and cocked an eyebrow. Tenney stepped closer to Jude without touching her, he leant in.

"I'll hold you to that promise," he said, his eyes twinkling.

**

At the campfire, the wolf was pacing anxiously, and Meg seemed agitated, but Stace was as calm as ever.

"Happy Birthday!" he said as the trio approached them. As the moon rose higher, the wolf and Meg became more fidgety. Aura looked on in concern.

"Are they okay?" she asked Stace.

He turned and smiled at her. "They will be," was all he would say.

They all sat together around the fire, but before they could talk about the events of the night before—the dragon flight and the psychic communication they had honed—the wolf loped away. Meg glanced up at the moon and back at Stace. He was about to say something when suddenly he froze. Meg followed the direction of his gaze as silently Stace stood up and moved away into the darkness.

Meg crept around to the trio. "We've got company," she whispered. "Stay behind me, okay?"

They nodded and stood up.

From the shadows of the woods around them, dark figures moved forward. Then someone laughed, a deep, guttural, evil laugh. It sounded familiar and yet wholly wrong. Aura shrank into her brother as one of the men stepped forward.

"We meet again, Elemental!" he said.

Aura shuddered as a figure separated itself from the shadows. "Callum?" asked Tenney incredulously. He hadn't seen him since the day he left for uni, and the boy looked wrong, deathly ill and emaciated. Dark light shone from his iris-less eyes. He didn't appear to feel the cold night air, his jacket open to reveal his bare chest. A poorly healed pattern seemed to have been carved into it. The people around the edge of the clearing all began to move forward. Their eyes were as black as those of the man in front of them. Black smoke wafted around their feet like a snake.

"They're the possessed," said Meg, never taking her eyes off the horde. The friends stepped back, their hearts beating a fearful rapport in their chests. As the dark man approached them, they saw a blur race around the edge of the clearing. Heads toppled and throats were ripped out until there was only the man, Meg, and the trio standing alive at the summit.

Stace stopped in front of the possessed man.

"Placidus..." he hissed.

"Fulcifer," Stace replied and lifted his sword high, about to bring it down on the demon. There was blood on the sword and running down his chest from his fanged mouth. His eyes burned red.

The demon sidestepped Stace's blow. He lifted his hands, and his nails became sharp claws. Stepping inside the sword arm, he quickly slashed at Stace, ripping through his shirt, before moving out of reach of the teeth.

"Haven't you heard, General? My name is Gallagher now. I have been watching your little group. My master wants the Elemental and has tasked me not to stop until I have her and her

Tether, and the weapon. I can smell it—it is close!" He laughed maniacally as, goaded by the ghoul in front of him, Stace charged forward.

Tenney, Aura, and Jude struggled to keep up with the fight, both participants moving faster than humanly possible. But when they finally parted from their macabre dance, they were relieved that Gallagher seemed to be losing, judging from the sword and bite wounds he had sustained. Stace thrust forward again. The demon screamed. The sky rent apart, and from the tear, a host of bodies spewed like lava, a legion of the possessed. The demons sprang forward, leaping on Stace's back. They pinned him to the ground.

The Gallagher demon crouched down over Stace as he struggled under the mass of bodies. "What did you do with it, Placidus?" he asked quietly, ignoring the sounds of the battle around him.

"Do with what, you bastard?"

The demon smiled and suddenly changed track. "You never did find out what happened to your family, did you?" Stace stopped struggling, his red eyes glowing. The demon realised that he had spoken the truth, and in doing so, he had found Stace's weak spot.

Gallagher laughed cruelly. "Let's just say, they made excellent target practice for my archers…" With a mighty roar, Stace threw off the demons on his back. He rose to his feet, but Gallagher was gone. In a swirl of violence, he turned and attacked the ones who had pinned him.

Meg drew a long knife from her boot and began fighting the demons coming at her from the side. Tenney shot forward and leapt on the back of one of the demons attacking Stace. He pried him off his mentor and viciously punched him hard on the jaw, a punch which would have cracked the jaw of a mortal but only caused the grotesque face to snap back and reform. Another demon came up behind him, receiving a punishing back kick from Tenney's booted foot. Tenney then dropped down into a low sweep, knocking the winded demon to the floor, and stamp kicked him in his throat, finishing him off. Black smoke rose from the unconscious body.

Jude yelped when a second demon crept up behind Tenney, its clawed hands ready to slice through his back. It moved as though it wasn't used to possessing a human body yet—its movements erratic, its control lacking. *Could there be such a thing as a young demon?* Jude wondered in the milliseconds it took her to tackle the she-demon. Like Tenney, she aimed a square punch at the woman's jaw. The demon screamed as smoke rose from her and dissipated into the ether.

Jude stood up and positioned herself back-to-back with Tenney. They were near the edge of the clearing, an embankment where a rampart for the fort had once been cut. The fight had taken them away from the fire. Away from Aura.

Aura watched all of this, feeling helpless, forgetting how to summon the dragon, her mind going blank. She felt all the blows Tenney received. She saw him standing and fighting with Jude, saw how well they worked together, each defending the other.

She witnessed Stace as the Roman General he must have once been, defeating demon after demon. His sword and his teeth never stopping. Never showing mercy.

And then she saw Meg, obviously weakening. There was something happening to her that was more than this battle as she doubled over in a howl of pain after defeating another enemy. Aura realised they were hopelessly outnumbered, and still she felt incapable.

A cold wind moved up her back, sulphur hit her nose. An evil laugh behind her ear. Aura turned and looked into the skeletal face of Gallagher. His breath stank of death. His black eyes glinting in the firelight.

He licked his lips and reached for her.

A black shadow leapt onto him, knocking him to the ground. The wolf had him. He tried to reach the demon's neck, but at this point on this night, the demon's strength was greater than that of the wolf.

Aura screamed as the demon grabbed the wolf by his throat. In a fluid movement, he stood up and shook the wolf violently. Aura saw the green in the animal's eyes dim as he took one last look at her. His suddenly humanlike eyes began to shut, begging her for forgiveness. A lifetime of love and loss flashed through them before they closed.

She knew those eyes; she had seen them before in the face of the stranger, and she finally understood. They were the same eyes that came to her sometimes in her dreams. Flashing before her were scenes from her past lives—a boy crawling from the bushes around her parent's garden, then a teenager and finally a young man, watching her grow up, only visiting for a few days each month. She saw his grief as time after time she vanished before his eyes. She knew him, she had known him for centuries.

"Hedge?" Aura whispered disbelievingly.

Then Gallagher flung the wolf away as if he was trash. The wolf landed in an unmoving heap beside the fire. Meg howled again in pain and crawled in the direction of the wolf.

-AURA! Tenney screamed into her mind, his concentration moving from the fight to his sister. Time slowed for Aura. She felt her heart break as she looked at the black form. Around his body, she saw the particles in the air move. They gathered and came to her open hand.

This time she knew what to do. She pulled the air into her and stored up their energy.

When Gallagher moved towards her, she released the energy blast, obliterating everything that got in its way.

Chapter 21

First night of the Full Moon Cycle.

Tenney's head pounded painfully. His neck felt stiff as he opened one eye. The moon, full and at its zenith, beamed down upon him. He tasted mud and blood in his mouth. Slowly, he forced himself to sit up, take stock, and try to remember what had happened.

He remembered the light, the burst of energy. His sister, her heart breaking, standing in the centre near the fire as she silently opened her clenched hands, releasing the energy.

Then he remembered tackling Jude as the blast took him off his feet. They fell together, tumbling and rolling down the side of the hill, hitting rocks, clothes tearing, flesh ripping, and then a second blinding flash. But this time, it had been inside his own head.

And then nothing. Nothing until the moonlight woke him.

"Jude…?" he croaked as he frantically cast his eyes around him.

He knew she had fallen with him, but where was she? Her dark blue bike jacket made it hard to see her in the moonlit night.

"Jude?" he called louder, stumbling to his feet. "JUDE!" He spun around at a sound. Something moved in the undergrowth a few feet from him.

"Tenney…" Jude rasped, raising a hand into the air.

He ran to her, scooping her in his arms, holding her to him, rocking her gently. She said something into his jacket. Moving back slightly, he asked, "What did you say?"

She smiled up at him. "Take me home."

**

Stace shouted to Meg – "GET DOWN!"

Meg lifted her head and saw what was about to happen. She hunkered down over the unmoving body of the wolf, protecting him, and keeping them below the level of the power.

The energy left Aura, bright and powerful. There was the blinding flash of light followed by a pulse as strong as an explosion. All the demon-men in the clearing that the blast touched evaporated, including Gallagher. His demon soul was seemingly obliterated into nothingness. Tenney, moving to protect Jude, was thrown back and down the side of the ancient hill.

When the light dimmed and the clearing returned to what it had been before they were attacked, Aura, the power spent, collapsed in the epicentre.

Meg, head close to the body of the wolf felt him take a breath. She put her hands deep into his pelt. Feeling his lungs rise and fall, slowly, but steadily, Meg felt a burst of pride at how strong the wolf was. The moon had nearly reached its zenith, and a familiar pain moved through her body and that of the wolf beneath her.

The clouds moved across the shining orb in the sky. Meg felt her skin tingle and move over her bones. She didn't have much time.

"Stace…" she whispered between painful contractions. Within seconds Stace was by her side. "Aura…" she said weakly.

Stace understood what she wanted him to do, and he moved to the girl, scooping her up he carried her to the wolf and laid her gently against his back.

With shaky fingers, Meg began to remove her clothes, before she would find it impossible to do so. The pain was beyond description now, every fibre of her alternating between fire and ice.

The wolf was waking.

She moved away from Stace as he stood over the sleeping pair. The waves of pain intensified. She couldn't help but cry out. No matter how many millions of times she had endured this, she still felt that she couldn't bear it.

She saw the black wolfs body shiver, his fur rolling along his body.

Meg heard a groan and saw Aura's eyes flutter open, locking them on to her. She gasped in shock, rolling back, her hand touching the body behind her. Meg cried out again. The wolf on the ground rolled over and opened his green eyes, his face close to Aura's. His fur began to fall off him, pink flesh showing through as the body changed. He cried out, his howl sounding more human, as the change neared its end. Meg howled in response.

The wolf-man turned away from Aura and looked towards the metamorphing creature that had been Meg. He reached out an arm, as he reached towards her his paw stretched into fingers, the sharp nails becoming stubby and softer. Meg's yellow eyes looked out of a brown, lupine face at the hand before collapsing to the ground in exhaustion.

"Mother…" croaked the body next to Aura. Aura looked at the naked man beside her, "Hedge…?" He turned to her his emerald eyes were wet with tears. The brown wolf that had been Meg recovered, shaking herself from her head to the end of her tail, and walked to them. He put one hand deep into the ruff of fur around the head of the wolf. His mother's fur.

Meg lowered her head, and he rested his temple against hers. They sat like that until Stace gently called her away. The wolf opened her eyes and stared at Hedge and Aura, before turning and loping off with Stace into the trees.

"Hedge…" Aura repeated his name timidly. He turned back to her and smiled from the side of his mouth. With a cry of relief, she went to him.

**

Together they staggered down the hill, the moon casting long shadows on the rocky path. The air was thick with the scent of pine and the distant howl of wolves. Jude stumbled, her legs giving way as exhaustion and pain rendered her momentarily immobile. Tenney moved to her, and without saying a word, carefully lifted Jude up so she was safe between his arms, her head resting on his chest, feeling his heartbeat through his torn hoodie.

"What about your sister?" she asked him, her voice barely a whisper.

Tenney closed his eyes and sought out his sister. She was safe, with the wolf.

"She's okay." It was all he needed to say. All he needed to know. He felt the thread that would connect them forever stretch to go with him, malleable and willing, no longer tight and breakable.

**

Hedge and Aura pulled back slightly from their embrace. "Hi…" he said, his voice soft.

Aura stared at him, her mouth moving like a fish. "…You're naked…" was all her jumbled mind could think to say as she struggled to comprehend that he was there, that he had always been there. He had never left her; she just hadn't recognised him until she had nearly lost him.

Hedge smiled down at her. "It's kind of one of the side effects of being a werewolf. No clothes." He laughed at her expression.

"But you're a wolf most of the time, how…"

"I was born during my mother's first change. You could say I'm a reverse-wolf." He tried to joke, but his eyes held a hint of sadness.

"Your mother? Meg?"

Hedge nodded. The moonlight came through the clouds, alighting on Hedge, making his tanned skin glow. Silvery scars criss-crossed his body, and Aura saw the bruises of the hand that had nearly throttled him, purple and violent, wrapped around his throat. She cried out and raised her hand to his cheek.

Hedge, unused to the gentle touch of a human, reared back slightly. Aura, leaving her hand in the space where his face had been, looked at him, and slowly he moved forward and touched his face to hers. They looked at each other as his hand snaked around the back of her head, his long fingers tangling in her hair. She mirrored his move, marvelling that this man who had been her companion throughout many of her previous lives, was real. Hedge leaned forward and kissed her deeply.

Aura responded. When they parted, both panting heavily from the influx of emotions they were experiencing, Aura realised that the choice was hers. There would be no going back. As if Hedge understood her sudden hesitation, he looked down and away from her. Aura felt her heart fill with love for this man who had saved her so many times, and she had never known.

She lifted his head up and gave herself up to him, body and soul.

**

"Will you come in?" asked Jude standing at the entrance to the hotel. "You're filthy. You can't go home looking like that. Whatever would your mother say?"

Tenney could see she was trying to make a joke, to hide the need not to be alone tonight. And he was a mess. So was she, if he was honest. Her long, curly brown hair held all manner of leaves and twigs, mud and blood marred the side of her face, leaving an ugly dark stain on her caramel skin. Taking her hand, he let her lead him into the hotel and up the stairs to her room.

It was a typical old-fashioned, chintzy place, in keeping with the style of the hotel. Her few belongings were kept in neat, ordered piles. A long mirror on one side of the large bed faced the door which led to the en-suite, a bath towel draped over it, partially obscuring the glass.

Seeing his furrowed brow, she quickly explained, "I can't stand sleeping in a room with a large mirror. Every time I move, I think somebody is in the room with me, so I cover them up."

Tenney could understand that. Sometimes, when he wasn't there, Aura would mention that she thought someone else was in the room, watching her. He made a mental note to cover up her bedroom mirror next time she slept alone.

On the small dressing table, papers and books were all piled together. Jude threw the keys down and caught sight of herself in the smaller mirror over the table and groaned.

"Oh, God!" she exclaimed. Her forehead was gashed, but not deeply. They had both sustained cuts and bruises tonight. Tenney came up behind her, gingerly rubbing a lump which had formed at the back of his head. She looked at him through the mirror, concerned. He assured her he was fine, that the bump didn't bother him. Then he turned her around and held her face, cupping her chin.

Jude felt her breath hitch. "Did I hurt you?" he asked, concern quietening his voice. She shook her head, but he held on to her, turning her face under the light, inspecting the gash.

"Do you have a first aid kit? Or TCP? Savlon even?" She shook her head.

She grabbed his forearms, "Don't go!" she begged. She felt she knew what his next remark would be. He would leave her, go home and get the things he needed. And she would be left, alone, with her mind and body spinning with a mix of emotions.

He breathed out, thinking aloud. "Have you got a tenner?" She nodded. "Wait here, I'll be 2 minutes." True to his word, he returned with a bottle of vodka from the bar and a clean cloth.

Looking at the cheap, half-drunk bottle, he smiled at her, a little of his cheeky humour returning. "I'll pay you back," he said.

"Don' worry 'bout it," she replied, imitating her father's accent.

Carefully, he opened the bottle and held it out to her. She dutifully took a sip, the warm liquid burning down her throat.

"Bleurgh," she coughed. "I've never liked vodka!"

"I'll remember that for next time," he said, deadpan.

Taking the bottle from her, Tenney upturned it into the cloth, and gently wiped away the blood, cleaning the wound. She gasped as the alcohol touched her, gripping his arm to keep herself steady.

Inadvertently, she breathed him in. He smelt like the mud they had rolled through, but underneath it there was an attractive spiciness. Her mind went off the pain as she let herself feel things for him. *He really was quite handsome, when he wasn't frowning*, she thought, recalling when she had first met him at the train station.

"Tenney," she began, "you know I don't think of you as a kid, don't you? I'm sorry I said that. I was just so angry at Stace for terrifying you. Well, for terrifying me, I guess."

She picked at some dried mud on his t-shirt. He took hold of her hand. He felt hot, and his breathing deepened. Anticipation caught hold of her.

"Jude…" he whispered.

"Yes…"

"It's okay. I know that now." He kissed her forehead.

"Jude," he whispered, throatily, holding her to him, he could feel each response her body made as his fingers delicately traced shapes up and down her spine.

"Yeah?"

"Do you mind if I use your shower?" The spell, not broken so much as put on hold, shifted. She laughed again, pushed him away, and brushed a tear from her cheek.

"Go for it," she replied.

He stood up and moved to the en-suite door. "Won't be long."

As he walked into the en-suite, Jude opened a drawer and found some sweatpants and a vest. She turned and caught sight of Tenney. He was moving within a small gap of reflective glass where the towel had shifted over the mirror. The door to the en-suite wasn't fully shut, and steam came through the gap.

Looking up she could see him under the jet of water, his hand running through his messy hair. She watched the muscles in his back, moving with him as he washed the dirt from his tanned body. Where the mud and blood sloughed off, she could see bruises and cuts, dotted all over his torso and arms. Some were from that night, but most were old, long in the process of being healed.

He turned around, his head tipping back under the water. Her eyes naturally moved down his chest, over his torso, to the dark line of hair from his navel, leading her eyes down, down…

Suddenly his eyes shot open. Jude blushed, and turned away from the mirror, pretended she hadn't been looking.

When the shower stopped Jude waited, her clean clothes in hand, for the door to open fully. Tenney stood in the doorway, a white towel around his waist. He held the door open for her. Clutching her change of clothes to her body, she squeezed between him and the door frame. He was still wet, and she could see the drops of water sitting on his skin, moving as he breathed slowly in and out.

She blushed again and moved past him.

**

Tenney began to dry himself. His back to the door to the en-suite. He heard her move about the bathroom, turn the shower on. He listened as the cubicle door opened and closed. He could hear her breathing, small moans of pleasure as the hot water hit her.

When she had walked past him in the doorway he could smell her unique scent. Lilies, he thought, and something fresh, citrusy, like grapefruit. But the end notes of her, the part that lingered and fired in his brain was simply, her. He knew that there was no other smell in the world, and no words that would be able to describe it, other than her.

He had never wanted someone as much as he wanted her. The way she responded to him, the looks they shared sent torment though his body as he fought to keep control. His heartbeat raced in his chest; his blood flowed hot until he could stand it no longer.

Letting his towel drop from his hands, he opened the door and stepped in.

Jude turned in shock as he walked into the steamed-up room. He locked his eyes brazenly on hers. She stood perfectly still, her hands had automatically covered herself, the water and soap falling down her body. He made himself wait. The choice would be hers, though he thought that if she turned him away, he might shatter into a thousand tiny pieces. He wanted her and he believed she wanted him to.

Jude closed her eyes once, taking a breath. Then she opened the cubicle door, welcomed him in.

**

Later, as they lay entwined together on the bathroom mat, Tenney began to whisper to her.

"She is coming, my own, my sweet;

Were it ever so airy a tread,

My heart would hear her and beat,

Were it earth in an earthy bed;

My dust would hear her and beat,

Had I lain for a century dead,

Would start and tremble under her feet,

And blossom in purple and red."

"Those words…"

"Maud," he whispered.

"Maud…" she replied as she turned back to him again, ignoring the feeling in her stomach that this may end badly. She breathed him in and allowed herself to take this new road.

The morning sun broke through the blinds.

**

Hedge looked down into Aura's blue eyes.

"How long do we have?"

"Less than 48 hours."

She held his face, tenderly. "Nothing hidden, ok?"

"Nothing hidden," he agreed as he fell into her.

Chapter 22

Tenney woke up. His head throbbed slightly, but it was bearable. Jude was wrapped around him, her warmth a comforting presence. They were still lying on the bathroom floor, the cold tiles a stark contrast to the heat of their bodies. The faint scent of grapefruit from her bodywash lingered in the air, mixing with the musk of their bodies. Pleasant memories of their night together surfaced in his mind, followed by the reason why they had ended up here.

He closed his eyes and sought out Aura. He found her quickly, and by the feel of things, she had had as much fun last night as he had. He nudged her gently, letting her know he was there.

-Ten?

-Hey.

-Are you and Jude okay?

-Yep. About as okay as you are, it would seem! He felt Aura blush.

-Who is he? Tenney couldn't quite mask his discomfort. The thought of his sister being intimate with a stranger, putting herself at risk, worried at him. Yet, everything he sensed from her told him she was okay, that she had wanted it. The protective part of him battled with the reality of what he was hearing and feeling from his sister.

-I'll explain it to you when you get here.

-Are you still at the Fort?

-Uh-huh. When are you coming? I'd like you to meet him…

"Is your brother okay?" Hedge asked her. The men's clothing in the back of the Land Rover made sense to her now, as he sat beside her clad in a dark t-shirt and torn jeans in the back of the vehicle. On his feet, a pair of loosely tied, beaten-up black boots. He didn't seem to feel the cold on his bare arms, despite the early morning chill that seeped through the vehicle's windows.

"What? How did you know I was talking to Tenney?"

He ran a finger down her nose. "This sort of crinkles up at the top. It was your concentration face when you tried to mind-speak to your sister, Livia. You seem to be able to speak to

147

Tenney much easier. It didn't crinkle quite so much. And then you smiled. So, I guess he's okay?"

"Yeah," she said happily, she thought she would give up eternity just to listen to his soft Welsh accent, "he's okay. He's with Jude." A thought occurred to her. She smiled again. "So, your real name is Wilfrid?" She looked at him with wide-eyed innocence, but he could see the mirth dancing behind the blue.

"Aaargh," he ran his hand down his face, "Mam told you, did she?"

"I've kind of just figured it out," she replied teasingly.

"I've been Hedge for as long as I can remember, which is a very long time." This time he chuckled nervously, half afraid of scaring her off.

"So why Hedge?" she asked, intrigued by the unusualness of his chosen name. She placed her hand over his heart, feeling the steady thump beneath her palm. The dark hairs that lay over the skin of his bare chest curled over the neck of his tee. His arms circled around her, and he rested his forehead against hers.

"It was what you used to call me," he whispered. She closed her eyes and had a vision of playing with a black wolf cub and then with a black-haired boy, but never at the same time.

"It was because after your change back to human form, you always seemed to slink out of the bushes…"

Hedge looked at her for a long time, he smiled again. "You're remembering."

**

Jude was still fast asleep in his arms, exhausted. Tenney looked down at her. He had never stayed the night with a woman before. With all the others, he gave them what they needed, what they wanted, and they reciprocated. But when they were done, he felt no compunction to stay. So, he didn't. He would often be gone long before they even woke up. Back to Aura.

But this time was different. He knew he didn't want to leave her. That he couldn't leave her. He brushed a strand of hair from her face, marvelling at how peaceful she looked. The events of the previous night played back in his mind – the laughter, the shared secrets, the undeniable connection. He felt a warmth in his chest that he hadn't felt in a long time.

-Aura, I think I'm in trouble.

-Why's that?

-Because I don't want to leave her.

-Then don't.

Tenney sighed, knowing it wasn't that simple. But for now, he would hold onto this moment, savouring the rare feeling of contentment.

**

"Urrgh," groaned Jude. "I'm gonna need another shower."

Tenney dutifully opened the cubicle door for her, ushering her in. He followed her and turned the spray on, hot. The water cascaded down their shoulders, starting to ease their aching bodies. The steam filled the small bathroom, creating a cocoon of warmth around them. He took the shampoo and placed some in his palm, the scent of citrus filling the air, and proceeded to lather it through her hair, careful of the wound on her forehead.

She did the same for him, her fingers gentle as they massaged his scalp. When she touched the bump on his head, he winced, and she looked at him with concern.

"Does this still hurt?" she asked him, her voice soft with worry.

She opened the shower door, handed him a towel, and wrapped one around herself before instructing him to sit on the loo seat. She stood behind him and looked under his hairline. A nasty swollen lump appeared across the base of his head, the bruise purpling.

"Do you have a headache?" she asked, her fingers lightly tracing the edges of the bruise. He shook his head in denial. He felt fine, the small ache he had felt upon waking long forgotten in the release of certain endorphins. Besides, he had had bumps before and didn't feel unduly worried about this one.

"Let me know if you do," she said, her tone firm but caring, "or if you go dizzy."

He turned back to face her, a playful glint in his eyes. "Yes Mam, Officer Marcello!"

She laughed, the sound light and musical, and swiped at his shoulder before he reached up to kiss her. Their lips met, and for a moment, the world outside the bathroom ceased to exist. The kiss was tender, filled with unspoken promises and a deep connection that neither of them fully understood yet.

**

They stood together at the Fort. Hedge fidgeted, his fingers tugging at the neck of his tee, stretching it until it became malformed. The feel of clothes on his back was an alien sensation, a stark contrast to the freedom of his wolf form. He couldn't help but feel restricted, but he knew Tenney wouldn't approve of his previous state of undress.

"Do you normally go naked then? During the Cycle?" Aura asked, noting his discomfort.

The Cycle, he had told her during the night, was how he and his mother referred to the 48 hours when they changed form.

"Yeah," he said, smiling naughtily. "But I am usually in much denser forests than here, where it's easier to hide. Plus, I don't want to make your brother any angrier with me." He chuckled, but Aura could see the underlying tension in his eyes. She gave a small smile, a little worried about what Tenney's reaction to Hedge might be. Aura changed the subject quickly.

"When was the last time you saw your mother?"

He thought for a while, his gaze distant. Time moved very differently for him. "I think the last time we were together was in the late nineteenth century. She left me a note saying that she and Stace had to go to New York with you. They haven't been back here since then."

Aura was amazed. Hedge hadn't seen his family in nearly 150 years. She leaned closer to him, letting him know she was trying to understand.

"Though, to say 'see my mother' is an understatement. We've never been human at the same time. Sometimes, for maybe a second, if we're lucky, we catch a glimpse of each other during the change. But that's all it is. A glimpse." His voice was tinged with sadness, and Aura felt her heart go out to him. Hedge's life must be so lonely. She didn't know how he bore it.

"That sounds incredibly hard," she said softly, her hand reaching out to touch his arm. "I can't imagine not being able to truly connect with your family."

Hedge looked at her, his eyes reflecting a deep well of emotion. "It is. But I've learned to live with it. You find ways to cope, to keep going." He gave her a small, reassuring smile, though it didn't quite reach his eyes.

"What does fahariad mean?"

Hedge looked at her, a moment of puzzlement crossing his face before he realised what she was trying to say, albeit butchering his mother tongue. He laughed. "What I said to you when we first met in this life?" She nodded. "I said *fy nghariad*. It means 'my love.'"

Aura blushed. "When was the last time you saw me?" Aura asked, her voice barely above a whisper.

"1850, I think? Not far from here actually. You and your sister were living in a hamlet near the Cwm Afon." Hedge's voice was soft, filled with a mix of nostalgia and sorrow.

Again, she was shocked. The revelation was almost too much to process. How could he have lived for so long, with his mother always watching over her, and never see her?

"Mam saw how close we had gotten back then," he began, his voice tinged with nostalgia. "We grew up together. Because I aged slowly, there were times in your many lives when we were children together. You would laugh and play, unaware of the Cycles I was bound to. Other times, you were like an older sister or an aunt, guiding me with wisdom beyond your years. And in other lives, I stood alongside Stace and Mum, guarding and training you and your twin from infancy, through youth, and into adulthood."

He paused, letting the weight of his words settle. The memories of countless lifetimes flickered in his eyes, a testament to the bond they shared across the ages.

Aura looked puzzled. How could he only look a few years older than her when he had been living in the world far, far longer? He saw her confusion and answered as best as he could.

"I believe it is due to my impermanence as a man and the fact that I was born this way. In one life, when you reached 17 and we were physically of a similar age, we finally admitted our love. Each new life that you lived, I had to wait until you were ready to receive me again."

He paused; his eyes distant as he recalled the past. "Then, one year, after we had danced the same dance which we had made our own over the centuries, things became, er, complicated. Your tethering was fragile in this life, your sister demanding more of you than any had before. You were torn between me and your sister. For five years, you battled between us for those few precious nights each month when we could be together."

Aura listened intently, her heart aching for the pain he must have endured. "Your heightened emotions and feelings for me were causing similar ones in her, but she would have no release. It began to fuel the instability the Tether feels when parted from the Elemental, only this was worse because it was a heart-based separation, not a physical one. Stace saw the distress my presence was inadvertently causing you and your sister." He paused, looking deeply at her, sorrow clouding his eyes. "I never meant to harm you."

She held him tighter, understanding how difficult it must have been. "And then, one stormy night, you came to me and the madness finally took hold of your sister. She staggered out of your home and fell into the Avon from the cliffs where the Suspension Bridge now stands."

Hedge continued, his voice breaking slightly. "The industrial revolution was in full swing by then, and families moved through the area faster and went anywhere. It was getting harder to keep track of you when you moved on."

He sighed deeply, the weight of centuries of longing and loss evident in his eyes. "My mother and Stace eventually got a lead that a family with twin baby daughters were travelling abroad to start a new life. You were a baby again, and I was physically a 23-year-old man-wolf. My heart was broken because I couldn't risk travelling for weeks across the ocean in wolf form. Mother warned me off you. Said that this was probably for the best. I agreed, thinking that it really was for your good."

Suddenly he shifted, uncomfortable, the guilt and betrayal he felt clear in his voice. "I've had other women since you." He looked down, unable to meet her eyes. She placed her hand on his cheek, encouraging him to carry on. "But I never loved anyone else. It was always you. It has always only ever been you."

She kissed him gently. "When my mother came to find me in these woods, just before the last full moon, I would smell you, living your life close by. That was the worst form of torture. But I kept my promise to her. I stayed away. Until I saw you, with your brother, at the Fort, that boy setting his dogs on your little fella. Then I knew that I couldn't let you go again."

"You still look 23," she said, nestling onto his shoulder. The warmth of his body was a comforting contrast to the cool morning air.

"Yeah, the ageing process, which was always slow, appears to have finally stopped. Not a bad age really to be stuck at." He smiled at his joke, but there was a hint of sadness in his eyes. The weight of centuries seemed to hang on his shoulders.

"But what about when I'm fifty and you still look 23?" she asked, genuine concern etched on her face. The thought of such a disparity in their appearances troubled her.

"Then I will still love you. And don't forget, you are Air." He kissed her. "You have the power to change your shape," a kiss; "your features," kiss; "you can look however you want to look."

This was a new development for her, one she would ask Stace about when he returned from wherever he had gone with wolf-Meg. Feeling slightly reassured, she let him wrap his arm around her shoulder.

"Wilf," she said.

"Oi!" he replied, playfully nipping her ear. She laughed. He loved to hear her laugh.

"When we were first at the Lodge, Tenney heard Meg whisper something that made no sense."

"What was it?" he asked, puzzled. He had trouble remembering what humans said when in his wolf form.

"He said it sounded like 'fill me'. Why would Meg want you to fill her?"

Hedge laughed, a loud, joyful sound that echoed around the clearing. "*Fili mi,*" he said.

"What does that mean?"

"My son. In Latin."

Aura looked at him in amazement. "You speak Latin?"

"Why do you sound so surprised?" he asked. "It was one of the languages of my childhood. Remember? I am sure, if you concentrated, you could recall all the languages you have spoken over the centuries."

Aura was still struggling with the concept that they knew each other, as children, in other lives. Even with the quick vision, it still couldn't quite resolve itself in her mind. It was another life for her. Then she realised, it was the same life for him.

She turned and leant against him, her back fitting comfortably against his chest, his arms entwined with hers. "Hedge, say something in Latin?"

He kissed her neck and whispered in her ear, "*Dormiam ego vos somniatis.*"

Aura shivered. "What does that mean?"

"'When I sleep, I dream of you.'"

A warm glow spread throughout Aura's body from her heart. "Hedge?"

"Yes, Darlin',"

"When Tenney's here, there's something I want you to do."

Hedge stepped back slightly, looking at her sideways. "Anything for you, Cariad." He smiled, switching back to Welsh again.

Aura was about to tell him what it was she wanted from him when she suddenly stiffened. "He's here," she said.

**

Tenney and Jude, hand in hand, crested the top of the track. The morning sun cast a golden hue over the landscape, the air fresh and filled with the scent of the earth and the trees. They had called in at the Wiseman house briefly, offering a tenuous explanation for Tenney and Aura's staying out all night. Martha was watching through the window as a coroner and paramedics wheeled a covered body out of the Old Man's house.

"What happened?" Tenney had asked, as he gathered some bagels, a carton of juice, and Bo's lead.

"The old man at the end of the Barracks - he died. It seems that the poor old guy had been dead for at least three weeks, and nobody noticed," Martha said, her voice tinged with sadness. "A person from a charity called in to do a wellness check and found him." Her head tilted to a man sitting beside an ambulance looking decidedly green. "I should have checked in on him, but he had become very abrasive, unkind even. Poor old guy."

Jude looked up at Tenney and was saddened to see his genuine sorrow at the loss of a familiar village face. She took his bag of food and waited for him by the door as he said goodbye to his mother. Moments later he joined her with Bo, and together they set out again to walk to the Fort. The path was lined with wildflowers, their vibrant colours a stark contrast to the sombre news they had just received.

As they reached the summit, Bo scampering ahead of them, Tenney's eyes immediately fell to Aura. She stood there, waiting for him expectantly, if with a little trepidation. Behind her, he saw a black-haired young man, standing deceptively casually as he watched them approach. The man's posture was relaxed, but there was an air of tension about him, as if he was ready for anything.

Tenney's eyes widened as flashes of this man – the stranger who had saved Bo – and his sister together danced before his eyes. His jaw clicked as he struggled to see past his protective nature. The thought of his sister being intimate with someone he didn't know, someone who was a stranger, still aggravated him. He knew that Aura had not been with a man in that way before. The idea of her first experience being with someone he hadn't vetted gnawed at him.

He took a deep breath, kissed Jude full on the mouth, telling her he'd be back in a moment. He walked past his sister, looked at her, smiled, and squeezed her hand. Then he kept on walking towards the young man.

Before Hedge could utter a greeting, Tenney had raised his fist and smacked him hard in the face. The sound of the impact echoed through the clearing, startling the birds from the trees.

Hedge quickly regained his composure. He breathed in deeply and squared up to Tenney. He was marginally shorter than him, but Tenney could see that he was much stronger. The girls by this time had run up to them, each of them placing a restraining hand on their men.

"Tenney!" Aura cried out, shocked at her brother's actions. "He's the black wolf! Don't you see? We just didn't recognise him!"

Tenney looked stunned. "You're the wolf?" he said incredulously.

"Yeah," replied Hedge, rubbing his slightly throbbing jaw. "Meg's my mum."

Tenney's mind raced as he processed this information. The black wolf that had been a part of their lives for a month was standing before him in human form. He felt a mix of anger, confusion, and a strange sense of relief. The wolf had saved Bo, had been a protector when they fought the possessed or when they were separated, but now, seeing him as a man, it was harder to reconcile those feelings with the sight of him standing so close to Aura.

"Why didn't they tell us?" Tenney demanded, his voice a mix of frustration and curiosity.

"It's complicated," Hedge replied, his eyes meeting Tenney's with a steady gaze. "They probably didn't know how you'd react. And honestly, they probably thought you wouldn't believe them anyway."

Aura stepped forward, her hand still on Tenney's arm. "We need to trust each other," she said softly. "We're all in this together now. The four of us."

Tenney took a deep breath, his anger slowly dissipating. He looked at Hedge, seeing the sincerity in his eyes. "Alright," he said finally. "But no more secrets."

Hedge nodded. "No more secrets."

**

The four of them sat in a circle, Tenney, Aura, and Jude sharing the bagels and juice around them. The morning sun filtered through the trees, casting dappled shadows on the ground. Hedge declined when the food passed his way, his eyes distant. Aura had noticed that the bruises around his neck had begun to fade away, the purpling skin now a lighter shade.

"I tend to heal pretty quickly," he answered her unspoken question, his voice soft but steady.

Bo lay beside Hedge, basking in the attention as he tickled his belly with his fingers. The dog seemed to know instinctively that Hedge was closer to his kind than anyone else, and he relished in it, his tail thumping against the ground.

"So, you're the child?" asked Jude, breaking the silence, her eyes filled with curiosity and a hint of apprehension.

"What child?" said Tenney, watching Hedge as he played with Bo. The Tethering connection between himself and Aura was saying that Hedge spoke the truth, but his brotherly instincts to protect his sister still battled within him. His jaw tightened as he tried to reconcile his feelings.

"Stace came to see me. He explained to me what he was. I assumed that Meg was the same. Then he told me that she had had a child, born with the curse in effect. I just imagined that this child would be the same as Stace."

"What do you mean?" Tenney's voice was edged with tension, his protective nature flaring up.

"Well, Stace is a vampire. I'm sure that you've figured that out already." Jude's tone was gentle, trying to ease the shock.

The pieces finally slotted into Tenney and Aura's minds, connecting at last. The way Stace stuck to the shadows in the day and grew stronger at night. How they never saw him eat. His pale skin, slightly cool to the touch. Each time Stace had shown his true self, Tenney was half gone with madness and thought it was part of it, a hallucination. They both felt like idiots that they hadn't realised this sooner.

"I just figured that Meg was a vampire too. So, you're a…?" Tenney's voice trailed off, his eyes searching Hedge's face for answers.

Hedge shifted, causing Bo to look at him with disappointment as he stopped stroking him. He got up, shook his whole body, and sat beside Tenney, the movement causing a rustle of leaves.

"Moon-cursed. You may say I am a werewolf," he finished for his benefit. "Mum is human for the whole month, apart from the 48 hours around the full moon. I'm the opposite."

"Whoa," said Tenney, quietly. "That's harsh." His voice was filled with a mix of awe and sympathy.

"Yeah, well it's all I've ever known." Hedge shrugged it off, though his eyes betrayed a lifetime of pain. "We're different to Stace. He needed to be put into a dark place, shut off from air and sunlight to change the first time. All we needed was the full moon. That just happened to coincide with the night a band of soldiers attacked the Fort – this Fort in fact." He tapped the ground with his feet, the sound echoing in the stillness.

Talking about himself made him feel uncomfortable, and this was the most he had spoken in many months. His eyes flickered with old memories, the weight of centuries pressing down on him.

"What happened next?" Tenney by now was engrossed in the story, his over-protective side calmed for a while as he listened to Hedge's history.

"My father was murdered the night Meg resurrected. When she returned to the ashes and ruins of her home, with a cub in her arms, the people who were left accused her of witchcraft, and we were forced to flee. She went to the Water Temple, where she met the goddess. She told me, in the letters she would leave for me to find, that the woman was beautiful, with skin the warm, dark tone of an oaks bark and shimmering golden wings. The goddess sent mum to Stace, who she promised would help us. And he did. He cared for me when mum was a wolf and raised me alongside his charges." Hedge looked sideways at Aura, his eyes softening.

"Hang on," said Tenney, "so you met my sister before?"

"Yeah, many, many times." Hedge's voice was filled with a mix of nostalgia and sorrow.

"How old are you?" he asked, not really wanting to hear the answer.

"I'm not entirely sure, but I think I was born around 150 AD. So, I guess I'm somewhere in the region of 1,900 years old. Give or take a decade." Hedge's voice was calm, but there was a deep sadness in his eyes, the weight of centuries of loneliness and loss.

Tenney heard Jude gasp. He knew that Jude was older than him, but when he looked at Hedge and Aura, how comfortable they were together. He realised that Jude's age didn't matter to him, not if his youth didn't matter to her.

Hedge and Aura had put their own age gap relationship into perspective.

Chapter 23

The buck grazed on the lichen under the forest's canopy, his ears twitching, scanning the land for any danger. Every so often, his antlered head rose up from the ground, his nose twitching, before resuming his meal. The animal moved further into the dim light under the trees, oblivious to the creature downwind from him.

Stace watched him closely, having hunted the animal through the dim light under the trees all morning. He didn't need to eat; the blood of the poor souls taken over by Gallagher's minions was still coursing warmly through his veins. But he needed to do something. What Gallagher had told him about his family opened the wound in his soul which had never fully healed. Their screams as he was dragged away from them reverberated around his head; the tear-stained face of his boy as he was forced to denounce his father flashed before his eyes repeatedly. They had been dead for many years, but the last piece of hope that they may have died in peace evaporated.

That morning, he had observed the youngsters talking at the Fort. He couldn't help but feel worried as he realised that Hedge was picking up where he had left off with Aura all those years ago.

Then there was Tenney; by far the strongest and most volatile Tether he had known. He didn't know what the outcome would be when he realised that he no longer held all of Aura's heart. It was then, as he contemplated only sadness, that he heard Jude laugh. Stace saw the way the boy responded to her, and he understood then that Tenney had already lost a part of his heart, just as Aura had lost a part of hers.

Jude was the key to their survival. He now understood why she was a part of this story. To act as a support to chain Tenney to the world and to her, so that he may Tether Aura.

The two couples were getting to know one another, swapping from serious conversations to great peals of laughter as one or the other said something funny. They threw sticks for the dog, tickled it, and laughed when it began to chase things they couldn't see. Occasionally Tenney would rub the back of his neck as though it was stiff or ached. Aura would look at him concerned, a telepathic conversation going on between them silently alongside the vocal one with the others.

Stace felt proud of them. They were learning fast and soon they would be able to try a longer distance again. For a longer period.

Stace felt confident they could do it.

He saw Tenney pull out his iPhone and hand it to Aura, who then began to film Hedge. He seemed uncomfortable, shying away to hide his embarrassment. She encouraged him to talk, saying that this was the favour she wanted him to do for him, reminding him of his promise to her. Stace smiled when he realised what Hedge was saying.

This incarnation of Air was by far the most compassionate, considerate of other people's feelings. That was good.

That was *very* good.

Her laughter rang out across the clearing.

Eventually the group were driven by hunger. He could hear Hedge's stomach rumble from here. *Foolish boy,* he thought, *he hadn't eaten properly before his change and now he is starving.* Stace remembered the terrible stomach cramps Hedge would experience if he ate cooked or processed food.

As a wolf for much of his life, his stomach was use only to fresh, raw meat and fish, or berries and other natural foods. He saw the boy's face twitch nervously when Tenney suggested they go back to his house and get a sandwich. He wandered how Hedge was going to get out of that one!

The answer presented itself quickly. The more time she spent with human-Hedge, the more she remembered of her past lives with him. She suggested that she and Hedge meet them at the house, after going to the butcher in the local town. Aura must have silently begged Tenney not to ask questions, as he readily accepted this odd request. The foursome, with the dog, walked away.

The buck moved again reminding Stace of his current objective. A few meters away from Stace, downwind of the deer, a great, brown shape leapt from the bushes.

She sprang at the deer, snapping at his hooves as he turned to run away. Stace moved to fence the fleeing animal in. Together he and Meg herded the animal to the place they wanted him to go. It was natural for the wolf to hunt like this, as a pack, wearing the poor creature down until she could bring it down and share the spoils. Stace was only too happy to oblige her.

Eventually the animal slowed, winded from the chase. The two predators cornered it between them and one of the forts ancient embankments. It lowered its head and breathed heavily;

some fight left in it. But it was too weak, succumbing easily as Stace walked to it and placed his hands on its antlers. He forced it to the ground. Its flanks heaved as it drew its last breaths. "Thank you," Stace whispered, deep respect for the animal emanating from him, a prayer to the antlered god, Cernwn.

Then he turned to Meg and nodded. The wolf lunged at the deer's belly, ripping it open, causing its internal organs to slip out. Greedily she dug in. Stace felt his fangs protrude. Faster than light he latched on to the animal's neck and drank from its artery.

Meg and he had walked together for nearly two millennia. She was his closest ally, his only friend. His family. They feasted together, trusting the other completely until they were both satisfied.

**

A weak black smoke moved through the trees. Finally, it pooled in a hollow near a footpath, and waited.

**

Hedge bit into the bloody, raw steak. He sucked greedily on the lines of white fat through the red meat. His human canines were sharper than those of other people, and he found it easy to tear into the flesh. It was a good piece of meat, and he was starving. Aware of his animalistic behaviour, he cast his eyes to Aura. They were sitting in the front of the Land Rover, in a secluded part of the forest, giving him the privacy he needed.

Suddenly, he felt very conscious of what he was eating, and how he was eating it. He turned away again in embarrassment. Her hand went to his knee.

"Hey," she said, "nothing hidden, remember?"

He turned back to her. She lifted her thumb to his mouth and wiped away a spot of blood from his lip. He smiled into her palm and kissed it before returning to his meal.

**

The house was quiet. Sam had been cajoled by his parents into joining Samuel at work at the Temple dig site, and Martha was doing her part-time shift at the Heritage Museum.

Tenney felt the throb at the back of his head. It had been getting steadily worse all morning. How he had managed to keep the severity of his pain from Aura, he didn't know, but she didn't pick up completely on how ill he now felt. He thought maybe the distraction of Hedge had a lot to do with it.

He shook his head, trying to clear it, reaching up into the cupboard for some paracetamol. His eyes blurred at the edges as he momentarily felt lightheaded. He shook it off again, rubbed his eyes before running some water into a glass to wash the pills down.

Next, he opened the fridge and pulled out the bread and butter. Some cheese, ham, and from the cupboard a jar of marmite. He put the bread on the board and began to cut doorstep slices from it. The bread seemed to move on the board, one slice turning into two as his vision went double. Rubbing the corners of his eyes with his thumb and finger did little to shift the sensation. The headache worsened, and he suddenly felt very sick.

The room spun as his legs gave way from under him.

**

Aura sat up in the car. Hedge, so attuned to the movements of her body, immediately sensed something was very wrong. She turned to him, her face pale and shocked.

"Tenney…" she uttered.

Hedge threw down the last of his meat out of the window and started the engine.

**

Hearing a thud from the other side of the kitchen, Jude looked up from the book in her lap.

"Tenney!"

Tenney was on his side lying in vomit, bloody froth at his mouth, his eyes rolled back in his head. She ran to him and held his head in her lap as the dogs whimpered beside him. She pulled her phone from her pocket and started to dial 999.

**

Hedge and Aura burst through the front door, running straight to the kitchen. Hedge, seeing Jude about to hit dial, shouted – "NO!"

She looked up shocked, "He needs an ambulance!" she cried out at Hedge. Aura was stroking Tenney's face, telling him that she was there, over and over and over.

"No," said Hedge, firmly. "We need to get him to Stace. Now!" His authority brokered no argument. Jude felt like she was seeing things from the outside in, unable to make sense of what was going on. Tenney had seemed fine. He was fine…

Hedge gently scooped Tenney up and with little effort hung his limp form over his shoulder in a fireman's lift. Without looking back, knowing that they would follow him, he ran to the Land Rover.

Aura scrambled into the back and Hedge laid Tenney gently beside her. She placed his head on her lap. The dogs, left behind, barked at them from the house as Jude climbed into the passenger seat. Hedge, jumping into the driver's seat, had the engine started before Jude could pull her door too.

Hedge took them back to the Fort.

**

Jude was the first to reach the clearing at the summit. She stood in the centre and yelled Stace's name. The others soon joined her, Tenney over Hedge's shoulder again, his sister clinging to his hand, talking to him constantly.

From the shadows of the trees, Stace appeared. His shirt looked bloodier than it had before, and it was still torn, but Jude felt relief at the sight of him. She didn't know what Stace could do for Tenney, but he had been around for a very long time. Maybe, at some point, he had trained as a doctor… Jude clasped at any option that might bring hope. She didn't want to consider that Stace would know how to help Tenney because humans were one of his main sources of food, therefore giving him an innate understanding of the human body.

He beckoned them over.

"What happened?" he asked as Hedge gently lay the unconscious Tenney down.

"He bumped his head, last night when he fell down after the blast." Jude didn't sugarcoat her words, worry clouding her judgment. Aura's face dropped when she realised that Tenney's condition was a direct result of her actions.

"Hey," shouted Stace at Aura, "This wasn't you. This was Gallagher. OK? Tenney's not dead. He has what's called a delayed concussion." She nodded her head sadly.

Stace gently slapped Tenney's face. "Hey! Tenney!" He called directly at him. "Tenney! Wake up!"

**

Tenney painfully opened his eyes. He saw Jude, her face tear stained. He tried to smile, but his mouth wouldn't work. He felt numbness spreading all down the left side of his body. Aura came into view next, her face as wet as Jude's from crying. The world around her went black, and she was the last thing he saw.

**

"Tenney!" Stace tried again.

"Stace," said Hedge. "You know what you've got to do. If you don't help him, Aura will disappear, and we will all have to start again. Who knows where she will end up this time. You've got to help him."

Stace didn't comment on the unsaid, underlying comment Hedge was making. Hedge didn't want to lose Aura, and the only way he could guarantee that wouldn't happen was to bring Tenney to Stace and ask him to heal him. Stace's hidden concerns that this may sever Aura from the world entirely if he died stayed within him. It was an impossible choice. He knew what the consequences were of healing a human with his blood. But the boy was dying, of that he was certain.

He had no other option.

Stace turned gravely to Aura. "I need to give him some of my blood."

Aura and Jude gasped. "No!" Jude cried, the legends about vampires making other vampires by sharing blood running through her mind.

"If I don't, he will die."

"What will happen to him if you give him the blood?" Aura asked.

"He won't turn," Stace said, looking directly at Jude, understanding her innate fear as dictated by the monsters in the movies. "I can promise you that. But his rage will come down on him, violently. For a while he won't be Tenney. But he will be alive. And in a day or two, he will regain his senses. But in the time when he experiences the bloodlust, he will be stronger, uncontrollable, and unpredictable."

"So, what do we do?" Aura asked, her composure slipping. She was searching for Tenney in her consciousness, but his voice was weak and far away. She was losing him.

"We tie him up, tight, and he stays here, with me. Aura, you had better stay, keep your cords around him, try and keep him calm. Hedge, you need to get Jude somewhere safe."

"No, I won't leave him!" said Jude, shaking.

"Jude, you promised to do what I said. I am asking you to stay out of things for your own safety. You must hold to that promise now. You will get him back; I promise you that."

"Let me see him," she begged. "Let me see him alive, and then, I promise, I will leave with Hedge."

Stace nodded his head, "But be ready to go when I tell you and go quickly."

He looked at Aura, "Are you ready?" She nodded once.

He lifted Tenney up and carried him through the shadows to the tree he had tied him to before. Hedge brought the ropes as the girls followed. The brown wolf appeared, her yellow eyes watching the scene as it unfolded.

When Tenney was secured, Stace lifted his head and spoke to the unconscious face.

"Tenney, I'm going to give you something. It will help you feel better."

He bit into his wrist and held it to Tenney's mouth. At first, nothing seemed to happen. Tenney remained unresponsive, his body limp and lifeless. Then, slowly, his throat moved. The blood flowed through his mouth and into his veins. It began to vibrate through his brain stem, firing off tiny sparks of energy, healing the blood, and mending Tenney's wounds. It covered his brain, sinking into the core of him, until it found his rage.

Tenney's body convulsed slightly as the blood worked its way through him. His muscles twitched, and his breathing became more laboured. The transformation was both fascinating and terrifying to watch. Aura and Jude stood nearby, their faces pale with worry and fear.

Stace's eyes never left Tenney's face, his expression a mix of determination and concern. He knew the risks involved, but he also knew this was the only way to save him.

Tenney's eyes fluttered open, bloodshot and filled with a wild, untamed energy. He looked around, disoriented, his gaze finally settling on Stace.

Chapter 24

Samuel Wiseman decided to spend his Saturday at the dig site, rising early that morning. He had seen Tenney briefly before he headed back out to rejoin his sister. Samuel hoped they were enjoying themselves. Martha had an early start at the local heritage museum. Sam, reluctantly leaving his games console, joined him on site. Samuel hoped that the fresh air this weekend would bring some colour back to his face. Sam seemed to enjoy their family trip to Caerleon the day before, although Samuel suspected it had more to do with having a day off school than anything else.

Sam seemed to be retreating into himself, and this worried Samuel. When he and Martha tried to engage with him, he just shrugged his shoulders, put the device away, and sat quietly until, exasperated, they left him alone.

Martha, after Samuel voiced his concerns for his youngest child, asked him what he was like at 16. Samuel had had to reluctantly concede that he had wanted to spend more time hidden away with his ancient history books or digging around the old Dobunni Fort or exploring the scowles, natural shallow pits where the Romans and Celts mined iron ore unique to the Forest.

Martha gently pointed out that the computer was Sam's ancient history books, his online role-playing games his version of digging around in the Forest.

"He'll grow out of it," she had said wisely, "when girls start to come into the picture, and he realises the real world is so much richer than any online world could be." She had patted him on his cheek and kissed him. Their relationship had only grown stronger with the births of the children, their love deepening into secure and solid foundations.

Samuel smiled at the memory as he gently scraped away with his trowel at the block of stone in the trench. The morning sun cast long shadows, and the air was crisp and cool, filled with the earthy scent of freshly turned soil.

The Water Temple had been discovered a year earlier. The opportunity to head the dig, funded by Bristol University, in the village of his birth was too great for Samuel to pass up.

Samuel remembered how he had looked forward to family nights in after a busy day of work now that he was primarily based in the village. He chuckled to himself at his naivety. Teenagers were never home early! The twins especially seemed to prefer being out, maybe with friends, maybe just by themselves, he was never sure. But there weren't as many family evenings as he had envisioned. Or hoped for.

But the dream had been a good one.

To add to his happiness, he would once more, after several years of lecturing, be 'on-site' working actively, being a detective of ancient civilisations again. Whilst Samuel enjoyed the teaching side of his career, he was an active man and would always choose the trowel over the pen when given a choice. He was the first person in the trench, the one who encouraged his loyal team to keep hunting.

As he worked, he felt a sense of peace and fulfilment. The rhythmic scraping of the trowel against stone was a comforting sound, a reminder of the past he was uncovering piece by piece. He glanced over at Sam, who was reluctantly helping with the dig. The boy's face was pale, but there was a hint of interest in his eyes as he watched his father work.

Maybe this will be good for him, Samuel thought again, hoping that the connection to history and the physical activity would help draw Sam out of his shell.

His imagination worked overtime as he envisioned the people who had lived and worshipped at the site. He was no longer simply analysing, summarising, and teaching. He was touching things that had been hidden for millennia, bringing them back to the surface. He still taught; regular groups from the University would come to his site for 'on the job' tuition. But it was the thrill of discovery that fired him.

Samuel turned his attention back to the stone slab. The site was definitely Roman, but what he was most interested in was what lay under the Roman. The manor house, upon which the site was found, was full of history in its own right. The house was built atop a Saxon Hall, which now formed its foundations and a basement. There had been a building on this site for over a thousand years, standing through plagues, wars, and prosperity.

It seemed that this place naturally drew people to it, and its location of the temple in relation to the wooded hill fort made Samuel want to answer the question of whether the temple was used by the local tribe, the Dobunni, before it was taken over by the invading Roman army.

And he could understand why. The Forest of Dean is an undulating triangle of land caught between the mighty rivers Wye and Severn. A raised basin, full of valleys and hills. Samuel joked that if you wanted to go anywhere locally, you would have to go either up or down; it seemed that there was nowhere which was truly flat. The local Foresters thought nothing of a house built on the side of the hills, their gardens reaching steeply up or dropping down from their homes.

If a person climbed to one of the viewpoints and stood at the 'top' of the forest, all they would see was a blanket of trees rippling out, onwards and upwards. The towns and villages hidden in the dells. Occasionally, a plume of smoke from a chimney would rise above the canopy.

A person who knew about different trees and had some knowledge of the history of the land could pick out the different eras of tree planting. The huddles of the giant Red Woods; the masses of long, straight, ordered lines of the conifers and evergreens planted originally to be masts on tall ships, demonstrated that forestry was still a major source of industry and employment in the local area. Then, if you looked closely enough, you saw the forms of the sweet chestnuts, popping up wherever the Romans had walked and discarded the nuts as they snacked on them.

Then there were the mighty, ancient oaks. The kings of the Forest. Some were so old, their bodies gnarled and warped by age. Samuel thought of the ring of trees around the site of the Fort where he had played as a child. The oldest tree had been affectionately known as "The Old Oak," and it was hundreds, maybe thousands, of years old.

But Samuel knew that it was underneath these blankets of green that the real history of the land, both the ancient and the more recent industrial, could be found if you looked carefully enough. Denebury itself sat in one of the plateaus cut into the hills. One side rose up towards the nearest forest town, the other side dropped sharply down toward the River Severn. The manor and the temple sat at the point of the drop. From the location of the temple, you could see all the way to the Cotswold Hills, the city of Gloucester, and the huge horseshoe bend in the river, which marked it out so clearly in satellite photos. On clear days, you could see across the border into Wales.

It would have been an important religious and strategic viewpoint, hence why the site had been used by different groups of people over the centuries from the Dobunni to the Romans to the Cavaliers in the Civil War.

Samuel's heart swelled with a sense of purpose and connection to the past. Each scrape of his trowel was a step closer to uncovering the secrets buried beneath the earth. He felt a profound respect for the people who had come before him, who had lived, loved, and worshipped on this very ground. The thrill of discovery was intoxicating, and he knew that this was where he was meant to be.

The dig began after the current owners of the manor dredged their pond, bringing the bust of a lady carved from the local sandstone to the surface. The find caused much excitement, and after more pieces were found, Samuel was asked to discover exactly who the bust was of, and why it was here.

It hadn't taken him and his team long to discover the remains of the temple, and to ascertain from its layout – its relation to the view of the river and the proximity of a spring which now fed the pond - that it was a temple to a water deity. From the distinctly female appearance of the bust, Samuel had deduced it was a temple dedicated to the goddess Sabrina, the roman name for the Severn.

The statue itself probably stood on this very same stone plinth that he was currently excavating. It stood just outside the entrance to the temple itself, and near the recently discovered fountain which was a conduit for the spring water. Samuel's imagination showed him what it could have looked like, in its heyday.

The effigy of the goddess welcoming pilgrims to her temple, beckoning them in to offer their prayers to her. It would have been an oasis of calm where people beseeched the goddess not to flood the land or prayed for a good harvest and the health for their families. Or maybe it was as a vantage point from which to watch the rivers strength and unpredictability as the famous Severn Bore travelled along it.

The bust of the goddess reminded him a little of Aura, her face seemed to follow the same delicate contours as her eyes peered sightlessly from their stone features.

Thinking of his daughter brought a grin to his face.

From the moment Martha had admitted to him that she was pregnant, all those years ago, his love for her meant that he couldn't see her abandoned, cast out by her family. When she accepted his hand, the children she carried became as much his as if they had been his own blood. Since that day, he had had over 21 years of happy marriage with the love of his life.

Martha had given him a tenacious, volatile, gregarious, funny, kind son and a beautiful, generous, worrisome, otherworldly daughter. Martha wanted to name their son after her favourite poet. She said it was important to her that he be called Tennyson. Samuel had suggested they give him the nickname 'Tenney' after the street upon which they had lived in Methuen, Massachusetts. In truth, he didn't know how he had come up with 'Aura', it had simply popped into his head as he held her for the first time after the shock of her birth. He was adamant that that was her name, like he had always known it was her name even before they knew she would be born.

They were both intelligent, good looking (sometimes he thought Tenney was too good looking for his own good, reminding him on occasions of the man whose genes he carried) and they had their own strong, individual, personalities. But they were the closest of siblings, Tenney's protectiveness of his sister often clouding his own judgement. But, Samuel knew, Aura could be just as overprotective of Tenney, although she went about it quietly and unobtrusively.

Occasionally, in the past, their closeness had caused some concern to the parents, but their being together was preferable to their being apart. He shuddered as he was taken back to the hospital room; his daughter dead on the bed; Tenney bursting in, radiating a rage he didn't think anyone could carry; and then the sudden calmness that had descended on him as his presence near her brought her back to them.

They were *his* children; from the moment they were born. Blood didn't come into it.

When Sam was born on the chime of the New Year a little over four years later, Samuel and Martha finally felt their family were complete.

Lost in his daydreams, he failed to notice the trowel digging deeper around the foundations of the stone. When he felt it snag on something, he was brought back to the present.

The trowel had caught on a piece of cloth. Lying flat on his belly in the bottom of the trench, he drew his tool kit closer to him and selected a soft bristled brush. Carefully, he wiped away the layers of dirt and mud from the material. His heart raced with anticipation as the cloth began to reveal itself. He could see that it had retained some of its rich, red colour. When he had cleared enough of the earth from it, he realised, judging from its depth, that someone had placed it there deliberately. An offering maybe to the goddess? He called his assistant, Nick, over, and asked for a tray. Meticulously, so as not to damage the material, he gently removed the cloth from the hole.

It was wrapped around something heavy, thin, and about one of his hands and a half in length. Buried then, he thought.

He carried the tray over to the work tent and placed it on a table. Pulling up a chair and using a gentle flow of water from a squeezy bottle, he gently separated the cloth from the object it housed. He focused on the material first, analysing it and studying it. He thought it must have been torn from a dress, and a very fine one at that. Small amounts of gold thread were woven through it, the material was thick and the original colour still vibrant despite its time in the ground.

More questions to be answered in the fullness of time. He handed the cloth to Nick for deeper analysis and turned his attention to the muddy object on the table.

"Dad?"

Samuel quickly looked up, his glasses sitting askew on his nose. He had forgotten that the boy was with him.

"I'm heading home."

"Oh, okay, Son," Samuel spluttered. He waved absently as his attention was drawn back to his find.

As he carefully cleaned it with the same attention to detail as he had shown the material, red and gold gradually revealed themselves.

"Oh, my god…" he said, shocked at what he had uncovered under the dirt.

He quickly picked up his phone and dialled the University, shouting for Nick to get the workers and the owners of the manor together!

**

Martha was sitting in the living room, Jess lying alongside her leg, watching *Pointless* on the telly. "Hiya Love," she greeted Samuel, who, still stupefied by the shock find, stood transfixed in the doorway of the kitchen.

"Aura texted me," Martha continued, oblivious to her husband's mood. "She and Tenney have been invited to go camping with a friend of theirs. Apparently Tenney called in earlier when we were out and collected some provisions. She says they hope to be back by tomorrow, but she'd let us know. They might stay a couple of days as they are okay and having a good time. How was your day, Love?" she asked, turning to Samuel, at last noticing the expression on his face. "What's happened?" She felt panicky, the last time he had looked like this it had something to do with the children…

"I found something, Martha. Something big. At the dig." He still couldn't quite believe it as he sat beside her.

"What did you find?" she asked carefully.

"Cloth from the dress of a presumably important woman from the Iron Age, woven with gold thread, red in colour. Possibly Dobunni. Buried, purposefully, at the feet of the goddess Sabrina."

Martha felt her interest rise; social, living, tangible history was her forte. "Yes…" she encouraged him, the quiz show forgotten as she sat forward on the settee.

"And…" he paused, looked up at her, finally smiling slowly, "it was wrapped around a gold dagger. The hilt had six blood-red rubies in it, three on each side of the grip. On the cross was the largest, brightest ruby I have ever seen and heard of. It positively throbbed in the light as I cleaned it. And down the blade, set into the gold, and descending in size as they neared the point, more of the same gems." He sat back against the sofa. "The style suggests that it is from the east, Turkey maybe."

Martha gasped, taking his surmising one step further. "Why was a dagger from Antioch, wrapped in a Celtic noble's dress and buried at a water temple in the Forest of Dean?"

From the telly, Alexander Armstrong responded to the applause of the audience: *"Congratulations! You have found a pointless answer…"*

Chapter 25

The world zoomed in and out of focus. The edges were cloudy, and the sounds dimmed. He felt groggy, disoriented. He wanted to lift his hand and wipe his face, but his arms wouldn't move.

Muffled voices came to him, incoherent, jumbled. He felt like they were trying to penetrate through water. He groaned. He felt… wrong. That was the only word for it.

He lifted his head and felt the rough bark of the tree behind him. A tree? How did he get here? Surely, he was in his kitchen at home. Again, he tried to get up, the voices still speaking at him becoming more fervent, each one talking over the other, nothing made sense. And then, one voice became clear.

"Tenney?"

In a flash, the world shot back into focus. Everything became sharper, brighter, and more beautiful. He heard the animals in the woods, the breathing of the she-wolf. The breaths of the people around him. Their hearts beating.

The sound of their blood flowing through their veins. He wanted to feel it, get closer to it. He wanted to drink it.

He moved forward to grasp what he wanted, but strong ropes held him back. He struggled again. Pulled forward. Nothing. The rage boiled up in him as he was denied what he needed to have. He screamed in fury, his body moving in a desperate frenzy to be free. Free to kill.

Free to kill everyone.

**

Aura moved back, away from her brother. His madness was screaming out of him. Hedge held Jude back as she desperately tried to move forward, to help him.

"What's wrong with him?" cried Aura to Stace. "What have you done?"

"He's drunk my blood. It's like a drug. It will heal him, but the process is hard, painful. He will have to face his demons, come to terms with the aspects of himself he doesn't like. All the while experiencing blood lust in a frail, human body. It won't kill him, but if we release him, he will kill us. Or try to."

The stunned group stepped back. "Hedge, take Jude away. She can come back in two days' time. He should be fine by then." Hedge nodded at Stace and turned to move Jude away when a thought occurred to him.

"Aura?"

She turned to look at him, her face wet with tears. Every part of him longed to be with her, to stay near her. "I'll be gone again… by the time this is over. But I won't be far away. I promise you." She smiled, sadly. This wasn't how he had wanted to say goodbye. "You'd better text your parents, explain that you're both away for a couple of days. That you'll be back soon." She nodded and pulled her phone out.

Hedge led Jude away.

**

They walked in silence down the slope to the Land Rover, the sounds of Tenney's screams following them.

"Has he done that before?" Jude finally asked Hedge.

"Yeah," he replied grimly. "London, Whitechapel to be exact. 1888."

Jude stopped momentarily as she associated that date and place with a murder spree that to this day still had people puzzling about.

**

Sam was certain he would be spotted by the policewoman and the dark-haired man. He pressed himself against the rough bark of the tree, holding his breath. The dark-haired man was unmistakable; Sam had seen him at the train station when Aura had suddenly fallen ill. The man had been there, urging Sam's parents to get Tenney back. And again, in the dim light of the hospital waiting room. The man's unnerving stillness had sent chills down Sam's spine until he just got up and walked out of the hospital.

As he had approached his home, he'd seen the man give Tenney a fireman's lift from the house. Tenney had looked dead. He saw them all pile into the Land Rover and speed off up the lane towards the ancient hill fort. They had been too preoccupied to notice him, so he went to the shed in the garden and grabbed his mountain bike. Pushing away from the curb, he followed them as quickly and as quietly as he could.

He had been just in time to see the man feed blood to Tenney. He was too far away to be able to hear the words they were saying, but he had seen the pale man bite his wrist and stick it in Tenney's mouth.

What the hell is going on? he thought. He needed advice. As quietly as he was able, he went back down the hill and found his bike.

Pulling out his phone before heading back to his house, Sam quickly pressed the messaging app and began to send his only real friend a message.

**

"Aura, try to connect with him," Stace instructed, sitting at a distance under the darkest shadows he could find. While Tenney was coming around, Stace had quickly changed his clothes, now looking as though he hadn't shed any blood or hunted a deer through the woods. He appeared the same old, calm and composed Stace she had come to know.

Aura closed her eyes and imagined the bright blue light that emitted from her, reconnecting it to Tenney. Gradually, his screams subsided, and he sat still.

"Ten?" she asked tentatively.

He snapped his head up, his bloodshot eyes boring into hers. "Bitch!" he spat, launching into a tirade of abusive words. Meg growled at him, but he didn't stop. Bloody spittle flew from his mouth as he bit through his lips.

He had been her protector, her saviour. Now he was her abuser. *This isn't him, this isn't him, this isn't him...* she repeated over and over in her mind.

Placing her head in her hands, the stress too much to bear, Aura wept.

**

The sun had finally started to go down. Stace, now freer to move, walked over to Aura. He sat next to her and wrapped his arms around her, just as he had done for two millennia. Aura responded to his comfort, moving closer to him, recognising him for who he was: her Guardian, her teacher, a father figure who had always walked beside her. The she-wolf stalked around Tenney, careful not to get too close, but never taking her yellow eyes off him.

Tenney started talking gibberish, hitting his head against the tree, his fingers flexing uncontrollably against the tightly knotted restraint. His eyes followed the wolf hungrily as she continued to pace around him.

Meg growled, deep from within her body. It was a warning: as strong and as mad as Tenney might be right now, she would always be stronger. And madder. She had the whole night and the next day before she would change back into a human again. The moon was at its fullest, meaning she was at the very peak of her wolf powers.

"It was 1887," Stace began, another story to explain things to his charge. Aura wiped her nose as she settled down to listen to him, willing to do anything to block out the sounds of her brother's insanity.

"I had to return to London from America. A friend was having trouble with his Elemental. She was an unpredictable, passionate person. Still is, I believe, but back then she was causing no end of trouble for the people around her. She and her sister were adept at getting what they wanted from men, and then leaving them destitute as a result.

"I arrived and helped him deal with the problem by bringing them into line, reminding them of their duty, their curse, I guess. I then decided to stay for a while, a holiday of sorts. You and your sister were still very young, and Meg was watching you.

"I had always liked London, and I had seen it change from the time it was still called Londinium. I had been there during the Great Fire, seen kings and queens rise and fall. I loved to see how it evolved. Changed. So, I stayed to help my friend and explore the city again.

"One night, the Elemental's Tether became ill. One too many dalliances had caused her to catch syphilis. She was dying. My friend was not like me, or Meg for that matter. He was another creature altogether. He couldn't help her. So, the Elemental begged me to save her sister.

"And foolishly, one night, I did. The girl escaped and went on a murderous killing spree, one that is still famous today as Whitechapel was never the same again. As the bloodlust wore off, she begged her sister to get her more from me. Then one night, the Elemental used her power to immobilise me. Before I could recover, they used a very sharp blade and cut my skin. The Tether drank from me until my wound healed up.

"The killing started again, and I was forced to put an end to it, even though it meant the Elemental would have to go through the rebirth."

"What did you do?" Aura asked quietly.

"I hunted her down, and I killed her before she could kill anyone else."

"What were their names?" Aura asked, fear for her brother striking her heart.

"The Elemental was named Bridgit."

"And her sister?"

"Jaqueline. But everyone called her Jack."

**

"Names are important for the Elementals," Hedge said, distracting Jude as he drove back to the village. Hedge was also aware that if she wanted him to stay, he would probably be a wolf before they headed back. "Although Aura seems to be the only one who keeps her name across the ages, the other Elementals choose names associated with their element. Bridgit means strength and exalted one. It was also the name of the Irish goddess of fire, poetry, and wisdom.

"'Aura' means 'soft or gentle breeze'. It also means 'glowing light.' She was always the kindest of the Elements, the one who cared the most about the humans on the earth. But she could be ferocious when she wanted to. She would join with her siblings and create hurricanes, typhoons, tsunamis, sandstorms. She could suck the air out of a place or breathe new life into it.

"At the beginning, the five elements worked together to replenish and repair the world, under the watchful eye of the Councillors. One day, Metal showed himself to a human, who spread the word about this immortal race of supernatural beings. The stories spread like wildfire and mankind started to worship them.

"Earth was the greatest, giving the world formation and foundation. Everything comes from the Earth. The creator made the first man with Earth's help, forming him from her mud.

"Water covers most of the globe and is completely necessary for the survival of not only man but all living things on Earth. The Elemental knew it and basked in his importance, becoming bold and arrogant.

"Metal was the strongest and, alongside Earth, the wisest. He had control over all the natural gifts of the world – ore, minerals, gemstones, and oil. Completely impervious; unbreakable. He professed himself to be their Leader.

"Fire was unpredictable, changing all the time, she literally had a blazing attitude towards all things. If something, or someone, pleased her, she would warm it gently, give light and the means to cook food, boil water. But if she was displeased, nothing could stop the devastation she caused.

"And Air…" Hedge trailed off and swallowed as he thought of Aura. "None of them would exist without Air. Water, we now know, is made partly of oxygen, fire won't burn without it, Earth wouldn't be able to sustain life, and Metal would be underground, unused, unknown."

Jude turned to look at him. His loyalty to Aura was clear in the passion of his voice.

"We are nothing without air. When they were finally caught by the Councillors, she was the first to be tethered, willingly, to a human. Then it was her sister, Earth. Her brother, Metal, fought but was overwhelmed by the Councillors and Tethered. Only Fire and Water proved the most elusive. But they were caught soon enough."

Jude could feel the tension headache tightening behind her eyes and was relieved when they finally stopped outside her hotel.

"It's ok," she said, massaging the spot between her eyes. "You can leave me here. I promise I won't go back. Not till he's himself again."

Hedge felt sympathy for her. But he understood her need to be alone. He knew it couldn't be long before the parents and brother returned home, and he needed to clean up the mess in the kitchen. Make it look like everything was ok, grab a change of clothes for Aura and Tenney. Already his mind was thinking about the next thing to do.

"Ok," he said, distracted as he realised that he would be able to spend his last day with Aura after all. "See you in a couple of days. Sort of…." He turned and smiled as she left the car and watched her enter the hotel.

**

Jude stood at the window and watched as Hedge drove away, the taillights of his car disappearing into the night. Flicking the switch to light the room, she felt an overwhelming emptiness settle in. The room seemed colder, lonelier than before. Her eyes fell on the photo of her parents on the dresser, a bittersweet reminder of happier times.

As she moved across the room, her foot kicked something. Bending down, she picked up a thick, white envelope. Embossed on the front was the logo in the shape of a diamond, and underneath, in fine cursive script, was her name and address. Placing it on the bedside table, she warily looked around her room. It was just as she had left it that morning with Tenney, housekeeping respecting the "Do Not Disturb" sign. The bathroom was in disarray, and the bed, rumpled from their exploits after their second shower, bore the marks of their presence.

She had made Tenney swear that he would come back with her and help tidy up, knowing full well it would probably have been left in a worse state by the time they were finished. Her heart stuttered as she closed the door of the en suite behind her. She tried to take her mind off him by beginning the monotony of tidying the room. But when she found the towel, he had wrapped around his waist, carelessly dropped at the foot of the bed, she finally collapsed and cried her heart out. Tidying the room no longer seemed important.

Halfway through the night, she woke up, having crawled onto the covers of the bed before falling into the deep sleep of the emotionally and physically exhausted. Her stomach rumbled, reminding her she hadn't eaten anything since the bagel that morning. It was too late to contact the desk, so she went to the kettle on the side and selected a sachet of hot chocolate. A cube of sugar would help sweeten it and provide some of the energy she needed to keep going. As she waited for the kettle to boil, her eyes went to the envelope.

Jude slipped a finger under the flap and pulled out fine hotel paper. Written by hand in the same cursive script, the note read:

Dear Officer Marcello,

Please be at Bristol Avon Gorge Hotel by 9 a.m. Sunday, 20th October. Ask for Humphrey Glendower.

At the base, written in very neat, precise lettering, as though the person leaving the message had had to spell out every letter, were words in a language Jude couldn't understand. She scrunched the letter up. The 20th was tomorrow.

It was still 11 days before the drinks convention when she felt sure she would find her mother. Glendower must have arrived at the hotel early and had received the message she left

180

for him. Maybe he would have some answers for her. She looked at her watch. It was nearly three in the morning. She knew it would take her less than an hour to get to Bristol, especially at that time of night, but she couldn't be here, not now, useless and incapacitated by loss.

She tossed the note at the waste basket. It missed and rolled under the bed.

Pulling on her bike leathers, she packed a small bag with some essentials, ready for an overnight stay if necessary. Jude left the room and all its memories behind.

Chapter 26

Hedge returned quickly from the Wiseman house back to Aura. He told her that he had cleaned up the kitchen and handed her a bag of clean clothes. He had also made sure that the dogs were okay, reassuring her.

Aura looked at Tenney as Hedge sat beside her. She didn't know how it had happened. How could Tenney, relaxed and happy, with only a slight headache, now be like this? Mad. Bloodthirsty. His whole personality had changed. She understood that it was the only way he was going to be saved, but she worried that he would crave the blood after it had worn off. Stace said it was like a drug. Highly addictive. Highly volatile.

"How does Stace know Tenney won't crave it? The blood? I mean, after this part, like Jack did?"

"He told you the real story of The Ripper then?" Hedge asked softly, putting his arm around Aura. Tenney, his head on his chest, mumbling incoherently, reacted to Hedge's simple act of possession, venting a tirade of foul, abusive language at him. Aura wished she could just shut it off. Instead, she focused on the blue light connecting them and tugged on it. The action had the desired effect and Tenney stopped talking. For a time.

"Yeah," she replied, shattered and devastated.

"Jack was basically a high-end street walker, already addicted to opium and easy men. Poor girl. She craved anything that made her and her sister feel alive, free. Stace's blood did that for her. And when she woke up from it, she didn't think about the people she killed, only about having another high like the one she had just experienced."

He shook his head sadly. "It was hard for Stace. He knew what he had to do. And he did it. When he gave his blood to Tenney, he went against everything inside him telling him no. But he did it because Tenney is important to you." Hedge smiled reassuringly at her. "Tenney's a strong lad. Because of that, I know he'll be okay."

"How can you be so sure?"

"Because you're his sister. And you'll make him okay." He kissed her tenderly.

The she-wolf snapped at Tenney as he strained towards Hedge and Aura, his corrupted brain telling him to separate them.

"Where's Stace?" Aura asked, desperately trying and failing to ignore Tenney.

"He's close by, don't worry." Looking for distraction, watching the wolf as she paced, Aura asked Hedge about Meg. "What's her story?" The she-wolf turned her head towards the couple. She seemed to wink at Hedge.

"Mam is originally from Antioch. She fled to Britannia after her uncle beat her aunt. She witnessed the abuse and picked up his ruby dagger. She slew the bastard before he could kill her aunt, or herself. She was 9 years old, or thereabouts." He felt Aura shudder at the thought of a child protecting her aunt in that way. He held her closer, the wolf shifting her glance between the young couple and the mad man. "When she and her aunt arrived on these shores, they travelled west until they found a new home with the Dobunni. The rest is history."

"What happened to her aunt?"

"She died shortly after hearing that we had been killed in the attack. Mam went to find her in Glevum, but we were too late."

"What about your mum's mum? Where was she when all this was happening?"

"She was an Elemental, who shortly after Meg's birth, disappeared when her twin died from a fever, leaving Mam to be raised by her their older sister. Mam's martyrdom proved that the Elementals could still parent night and moon creatures even after they were Tethered. I am the proof that the children of Elementals can beget the same creatures. Stace is careful, he doesn't want to be the father of too many of his kind. I assume Mam is careful too. At least I haven't heard of any siblings."

His mother harumphed from across the clearing.

"Anyway, after the death of my father, and the trauma inflicted on her, well, on us," he reflected, "After all that, Mam has preferred the company of women. Stace is the only man I have ever felt my mother truly trust like a brother." Aura couldn't help but glance at her own suffering sibling. Hedge continued, "Occasionally Mam will meet her mother, in her new form. But she's not really her mother, you know. It's complicated."

Aura's heart began to race, the sudden rush of blood causing Tenney to tense up again. "Hedge! It's not me, is it?" She was truly frightened that she might be related to him.

He roared loudly, "Hell no!" he continued laughing. She slapped him lightly, almost playfully. "Mam's a daughter of Earth – not Air!" Amazingly, on this impossibly sad night, Hedge had managed to make her smile.

**

Stace sat on a bough high up in a tree surrounding the captive and his guardians. He felt the cold breeze brush his colder face. Winter was nearly upon them. The group on the ground were settling into their night vigil. Every so often Tenney would rant and rave. But mostly he sat, slumped, head bowed, his back against the tree. But Stace knew he wasn't quiet. He could hear his own blood pulsing through the boy's veins, burning him up, making him crave something he should never have.

He had been careful with how much blood he had given him, but it wasn't an exact art, and each person was different. Too little and it would have been pointless; the illness would have returned as soon as the blood left his system, killing him quickly. Too much and he would be too strong to control. Stace knew it would be difficult to control a man like Tenney in that state if he broke free.

When a nightwalker was reborn, they very soon learned that their body had changed. Externally, they grew taller, stronger, and leaner. Their skin became harder and colder as their circulatory system slowed down to only a few beats of the heart a minute. Some old scars became more prominent, but new scars disappeared within minutes or hours of receiving the wound.

Internally, the change was far more dramatic. Bones became harder yet lighter, ligaments faster. Their hearts became stronger and needed less oxygen, so they could move faster than light when they wanted, or needed, too. The skull and jaw allowed for the new set of fangs which would drop down at a moment's notice, and then go back just as quickly. Their mental acuity and digestive system changed dramatically, allowing for a new diet, and the mindfulness to accept it. They could learn to control the blood lust, the blood rage, and find a modicum of peace if they wanted to. Eventually. He was the living proof of this.

But a human being didn't change physically from the blood. They experienced a momentary time of vampirism, revelling in the freedom of knowing you could kill, and not care. At least not until you came out of it on the other side. And then you felt the guilt squash you down, and the only thing that would help was more of the same blood-drug.

He was worried, which was why he had decided to sit here, close enough to watch and help, but far enough away that he could think and pray to his own gods in peace. Tenney was unusually strong already, and the speed into which he fell into the separation rage was startling. The blood worked by healing that which was hurt, but it also exacerbated the person's own psychosis.

That was also why he kept Aura close, knowing that Hedge would do everything in his power to protect her. She was the embodiment of Tenney's best side.

Stace closed his eyes. He turned his face up to the dark night and prayed. Prayed that Tenney's uniquely strong bond with Aura would bring him back to them again. That his fledgling relationship with Jude would remind him of his humanity. There was something about the boy that made him like him, something more than just being Aura's Tether. He surprised himself when he realised that Tenney was like kin, more than any tether he had worked with before. He would do anything to protect those he counted as kin.

**

Tenney was desolate. His whole body burned. He was in pain. Masses of pain. Agony coursing through him with every beat of his racing heart. And he was so hungry. Everyone had abandoned him and were ignoring him, denying him what he needed. It was all he could think about.

Even his sister, his closest friend, had abandoned him. The bitch. With her wolf mutt she didn't care about him anymore. Her own twin. She should be grateful. He was the reason she was even here in the first place. He wanted to kill her for abandoning him like this.

These thoughts circled through his head, driving him deeper and deeper into his lunacy.

All of a sudden, he heard a new sound. A heartbeat. Soft and fast. He stilled himself. The mouse, oblivious to the goings on around it, crawled over his legs, up his chest.

**

The next morning Aura woke up to a light drizzle. The sun was fighting to shine its light through black clouds rolling across the trees, making the ground dim in places. Through a small gap in the trees, she could see that a fog lay in the valley below, covering the village. Someone had covered her with a waterproof jacket and moved her under a low hedgerow.

She sat up, momentary confusion settling on her before she berated herself for falling asleep. Then she heard shouting from a short distance away.

She placed the jacket over her shoulders and ran into the clearing. Tenney was pulling on his ties again, his veins standing out, his eyes looking more bloodshot than before. The she-wolf was pacing around him in an agitated semi-circle, backwards and forwards, backwards, forwards. Aura could see the trampled grasses where she had walked the same route, possibly for a few hours.

Hedge stood, between his mother and Tenney, in a low stance, his left leg out the front, his back leg firmly grounded. His hands were held up, fencing himself off from her brother. He spoke calmly, quietly, trying to placate Tenney.

Tenney stretched forward, closer still to Hedge. Every muscle in his legs, torso, shoulders and neck straining to get away, to attack the man in front of him. The ropes gave slightly. Aura stifled a scream. Meg hunkered down ready to pounce. Hedge danced out of the way.

He spotted Aura, and subtly nodded his head to the side, to a safer place, and somewhere in Tenney's eye line so he could see her. The blue cord of light was a little weaker than it had been before she fell asleep. She tried to fix it, but Tenney, for the first time in their lives, began to resist her.

She ran around to look him in the eyes, but the sudden movement only caused him to get madder. She saw blood in his spittle from his mouth. *He must've bitten his tongue!* She thought.

He screamed forward again, the ropes stretching and fraying. He flew backwards, landing with a thud against the tree as Stace pinned him down, smoke curling where the few rays of morning sun hit him. But Stace ignored his own pain, talking quietly to Tenney, face to face, trying to calm him down.

It had no effect.

All at once Stace got kicked back, flying a few meters into the clearing before skidding to a stop. Tenney rose to his feet, panting deeply. He took a firmer hold of his ropes and pulled. They came away from the tree, the strain too great for them to hold anymore.

Immediately Tenney pounced on Hedge and went for his throat. Meg launched herself at Tenney, desperate to protect her son, but Tenney blocked her, sending her tumbling backwards. Stace, the sun causing his burn scars to spread, sprang up and ran at Tenney attempting to knock him off the body beneath him, but Tenney was too far gone. Hedge, using all his strength, pushed Tenney's face away, and tried to wriggle free, but his adversary was too strong. Too determined.

Aura felt the world slow, each second stretching into an eternity. She saw Stace stand back up, his movements sluggish and laboured. Meg, shaking herself as she staggered upright, seemed to move in slow motion, each hair from her head to her tail swaying as if underwater. Hedge was losing his battle with Tenney, their struggle a chaotic blur in the periphery of her vision.

Stace's face was red and raw, the sun's rays causing his skin to smoke gently. He turned to face her, his mouth wide open in a silent scream, his eyes filled with desperation. He began to run towards her, his movements exaggerated and slow, as if wading through thick syrup.

Aura's mind detached from her body, her consciousness floating above the scene. She saw only the threat, the imminent danger that had to be stopped. Her Elemental self surged to the forefront, a primal force of nature. She raised her hand, pointing it at Tenney with deliberate slowness. With a flick of her wrist, she commanded the wind to push him back. Tenney flew through the air, his back slamming against a tree, his feet dangling a foot off the ground.

Her hand remained outstretched, her fingers curling into a fist. As her fist closed, Tenney's eyes bulged, his mouth opening in a silent scream. She was cutting off his oxygen, the air around him becoming a vacuum. His eyes rolled back in his head, his body convulsing as he took one last desperate gasp for air before going limp.

The world around her dimmed, the edges of her vision darkening. Aura's hand fell to her side, her strength ebbing away. Her lungs felt like they were being squeezed shut, and she collapsed to the ground, the world fading to black.

Chapter 27

Jude rode through the early morning mist, the Severn Bridge looming ahead as she approached the M4/M5 exit. The steady thrum of her bike's engine beneath her was a comforting rhythm, a reminder of the freedom she craved. For the first time in days, her mind felt clear, the worries that had plagued her fading with each mile.

She still had a few hours before her meeting, leaving her with a choice. She could turn off the M4, head south down the short M32 through the bustling streets of Bristol City Centre and find a quiet café near the hotel to pass the time. Or she could continue down the motorway, enjoying the light traffic and the open road, before turning back in time to reach Bristol.

As she twisted the throttle, the decision felt symbolic, a small act of control in a world that often felt chaotic. She chose to ride east, chasing the golden hues of the sunrise, letting the promise of a new day guide her path.

**

The Elemental being was free at last. She had no ties, no worries. All she had was herself and the element that sustained her. She saw the air as it moved around her, through her. The creatures of this realm of sky and space called to her, sharing what they saw and heard—the birds singing to the dawn, the insects rustling in the foliage, and a solitary horseshoe bat, caught out too long after dark, making its way back to its colony.

She saw the essences of all living things glowing in halos of different colours around them. She saw the truths that people hid, their darkest secrets laid out before her clearer than day. An owl watched her from a tree, its moon eyes boring into her.

She remembered green eyes doing the same thing and felt her unseen heart thump. She remembered touch. *Thump*. Laughter. *Thump*. Heartbreak. *Thump thump*.

There was movement near her, something from the solid world. She drifted around, her body nothing more than a shimmer of breath on the breeze. A child of her sister, Earth, was moving over the body of a small blonde girl, trying in vain to blow life into her lungs, his mouth crushing hers in desperation. His glow were the colours of death and grief, bursting from him in blacks and sickly greens. His dark hair obscured his face, but she could see his hands cupping the back of the girl's head, her chin, as though his touch would revive her. She felt a tingle on her ethereal face, mirroring the places he touched the girl. Then he shouted a name. A familiar name. Her name.

Another of his kind paced anxiously around him, helpless to do anything in her form. Her glow was a sickly yellow as she panted with anxiety.

Turning, she saw another figure leaning over a second limp, lifeless body, this time a man who smelled of blood and strength. One who had walked in the world for millennia. She recognised him as a son of her brother, his powerful arms pressing down on the chest of the body beneath him. Like the other man, he was attempting to revive the body by blowing air into his lungs. As he blew, his glow flickered in a succession of colours—red for determination, blue for hope, and grey for despair—as he tried to restore the life lost in the boy on the ground.

There was something about this prone body that caught her attention. She knew his form better than she knew anything else in the world. She floated closer, hovered over him. When the son of Metal moved away, finally defeated, she used the opportunity to look closer at the body's face. His features were ones she knew—the curve of his bowed lips, the line of his nose, the purple bruises around his jaw. Gently, she blew one of his eyelids open, unconcerned with the man beside them. She saw bloodshot hazel eyes framed by long dark lashes.

The eye softly closed again. She floated back, away from him as something within her started to clench and unclench. Loss threatened to overwhelm her spirit as she thundered in dark blues. She wanted to scream, to fly away and leave this sorrowful place. It was her fault. He was lying here because of her.

She felt guilt begin to weigh her down. She thought nothing could weigh her down—she was Air! A free spirit, an Elemental. She grew angry as new emotions and memories coursed through her. A small tornado began to form in her wake, making the autumn leaves take flight and the clouds blow in, finally obliterating the power of the sun and turning the day dark.

"Aura?"

Riding the wind, she flung herself around to look at the spirit of the man dead on the ground. The ghost of her lost soul.

**

"Hedge…" Stace moved back from Tenney's body. He had seen the eyelid flutter open, felt the breeze on his skin, warmer than the morning air should have been. The sudden tornado of leaves across the ground. He felt his strength return as the sun vanished behind the onset of heavy clouds.

"HEDGE!" he called louder this time.

Hedge was holding Aura's lifeless body to him, trying in vain to bring her back to life. After she had cut off the air from Tenney's lungs to stop him from trying to kill Hedge, she had inadvertently killed herself in the process. She had given up her life, and the life of her beloved brother, to save him.

He felt wretched. His heart was shattered into a thousand pieces, irreparable. His blood pulsed with the pain of his loss. He was desperate to join her, but he was just as immortal as she had once been.

Stace grabbed him and shook him out of his stupor. "HEDGE!" he screamed, slapping his face before grabbing his chin, making sure that his green eyes were focused on what he was trying to tell him. "Hedge, she's still here!"

Hedge's glow flickered with a spark of hope, a faint bright green light amidst the darkness. He looked around, searching for any sign of Aura's presence, his eyes wide with a mix of fear and longing.

**

Jude sped down the motorway in the early morning, the cool air whipping past her as she expertly navigated through the light traffic. The hum of the engine beneath her was a comforting constant. Her bike was her sanctuary, a place where she could clear her mind and feel in control. The ride had done wonders for her mood, though it didn't take her mind off Tenney and what was happening to him and her new friends back at the fort.

As she approached the junction, she indicated left and smoothly turned onto the roundabout. The city of Bristol loomed ahead; its skyline tinged with the soft hues of dawn. She reminded herself that this meeting could be pivotal in her search for her mother, and she was determined to see it through. Her heart pounded with a mix of anticipation and anxiety, but she steeled herself. Determined to get something right, she tightened her grip on the handlebars and pressed on.

**

"Aura?"

"Ten?"

"What happened?"

"I killed you. I killed us."

"What?"

"You had gone mad, filled with bloodlust. I knew that I was the only one who could stop you. I'm sorry, Tenney. I didn't know what else to do."

The spirit and the Elemental floated towards each other, still connected by millions of blue threads of light, every inch of them intertwined.

"What now?" asked Tenney.

"I don't know. Maybe we have to make a choice."

The Elemental felt sure that he would choose to sever himself from her, to let her go, freeing her from the guilt of killing the other half of her soul. He would die, but she would be free— free from all the pain of a human existence. No more rebirth. No more being anchored. Free to fly, free to influence the very fabric of the universe around them. She could be powerful again, unrestrained by human emotion.

She turned her head away from the spirit, catching another flash of bright green. The man covering the body of the blonde girl had looked up. Tears had fallen from his emerald eyes, eyes that were like green beacons beckoning her home…

She gasped as she remembered him, and intense human feelings rushed into her. She suddenly felt more substantial and began to warm through.

"Aura?"

She turned back to the ghost of her soul.

"I am not ready to leave you - I choose you. I will always choose you. I wouldn't be me without you. I love you, Aura, no matter what you've done. And I know that you love me. And you love Hedge. You must remember that love, sister."

She looked back at him and felt a sudden magnetism as they were drawn together, melding together, mending their fractured soul.

From below them, the daughter of Earth growled.

**

Stace shook Hedge's shoulder and pointed to where Meg was growling at the air. A slight blue shimmer could be seen above her nose.

"They are right there," he said, his voice urgent. "They're in the *inter duo mundos* - the between." Hedge nodded once, his eyes filled with determination, before looking down at Aura, still cradled in his arms. His tears hit her face, leaving tracks through the dust that had settled on her.

Stace walked over to Tenney. He lifted him up, the ropes hanging from his bloodied wrists, and as the sun began to shine again, he carried him back to the safety of the shadows. Under the tree where Tenney had been tied up, Stace saw the bloodless husk of a mouse. The sight made his stomach churn.

Stace berated himself for not keeping a closer watch. Such a small amount of blood shouldn't have been enough to cause that sort of strength in Tenney. He must have some Elemental blood in him, Stace thought. If that was true, he couldn't say how many generations back someone in Tenney's family tree had been born to an Elemental, or how diluted his DNA was. Depending on which Elemental Tenney was descended from, it would dictate what creature their progeny would become. Nightwalkers and the Moon Cursed were only two types of creatures born from the ancient gene pool.

If he did have a trace of Elemental blood in his body when he died, he shouldn't turn, despite dying suddenly and violently. But the thought troubled Stace, raising more questions than answers.

Hedge carried Aura's cold body over and laid it next to Tenney. He looked at Stace, his eyes filled with a mix of sorrow and determination. "We have to find a way to bring them back," he said, his voice barely above a whisper.

Stace nodded, his mind racing with possibilities. "Talk to her Hedge." he said, simply.

Hedge brought his mouth to her ear and whispered all the things he wanted to say to her—all the ways he loved her, his hopes for their future, his plans. He laid one hand over her heart and told her that his heart was hers, had always been hers, forever.

**

Jude pulled up in the centre of Bristol, the roar of her bike cutting through the early morning bustle. She had time to stop, before riding the short distant to the hotel overlooking the Clifton Suspension Bridge. The city was in the throes of rush hour, with the shopping mall, Cabot Circus, just starting to open for business. She glanced at her watch. 8:30 am. Perfect timing.

She wandered into the shopping centre, the aroma of freshly brewed coffee guiding her steps. The hum of conversations and the clatter of store shutters opening filled the air. She firmly pushed all thoughts of Tenney to the back of her mind. He was in good hands, and when she got back, when he was better (he had to get better!), they could pick up where they left off.

Right now, she had another job to do. She took a deep breath, steeling herself for the meeting ahead.

**

The embracing spirits felt their connection grow exponentially. They remembered their lives together; they remembered love and forgiveness. Aura could hear Hedge whispering to her human body.

"Ready?" she asked.

Somehow the spirit had retained its megawatt smile. Pulling back slightly so she could see the grin, he answered her.

"Ready."

**

Hedge was giving up hope. He kept whispering to her, waiting for some sign of movement under his palm. But nothing happened. He looked into her face, trying to memorise it. He doubted that she would be reborn. This time was different; an Elemental had never killed their Tether before. The shimmer above his mother's head vanished.

He kissed her frozen lips one last time, something for him to carry with him for the rest of his unending life.

Aura breathed him in. Her heart began to beat as her lungs moved. She opened her eyes, swirling blue miasmas meeting emerald, green.

**

"Urrrgh, my head!" Tenney sat up abruptly. The move was so sudden, so unexpected, that Stace fell backwards out of his vigil, nearly landing back in the sunlight.

"Tenney!" he cried out.

"Yeah," Tenney spoke groggily, his tongue thick.

"Look at me, boy," Stace grabbed his face.

"Ow, careful, man!"

Stace looked into his eyes. The blood was fading from them, and they looked clear. He steeled himself for the next question.

"Tenney," he said carefully. "Are you hungry?"

Tenney thought about it for a second. "Yeah. Starving."

"What for?"

"Huh?"

"What are you hungry for?" Stace asked, impatience and concern making it sound harsher than he intended.

"Well, if you must know, I would kill," Stace drew in a deep breath, "for a cheeseburger. Loads of gherkins, fries, and a strawberry milkshake."

Relief caused Stace to laugh. He laughed as he hadn't laughed for a long time.

He looked over to Aura. Hedge was holding her so close to his body, rocking back and forth, that Stace was worried the strength of his embrace would be enough to kill her all over again. He smiled and nodded his head towards them, causing Tenney to look over.

"Ah, geez," he tutted, holding his head in one hand. He felt like he had the worst hangover ever. "Can't you two get a room?"

Aura pulled away from Hedge, smiling widely. Hedge sat back; relief etched over every part of his face as he let her go to her brother. As Tenney held his beloved sister tight to him, their bonds of light growing stronger and stronger, their two souls becoming one, he caught sight of his hands.

"Er, Aura," he said, puzzled. "Why have I got ropes around my wrists?"

**

Jude walked into the hotel, the coffee having helped to clear her mind and prepare her for what was to come. The lobby was bustling with activity, guests checking in and out, and the faint sound of a piano playing in the background. She approached the receptionist.

"Officer Jude Marcello, here to see Mr. Glendower," she said, her voice steady.

Behind her, a man rose from an armchair. "Ah, Miss Marcello. You made it," he said in a soft, Scottish accent, his eyes warm and welcoming.

She turned to him just as her phone buzzed inside her breast pocket.

"I'm sorry, excuse me one moment." She fumbled as she pulled the phone out, her hand shaking slightly. It was a missed call from Tenney's phone. It must have been Aura, calling with an update. She'd call her back after the meeting. Switching off the phone, Jude turned back to the man.

"Mr. Glendower. Thank you for agreeing to see me."

She held out her hand and walked over, her mind racing with anticipation and a hint of anxiety. This meeting could be pivotal in her search for her mother, and she was determined to make the most of it. It might finally help her understand her mother's reasons for investigating this man, and perhaps, uncover the secrets that she knew instinctively had been hidden from her for so long.

Chapter 28

Glendower led Jude through to a private sitting area. The room was expansive, with distinct sections created by the strategic placement of wingback leather armchairs around low coffee tables. This arrangement provided a semblance of privacy for the hotel guests. The walls were adorned with rich, dark wood panelling, and the floor was covered in a plush, deep red carpet that muffled their footsteps. Soft, ambient lighting from ornate chandeliers cast a warm glow, creating an atmosphere of understated luxury.

On one table, a large crystal decanter of water sat upon a gleaming silver platter, flanked by two delicate glasses. The table also held a selection of croissants, jams, and butter, arranged with meticulous care. Jude's stomach rumbled audibly at the sight of the food, a stark reminder of her hunger which her earlier drink hadn't satisfied. Glendower's eyebrow arched slightly at the sound, and he extended a hand towards the breakfast spread.

"Please, Officer Marcello, help yourself if you are hungry," he said, his tone gentlemanly and inviting.

A small man with slicked-back hair and a hooked nose approached them. He was dressed in a formal "penguin suit," complete with a waistcoat and tails, and he deferred to Glendower with a slight bow.

"Can I get you a hot beverage, Sir? Madam?" he inquired, his voice polished and professional. Jude couldn't help but think he looked as though he had just stepped off the set of a Georgian period drama.

Glendower shook his head as he reclined back in his seat, crossing his leg in a way that revealed a flash of blue sock between his polished black brogues and trouser leg. Jude requested a coffee from the butler and selected a croissant, opting to eat it plain to avoid the risk of getting jam on herself.

As she took a seat, Jude couldn't shake the feeling of being out of place. The opulence of the room, with its luxurious furnishings and refined atmosphere, was a stark contrast to her own dishevelled state. She felt acutely aware of her hot, sweaty skin from the bike ride, the restrictive nature of her leather jacket, and her hair likely flattened from her helmet. The exhaustion from her worry about what was happening and what had happened both in her family and with her friends in the Forest weighed heavily on her, making her feel even more out of sync with her surroundings.

Despite her discomfort, Jude was determined to maintain her composure. She straightened her posture, adopting a professional demeanour. Her eyes scanned the room, taking in every detail, while she forced herself to focus on the task at hand. She couldn't afford to let her guard down, not even for a moment.

After the butler had left, Glendower leaned back in his chair, crossing his legs and steepling his fingers. He smiled magnanimously at her. Jude estimated he was in his late 50s, perhaps early 60s, but he possessed that youthful air that only the very wealthy seem to maintain. His body was in good shape, his suit impeccably tailored. His eyes were an unusual shade of grey, reminiscent of storm clouds just before they unleash their fury. His hair, also grey, was styled in a manner that reminded Jude of George Clooney, adding to his debonair appearance.

"So, Miss Marcello. How may I help you?" he asked, his voice smooth and composed.

Jude couldn't quite suppress a shiver of exhaustion and quickly swallowed a yawn behind her hand, pretending to look around the grand hotel. Drawing in a deep breath, Jude fell back on her professionalism, adopting her best police-woman attitude. No nonsense, no faffing about. Get straight to the point. Get the answers you need. Listen and observe everything.

Then get back to Tenney.

"Thank you for replying to my message. I have some questions."

"About your mother, I believe?" His accent was Scottish, but not broad. Jude wondered, yet again, how her agoraphobic mother had anything to do with this man and his company. But that question would come.

He continued, "I'm sorry it has taken me so long to extend an invitation to meet with you. I've been out of the country. Family business." He smiled at her again. Glendower was in total control; every move he made was considered and careful. Jude got the impression that he would quickly consider his answer to all her questions, which made her wonder how much of what he told her would be the truth.

"Yes, my mother. Raechael Garbling-Marcello. She's been missing for some time from her Lincoln home. I went there after I hadn't heard from her for a month. I later received an answerphone message from her, suggesting that she may have been investigating you or someone in your company."

"You're sure she's missing? Not on holiday, or visiting friends? Away with your father perhaps?"

Jude bristled at the cross-examination, and then felt the usual shudder of repressed grief and isolation when someone mentioned her dad. The butler returned with her steaming cup of coffee. Taking it, she took a sip of the hot, strong liquid and prayed it would help her to focus. Glendower watched her, his grey eyes following her every move as she bit into her croissant, using the time to formulate an answer, one which didn't involve her reaching over and smacking his ever so slightly condescending smile off his face.

Glendower seemed to know what she was doing, weighing her up as much as she was weighing him up. He waited patiently.

"My father died." Glendower gave a murmur of sympathy. "Since then, my mother has been a recluse. She wouldn't just up and leave."

"And why did it take you so long to realise she had gone?" Jude bristled again, but Glendower seemed genuinely intrigued.

"Since my father's passing, my relationship with my mother has been…" she swallowed guiltily, "strained. She is fragile, Mr. Glendower." She took a sip of her drink and felt the caffeine buzz finally start to work.

Glendower leant forwards, his elbows on his knees, his hands at his face, thinking. "What did you say your mother's name was?"

"Raechael Garbling-Marcello." She spelt it for him; it was so unusual. About the only thing exotic about her mother, she thought.

"Ah, yes. I remember now. I think a lady going by that name wrote to us several times, asking to meet."

"Did she say why she wanted to meet you?"

"She said it was about the water. I mean, that is fairly non-descript in my line of work." He laughed.

"What is your line of work, Mr. Glendower?"

"We source and bottle fresh, highland spring water, straight from our Perthshire Spring. We send it worldwide. We've won numerous awards for it. Maybe your mother wanted to tell us how much she enjoyed it!"

Jude again fought the urge to slap the smile off his face. She took another sip of coffee and composed herself.

"Would you be able to get me copies of her letters?"

"I will see what I can do." Glendower smiled broadly, his eyes quickly flitting across her body. "Officer Marcello," he stressed her formal title, "may I invite you to try some of our water? It really is exquisite. And if you don't mind me saying, you seem rather jumpy from the coffee."

Jude just wanted to get away. Call Aura back and see how Tenney was. She felt stupid for thinking that she might be onto something here.

Jude looked at the man sitting across from her. She followed his eyes as they glanced at the crystal clear, cool water. If it meant she could get away quickly, she should take a sip, massage his ego, and then jump back on the bike, and back to the Forest. Her overnight bag was a wasted extra.

"Sure," she said, a little grudgingly.

From out of nowhere, the small butler appeared and poured some of the clear water from the crystal decanter into a glass. She took a sip and felt it fizz pleasantly on her tongue. She took another sip. It really was quite delicious.

Suddenly Jude felt very tired, her limbs grew heavy as she raised a hand to stifle a yawn. The virtually sleepless night spent with Tenney, followed by a stressful day and only a couple of hours of fitful sleep last night, broke through the caffeine and finally caught up with her. She felt her eyelids begin to droop.

The last thing she saw as the butler lifted her effortlessly from the chair was another figure uncurling himself from a separate seating area, hidden by the high-backed chair, and Glendower moving to speak to him.

**

"I still can't get hold of Jude," said Aura, her voice tinged with worry.

Tenney was pacing the clearing, his hand running through his hair the way he did when he felt anxious or was deep in thought. Hedge had found some bandages in an old first aid kit in the back of his car, and Aura had gently wrapped them around the deep rope burns on Tenney's wrists. As he lifted his hand, she could see one of the burns peeking out from the sleeves of the jumper Hedge had brought back from their house. The burns weren't the only reminder of the struggle he had been through. Every so often, Aura saw Tenney run his tongue around his mouth, as if trying to get rid of the taste of mouse.

"Something's wrong," he said, certain that Jude would have been in touch by now.

Hedge, sitting behind Aura as she leaned back on him, said, "You don't know that, mate. She might've just gone out on that beast of a bike."

Tenney stopped and looked at them. Aura called it his Peter Pan pose—legs apart, hands on hips, head up and determined-looking. "No, I feel it in my gut. Something's definitely wrong."

Aura shifted uneasily. Since they had returned to the solid plane of existence, her connection with him was stronger than it had ever been before. Neither of them needed to concentrate to speak telepathically anymore; they did it as naturally as breathing. She could feel everything that he felt; heard his instincts screaming at him as his gut churned in concern.

"Hedge, I think Tenney and I are going to have to go and have a look, at least at her hotel."

Hedge looked at her. "I'm not letting you out of my sight. I've only got about 13 hours left, and I wanna spend them all with you." He stopped her from answering him. "So I'm coming with you. Deal?"

Tenney squatted down in front of them and gave a cheeky smile. "You know what, I'm liking you more and more. I'm starting to see what my sister finds so attractive." He winked at him playfully. Hedge threw his head back and laughed.

"Ah, bugger off, mate!"

Aura was beyond happy to see the two most important people in her life finally getting along.

The trio headed down the track to the Land Rover which would take them to the village, making plans to find Jude. From the shadows of the trees, the nightwalker and the wolf watched silently as they walked away.

**

"So how do we get in?" Aura asked as they eyed up the hotel entrance.

"Which room is hers?" Hedge asked, taking in all the windows at the front of the building.

"Room 8. It's the one over the old carriage arch," Tenney pointed it out.

"Ok dokey," said Hedge. "I'll see you up there." He slipped from the car, closing the door softly.

"What's he going to do?" Aura asked.

"Don't kn…" Tenney was barely finished speaking before Hedge, casting a careful eye around as he used all his senses to determine that no one apart from the twins were watching, leapt high up at the wall. He seemed to be able to find invisible foot and hand holds as he scaled it like Spiderman. From his position parallel to the window, he shimmied along the wall and over the archway. When he reached the window, he jimmied it until he was able to lift it up and slipped inside.

"Now that was cool," Tenney said in quiet awe.

"Ok, hotshot. How do we get in?" Aura asked.

"Can you summon some air or something? Lift us up and in?"

Aura shook her head. "Not after this morning. I'm going to need more training before I unleash those powers again!"

"Yeah, know what you mean." He squeezed her hand. Neither of them wanted a repeat. From around the corner, the postman appeared. He was sorting out his pile of letters when the hotel door opened, and the receptionist greeted him.

"Oh yeah," said Tenney. "I know how we can get in."

Aura stifled a groan as she thought about what was to come next.

**

Debbie Arthur was bored. Her morning shift was almost over, and it had been long and dull. She collected the letters from the postman, *my highlight of the day*, she thought sarcastically. The hotel was virtually empty, one of the guests having left '*maybe for one night, who knows.*

But I will be back!" That was early in the morning. Derek, the night porter had filled her in when she had started her shift.

She pulled out her bar of dairy milk, hidden in one of the drawers, when the front door opened. She quickly dropped it and smoothed down her top. Tennyson Wiseman, the object of her, unrequited, affection at school had unexpectedly walked in. And he was smiling at her.

Her heart raced as he walked right up to her. "Hi," he said, beaming down at her. "Debbie, isn't it?" Debbie blushed, her nose crinkling slightly. "I don't know if you remember me?" He said. "I think we shared a class at school?"

"Ph ph physics…" she stammered.

"That's it!" Tenney seemed genuinely pleased that she remembered. "See Aura, I told you she'd remember us!" It was only then that she spotted his mousey sister, hiding behind him like always.

Debbie couldn't believe that someone like Tenney had a sister like that. A freaky creep who seemed to always be there, stopping other girls from getting to know him better after they'd had a quick tumble behind the art block. *Well*, she thought, all *the other girls except me.* And she blamed Aura for that. She smiled inwardly as she remembered that that was the name she had created for the waif-like creature, living off Tenney like a parasite. The Creep.

"That's great, Ten," the sister said.

"Oh, go away Creep," she muttered under her breath.

Debbie, desperate to get his attention back on her, gave into impulsiveness, and placed one of her clammy hands over his. Tenney turned back to her, pretty quickly she thought, pleased with herself. She thought she heard his sister stifle a laugh.

"So, er, *Ten*, what can I do for you?" she smiled at him, she hoped seductively, completely missing the miniscule tensing of his jaw as she called him 'Ten'. He quickly recovered and leant over the counter.

"Say, Debbie, a friend of ours is staying here," he fixed his hazel eyes on her, taking all of her attention. "Do you know if she's still here?"

"Sure *Ten*, what's her name?" she batted her eyelashes at him, completely under his spell.

"Jude Marcello, room 8."

"Er, yeah. She went out. Early this morning. Don't know when she'll be back."

"Did she leave any messages for me, or a bloke named Hedge?"

"No, I don't think so… But she sneaked someone in two nights ago," she whispered conspiratorially across the desk to Tenney. "Probably this Hedge guy you mentioned. They left the room in a right state!"

This time Aura did laugh once out loud, unable to contain her mirth as Debbie grasped hold of completely the wrong end of the stick. Tenney turned to Aura and widened his eyes as he communicated his embarrassment with her. Aura turned away to flick through the tourist attraction leaflets, trying desperately to hold back the laughter.

"Ok, Debbie, did she receive any messages?"

Debbie caught the blush and thought it was because he was embarrassed by his sister's rudeness. She puffed out her chest as Tenney turned back to her. "Yeah, she did, yesterday. But I didn't take it though."

He briefly looked back at his sister again. Then turned his megawatt smile on her, full beam. Her knees felt weak. He placed a hand over hers and patted it. "Aura leant something to Jude, and she really needs it back. Can we just pop up there and have a quick look, see if she's left it?"

"I shouldn't really…"

Tenney lent further forward, his natural magnetism overwhelming the girl. Aura had to keep her back turned to him, her shoulders were shaking as she raised her hands to her mouth, trying to restrain the giggle.

"Pretty please?" he purred. "We'll only be 5 minutes."

Debbie blushed again. "Oh, ok. Only 5 minutes though, else you'll get me in trouble." At the last word, she licked her lips and batted her eyelids again, thick clumps of mascara moving over her eyes.

"You, Debbie, are a star!" Tenney leant over the counter and whispered in her ear. His warm breath seemed to caress her cheek, and she felt the blush rise to her forehead. With a slightly shaky hand, she handed him Jude's room key.

**

"So, what did you whisper to her?" Aura murmured to him as they climbed the stairs.

Tenney's flirtatious look had changed rapidly to one of determination and worry. "I told her I'd tell her something special when we came back downstairs," he said grimly.

Aura raised an eyebrow. "And what's that going to be?"

Tenney sighed. "I'm still deciding."

Aura nodded. She had heard what Debbie had muttered under her breath, and she was impressed that Tenney hadn't reacted there and then. Hopefully, these few minutes would give him time to calm down. They reached the door to Room 8, and Tenney inserted the key, turning it slowly. The door creaked open, revealing the room inside. They both took a deep breath, ready to search for any clues that might lead them to Jude.

**

Hedge slipped into the room and almost immediately reeled back from the aroma. To his sensitive nose, it was overpowering. Diesel was preferable to what he could smell, and it was worse in the bathroom. He decided to leave the window open.

Forcing himself not to think about the strong unified smells of Tenney and Jude that permeated everywhere, Hedge began looking around the room. The maid had been in, and the faint whiff of furniture polish mingled with the other smell. Fresh towels lined the rails in the bathroom. The safety chain on the door was broken, as though the door had been pushed inwards by someone very strong.

He drew in a deep breath, working through the other smells in the room and detected the faint whiff of Stace. He must have visited Jude. Next, Hedge opened the small fridge. A three-quarters drunk bottle of vodka, and some boxes which read 'Etanercept' and showed an image of what looked like an epi pen. He couldn't tell if she had drunk anything from the assortment of neat packets of teas, coffees and sugars next to the kettle as they had already been replenished. He wouldn't have blamed her if she hadn't. The few times he had stayed in a hotel, he had nearly thrown up as his stomach recoiled from the horrible smell that came from within the innocuous little sachets.

He flicked through the papers on the dressing table, letters and diary entries, written in a flowery script which he couldn't quite associate with Jude. Some written in a language even he couldn't read. A silver-framed photo of a man and a woman sat next to the papers. Before he could look too closely at it, he heard Tenney and Aura walking up the stairs and turning the key in the lock.

Tenney hesitated before he crossed the threshold. His eyes flickered over the room, alighting quickly on the door to the en-suite. Hedge laughed softly, "Smooth work, man!" He had heard the way the girl clumsily flirted with Tenney, and Aura's restrained laughter. Tenney gave a small, crooked smile, his mind on other things.

"Find anything?" he asked.

"Not yet. It's been cleaned and tidied by the staff." Hedge paused and looked at Tenney sideways, "smells like you had fun though!"

Tenney showed enough gumption to look embarrassed. Aura walked up to Hedge and gently swatted his arm. "Stop teasing him!" she laughed.

"We've got less than 5 minutes, so we'd better start looking." Tenney started to rifle through her drawers. Hedge turned to start looking in her bedside tables. Aura went to the dressing table and the pile of papers. She gently touched the photo of Jude's parents. They looked so happy together. The woman was stunning. Her golden almond skin radiated a glow that the camera had somehow managed to capture as she laughed, leaning back in the arms of a man, one hand cupping his chin as he looked down at her. His hair was greying, but flashes of russet could still be seen in the stubble around his face. On his head, he wore a cap with the orange Mets logo stitched on. His eyes sparkled with love.

As Aura turned away, she knocked a sheet to the floor. Stooping to pick it up, she spotted a balled-up piece of paper under the bed. She lay down and reached under the divan to grab it.

Unfolding it, she read the note. "She's gone to Bristol," she said. Tenney took the note off her. Hedge nodded to them.

"Right-ho, I'll meet you in the car." He paused when the local clock tower struck midday. Twelve hours left… "We'd better find her quickly though. Don't know what Bristol will make of a big, bad wolf wandering its streets!" And with that, after a quick look, he jumped from the window.

Aura ran across the room to look out. Hedge had landed softly; he turned, looked up, and gave her a little mock salute above a wide grin, before sauntering over to the Land Rover.

**

As Tenney and Aura walked past reception, Debbie gave a little cough. She'd had just enough time to apply a bit of lippy to make herself look good for him. Tenney turned back to her. She took a step back from the counter. He wasn't smiling anymore, his expression dark, thunderous.

He slammed the key on the counter, rested both hands in tight, white fists on its surface and leant forward, a cruel parody of the flirtation from just a few minutes before. "I was going to tell you something, wasn't I?" His voice was quietly threatening as he struggled to hold back his distaste. "If you ever call my sister a creep, or you and your little shitty friends laugh at her behind her back again, I'll be back. And I won't be nearly so nice. If you're really unlucky, it'll be the wrong time of the month, and her boyfriend will come with me. Trust me, I'm a pussy cat next to him. He's, well," Tenney gave a short, sharp laugh, "he's a beast."

Without a second glance back at her, he walked to the door, putting an arm around Aura's shoulder and guiding her out into the autumn afternoon.

-*Better?* She thought.

-*Better*. He replied.

**

When they got back in the car, Aura gave up the front seat to her brother. Hedge held his fist out to Tenney, and he bumped it back. He'd heard Tenney's threat, and he wanted him to know that no matter what, whatever form he was, he had his back as far as Aura was concerned. The unspoken pact of male bonding echoed around the car.

Aura rolled her eyes at their bravado. "So where to?" Hedge asked, starting the engine.

"The Avon Gorge hotel, Bristol." Aura replied.

Chapter 29

A teenager from the village walked along the footpath, headphones ramped up to top volume as they made their way home following the shortcut from their new girlfriend's house. They didn't see the shadows in the hollow move beneath rocks and mud.

They were totally oblivious as it followed them insidiously. It moved like it had a conscious mind, slowly weaving between the blades of grasses, the fallen leaves, the trunks of the trees. Something must have alerted them, a prickle down their spine maybe, for they stopped and looked behind them, certain that something was following them. When they saw nothing there, they turned back, and screamed as a black figure made of smoke rose up in front of them.

Their scream was cut off as the smoke shot into their mouth.

Gallagher looked out of their new eyes. Their eyes turned black as thoughts of revenge ran through their new synapses. They wanted death. Death to those who had defeated them twice.

The demon stepped away, ready to begin their search again and contact their brethren. This time their army would be undefeatable.

**

The Land Rover thundered down the motorway, its three passengers discussing what they might find and what may have happened to Jude.

"Try her number again, Ten," suggested Aura.

He pressed the last number dialled and listened to the rings before the generic EE answering service kicked in. He shook his head in the negative. He barely knew her, and yet since that fateful 24 hours in Lincoln a month ago, they had experienced so much together. So many revelations and new understandings; new shifts in the world they had all taken for granted.

Tenney raised his hand to rub his forehead, suddenly tired as he felt the bandage pull slightly on the rope burn. The hand slipped through his hair and ran around the back of his head. It was smooth where the bump had been; Stace's blood had healed him. His body had never looked, or felt, so healthy. All his injuries sustained in the last month had been healed—apart from the rope burns around his wrists. He suspected that even those could have been worse. Judging from the depth of the injuries and going by the reports of his insanity and strength, he was sure that the ropes would have cut down to the bone. In fact, he felt lucky that he hadn't completely severed his hands.

When he came to, Stace sitting out of the sun's light, had told him what had happened. His heart clenched when he thought of how worried Jude must've been. She probably thought she had another day before he was 'safe' to be around again.

That thought made him shudder. He knew he had a dangerous side, one which he had been forced to face during the blood lust. He never thought he would be capable of using it against people he cared about deeply. His sister. Jude. He would have to listen to Stace, really try to learn to make his issues less damaging to his loved ones, his family, and his friends.

Stace had saved him; but then, so had Aura when they found each other in the – what had Stace called it? The *inter duo mundos*. And so had Jude. When she found him broken at the train station, he hadn't paid her more than a cursory glance, another obstacle to break through to find himself again. He couldn't understand how, or why, a smart, generous, gorgeous lady like her, after a bad start, a rough middle, and no guarantee that life would ever be 'normal' again, would want to know him. Let alone want to be in a relationship. If she ever found out some of the things he had made himself do to protect Aura, it might break this fledgling something that was happening between them.

-She'd understand, Ten. Aura's voice in his mind reminded him that his thoughts weren't his own anymore. He also felt the guilt she experienced when she thought about those occasions when he had, basically, given himself to protect her from narrow-minded people. Tenney wasn't so sure she would.

-You'll never be put in a situation like that again, Tenney, Aura promised him.

It should have taken them under an hour to get to the Clifton Suspension Bridge. It took them closer to two. There had been an accident on the junction at Cribbs Causeway, the other mall on the outskirts of the city, causing a tailback up the M5. They all felt tense, each one aware that time was running out for Hedge. As they finally passed the accident site, they each scanned the scene, looking for any sign of a blue and silver motorcycle.

Tenney felt the tight band around his chest ease as they saw no evidence that Jude had been caught up in it. Aura reached forward, and for the rest of the journey kept her hand on his shoulder, her palm glowing blue as she connected with him.

Finally, they paid the £1 toll and crossed the Victorian Bridge, finding a parking space on the street just down from the hotel. The city, even the very edge of it, felt oppressive after the space and the air of the forested countryside. Aura took hold of Hedge's hand as his heightened senses worked on overdrive, trying to assimilate all the sights, sounds, and smells into his brain. He hated overpopulated spaces. He reminded himself that this was important to her because it was important to Tenney. That made it important to him too. He was determined not to waste any precious time by not being near her. So, he walked on, feeling her squeeze his hand, and did his best to ignore all the commotion around him.

As they crossed the busy road, they spotted the silver and blue Yamaha, parked near the entrance of the hotel.

"She's definitely here then," said Tenney.

The doors opened for them with a whoosh, and they walked into the foyer.

**

Jude felt soft pillows under her head. A light duvet covered her. She felt groggy, the sort of tiredness you only feel after a long sleep. Her joints were stiff as she remembered she had skipped medication over the past few days. Where was she? The last thing she really remembered was drinking the water…

She sat bolt upright. Had she been drugged? She looked down, under the covers. Her jacket had been removed and hung neatly over the back of a chair, her boots placed beneath it, but they hadn't removed any other items of clothing. She breathed a sigh of relief. Not rohypnol then. She had been at the scenes of crimes where girls' drinks were spiked with the date rape drug. It wasn't something she wanted to happen to her. The relief she felt was immense.

She sat up and surveyed the room. It must have been one of the nicer suites, she realised. It consisted of the bedroom, a bathroom, and a separate sitting room with two large soft sofas positioned around a glass coffee table. There was a large flat-screen TV on the wall. The dim sounds of the street echoed up towards her window, but all she could see were the tops of the buildings around her. Penthouse? she wondered.

The door to her room opened. A man in a black suit, white gloves on his hands, walked in. She stared in disbelief as the butler who had served them downstairs stood before her, his hands clasped behind his back. He gave her a small dip of the head and said, "Ah, Miss is awake." His accent was proper Queen's English, sharp enough to cut steel.

"Why am I here?" she asked him, her throat dry from sleep. Jude swung her legs out of the bed. On the table next to her sat a thick envelope, her name in black calligraphic letters across the front.

"You fell asleep, Miss. Mr. Glendower instructed you be brought here to rest. He has had to leave, and for that, he offers his apologies. But he asked me to tell you that you are free to use the room for the rest of the night. And to help yourself to the amenities of the hotel." He bowed slightly as he got to the end of his instructions.

Now Jude was really confused. "What's your name?"

"Frommes, Miss." He tilted forwards again.

She looked at her watch. It was well past 2 p.m.; she'd been asleep for nearly 4 hours. Jude considered her options and immediately thought of Tenney. He was probably still under the influence, and she would be turned away from the Fort if she even got within half a mile of it. She turned back to Frommes.

"What was in the water?" she asked.

"Pardon me, Miss?"

"The water. That Glendower gave me? What was in it?"

The man looked at her like she was barking mad. "It was water, Miss. Pure, Highland Spring water. Nothing else was in it."

She laughed, embarrassed. Of course it was only water! She had been so tired, and the large leather chairs had been so comfortable that it was perfectly plausible that she may have succumbed to her exhaustion. She felt mortified that she had fallen asleep, in front of a suspect at that. No, she thought. Not a suspect—a lead! But that lead had gone nowhere.

Disappointment weighed her down. She looked around the room again. Maybe a night away from it all was what she needed. Get her mojo back.

She stood up. "Thank you, Frommes."

"Is there anything I can get you, Miss?" he asked. Jude scanned the room and spotted her overnight bag on one of the armchairs in the room, her bike helmet next to it. "No, thank you," she said.

With that, he bowed again and left the room, giving a slight flourish as he closed the doors.

Jude went to her jacket pocket and found her phone.

**

Tenney walked straight up to the receptionist, his confident stride and easy smile immediately drawing her attention. As he spoke to her, charming her as effortlessly as he had Debbie, Hedge shook his head in amazement. "Has he always been able to do that?" he asked Aura, his voice tinged with disbelief.

Aura laughed, her face lighting up with a warm smile. "Ever since he was a toddler and charmed the old ladies in the park to give him sweets or a penny," she replied, her eyes sparkling with fond memories.

"It's a real skill," Hedge said in awe, watching Tenney work his magic. "Hey!" he jumped back slightly as Aura pinched him playfully.

"Not always," she replied, her tone becoming more serious. "I remember at school; all these girls would follow him around. All the boys wanted to be his best mate. But he was oblivious to them. It was always just me and him, which made some of them jealous. They bullied me because I was his sister. It was worse when we were teenagers. I always begged him not to do it, but Tenney did what he felt he had to do to keep people like her off my back, by giving them what they claimed they wanted." Hedge saw the pain in her face as she told him of Tenney's sacrifices. "They wanted him, so that's what he gave them."

He quickly understood what she implied. He knew that for Aura, he would, and had, gone through hell for her. For Tenney to sleep with people he hated simply to keep her safe, well, not many people would give up themselves like that. Tenney shot up some more in his estimation.

Tenney walked back to them, his expression serious. "Glendower left a few hours ago. Apparently though, his room is still being used. Lisa," he nodded to the receptionist, who was smiling at Tenney's back, slightly flushed, "is going to call up to his suite, find out if Jude is the one staying there."

They watched as Lisa picked up the phone and dialled a number. Tenney walked back over to her, waiting patiently as she held up a finger, asking him to wait. She replaced the receiver and took out a hotel business card and a pen.

"She's told him that the occupant is on their way down," said Hedge. "And now she's giving him her number…" Aura laughed again, the sound light and carefree.

Hearing the lift doors open with a ping, Tenney turned to them. He saw Jude step out; her hair flattened on one side as though she had been asleep. She wore her jeans and a white vest, and he smiled when he noted her socked feet. She had been in such a rush to get down to him, she hadn't bothered to put her boots on.

For a moment, time seemed to stop, and they looked at each other. Aura felt the air crackle with tension, and then, in a few fast strides, they were together, embracing passionately.

Lisa at the desk's mouth dropped open in surprise.

**

The four of them spent a few hours in the suite of rooms, catching Jude up on the events of that morning. She had taken off her jeans and was now wrapped up in one of the hotel's soft, white robes. Leaning her head on Tenney's shoulder, a solitary tear rolled down her cheek as she heard how close she had come to losing him. She resolved that she would stand up to Stace if it ever happened again. There was no way she was going to leave Tenney. She also made a mental note to remember that Aura could, quite literally, take your breath away. She looked at her with a newfound respect, tinged with a little, healthy fear.

They all made the most of Glendower's suite and his all-expenses-paid generosity. Tenney, Jude, and Aura indulged in cheeseburgers and fries, while Hedge stuck to a blue steak. Nobody commented on his unusual eating habits. Aura had already filled Tenney in, and Jude had figured it out. If she was a wolf for most of the month, she wouldn't want to eat overcooked meat as a human.

Jude then told her friends more about her mother, how she was sure something had happened to her. She explained her need to find her.

"Why here though?" asked Tenney.

"I was following a lead," she replied. "Mum left me a message mentioning Glendower by name. Mum had written several letters to Glendower Springs, some asking to speak to the

CEO. I think she was on one of her crusades, her conspiracy theories." The ways of her mother still puzzled her. "When I received the message inviting me here, I felt I had to. I was going crazy in that hotel room, not knowing if you'd make it or not." Tenney held her close and tenderly kissed her forehead. "I'm coming back for the drink's convention in a couple of weeks' time. I think Mum will be here for that."

He suddenly had a thought. "Aura, do you still have that message that Jude received?"

She nodded. "Yeah, I'll get it." Shifting slightly beside Hedge, Aura put her hand in her pocket and pulled out the scrunched-up piece of paper. There was an odd feeling in the room, a slight unease, as though something dark had been there before they arrived, its malevolent presence lingering like a gas.

-Aura?

-Yeah, I sense it too.

Aura handed Tenney the crumpled note. *-Maybe we're just tired?* As he took the note, he gave a half, crooked smile, a shadow in his eyes.

-Probably. It's been a long couple of days. He smiled again, trying to add reassurance to his features, glad that Hedge and Jude were none the wiser about their concerns.

He looked at the bottom at the extra paragraph of carefully written gibberish. He couldn't make head nor tail of it, but Hedge might.

"Looks familiar," Hedge said, taking it from Tenney's outstretched hand and scratching his jaw. They had all noticed that Hedge was getting fidgety, that he would need to leave soon if he was going to make it back to the relative safety of the Forest. "I can't quite place it though. Sorry, the brain gets a bit foggy around this time." Aura slipped her hand into his, giving it a squeeze, feeling the soft shake as he tried to hold it together.

"Let me see it again. I only really looked at the main part of the message back in Denebury." He handed it to Aura. "What do you mean gibberish?"

"I mean, nonsense, twaddle, idiocy."

"Yes, thank you, Ten, I know what gibberish means." He grinned at her. She looked back at the note. Suddenly the 'gibberish' made perfect sense to her, like another piece of her had slotted back into place. "I mean, it's not gibberish, not anymore. It's as clear as day."

The other three sat up. "You can read it?" Jude asked, the little knot of fear and awe tightening in her stomach.

"Yeah, it says '2 Peter 3:10.'

'But the day of the Lord will come like a thief. The heavens will disappear with a roar; the elements will be destroyed by fire, and the earth and everything done in it will be laid bare.'

"Well, that doesn't sound good," Tenney said after a few seconds for the passage to sink in.

Jude sank back into the sofa, her brain trying to puzzle the pieces together. "Call me mad, but I am starting to think all of this," Jude waved her hands around the room, encompassing the people, all the events that had brought them here, and the space itself into her meaning, "has something to do with my Mum. Which means Glendower was lying."

**

Hedge had started to pace the room, his fidgeting becoming more pronounced. Aura glanced at her watch: 9:38 PM. They had stayed too long, enjoying each other's company, trying to figure out the connections, what it all meant for them, and what they were going to do next.

She looked at Tenney. -*I've got to get him back.*

-*I know.*

-*But Jude's shattered, and you shouldn't leave her, but Hedge can't stay here. I'm not sure he could drive in this state.*

They both looked at Hedge. He was beginning to behave in an animalistic way, jumping at sounds they couldn't hear, growling low in his throat when somebody walked past the room. His eyes held an extra glint, one which signified the feral creature he would be in a couple of hours' time.

-*What are we going to do?* she asked him, though she already knew what he was going to suggest.

-*How's the cord?*

-*Strong and bright, flexible.*

-I think we need to try it out. Stace did say that the next thing was to go further away from each other, and for longer. He smiled at her, reassuring her that he felt fine. *-I'll stay here with Jude; you take Hedge home.*

Aura bit her lip in concern, torn between her heart and her soul, even though her soul had given her permission to follow her heart. Tenney saw this internal battle inside her. *-How about I promise to be home early? 8 AM.*

-Make it 7, and you've got a deal.

They smiled at each other, the others unaware of the exchange between them. *-We've got to try this, Aura,* he said.

-I know. I just can't lose you, Ten, not again.

He stood up from the sofa and she followed suit. They hugged, long and hard, sealing their bond, until he released her, and she turned to Hedge.

"Come on," she said. "We're going."

Jude, her eyelids drooping, made herself stand up. She stretched, yawned, and made to get her clothes and her bag, helmet, and boots.

"Not you guys," Aura laughed. "Just me and Hedge."

Jude gratefully sank back down into the enveloping cushions of the sofa, her weary shoulders relaxing. "You're sure?" she asked the twins.

"Yes," they both replied, looking each other in the eyes.

**

They waved Hedge and Aura off down the corridor. Aura had to support Hedge; her arm wrapped around his waist. He was shaking visibly now, struggling to walk on two legs, but Aura managed to support his weight, Tenney suspecting that she was manipulating the air somewhat. Jude turned as she heard footsteps approaching from the other end of the corridor.

Frommes wandered up to them. "Is there anything else I can get for you, miss?"

Jude leaned against Tenney, glad beyond words that he was here. With her.

"No, thanks, Frommes," she said. "Good night."

"Good night, miss, sir." He bowed, yet again, and turned back down the corridor.

Tenney pulled her back into the room. He held her close to him, running his hands up and down her back. He felt her sob, once. From worry. From exhaustion. From missed opportunities. He held her face in his hand, his other wrapped around her waist, and wiped a tear away with his thumb.

She smiled and gently disengaged herself. As she turned away, she caught sight of the thick, expensive envelope.

"I forgot all about this," she said, as Tenney flung himself on the bed, propping himself up on one elbow, watching her.

"What is it?" he asked.

She slipped a finger under the flap and opened the letter. An embossed card slipped from within. Her name was written in the same calligraphy as was on the front of the envelope.

"It's an invitation. From Glendower. He's invited me to the Fireworks party. At the Avon Gorge Hotel. It's during the convention."

"That's soon, right?" he asked. "Any mention of a plus one?" She smiled at him, put the invitation down, and walked towards the bathroom.

"Now where are you going?" he asked.

"I'm going to have a bath," she said, beginning to remove the robe. She looked over her shoulder coquettishly.

"You coming?"

Tenney had never moved so fast.

Chapter 30

Tenney and Jude left very early the next morning, returning to the Forest well before 7 a.m. Jude managed to get a few solid hours of sleep, lying in Tenney's arms in the massive bed, but he was restless. He felt Aura's unhappiness like a lightning bolt just after midnight. She had tried to shield him from it, but their empathetic connection was too powerful to hide their strongest feelings. He felt her transformation into the dragon, saw the land fly by through her eyes, and heard her bellows of grief as though they were his own.

For the first time, Tenney felt torn. Torn between his sister, who was the other half of him, and the beautiful woman who had him under her spell and was lying next to him. Fortunately for Tenney, this same woman was compassionate and understanding. She insisted they return to Aura sooner rather than later.

So, at 3 in the morning, they crept from the hotel and rode back to Denebury. "Home or Fort?" Jude asked.

Tenney closed his eyes for a second and felt his connection to Aura, as strong as if they were next to each other, the reassuring cord telling him it could never shatter, never fray again.

"Home," he said.

**

Frommes watched them from the window of the suite. The rooms bore evidence of their presence. Water still pooled around the bath where it had cascaded down the sides from their splashing; the bed showed the shapes of their bodies where they had lain. The bin was filled with the detritus of a fast-food meal, the smell of raw meat wafting from a plate stacked on the side. A short note on the back of the room service menu thanked him for his care and Glendower for his generosity.

He clenched his fists and breathed in through his nose. He had played his part well. He had been courteous, polite, and helpful. He had left her alone, to an extent. But how was he to know that the others would arrive to find her? His spies had told him that the Tether was incapacitated by blood lust, the Elemental too involved with him to ever leave his side. And the wolf…

Frommes nearly retched at the thought of the filthy mutt being here, in these rooms. His eyes darkened at the thought of the mongrel's presence. His instructions from his boss were to keep the woman happy and, through kindness and servitude, try to win her over, planting seeds of doubt about her companions. Encourage her to the party. Let the next part of the plan unfold. And now he had to report back that the night had not gone as expected.

He was furious with himself. This momentous time in history should have gone differently. He knew who was to blame: the bane of his life, the wolf-bitch and her pup.

Black smoke wafted around his feet.

**

Tenney kissed her neck between the top of her jacket and the helmet. "I'll see you later, yeah?" he said, swinging his leg off the bike.

"Definitely," Jude smiled back at him. "I hope Aura is okay?"

Tenney just smiled grimly. He gave her a small wave as she pulled away, heading back to the cottage. He turned and let himself in through the front door.

Creeping up the stairs, after quieting the dogs as they sleepily raised their heads, he tiptoed past his parents' and brother's rooms. Tenney looked at the two doors at the end of the corridor and opened the one on the left.

Aura stood at his bedroom window, looking down at the garden, his duvet wrapped around her bare shoulders. He walked up to his sister and wrapped his arms around her. He knew she would be here, among his things, so she could fool herself that he was with her physically as well as spiritually.

She leaned back into him, her shape fitting his perfectly. They let their souls touch and took comfort from each other. In the garden, two bright green eyes framed by a black lupine face looked up at them.

**

The house was a frenzy of activity when the twins finally made it downstairs later that morning. Martha, usually the last to be dressed and ready for the day, was in a pretty, floral dress and a loose, flowing cardigan, instead of her customary jeans and fleece. She gently patted Tenney's cheek as his eyes widened.

"Yes, son, I am a woman after all!" she laughed, pouring a cup of coffee.

Their father came through next. "Martha! I've lost a boot!" Even he looked smart. Well, smart-ish. He wore clean dig clothes, consisting of a flannel shirt over a grey tee and multi-pocketed combat-style trousers, but the top of his shirt was held closed by a loose tweed tie.

"It's by the door, Samuel!" she replied, exasperated.

The twins stood in the middle of the kitchen as this maelstrom of activity whirled around them, neither having any idea what it was all about.

"Er, Ma," Tenney finally asked, "what's going on?"

"While you and your sister were off gallivanting with your friends, your father made a huge discovery!" The twins shared a look when their mother described the last few nights as 'gallivanting'. They were glad she would never know what sort of 'gallivanting' they had been getting up to.

She carried on, the coffee hyping her up as she warmed to the subject of bossing her children around. "You two need to be dressed and ready in 15 minutes! Sam's been given special permission to have the day off school. This is an important family occasion!"

"What about breakfast?" Tenney asked, running a hand through his hair, his stomach rumbling. That was when their mother caught sight of the bandages around his wrists.

"Oh my god! Tennyson Deakin Wiseman! What's happened?"

Tenney looked suitably abashed. Aura had changed them just before they came downstairs, as he had somehow let them get wet the night before. He pulled down his sleeves, but his mother was quicker and pushed them back up to his elbows.

Aura came forward and placed a hand on her mother's arm. "Ma, he…" she began.

Martha turned on her. "You! Go and get ready! And get Sam moving off that wretched computer! I want you both ready and down here in 15 minutes sharp!" She didn't want Aura and Tenney ganging up and making semi-plausible excuses. She wanted him to tell her the truth. "Now Aura! GO!" Martha none too gently pushed a hesitant Aura towards the stairs. Tenney was left alone to face the fearful anger on his mother's face.

When Aura, sending a helpless apologetic look at him, had gone, Martha, who barely reached her son's shoulder, stood in front of him, blocking his exit, her hands on her hips and a face that said, don't mess with me, Son! He drew in a breath, ready to face her.

"Well?" she asked.

"It's nothing, Ma. Honest." Flippancy was his first line of defence.

"Don't you try that with me! Someone doesn't wrap bandages around their wrists and say it's nothing!"

Tenney rubbed his face. Sometimes a little bit of truth helped sweeten the lie.

"We went out, as you know, and, well, we got a little merry…"

"At the pub?"

"Er, no, we actually ended up in Bristol…"

Martha let that one go, deciding to tackle one issue at a time. That subject was about having the manners to tell their parents if they left the Forest, especially while they lived with them. She raised a hand and controlled her breathing.

"OK. So, what happened in Bristol?"

"Well, you know…" he said, a twinkle in his eye.

"No, Tennyson, I do not know." She felt angry now.

"Well," Tenney hoped Jude would forgive him for this, but it was the only way to get Martha off his back. "Well, Jude and I kind of hooked up." His mother's face went a puce colour. "And Jude likes to play games… like cops and robbers…" he let the innuendo slip out. His mother's face seemed to turn a little green. She raised a hand to her lips.

"Is that why Aura was home before you?" He should've known his mother would hear them come in.

"Er, yeah, I guess…"

Suddenly, Martha's anger was redirected at a new target. "When I see that woman, I'll kill her! Using a younger man like that! It's sick! And to think! She's a policewoman!"

Tenney felt bad, using Jude to take some of the blame. But it was better than telling her that he had nearly died from a head wound after his sister caused him to fall down a hill using a supernatural power blast of pure energy. That he had then drunk from a 2000-year-old vampire, been tied to a tree after developing a raging homicidal blood lust, and then nearly died again. And because of Aura's immense power, Martha had come very close to being a mother of one. She would never know just how close she had come to losing both of them. Again.

"Sorry, Ma," he said, giving her his wicked slow grin. Later, he would tell Aura that he couldn't help himself as he said, "Oh, but Ma! It was so much fun!"

Their mother turned back to him with a loud exasperated GRRRRR, picked up a tea towel, and shooed him to the stairs. Samuel came rushing in, both boots on his feet, jacket half over his shoulder.

"What's wrong?" he gasped. "What's happened?"

"Tell your son to get ready, and dress smartly! He only has 5 minutes!" With that, she returned to the kitchen, fury radiating off her in palpable waves. Jess, in her bed, having watched the whole exchange, stared up at her with baleful eyes.

"What have you done now, Tenney?" Samuel asked, resigned to his semi-wayward son's antics. Tenney laughed up the stairs, trying to force some joviality into the sound. The laughter stopped when he reached the top. Leaning back against the wall, he pulled out his phone to warn Jude.

Tenney looked up as Sam left his room. He too was looking down at his phone, deep in a conversation of his own. Both brothers looked sheepish, like they had been caught doing something they shouldn't. They quickly pocketed their phones, mirroring each other as only siblings can do.

Tenney laughed nervously. "Sammy," he said.

"Ten." Sam seemed to fidget, their easy relationship from the birthday trip to Caerleon forgotten. He couldn't shake the image of Tenney, tied to the tree with blood dripping from his mouth. The recent revelations about his siblings had left him spinning. Thank goodness for Theo, he thought, remembering the speed with which Theo had replied to him after he had described the scene at the Fort.

Theo: *Stay calm, Sam.*

The three dots at the bottom of the chat box blinked for what felt like an age to Sam.

Theo: *We'll work out what's going on together.*

"Do you know what all this is about?" Tenney asked him, trying to act normally despite the tension.

"Yeah, Dad found something at the dig. The local news people are coming up to the manor house to see what's going on."

"What did he find?"

"Some kind of knife, I think." Sam shrugged his shoulders self-consciously. "But Mum is keen that we all show our support. She reckons it's a big deal for Dad."

From the kitchen, they heard their mother yell up to them, "KIDS! COME ON!" Tenney let out a breath.

"Better get going, I guess," he said as he headed down the corridor to his room. He turned at the last moment. "Sam?" Sam stuck his head around the banister.

"Yeah?"

"Whack some bread in the toaster, would ya? I'm half starved!"

Sam rolled his eyes.

**

Aura, in a blue dress and thick turquoise cardigan, buttered Tenney's toast and handed it to him as he pulled his fleece on over his shirt and jeans.

"Thanks!" he said, spluttering breadcrumbs as they locked the front door and headed down the path. Their parents were in the front of the car, Sam was in the back, on his phone again. The dogs were brushed and placed in the boot, so they didn't shed hair on their 'smart' clothes. Bo stood excitedly with his front feet on the boot hatch, looking out at the world from a different vantage point.

Tenney opened the door of the old estate car, let Aura slide in, and then followed her. He lifted a booted foot up, knocking his father's seat.

"Watch it!" Samuel called into the back.

"Sorry," Tenney sprayed yet more crumbs out of his mouth. He was dismayed to see his mother was still upset about his remarks, her face turned resolutely away from him, a loud 'tut' coming from her lips.

Aura squeezed his knee and rested her head on his shoulder. She was shattered; he knew she hadn't slept much in the night. He wondered if it would be like this every month. Hedge reverting to wolf-form, Aura crying herself to sleep in his bed as he held her close, letting her know he was there, that he would always be there for her.

He linked his fingers through hers as the Wiseman family set out on the short drive to the Water Temple to revel in their father's discovery.

**

The young person with black eyes walked to the Temple, a steady flow of black smoke in their wake. A crowd of people had gathered at the site.

A cameraman yawned.

Perfect, thought Gallagher as they walked their host to a quiet corner and shed their body.

**

Samuel struggled to find a parking space, the area blocked off with large expensive cars, older vehicles probably belonging to fellow architects, and some news vans from local BBC and ITV stations, as well as the local newspapers, The Forester and The Citizen.

He drew up as close as he could and nervously encouraged his family out of the car and up the drive. Martha had found a smile and plastered it on her face. She had requisitioned Sam's phone and told Samuel to tell Tenney to behave. The dogs were leashed at Tenney's side, and he had strict instructions not to let them bark or run amok. Aura smiled brightly, only her twin seeing the deep sadness in her eyes.

-*Give some of it to me,* he asked her.

-*It's mine to carry,* she replied, grateful for his concern. -*If I don't have it, then he would be nothing more than a dream, a memory lost in time.* He put an arm around her shoulder.

"Don't go too far, okay? I don't think we should separate right now."

"Okay," she agreed quietly so only he could hear her.

The crowd erupted into loud cheers and applause as Samuel appeared around the bend, his family behind him. The representative from the archaeological department at the University separated him from his family and brought him forward in front of the press and people gathered.

The mayor stood there, ready to shake his hand. The owners of the manor, one of them was laughing loudly, holding a glass of champagne at the ready, acting like it was really their find that was being celebrated, while his husband looked on bemused. There was the obligatory local zed-list celebrity feeding off the back of the publicity. "Oh, I love history an' all that!" she cackled to a reporter. Tenney shuddered as he shouldered his way through the crowd, Jess beside him and the smaller Bo in his arms so he wouldn't be trampled on. Aura, Sam, and Martha followed as he made a path for them. They found a spot near the front and lifted their eyes towards the raised dais.

The mayor had begun to speak. "It is with great privilege that I introduce the leader of this site, the maestro of this endeavour" (Tenney and Sam stifled a snigger) "a personal friend" (a roll of the eyes) "and discoverer of an important piece of Forest history, Professor Samuel Wiseman!" The crowd dutifully applauded as Samuel, embarrassed, walked forward.

He coughed, clearing his throat. "Er, yes, er thank you, Mr. Mayor, for the kind, er, words. But this find wouldn't have been possible without my team." He drew the crowd's attention to the small group of archaeologists at the sidelines. "My assistant, Nick," he nodded to his friend. "Bristol University for letting me come and work here and funding the project," the University rep smiled magnanimously, giving a little thumbs up. "And the Misters Smith-Frobisher, whose land we have pretty much destroyed to find the wonders beneath," the owners of the Manor stepped forward in front of the cameras, waving their glasses, the zed-lister shuffling into view behind them. Samuel steadied himself and looked down at the people he loved the most in the world.

"But my greatest thanks go to my family, my sons Tennyson and Sam, my daughter Aura, and my beautiful wife, Martha." One of the dogs barked; the crowd laughed. "Yes, I hadn't forgotten you, Jess and Bo." He played to the crowd. "But in all seriousness, without their support and encouragement over the years, I wouldn't be here now, working at this dig in the village of my birth. I am a very lucky man." Martha wiped a tear from her eyes and mouthed "I love you" towards him.

Samuel smiled at her and continued, "It is now my great pleasure to show you items of important historical and cultural significance for this area. The first is a piece of fine, woollen cloth, dyed a deep rich red, and threaded with gold. We believe it was worn by a Noble Lady, possibly of the Dobunni tribe who lived near here, possibly as far back as the beginning of the first century. I discovered it buried at the feet of the goddess Sabrina." He paused. "It was wrapped around something of huge significance. Inside its folds, we found a dagger. A very rare dagger.

"Preliminary dating of this, frankly stunning artefact, suggests it is much, much older than the material it was wrapped so carefully in. Why it was buried here, we may never know. But the fact it was buried here suggests that this Temple was used by both the Celts and the Romans, and it held significant religious and spiritual connotations for both peoples."

Samuel stepped back as Nick came forward carrying a covered box. He placed it carefully on a plinth before Samuel removed its cover. The crowd gasped as he revealed the lightly polished yellow gold, long dagger lying atop the red material, in an airtight presentation box. The archaeologists had discovered that the blade was still keen, sharp enough to draw blood if mishandled. But it was the vivid red rubies studded solidly in its hilt and blade that drew the eyes of the onlookers. Its rarity was unquestioned. Its beauty undisputed. Its importance, unparalleled.

Tenney and Aura didn't think of these things when they saw it. Their faces paled as they felt their bones quake in some deep, ageless part of themselves. Their unified soul, their very DNA, knew the ancient relic. Tenney rubbed his chest as images from his nightmare flashed before his eyes.

The stones called out to them of separation.

The blade spoke of death.

Chapter 31

The reporters leapt into action, their phones set to record what was being said, the cameras zooming in and out on the relic, the people on the dais, and the happy family at the front of the crowd. As the crowd swarmed and the dagger hummed, Tenney ushered Aura away. They felt a sense of claustrophobia pressing down on them, squeezing them and bringing an edge of darkness to their field of vision.

Martha, her eyes on Samuel, barely noticed them leave. Only Sam, watching from the sidelines, saw them go, a puzzled frown on his face.

A raised bank ran between the manor house gardens, where the press event was taking place, and the field housing the Water Temple site. Along it ran a line of ancient sweet chestnut trees—the very same ones that grew from nuts discarded by Romans as they walked, eating the sweet chestnuts and dropping some, which then took root. Tenney helped Aura up the bank, the dogs trotting beside them, as they headed for one of the trees furthest away from the throng.

They both felt sick, dizzy. Bo, happy to be out from the legs of people, jumped about on the end of the lead. As Tenney bent down to unclip the dogs from their leashes, he felt the blood rush from his head. The world moved in and out of focus as he felt his sense of balance leave him. Aura supported him, as he supported her; together they made it to one of the trees where they dropped heavily to the ground, both panting.

"What the fu…" Tenney started, running his hand through his hair.

"I don't know. I've never felt like that before," Aura gasped, the air heavy on her chest. "At least, not when I'm with you. I've felt it when you've gone, but never near you." He drew her closer as they lay on their backs, watching the clouds scud across the skies through the chestnut's leaves.

They could hear the crowds, the milling of the people, and the sporadic bursts of laughter dulled by the rise of land. They felt the cool autumn breeze on their faces, both aware that they were well into October now; winter would soon be officially here. In front of them, they could see the river winding its way through the valley, the Cotswold Hills shrouded in low cloud, and Gloucester Cathedral standing in the centre, proud of its city and the land around it. Behind them was the dig site, white tents protecting some parts, others left open, trenches cut into the earth. A large mound of dirt, waste dug from the trenches, stood to one side like a mini hill.

Bo played happily near them, chasing the falling leaves, gathering feathers in his mouth, spotting make-believe threats and standing to attention, before wagging his tail and returning to the leaves. Jess settled beside them, drifting off to sleep. Slowly, after being quiet with each other for a time and letting the peace of the view wash over them, they felt their steadiness return. The sickness passed and the world stopped spinning.

-*This is the first time we've been like this for a while,* Tenney remarked silently. -*Just you and me and the dogs, with nature. Nothing else to distract us, as happy as those distractions make us,* he added cheekily.

Aura slapped his chest. -*Why is everything so complicated now?* she asked.

-*Because we're finally learning who we really are. We're finally waking up to the world as it is, and not as we want it to be.*

-*I wish we could go back. Back to the days when we were ignorant, when we were simply Aura and Tenney.*

-*Aura! We've never been simply anything. We've always been one. Complementing each other, making up for the other one's weaknesses and strengths. If we must experience these supernatural wonders, I'm glad we can experience them together.*

-*Always together?*

-*Always.* He kissed the top of her head. -*I'll do anything for you, to protect you, Aura.* And she knew that he would. Their history had shown her that he would.

"What are you doing?"

The twins sat up abruptly. "Sam, hi!" said Aura, trying to sound cheerful.

"What's wrong?" Sam asked them.

"Nothing," said Tenney. "We just felt a bit sick, that's all." He smiled at his little brother. "Everything alright down there?"

"Usual boring stuff," said Sam. "Apart from when one of the cameramen dropped his equipment. The reporter gave him a right telling off before he ran off like a girl!" Sam joked, one of his rare smiles spreading across his face.

"Oi!" reprimanded Aura.

"Anyway, Mum said you must come back. Dad wants to take us all out for lunch."

-*We're going to have to find Stace,* Aura said silently.

Tenney gave her a subtle nod of his head and pushed himself up, lending a hand to his sister to help her stand. He whistled to the dog, clipping him back onto the lead and gently removing the fragments of leaves and feathers from his soft mouth.

"Has Dad put that dagger away?" he asked Sam, nonchalantly.

"Yeah, why? Did you want to take a closer look?"

"No!" Aura and Tenney said together.

**

Gallagher, having taken over the body of the cameraman, was tired. The man's will was stronger than he had anticipated, and he had fought him. But Gallagher knew how to get what he wanted, and he bent the man to his will. The teen he had left had risen groggily and stumbled away, confused and probably mentally scarred for the rest of their life.

Gallagher didn't care. He watched the Tether and the Elemental slip away through the crowd and over the bank out of sight. They had moved as though they were ailing from something after the man had pulled back the cloth. Gallagher didn't know yet what the object was as he battled the former inhabitant for control of the body. He itched to follow them, finish them once and for all.

But his instructions were to stay here. Watch, don't touch. Report back.

He growled in frustration, the sound man near him taking a step back. "You okay, Bob?" he asked nervously.

"Yeah," said Gallagher.

He picked up the camera, turned it on to the people on the dais, and zoomed in on the object in the case. His shock at seeing it was so great, the camera fell to the ground, the lens smashing.

"You clumsy idiot!" shouted the sound man.

"It can't be!" Gallagher whispered.

But he knew it, he recognised it. The last time he had seen it was in the hands of the she-wolf as she defended the children of the fort. The gold and the red glinting from the torchlight as it drank the blood of those she had slain, before his own blade caught her through her belly, skewering her and her unborn child to the floor, the blade lost beneath the folds of her red dress as he had turned to defend himself from the attack by her husband.

Ignoring the sound man's protestations about the cost of the camera, Gallagher stepped forward. The reporter stood in front of him, telling him to leave, thanking him sarcastically for ruining the biggest story this month. He was oblivious to the man and the sounds of laughter coming from the humans around him, the cackle of the plastic woman.

All he saw was the object he had lost millennia ago, but it had found its way back to him. He spun on his heel and ran towards the road.

**

The Wisemans drove deeper into the Forest, to an old pub set back from a lane so that it sat in the woods, an island surrounded by trees. It was one of the public houses built to cater to the miners and their families working at the local, now defunct, coal mine. A small grouping of houses sat just below it. In its grounds was a large pond and a terrace with picnic benches and umbrellas. It was one of their favourite places to walk to on a summer's day. They all sat inside, Jess and Bo getting as warm a welcome as they did when the Landlady recognised them.

They spoke about Samuel's find, Martha temporarily having forgiven Tenney for his earlier remarks and innuendo. Silently, Aura and Tenney made plans for that evening.

**

Jude was waiting for them at the end of a forestry track ready to walk to the Lodge. She smiled when she saw them, her heart skipping at the sight of Tenney. He carried his rucksack over his shoulders and a bright torch in his hand. Aura embraced her warmly, thanking her for getting Tenney home last night. Tenney kissed her long and hard. She felt a little embarrassed in front of Aura, but she just rolled her eyes, saying, "Come on, love birds! Let's go before it gets any darker!"

They walked up the track, the light from the torches showing the way. Green eyes appeared through the trees. The black wolf caught up with them, rubbing his body against Aura's legs, rolling his head in her hands. She stroked him, kissed his head, and walked beside him, one hand deep in his pelt, towards the house.

Jude marvelled that this wolf was Hedge, and Hedge was the wolf. She watched the couple, separated by species but together in heart, and held tightly to Tenney's hand. She felt very lucky that this man was a man, would always be a man, and that they could walk together hand in hand under the stars.

A thought occurred to her. "So why do I need to keep away from your mum?" she asked him.

Tenney looked sheepish. "Oh, er, yeah, I kind of need to fill you in about that…"

Aura laughed aloud as she heard Jude exclaim, "You said what?"

**

Stace and Meg, who was human once again, watched as the four walked up to the lodge. They made quite the quartet, he thought. His sensitive hearing picked up snippets of their conversation as they spoke about everything except what was truly on their hearts.

Hedge, now fully wolf, probably didn't understand much, but he seemed happy, walking beside Aura, basking in her glow.

Stace thought back to the night before, the screeching of the tyres as Aura pulled up at the parking area. Hedge doubled up in pain lying in the back of the Land Rover. His changes were always worse when he was trapped within humanity, stressed because he couldn't do it quietly, unobserved. Meg had once told him that the change was a deeply private experience.

"It's like you're being pulled inside out, and all your flaws and weaknesses are on show. It's not something you want people to see, no matter how understanding they may be about it," she had said to him.

Meg had paced anxiously as Stace lifted Hedge from the vehicle and carried him to the copse of trees. Aura helped him undress, carefully folding his clothes as though doing a mundane task would help keep the reality at bay. Just before he changed, he looked first at his wolf mother, and then at Aura, and whispered, "I love you both." His last words before he could speak no more.

After the change, when Meg stood a woman and Hedge a wolf, Stace explained to Aura, as sympathetically as he was able, what happened next. "Hedge will be struggling with the reversion back to animal. He'll need some time to adjust, to find the balance. And he needs to hunt. Meg will stay here; she too needs to adjust, and she'll wait for him to return from his feast. But you need to go. Go home, get some rest. We'll be here tomorrow."

Aura nodded; her throat closed with grief. He saw her shimmer, her form change. The dragon bellowed once and flew into the sky.

After Hedge had eaten, he hadn't returned to his mother, but to Aura, watching her from the garden of her home.

Stace felt Meg shift as they came closer. He knew she felt rejected, her son choosing another over her. He also knew that she realised she had no right to those feelings. She and Hedge had never been together, the same species, at the same time since she birthed him. She had left him for decades, sometimes centuries, to fend for himself while she cared for another. Hedge had grown up, effectively, as an orphan. No home. No family. No real human life. If he chose to make what little time he had each month with another, she could not protest.

In fact, Stace was amazed that Hedge showed any feelings for his often absentee mother. If his sons had lived, all those centuries ago, he would have moved heaven and earth to walk beside them. Watching Tenney walk towards him, he saw similarities to his eldest son's swagger, his fake bravado. He wondered what he would have been like had he reached Tenney's age.

He shook himself free of the memories. They were dangerous things in an immortal's life, threatening to drag you into them, pull your mind back from the present. The youngsters approached.

"We have something to ask you, Stace." Straight to the point, he liked that about Tenney.

Seeing Jude and Aura shiver, Stace suggested they might be more comfortable inside. They went into the room with the large fire. From his rucksack, Tenney produced a thermos of tea, some sandwiches, and blankets. Jude, amazed at his ingenuity, smiled when he was forced to admit that it had been Aura's idea. "That makes more sense," Jude teased him.

Aura loved seeing them together, witnessing how happy Jude made her brother. She knew he was falling for her, even if he wasn't ready to admit it. Tenney had never had a real girlfriend - just blips, he would say. For Tenney, sex was a tool to get what he needed or to give someone what they wanted so they'd leave Aura alone. Once, Aura asked him if he knew how many girls he'd been with. She had lost count sometime during their second year of Sixth Form College. He ran his hand through his hair, thought for a moment, and said, "Don't know. Don't really care, if I'm honest."

And she knew he didn't care. Jude was the first one he actively sought out, the only one he looked forward to seeing again. The only woman who excited him in that way. Aura felt happy for him, relieved that Jude understood their unusual relationship. She remembered a short-term boyfriend she had after they left school. He couldn't handle her closeness with Tenney. When he asked Tenney to back off, Tenney punched him. She never saw him again.

Tenney served the tea. Meg's eyes rolled back in pleasure as the hot, sweet liquid flowed over her tongue. With a gentle mental nudge from Aura, he asked Stace about the dagger.

"Can you describe it?" Stace asked. "Yeah, long, yellow gold. Rubies all along the blade and hilt. Wrapped in red cloth, probably a lady's dress." Tenney paused, his eyes flicking to Aura for support. Absentmindedly, he rubbed his chest, the spot above his heart. "It's the same blade I see in my nightmares."

"The one that flies towards you?" Stace asked, surprised. Tenney nodded once, his face pale as his fingers slipped from his chest. "It sounds like a dagger that was once in my possession. I took it from the demon who killed me, after I returned to the world in my new guise. You've met him, and I hope you destroyed him."

Aura remembered the powerful blast she had emitted when the demons were attacking Hedge. She saw the body of the boy who had once tormented her explode into dust. Stace continued. "I had no use for it, and its presence only reminded me of that terrible night. So, I gave it to a trader from Antioch."

Stace stopped when Meg gasped, her mug dropping to the floor, spilling warm tea across the old wooden floorboards. She had paled, her eyes flicking to Stace's, her hand shaking. Hedge sat up on his haunches, aware of his mother's distress but not the cause. He whimpered quietly until Meg gently stroked his nose. She spoke to him softly in Latin, and he lay back down beside Aura.

"Meg?" Stace asked. She turned to him, then back to Tenney and Aura, her face as white as a sheet despite her efforts to regain composure while calming her son. "You say your father found it, buried at the Temple?"

"Yes," Aura said. "Buried at the bottom of a plinth where he thinks the goddess's statue was placed."

"Oh no…" she whispered into her hands.

"What do you know about it, Meg?" Stace asked calmly, though Aura could see the tension in his jaw.

Meg's yellow eyes widened as she turned to the siblings. "How did you feel when you saw it?" she asked.

"Sick, dizzy. Like it was alive. It hummed. It felt like separation. Like death." Both she and Tenney shuddered at the memory.

"It's called 'Χερουβίμ Στιλέτο,'" she said in flawless Greek. "Roughly translated, it means 'The Cherubim Dagger.' It is filled with blood rubies cut from one mighty stone, forged at the dawn of time alongside three other gems. The Councillor who fell split the ruby and forged it into a blade of gold. The rubies grow redder with each life the dagger takes. I brought it with me after using it to kill my uncle. It was my talisman, my reminder that I couldn't be cowed or beaten again. Then I wrapped it in a strip from my finest red and gold gown and buried it after I was banished with my son from our home."

"You buried it?" Tenney looked at her in disbelief.

"Yes. At the feet of the goddess, by the edict of the Councillor. She told me I couldn't carry it, that its power was too great. It is a weapon that was prophesied to one day separate souls from bodies—a very specific type of soul. It was the Enemy's last attempt to wrest control from the Creator." Meg paused, her eyes steely. "She said a time would come when it would be found again, and that would spark the beginning."

"The beginning of what?" Aura asked tentatively.

"Of the end," she replied.

Chapter 32

They barely spoke as they walked back to the village, at least not aloud. Tenney kept his arm almost constantly around Aura—her shoulder, her waist. It was as if he had to keep touching her, or they would disintegrate. Vanish.

Jude had to admit, Aura didn't look well. The loss of Hedge and now the fear of losing her brother had diminished her somehow. Her skin had taken on a translucent sheen. Any happiness they may have felt shattered because some stupid artifact had been discovered, one that might herald the end of all things.

When they reached the junction that led one way to the Wiseman house and the other to the hotel, Jude wanted to ask Tenney to come back with her. Hold her. Make love to her. But she knew she couldn't. Shouldn't. Her heart felt like it would shatter if she asked him, and he refused. So, she bid them good night, said she'd see them in the daylight, and walked away.

When she turned around, they had already gone, only a pair of green eyes watching, always watching from the shadows.

Jude let herself into her empty room. She took a shower, trying to wash away the sorrow, then pulled on her gown and cleaned her teeth.

Drinking a glass of water, her eyes fell upon the dressing table, to the photo of her parents. They looked so happy, serenely smiling at each other. Next to it was the pile of papers, her sole clues to finding her missing parent. Atop them lay the thick envelope with the party invitation. She fingered the curved lettering, the precise nature of how Glendower had written her name.

Glendower was a puzzle. He obviously knew far more than he had let on, but she wasn't convinced that he had much to do with Rae's disappearance. Uncertainty about the role he played in all this made her stomach flip. Frustration coursed through her after everything that had happened, was happening, her ineptitude to really help the people she loved the most. She screamed in dismay, her burdens feeling too heavy for her shoulders to bear anymore as she swept her hand through the papers, scattering them across the floor.

She sat on the end of her bed and wept. She wept for her mother, her father, both lost to her. She wept for Aura's pain, for her immense hidden power that held so much terrifying sway over so many people. For Hedge, only living as a man for 48 hours a month. The unfairness of it all. But most of all, she wept for herself. For falling in love with someone nearly 10 years younger than her. For jumping in like a hero, trying to save the day and becoming embroiled in something so far out of her comfort zone, she felt like she was stratospheric.

She wept and wept and wept.

Until there was a gentle knock on her door. She jumped, her eyes red-rimmed, and looked at her phone's clock. 4:13 a.m. Her senses went into overdrive, remembering the uninvited visit from Stace. She picked up her can of deodorant, confirmed the repaired security chain was firmly in place on the door, and looked through the spy hole. Nobody was there.

She really needed a good night's sleep. The tiredness was another burden on her shoulders. She turned away from the door and walked back towards the bed.

Another knock. This time she spun around to the door, determined to get to the bottom of who was playing silly buggers. She opened the door as wide as the chain would let her. "Listen, dick, stop messing around and get away from my door!" she said in a forceful whisper.

"Jude?" a voice whispered back.

Jude gasped, shut the door, and released the chain.

"Tenney?" she asked, amazed that he was there. He looked as tired as she felt, his eyes red-rimmed, his hand in his hair.

"Aura told me I was being an idiot. Told me to come over and apologise. She said if I didn't, she would drag me round herself." Jude tried not to smile and quickly wiped a stray tear from her cheek. He shot forward, his hand cupping her face, feeling the moisture there. "Oh god! I'm so sorry." His heart cracked as he saw her distress.

This time she tried to smile, but instead sobbed. He pushed her back into the room, shutting the door with his foot, one hand on her face, the other at her hip. He stroked her cheek, softly, softly.

"Where's Aura?" she asked. "How's she coping without you?"

"I stayed with her until she fell asleep, as she asked me to. But she's with me, here," he touched his heart, never letting go of her face; "and she's here," he touched his head. "She's with me all the time. And I'm with her. I'll know if she wakes up and needs me, and I'll go to her. You understand that, don't you?"

He looked at her beseechingly. She nodded, still too choked up to speak. He kissed her, a desperate kiss. It was a kiss that said he was right there, with her, at that moment. When he pulled back, Jude felt like he had drawn some of the air out of her lungs. "And besides," he said, his trademark smile on his lips, "I kind of let the big bad wolf in…"

She laughed once. "You didn't! I thought Hedge the Wolf didn't like being indoors!"

"I kind of got the impression in Bristol that he would bear any pain, any discomfort, for my sister." He smiled again. "Aura says he's lying by the side of my bed, snoring! She's got the other two dogs up there too, Bo watching Hedge carefully. I think Aura has a rival for Hedge's affections." He teased her again. She playfully slapped his chest. He kissed her once more, pushing her further into the room.

Tenney stopped and looked down when his foot reached the strewn papers across the floor. "What's all this?" he asked.

"Pure, unadulterated frustration," she replied, resting her forehead on his chest. He crooned a hum deep in his throat, the sound reverberating through her head, down her spine.

"How long have we got?" she asked, fingering the zipper on his jacket.

"An hour, maybe an hour and a half. Mum would go ballistic if she caught me sneaking out again."

"Good," said Jude. "Don't suppose you know a cure for frustration?" She smiled up at him, biting her bottom lip.

"Ah, well you see, Officer Marcello, I know the best cure," he began unfastening the belt of her gown, "for all sorts of frustrations." His hands slipped inside the gown.

**

Jude fell asleep quickly, a deep, satisfied sleep. He watched her for a few moments, taking her in. A stray lock of curled dark hair fell across her face, and he gently moved it, wrapping the black curl around his finger. She instinctively turned towards him. The urge to wake her up was almost too much to bear, but when she nestled deeper into the cushions, a pleased groan escaping her lips, he recognised that sometimes sleep was better than sex.

Gently, he kissed her cheek, the taste of dried tears on his lips, and extricated himself from the bed. He found his jeans on the floor and pulled them on. As he looked around for the rest of his clothing, his eyes fell on the mess of papers on the floor.

Tenney looked closer. There were letters addressed to one 'R. Garbling-Marcello' from a representative of Glendower Springs, explaining, again, the company's policy on how their water is sourced. Moving some of the pages aside, he found a diary. Opening it, he saw the pages filled with a strange script, the language unreadable. He wondered if Jude's mother wrote in code or knew a foreign language. But nothing in the pages looked familiar to him; they weren't written in Cyrillic, Arabic, or any East Asian script. He couldn't work this out by himself, so gently he nudged Aura. When he felt her stir, he asked her to look through his eyes at the spread of papers.

-*Have you apologised?*

-*Yes, twice.* He felt her laugh. -*Look at these, Aur, what do you think?*

-*Glendower – wasn't that the name of the man she met in Bristol?*

-*Yeah.*

-*Is the R her mum, do you think?*

-*Probably. Looks like she held a real grudge towards this Glendower and his company. One of these letters reads like it's the umpteenth time they have had to reply to her. Do you remember that Bible verse?* Aura didn't question his change of tack, just answering him naturally;

-*Something about the Lord coming like a thief, elements destroyed by fire, heavens vanishing. Basically, the end of the world.*

-*That's what I thought… And look here, can you see the watermark?*

-*Yeah, what is it?* It looked like a dragon, but without wings. It was almost eel-like, its body and tail long and sinuous, with two legs protruding from the shoulders ending in clawed and webbed feet.

-*It looks like it's swimming, doesn't it? I've never seen a creature like it though. But Aur, doesn't it remind you of something?*

-*Yeah,* she said, - *on Stace and Meg's business card. But that was a dragon, like me.*

-*What if this Glendower knows something about our kind?* he asked, tentatively. Aura was silent. Then he heard her get up and move around the room.

-*Ten! I just heard Dad get up for the loo! You've got to get home! NOW!*

Tenney dropped the page and hunted for the rest of his clothes, pulling them on quickly.

-*What are you doing?* he was alerted by her frantic movements.

-*I'm trying to encourage Hedge out without alerting Dad to the whacking great wolf in your room!* He laughed silently at the comedy of errors. As he turned, his foot nudged a thicker piece of card. The invitation. He bent down and picked it up, looked at it, an idea forming in his head. Quickly, he found a pen and wrote on the envelope, propping it up against the photo. He turned back to the room, one last look at Jude, and quietly left.

**

Jude woke up, feeling refreshed. She had managed to get a good five hours of sleep and felt much better for it. She stretched out her body, remembering the feel of his hands on her. She wasn't surprised to find him gone, but she missed him nonetheless.

Jude reached down beside the bed and picked up her robe. Turning, she surveyed the papers that had once been on the floor. Tenney had piled them up and placed them back on her dresser. Her eyes went to the photo of her parents, resolving yet again to keep looking for her mum. It was then that she spotted the envelope, the new biro scrawl across the top of it.

J,

I'll sort out a nice suit for this shindig, I may even find a suitable tie! Think we should go, probably be a laugh :)

Love, T x

P.S. Didn't want to wake you. It was hard though—you looked beautiful. See you later x

**

A mass of people arrived at the ruins of the Dark Hill Ironworks in the heart of the Forest of Dean. They gathered at the base of the ruins, looking up as though facing a massive stage. From a tunnel that led into the heart of the once-thriving industry, now over 150 years abandoned, strode a man with black eyes, a cloud of sulphurous smoke swirling around his feet.

Gallagher pointed at his most trusted soldiers, and together they formulated a plan to reclaim their most important weapon.

Chapter 33

Meg, dressed in black skintight jeans, black boots, and a black jacket, stood at the summit of the hill, her arms crossed, and her legs braced in a wide stance. By her side stood the giant black wolf, and at her feet was a large bag. She looked formidable, the breeze moving her short hair, her yellow eyes staring at the trio as they crested the hill.

Tenney and Aura exchanged glances, readying themselves for the day's lesson. Jude walked to her usual vantage point, a fallen tree at the side of the clearing, to watch from a relatively safe distance.

"Aura," Meg said, drawing her attention. "You need to learn control, so you don't let your feelings overwhelm you and take over. You could have immobilised Tenney, judged when he was about to pass out, and stopped. Instead, you let it get control and took it too far."

"Hey!" shouted Tenney, his instinct to protect her making him speak out.

"No, Ten, she's only telling us as it is. As it was. It's okay." Aura placated him.

He stood down, and Meg continued. "If you or Tenney are faced with the dagger and you lose control again, it will be easier to separate you because you, and he, will be vulnerable. The reason that you have a Tether is so that you are always aware of your connection to the physical world, aware of the repercussions of using your powers. But also, so that you are equally aware of the repercussions of not using your powers.

"You will always be stronger together because Tenney is your link to the tangible. But you can't always be together physically, so we need to ensure you are strong and Tenney is protected when you are apart. That includes being protected from others, but more importantly, protected from himself. Remember, if Tenney dies, it's game over."

**

Stace, walking through the dark places of the woodland, was able to cover much of the land between the Fort and his destination without touching the full force of the autumn sun. Occasionally, he was forced to sprint at unimaginable speed across the roads that crisscrossed the Forest, a blur in front of passing cars. He knew where he was heading, where he needed to go to plan. To think about the coming night, the repercussions if they were successful, and those if they were not.

It was all different this time. She was different, her Tether unusual. Unique, he supposed. Things were moving fast, changes were happening, and Aura and Tenney were smack in the middle of it.

The church in the woods, reachable only by one long driveway or a footpath through the surrounding woodland, appeared through the trees. Behind it loomed the old vicarage. On one side, a gated car park; on the other, some allotments. The graveyard across the drive from the church seemed to become part of the woods.

He saw the upturned rivets of grass where the wild boar had been. He had hunted their ancestors that roamed these woods in his long first life. These boars were reintroduced a couple of decades ago; they were a nuisance, many of the locals felt. But Stace believed that he saw how the Forest was slowly reclaiming the land, returning to how it once was. If the people realised that wolves were now roaming the lands, the boar would be the least of their worries.

A small flock of the free-roaming sheep, so common inside the Forest itself, looked up from grazing the verges that lined the drive, gauging if he was a threat. His tastes didn't always go for mutton; he had always preferred venison. They were safe from the predator in the shadows.

The church was another hidden building, like his Lodge. A newcomer would only know it was there if they stumbled upon it unexpectedly or set out to find it specifically. The church signs at the foot of the driveway promised people it really was there, but they still had a bit of a way to go to reach it. Stace stood at the gate that separated the church drive from the footpath. He saw that there was one car parked nearby.

There wasn't much shade between him and the church porch. Stace realised that he would have to run, something he was loath to do if there was a chance he would be witnessed. Humans didn't take too kindly to the sudden appearances he was prone to make. He closed his eyes and listened. He heard the mice in the undergrowth, the buzzard in the sky. He heard the repetitive munching as the sheep continued eating the grass. A couple of people were deep in the graveyard away from the drive, replacing the flowers on the grave of a loved one. In the distance, he heard a man walking his dogs towards the church, but Stace gauged that he was still a way off.

Stace turned his focus on the church. One heartbeat. Female. He listened closer, trying to gauge her placement in the building, making sure she wasn't near the porch when he suddenly appeared. He was safe. She was in the back of the church.

He looked up, the clouds moved over the sun, partially covering it. Pulling up his hood, he ran for it. Even in the few seconds he was out of cover, he felt the sun's rays hit him, knowing that when he stopped his face would be mottled, red, and sore. He also knew that in an instant he would look normal again. The longer he was out in the sun, the longer it took to heal.

In one fluid motion, he opened the door and stepped into the cool porch. He breathed deeply. The familiar smells of worship assailed him: wax from the candles, autumn flowers arranged on plinths and in vases. He smelled the people who had passed before him, the musty smell of the books—hymnals, Bibles, and orders of service. He detected the faint whiff of incense, but not much. This wasn't a high Anglican church, so the use of incense was not a common occurrence.

The building itself was octagonal in shape, with whitewashed walls. Very simple, the only nod to art was the painting of 'Christ Mocked' in the centre of the ornate white and gold gothic reredos. He was flanked by the Ten Commandments, a reminder of the Son of God's sacrifice, and the expectations of his followers. The door to the vestry stood open at the side, and Stace could hear the heartbeat coming from within.

Quietly, he took a pew and contemplated the painting of Christ.

The vicar, a lady in her early sixties, moved out of the vestry, shrugging on her coat. She started slightly when she saw the man, sitting unnaturally still in one of the pews, but quickly composed herself. It was common in this church, which was open every day, for a parishioner, holidaymaker, or hiker to take refuge inside. Find space to pray and talk to God. Or just to have a look around.

Stace smiled at her, nodding his head slightly. She returned the smile and, realising his need to be alone, said a quick "Good afternoon," and walked towards the back of the church. The man in the woods, his dogs tugging at the end of their leads, had come into the porch. He heard the vicar greet him warmly. He turned to look at them over his shoulder and saw her proffer her cheek for a kiss. Her husband, he guessed. The dogs greeted her with enthusiasm before returning to smelling the ground.

And then Stace was truly alone. He knelt, closed his eyes, and began to recite his old prayers in his old tongue. He asked for the souls of his murdered family to rest in peace. Then he prayed for his own salvation, for forgiveness for all his unforgivable sins. He prayed for Tenney and Aura, for Meg and Hedge, and for Jude. He prayed that they would have the strength and courage to face what was coming as a team. And then he sat and waited for an answer that he knew would only come when it was ready to be given.

"I haven't heard that tongue in a long, long time," said a man's voice from beside him. He hadn't heard him come in, but he shouldn't have been surprised. He finished the prayer and pushed himself back onto the pew.

"What name are you going by this time?" he asked in greeting.

"Oh, I don't know." The man thought. "How about Paul, in honour of the saint of this church?"

Stace shook his head in wonder at how flippant this powerful creature could be. He turned to look at the man. He was tall and slim. His face was lean, but not unattractively so. He was smiling with perfect white teeth, a twinkle in his golden eyes. His hair was short, almost military, but not quite; there was a well-maintained quiff hanging slightly over his forehead. He wore jeans and a casual blue jumper over an open-necked shirt. Black, polished shoes, crossed at the ankle. He was completely relaxed.

"Ok, 'Paul'," Stace couldn't quite hide the mockery in his voice. "What are you doing here?"

"Oh, Eustace! Don't sound like that!" His voice was mellifluous. Powerful, but gentle. "He heard you, you know? I'm here to help, offer some words of advice. And I have a little message for you to pass on."

Stace didn't quite trust these creatures; their history was too long. Too painful. The only one he trusted had apparently abandoned him, refusing to acknowledge him when he had begged for help.

"What do you want, Paul?" Stace's patience was wearing thin.

Paul looked at him. He really looked at him, shedding the layers that Stace had worked so hard to put into place, and getting right down to the soul of him.

"I can't tell you that your children didn't suffer. I'm truly sorry." Stace tensed up. "But I can tell you that you are right, the balance is shifting. Things are moving towards a conclusion. A choice. The Elementals will be together again, and you will need to stop them from becoming the Titans they once were. You will have a decision to make." He paused, shifted fractionally to take in the beautiful simplicity of the church.

"You will have help, I promise you. Your guide will reawaken to her responsibilities. She will aid you once more." Paul stood up and moved to the rail separating the altar from the rest of the church. The sunlight through the two clear-paned windows on either side of the reredos shone on him. Diffused through the glass, the rays seemed to be drawn to Paul. Stace could see the dust motes dancing in the beams as the peace of the church settled around them.

Paul gazed upon the painting of Christ, totally captivated by it. "He had to suffer so much for the souls of mankind," he said suddenly. Stace had begun to worry that he had forgotten he was there. Time moved differently for creatures such as him; a decade was over in a second, but a second could also last for a hundred years. They observed life, only interceding at pivotal moments, *or at times when they felt they could interfere and get away with it*, Stace thought sceptically. He knew that for this particular being to be here, today, just before they were going to risk everything to reclaim the dagger, something was going to happen. That knowledge made him uncomfortable.

"Yet he did it, even though he was afraid, in pain, alone for a time. Will you be able to do the same thing, Eustace? You will need to keep your head when all around you are losing theirs. You must be ready for the challenges you alone will face. Will you be ready to be fully The General again, and not the teacher?" Paul asked as though it was a rhetorical question. Stace didn't answer. He didn't appear to have expected him to.

"It's a pretty good likeness, really," he said of the painting. "Well, I mean, I've seen worse," he smiled over his shoulder at Stace.

"The message?" Stace asked. Paul turned back to him, a puzzled look on his face, before he remembered it again. "When you see my sister, tell her all she has to do is ask, and she shall receive."

With that, a huge pair of golden wings appeared behind him. There was a small flash of light, and the creature known as a Councillor disappeared.

Stace shook his head, trying to shift the blobs of light from his eyes. "Flipping Angels," he muttered.

**

Meg had Tenney doing some drills, running up and down the hill, trying to work off his excess energy and anger, learning to control them through mindless, physical activity. The wolf ran alongside him, enjoying the exertion.

Meanwhile, Aura sat in the centre of the clearing, her eyes shut, breathing deeply. Meg wanted her to sense the air, to feel its movements, and have Aura use the air to stop her from approaching. Meg was stealthy; the first few times, she managed to tap Aura on the shoulder before she realised she was there.

"Stop worrying about Tenney," she said. "He's fine, and your connection is telling you he's fine. The mistakes of the past must be forgotten. He won't lose control; you won't become ill. Have faith in your bond and concentrate on the air around you."

This time, Aura felt Meg approach. She saw the air bend around her as she crept up. Aura pointed at her, but it wasn't enough. Meg pounced again.

"Stop me, Aura!" Meg said again. Aura heard Tenney, starting to puff as he came up the slope. Aura opened her eyes and looked at him as Jude held out a bottle of water. She wished that she could do as Meg asked. Hedge, his long tongue hanging from the side of his mouth, now lay next to her. Aura, her eyes fixed on Tenney, ran her hand through his coat and felt him shiver under her touch.

Meg stared at her, her yellow eyes glinting, before she moved off into the trees. Tenney was laughing softly with Jude. Aura closed her eyes, sensed the air around him, saw the pull of attraction between them, and the bright blue cord that would forever link her to her brother. And then, from the darkness of the trees behind them, she saw the air move around another figure, creeping up behind him. The shape of a short knife, pointed towards Tenney, cut through the air.

Quickly, she raised her hand. The figure stopped, as though hitting a wall. She twisted her hand, so the palm faced the sky, slowly closing her fist, and moved her hand savagely away from her brother. The figure lifted into the air and then flew backwards, hitting a tree.

Alerted by the sound of a body hitting wood, Tenney spun around.

246

"Meg!" he exclaimed. Aura opened her eyes. She saw Meg, sprawled out at the bottom of the tree, rubbing her head, the small paring knife fallen at her side. Hedge, lying on his belly near Aura, looked up, his ears erect and his tongue lolling. He seemed to be grinning!

"Meg!" Aura shuffled to her feet and ran over to where Tenney and Jude were helping the woman up. "That was you? I'm so sorry! I saw the knife, and I kind of just reacted!"

"What knife?" asked Tenney, puzzled.

"So, we've established that when someone you love is in danger, you have no trouble summoning your powers, but when it is your own life, you're more circumspect?" Meg looked very pale, her hand on her head.

"I'm so sorry, Meg!" said Aura, shocked at what she had done.

"I'm fine. But you," she was pointing at Aura, "need to learn to use your powers in defence of yourself as well as of others. If you are defenceless, how will you save those you love around you?"

"I think it's time for a quick break, don't you?" said Jude.

**

They sat on or around the fallen trunk, sipping from cups filled with the contents of a thermos of tea. Aura looked at Meg, who was deep in thought. She no longer rubbed her head, explaining that she healed very quickly.

"Ten," Aura asked. "Can I have your phone?"

Tenney looked at her and smiled. He knew what she wanted to do as he reached into the pocket of his jeans and pulled out the iPhone. Aura moved around and sat beside Meg. She jumped slightly, shaken from her thoughts. Aura accessed the video app on the phone, held it out to Meg, and pressed play.

On the screen sat a black-haired young man. He was looking away from the camera. In the background, she heard the soft murmurings of Tenney and Jude. Closer to the camera was Aura's voice, a light laugh followed by an instruction: "Hedge – say hullo to your Mum!"

The black head turned, squinting in a beam of sunlight. He casually ran his hand through his hair as he leaned back on one elbow and stared right at the camera, his green eyes flashing with mirth. He waved once at the camera and spoke. "Hi, Mam!"

Meg gasped. She had never heard his voice with the ears and mind of a human. She brought a hand to her mouth as a tear fell from her eye. She was oblivious to the others watching her; she only had eyes for the figure on the small screen in front of her.

"Say something else!" Aura instructed from behind the screen.

"Ok," he began. "Er, hullo, this is Wilfrid" (a laugh from his friends, followed by a look of playful annoyance from her son). "I think you are currently off hunting with Stace, and I am, well, I am me, I guess." He looked down at his hands. She knew the feeling of finally being herself again. She imagined it was tenfold for him.

"Tell her what you've been up to." Aura again.

"What, everything?" he teased.

"Oi!" she heard Tenney in the background. "That's my sister!"

Hedge laughed! Meg found that the sound was magical to her, his voice mesmerising. She swore to herself that she would remember its cadence forever.

"It's no worse than what you two must get up to, Mate," he teased back at his new friend. This time Tenney laughed, and it was Jude's turn to sound outraged. Aura quickly brought Hedge back to the camera and his message.

"This is very new for me. We've only been able to communicate through letters before. And misremembered messages via Stace. You know how bad his memory can be!" She smiled, knowing that Stace's memory was anything but bad. "Well, I've been in Europe, the Dolomites, the Alps. Siberia. Had to be a bit careful there. They really don't like wolves! I was just wandering around, I guess. I got back here a couple of months ago, during the August full moon. I cut it a bit close though. I only just managed to drive here from Dover before changing. I've been wandering around, reacquainting myself with this place. And then I found you and we found Tenney and Aura. Then Stace showed up, and bam." He hit his palm with his fist, "Reunited again!"

He paused, looked down at the ground, then spoke again. "I won't lie, Mam. It's been tough. I miss you, even though we are never really together. I miss my human self when I'm a wolf, especially now I've found Aura again. But I miss the freedom of the wolf when I'm human. It's the only life I've known, and I've tried to make it a good one. I've seen things, witnessed things, people can only dream of. And I've learned to live in the moment, so, I guess, right now, I'm the happiest I've ever been. I've got new friends who accept me and my, er, quirks, and I'm totally," he began to get up, crawling towards the camera, "bona fide," closer, "one hundred percent," he was so close she could see the different shades of green in his emerald eyes, the beautiful human flaws in his skin, "infatuated with Aura!" The camera fell back, the screen showing sky, as he held Aura, who was squealing, close to him.

Tenney and Jude laughed as the couple wrestled, Aura reaching for the phone. Meg's heart caught when she saw the look in his eyes as Aura finally reclaimed the it. The last time she had seen that look from green eyes in a face that he resembled so strongly, had been her last night with Bodvoc, before her death, when she was still completely human, he was alive, and their child was safe in her womb.

"Say goodbye to your Mum!" said Aura, laughing again.

Hedge turned from her and smiled happily through the screen at Meg. "*Vale Matris. Te amo.*" He smiled at her sadly. She saw now that his eyes were old, tired even. Suddenly, from the edge of the screen, Tenney ran behind, slapping Hedge, tagging him. He began to rise, about to chase Tenney and tag him back. There was more laughing, and the screen froze as it reached the end of the recording.

Meg stared at the picture of her son, caught in time. Happy. Carefree, and so very handsome. She saw the right mix of herself and his father, whose features, until this moment, had been fading in the mists of time. She caught a sob before it could be released, hurriedly wiped her eyes, and turned back to Aura.

Her sympathetic look was almost too much to bear. "Thanks for that," she said, handing the phone back to her. She began to get up, compose herself, her wolf child looking at her, his head cocked. His eyes were the same as when he was human. They were the only part of him that didn't change, she realised.

"We can send it to you if you like?"

She looked down at Aura and gave a small, sad smile. "I'd like that. Thank you."

Then, getting back to the business at hand, she reached into her bag and produced two mirrors. "Right!" she said, signalling the end of the break. "Let's practice communication."

Chapter 34

Tenney watched his father across the table, listening intently as Samuel spoke animatedly about the discovery of the dagger. It was rare to see him so excited.

"Do you know what this means?" Samuel asked.

The children chimed in together, "That the Dobunni and the Romans shared some beliefs. That the Dobunni were an important tribe. That the Forest is finally getting the historical interest it deserves." Samuel looked amused.

"I'm talking about this a lot, aren't I?"

"Don't listen to them, love," said Martha, resting a hand on his arm. "We are all very proud of you."

Samuel smiled warmly at her. "Thanks, love." They were proud of him. Tenney found it hard to swallow the last piece of food on his plate. He glanced at Aura.

- I know, she said. *-We're going to break his heart tonight. But we have no choice.*

Tenney smiled grimly at her.

After the meal, they asked to be excused, claiming they had plans to meet friends. "It better not be that policewoman!" Martha called after them. Tenney rolled his eyes.

"Have you got the key?" he whispered to Aura as they put on their boots.

"Yeah," she replied, patting her coat pocket.

When they had returned from the Fort, Tenney had kept Samuel busy with small talk while Aura found the key to the safe in the Manor House, hidden in one of his bags. He wouldn't miss it until morning, so they only had tonight. Meg had called the owners, telling them that they had won a prize - a classical concert in Cheltenham with an overnight stay at a hotel.

The plan was set. Together, they left the house, calling out goodbye as they exited the front door.

"TENNEY!" He turned at his father's shout, seeing Samuel dash out of the house in his slippers, waving his hand. Panic gripped them as they thought he had discovered their theft of the key.

"He knows!" whispered Aura. Tenney positioned himself in front of her, ready to face their father's wrath.

"Tenney! Ten! Son!" Samuel didn't sound angry. He caught up to them, breathing heavily. "Ten, I just need a quick chat. Aura, do you mind? I think this needs to be done alone, you know, man to man…"

Aura felt relieved they hadn't been caught. "I'll meet you at the pub, Ten," she said. Jude was waiting for her at the end of the drive, watching as Tenney and his dad talked outside the front door.

"What was all that about?" she asked.

Aura smiled. "Dad's giving Tenney the talk!" she laughed as they walked down the lane towards the village.

"So, er, Tenney. We haven't really had the chance, you know, to, er," Samuel coughed, the awkwardness of the situation making his throat dry. "Well, you see, the thing is, your mother asked me to just come out, you know, make sure that you know what you're doing. And, er, give you these."

He handed Tenney a few small pouches. "Now, I, er, know they're nothing fancy, or, er, anything. But, well, they will keep you and, er, Jude safe." Samuel let out a breath he had been holding, relieved to finally fulfil his fatherly duties to ensure his children were safe in all things.

Tenney felt the blood rush to his face. "Dad," he said, no jokes in his voice as he couldn't find any humour in the situation; it was so embarrassing. "I'm 21."

"Yes, I know, son, but, well, you spend so much time with your sister and you've never brought a girl home before, so, well, your mother and I were never, you know, a hundred percent sure that you had, er," he coughed, "had the experiences other boys and girls may have had." Samuel looked at his son from under his eyebrows, trying to inject some gravitas into the situation, and ignoring the feeling in his gut that he was making a terrible misjudgement.

Tenney ran his hand through his hair. "Dad," he finally said after considering an appropriate answer, and realising that he couldn't lie to his father, not when he was about to commit such a huge betrayal. "You should have had this chat with me when I was 15."

Samuel stood still as he tried to absorb what Tenney was saying, not quite taking it in. In seconds, he was trying to reconcile what he was hearing his son, his child, say to him. "Oh…" and then a louder cry of "OH!" as he realised what Tenney was implying, and the pieces finally slotted together to produce a picture, slightly different from the one he had always known, of his child.

"I've got enough of these and had enough experience to know to use them. There won't be any girls knocking on the door, announcing they're about to make you a grandad." He smiled gently, trying to soften the blow, and handed the condoms back to his gobsmacked father.

"Aura…?"

"Aura can handle herself. She takes precautions too." Tenney felt bad for shattering his father's fantasies that they were still the chaste children he imagined them to be. "So, er, Dad, can I go? Catch up with Aura and Jude?"

His father rallied and tried to retake some control of the situation. Their faces were both red from the embarrassment of the conversation. "Yes, son. Of course. Here, buy yourselves a round of drinks." This time he handed Tenney a couple of twenties. "Maybe, er, two rounds?"

"Yeah, thanks, Dad." Tenney turned to go, poking his tongue out at the two girls laughing under a solitary streetlamp on the lane.

Samuel turned back to the house, walking very slowly. He suddenly realised that there was so much he didn't know about his children. The thought left him feeling bereft; how had he missed the fact his son was sexually active from such a young age? And Aura—his beautiful, innocent daughter… It was all too much. As he reached his front door, he took a deep breath and entered the house.

Martha stood in the front room, anxiously wringing her hands together. "Well?" she asked as soon as she saw him. "Did you talk to him? Did he take them?" Samuel put his hands on her shoulders.

He decided to lie, to protect her. "Yes, love. He's okay. He took them."

"Oh, thank God!" she said, relief making her collapse onto his shoulder. He stroked her hair, kissed her head.

"He knows exactly what he's doing," he whispered.

**

They stayed in the pub until closing time, enjoying each other's company and wishing Hedge could be there to make them complete. The girls teased Tenney, as Aura had linked to him and witnessed the entire awkward conversation, recounting it to Jude in real time.

"You mean your folks never had the sex talk with you before?" Jude asked incredulously.

They shook their heads. "Well, not properly. I think they kind of assumed the school would do it, or if they didn't make a big issue of it, then we wouldn't go out looking for it," Aura explained.

"But 15? That is kind of young," remarked Jude, her cop brain not quite able to shut down. Tenney looked at Aura. -*This could be the right time to tell her, Tenney*, she thought. He raised his eyebrows and folded his lips under his teeth before taking a sip of his pint.

"Aura was very badly bullied at school. I couldn't always be there to protect her, and as we progressed through the years, we were made to take different subjects. I was into sports, star player in rugby and stuff." Jude thought he didn't sound particularly pleased with the accolade.

"Anyway, if you were good at sports and won the school prizes, then you were the most popular kid there. For the students and the teachers. Aura liked her art and history. Sport never interested her. So, rumours spread that she was holding me back, hampering my chances, and therefore the school's chances. The head teacher even called me into his office one day and suggested that I might want to gently try to cut some of the sibling ties with her. If she hadn't been outside his door keeping me calm, I would have been expelled for knocking him out.

"Then one day the bullying got worse. She was called The Creep, tripped and pushed in the corridor. I'd find spit in her hair, an upturned can of coke in her school bag." He clenched his fist as he struggled to rein in the anger he felt at the memories. "One day, Aura came to me, her face bloodied and her clothes torn. This one girl had pushed her down a flight of stairs. All the bullying happened when I wasn't around, and when I was around, this girl would try and flirt with me, make nice with Aura. And then chuck a bit of chewed gum at her or something. So, I did what I had to do to get her and her little minions off Aura's back."

"What was that?" asked Jude, horrified at his story. Aura sat there, watching Tenney closely.

Matter-of-factly, his eyes never leaving hers so that he could gauge her reaction, Tenney said, "So I started paying attention to all the girls she hung around with. All except for her. I gave them all what they wanted and ignored her. They left Aura alone for long periods of time, but the bullying always started up again, led by this girl. So, I'd go through them all again."

"What about the boys?" Jude asked, worried slightly about how far he would go to ensure Aura stayed safe.

"I'd miss a kick, drop the ball or something. If they wanted me to play well, then they left Aura alone." Tenney took another sip of his drink. He continued to look straight across at Jude. "I'll do anything to protect Aura. Protect the people I love the most." His eyes bore into hers as he stressed the end of the sentence.

Jude believed him.

**

They walked through the night towards the manor house, each lost in their own thoughts.

"I was 23," Jude suddenly announced.

"What?" asked Aura, puzzled by the seemingly random proclamation from her friend.

"I was 23," she repeated. "When I lost my virginity. I didn't want to just, you know, give it up to anyone. Mum has very firm ideas about pre-marital sex. It kind of rubbed off on me. Anyway, one day I just did it to see what all the fuss was about."

Tenney looked at her, and she smiled up at him, suddenly shy. He glanced down the road and saw Meg and Hedge waiting at the small roundabout.

"Aura, go on ahead, we'll catch you up, okay?" She grinned at him, turned, and walked away.

Tenney looked up and down the street and saw the dark alleyway that led to the housing estate. Taking hold of Jude's arm, he gently guided her down it. When they reached a dark spot where neither the streetlights nor the single weak bulb in the alley reached them, he pressed her against the pebble-dashed wall and kissed her. It was so deep she felt her legs turn to jelly, only his body and the wall keeping her upright. He pulled back, and she held his face in her hands, barely able to see him in the shadow of the passage.

"I never really knew what all the fuss was about, until you," she uttered, breathless.

**

Twenty minutes later, still straightening their clothes, they met the others at the gated entrance to the manor house.

"Where's Stace?" Tenney asked Meg.

"He's been watching the house, making sure the owners left. He's disabled the security alarms and cameras," Meg replied. They could all see she was focused. Jude, conscious of her precarious position in the police force and the illegality of the job at hand, shifted uneasily on her feet. She didn't need to know any more about the burglary than she already did, but she wasn't surprised that Stace would have the skills of a cat burglar.

Meg looked down at Hedge. "*Nunc igitur vade!*" she said, nodding her head up the drive. The wolf sloped off in the direction of the manor. Then she turned back to the trio. "You know what you're doing?" she asked. They all nodded, adrenaline pumping through their veins.

Jude was elected to stand guard at the gate, out of sight, and call Tenney's mobile if anyone should approach. She kissed him, wished them all good luck, and hid herself away, mobile at the ready.

Tenney, Aura, and Meg began to walk up the drive. The wolf met them halfway and turned back on his heel. "That means it's safe, no one's there except Stace," Meg said.

They rounded the front of the building. It was Jacobean, flat-fronted with three floors and seventeen diamond-leaded windows. A porch jutted out from the front over the heavy oak door. There were many myths and legends about the building; stories of ghosts and blood stains from the civil war that wouldn't disappear no matter how hard a person scrubbed the floor. Aura involuntarily shivered, and Tenney rested a hand on her shoulder. She should have been relieved - ghosts weren't real. But then again, a month ago neither were vampires or werewolves.

When a bat flew over their heads, Aura emitted a little shriek.

-*What the hell was that!?* she exclaimed silently.

-*Greater Horseshoe Bat*, Tenney answered, smiling at her reassuringly. Aura quickly closed her eyes and felt all the creatures that flew in the night: the barn owl gliding silently through the sweet chestnuts and out over the temple site; the great bats, lots of them, catching night insects. There was nothing to be afraid of, she realised. She reopened her eyes and saw the shape of the wolf nearby. And then a dense patch of black, something darker than the night shadows, stepped forward.

"Let's go," Stace said.

**

Stace jimmied open one of the old windows, holding it as Meg, as agile as her son had been at the hotel, silently leapt in. Stace helped Aura over the sill, and Tenney followed her, his height making it easy for him. Stace then slipped in soundlessly after him, landing softly. Hedge paced the area outside the window.

They all wore a similar combination of jeans and dark, warm jackets or hoodies, soft-soled trainers, and gloves. Aura had pulled one of Tenney's beanies over her blonde hair and noted that Stace wore something similar.

The curse of the bright-haired, she thought. Tenney smiled at her, laughing silently, his brunette head blending in with the darkness of the night.

The house was totally silent as they looked around at their surroundings. They were in the dining room, a long black table with silverware displayed upon it as though the owner was expecting to host a banquet any minute, running down the centre of the room. There was a large fireplace on the back wall.

"Where's the safe, Aura?" Stace asked.

"Upstairs, in one of the bedrooms. There's a priest hole."

He nodded once. "Lead on," he said.

Aura tiptoed across the dark wooden floors and opened the double doors leading to the hallway. She turned right, away from the front door, towards the back corridor. She turned right again towards the staircase that led up to the first floor. Her father had brought her here several times, delighting in telling her all the stories that surrounded the place. The history of all the different buildings that had stood there—from the Saxon Hall to the Norman house, to the current building. He told her about the Cavaliers who used it as their base, and the skirmish with the Roundheads that led to the famous, ghostly blood stain. That had happened in the dining room, she remembered with another shudder.

Tenney touched her shoulder. She turned, gave him a quick look to reassure him that she was okay, and made her way up the stairs. At the top, she followed the corridor down to the last bedroom and opened the door. The owner had made this room into a study, which didn't surprise her. She wouldn't have wanted to sleep in a room with a priest hole.

The wooden-panelled room was dominated by a large black, ornate Flemish fireplace. Stace recognised the release mechanism for the door. He had seen these kinds of fireplaces before, and he instinctively moved to one panel to the right of the fireplace. He felt down its edges and pushed a certain, hidden spot. The secret door opened in the panels to the right of the fireplace, revealing the priest hole beyond.

"How did you know it was there?" Tenney asked, amazed.

Stace turned back to him and gave a smile that would have rivalled one of Tenney's in the mega-wattage stakes.

"I've hidden in a few myself," he said. "Hunted people down to them as well," he added, almost as an afterthought.

Meg tensed up and looked around the room, past the buzzing computer monitor and the accoutrements of a man's office, towards one of the windows. She had smelled something, something foul. Something was wrong.

Inside the small space of the priest hole was a stone seat, and opposite it, a safe. Aura pulled out the key. She flourished it, was about to say, "Ta-da!" when she saw Tenney's expression.

"We're not going to need that, Aura," he said.

She pushed past him. The safe's door had been ripped open. The dagger was gone.

Meg whipped around. There was a movement above the window! A black shape materialised and crawled down from the ceiling. The possessed man hissed at her, broke the window, and climbed out and up towards the roof. She ran after him. Below the window, Hedge howled, agitated, pacing back and forth and looking up towards the room they were in.

Meg gracefully pulled herself out of the window and followed the creature to the roof as Stace sprang into action.

"Tenney!" The General revealed himself, using his commanding voice. "Phone Jude. Tell her to stay hidden! She must NOT try to apprehend anyone she sees! OK? These demons are powerful, no matter how human they may seem." Only the strongest of the demon horde could make their host body disobey the laws of gravity and crawl over ceilings and up walls.

Tenney nodded, already pushing the speed dial for Jude's phone. Stace continued to issue instructions: "Take Aura out, get her away, tell Hedge to keep her safe. Then find Jude. We'll meet you back at the church." The demons wouldn't dare to step foot on sacred ground. He hoped. "Ok?" Again, Tenney nodded. The phone connected, he spoke quickly to Jude, and hung up just as Stace leapt onto the sill and, in one mighty jump, pushed himself out of the window and up two floors to the roof.

"Aura – come on!" he grabbed her arm and together they ran back down the stairs and out through the window in the dining room. They found Hedge. Tenney quickly hugged her and spoke clearly and succinctly to Hedge, like he would when training the dogs. Then he stepped away and watched them run across the lawn towards the fields beyond. For the first time in his life, he trusted his sister's life to another. He trusted it to the wolf.

Chapter 35

Hedge encouraged Aura down the slope from the Manor House's gardens. He leapt over a fence dividing the property from the field between the church and the house, waiting semi-patiently for Aura to clamber after him.

"Ahhhh!" Aura cried out, struggling to pull her leg over the top bar of the fence. The farmer had wrapped barbed wire around the wood to deter people from getting too close to his prized animals. In her panic to get across, Aura fell forward, her chin landing painfully on the wire. One of the barbs tore upwards towards her lip, and blood began to flow down her chin and neck.

Hedge, incapable of helping her, paced anxiously in front of her, whining softly. His ears were erect, his nose constantly sniffing the air. He smelled her blood—metallic, rich, and powerful. Then he smelled the possessed men who were making their way towards them from the shadows. The last thing he smelled was the bull moving towards him, ready to protect his females.

Aura looked at Hedge's green eyes and whimpered slightly. Her torn face throbbed, her hands coated in blood. She pulled her leg over, ripping through her skinny jeans and adding to her wounds with a gash from the back of her knee down her calf. She fell awkwardly in the mud. Hedge yipped, highly agitated.

"Okay, it's okay. I'm okay!" She pushed herself up, held her jacket sleeve to her face, and hobbled after Hedge towards the church.

**

"Tenney!" Jude whispered as loudly as she dared from her hiding place. He saw her head poke out from behind the woodpile near the garages and jogged over to her, feeling immensely relieved to see she was okay.

"Where's Aura?" she asked, casting her eyes around.

"We had to split up." Jude could see that Tenney didn't think very much of that idea. "Stace and Meg followed the man-thing onto the roof. Aura's with Hedge. We're to meet them at the church." Jude nodded, watching the driveway. "Man-thing?" she queried.

"There was one of those demons in the room." Tenney looked shaken but determined. His jaw clenched as he clamped his teeth together, one hand on Jude's knee as they hid together, peering back up the drive. She was learning to read his tells. This one said he felt weak, powerless to help anyone but also determined to try and save those he loved.

"Did you get the dagger?" she asked.

He shook his head. "We were about 30 seconds too late."

"Dammit…" she was about to add more when a movement caught her eye. Quickly, she pulled Tenney down behind the woodpile. He fell heavily on top of her.

"You know I'm all for an outside fumble, but I really don't think this is the time or the place." He smiled down at her. Even in a state of peril, he still resorted to humour if possible, to try to alleviate the situation.

"Gerroff!" she whispered, shoving him up and off. The sight of a group of men walking down the driveway made all her instincts scream that they had to stay quiet. She raised her finger to her lips, "Shhhh," she blew through her lips, and pointed.

Tenney then saw the men. There were four of them. One of them towered over the others; Tenney thought he must be close to seven feet in height. He wasn't used to having to look up to anyone. But the disconcerting thing was that the four men seemed to have stepped straight from the shadows. One minute the driveway had been clear, the next they appeared.

"How'd they do that?" Tenney whispered.

"I don't know, but it might explain how Stace, Meg, and Hedge weren't alerted to their presence," Jude whispered back, solemnly.

"Ahhhh!" Tenney gasped loudly, holding his chin. He held his hand up, expecting blood. Nothing was there, but the pain was excruciating, throbbing through his jaw and up his face. Jude turned to him in shock.

"What happened?" she asked, alarmed.

"Aura…" Tenney spluttered, before grabbing his right calf, his face screwed up in pain. "She's hurt!"

"What?" To Jude, it looked like Tenney had received the injury. She held his face and scanned it, looking for a cut, blood, anything. "How?" Before he could answer her, a cold, deep voice spoke to them over the woodpile.

260

"Hello, little mice." The giant smiled as he stared down at them through his black eyes.

**

The two demons could smell the blood. Emerging from the shadows, they were drawn to the rich, red liquid spilt on the fence and barbed wire. Effortlessly, they crossed the fence and made their way across the fields. They didn't rush. The girl was limping, struggling over the rutted, cow-patted terrain.

Their prey was well within their reach.

**

Stace surveyed the view from the rooftop. He saw the chimneys rising from the older Jacobean wing and the more recent, smaller Georgian wing, which jutted out from the side, forming an L shape. Meg was crouched beside him, sniffing the air.

"How'd they get past you?" she asked quietly. There was no scorn or derision in her voice. They had eluded her as well.

"I don't know. Gallagher is one of the original demons, and it was his dagger we were trying to steal. But that was a new trick of his—to be in the building with us, let alone the same room." Stace was angry with himself for putting them all in such danger. Automatically, he fell back on his training from two millennia ago, trying to present a calm, authoritative, clear-headed leader. Meg could tell that it was a hard task for him.

Silently, she nodded over the roof. "He's over there," she said.

"Good." Stace snarled, his composure beginning to drop slightly as his fangs descended.

They leapt after the shadow.

**

Aura was struggling. The field was churned up, her leg and face were in agony. Hedge circled around her, shepherding her forward, nudging her if she slowed too much for his comfort. The boundary wall between the field and the church seemed a very long way off. She turned around to look over her shoulder; the shadowy men were gaining, and they seemed to take pleasure in her flight and their easy hunt. She heard a cruel laugh reverberate over the field.

Turning back, her foot slipped in a cowpat, and she fell painfully on her back, staring up at the starlit sky. The ground shook as the men finally ran towards her.

Aura felt Hedge's wet nose on her face, under her neck, trying to encourage her up. She rolled onto her side, pushing up painfully to her good left knee, her bad leg stretched out behind her. Her face was coated in the mess and dirt of the field, and filth was getting into her wound. She pushed herself up, but her right leg buckled under her.

Hedge yipped at her again. She tried once more, fear and adrenaline giving her the extra strength to stand. She began to limp away again.

The men were gaining. She could smell the sulphur over the other scents of the field, and she knew that she wasn't going to make it. She tried to find the dragon, to call on the pulse of power, but she couldn't remember how to do it. She felt delirious, fear and pain clouding her mind.

Then she felt an invisible vice around her neck, cutting off her blood supply. The world began to spin and go black. Her last sight as she fell to the ground was of the black wolf as it launched itself at one of the demon-men, ripping out his throat, before the other stabbed him in the ribs with a switchblade.

Her last thoughts were for Hedge - and then Tenney.

**

The giant pulled them roughly from the woodpile, his strong hands holding the struggling pair by their necks. Jude was forced onto her tiptoes, trying to stop herself from being dragged through the gravel. She tried to prise off the hand from around her neck, but the steel-like fingers and thumb were clamped from behind. She could feel them pressing on her carotid arteries, restricting the blood flow from her heart to her brain. She knew she wouldn't have long before she passed out. Or worse.

She turned her eyes as far to the left as she could, trying to spot Tenney. Being much taller than her, he was being pushed as much as dragged. He too was trying in vain to release the vice-like hand.

The giant brought his nose close to Jude's neck. He drew in a long sniff, a snake-like tongue flickering out, licking her jawbone. She felt a numbness spread out from the area, like his saliva—a last remnant of a body as good as dead—wanted to kill living flesh. She wanted to retch, but the hand never relaxed its grip on her. She was powerless.

She heard Tenney's outrageous cries, his struggles to come to her aid. She heard the giant's laugh and his little friends egging him on. Then one of them, Jude thought he must be the smart one, spoke up. His face was weasel-like, the cheeks sunken due to some missing teeth, and he spoke in a harsh, rasping sound that felt like thousands of spiders crawling up and down her skin.

"Gallagher said not to kill the Tether. But we can do what we like to the girl." He licked his dry, cracked lips.

Jude's heart began to race as she felt the panic rise. She tried to struggle some more, kicking out at the giant's knees, anything to get herself and Tenney away. The demons simply laughed at her futility. The fingers pressed harder on her neck, and the numbness was spreading, the blackness rising across her eyes.

Tenney fainted as his brain was denied oxygen. The giant didn't know what to do. He'd just been told not to kill him. He hastily dropped Tenney and Jude, looking at his comrades with a stupefied expression on his face.

Tenney, completely boneless, fell in a heap on the ground. Jude quickly scrambled over to him, felt his head, and checked his pulse. It was weak, but it was there. She lifted his eyelid, ignoring the demon-men as they argued about what they were going to do. The giant sounded genuinely terrified of the repercussions of his brutishness, but Jude wasn't listening. Tenney's eyes were no longer the beautiful hazel she was coming to love, but a swirling blue miasma.

A blue like Aura's.

**

Stace leapt at Gallagher, knocking him to the tiles. He reached down to tear out the demon's throat, to finish him until the next time Gallagher resurfaced, but he wasn't fast enough. A second demon leapt from nowhere, landing on Stace and causing him to fall off Gallagher.

It was a she-demon, small but as strong as a nightwalker. In her hand was a vicious machete, which she brought down towards Stace. He managed to stop the strike with both his hands, struggling to prevent the blade from slicing through his neck. It was dangerously close to a strike that could incapacitate him for days or, possibly, end him completely. He had to make a decision quickly: hunt Gallagher or defend against her. In the end, there really was only one choice, his eyes quickly taking in the battles around him.

So, he fought her.

Meg had sneaked up behind Gallagher, having mastered the silent walk. Most foes never knew she was there until she had a knife pressed to their throat.

But Gallagher was not one of these foes. Without even looking back at her, he delivered a punishing back kick. Meg stumbled back a few steps before adopting a new low stance, hands raised in a guard. Gallagher laughed, then charged. Meg threw him, using his own momentum to push him to the tiles. Gallagher rolled and stood back up. Meg glanced quickly to see Stace still battling with the she-demon above him, the machete points dangerously close to his neck. Then Meg turned back to Gallagher. Using her wolf agility, she jumped from one sloped roof to the next, the momentum aiding her in delivering a spinning kick to Gallagher's jaw and neck.

It should have killed him. She heard his neck snap and then the crunching, grinding sound as he turned his head slowly back to look at her. She saw the unnatural bend in the neck and the crushed windpipe. He smiled grotesquely. He still wore the cameraman's body, but now it was beginning to decay, his last vestiges of humanity having begun to die when the spine broke in two, only the demon's indomitable spirit holding him up. *What the hell is going on?* Meg thought.

The demon brandished the Cherubim Blade, its rubies gleaming in the starlight. He waved it in front of her face, taunting her. "I've waited two thousand years for this dagger to come back to me," he rasped, his voice barely audible to human ears due to the broken voice box, but as a werewolf, she could hear every word.

"You killed my brother with it, in Antioch. He should have stuck to the command, get the blade and get out. But he had to have some fun with that aunt of yours." He laughed again, as if the beating of her adoptive mother was a sweet, funny memory. Meg felt herself rising to the bait.

Stace finally managed to push the she-demon off him. He sunk his teeth into her neck, flesh tearing savagely, blood flowing. But the girl wasn't quite dead; she raised the machete and pushed it through Stace's neck. They both fell, as though in an embrace, upon the tiles of the

264

roof. Black smoke rose from her eyes, nose, and mouth and moved on, leaving the vampire as though dead.

"Oh, dear," Gallagher whispered cruelly. He smiled again. Meg could see a piece of bone sticking out from his neck. *How can he still be here?* she thought desperately. She swallowed, kept her stance low, her guard up, never taking her eyes off Gallagher.

"You know," he said, "if you hadn't killed my brother, your uncle as you believed him to be back then, I wouldn't have been forced to kill you trying to get this back." He waved the dagger again in front of her face, like it was a trivial thing. "And you and your boy wouldn't be slaves to the moon. So, really, all of this is your fault. Entirely."

He gripped the dagger more firmly and mimicked her stance.

Unable to bear his taunting any longer, Meg attacked first, sending out an inner crescent kick, trying to dislodge the blade from his hand. Trying to shake herself free from his words, and the truth they contained. He jumped back before she could make contact. And then he lunged. She barely had time to block him before the blade cut her.

She rapidly punched the pressure points in his arm, but it wouldn't deaden, his broken neck stopping the nerves from reacting. She elbowed him in the nose, blood spraying out, but still he kept coming. From the field, she heard a yelp—Hedge! Gallagher used her momentary distraction to lunge forward again. She barely moved fast enough to dodge his strike.

And then the house began to shake under her.

**

Tenney met Aura in the field. They looked around, seeing the stars and feeling the night breeze. The cows and the bull were lowing angrily at the back of the field. They saw the dark shadow-people closing in on the body in the mud. The green aura around the form of the wolf shone out like a beacon of light around its prostrate form.

Aura reached for Tenney's hand. She was glad he was with her. She didn't think she could do it alone. He smiled at her, encouraging her.

"I've got to do this, Ten."

"I know."

"Will you wait for me?"

"Always."

She looked at the field, imagined the winds behind the bull, and created a whip of air that smacked the bull's behind. Outraged already by the imposters in his territory, he bellowed and charged.

The shadowed figures didn't spot him until he had tossed one of them high into the air, killing him instantly, his demon smoke shooting out of him with a scream. Noticing that the wolf was in the path of the bull's rampage, Aura created a bubbled force field around the animal. The bull leapt right over him before turning to charge again.

This time, she put a bubble over her human body, protecting it. Feeling herself begin to weaken, Tenney sent her his strength, but she knew it was finite.

"Dragon?" he asked.

She shook her ethereal head. *"No."* She needed her corporeal form to create the dragon. In this form, it would kill them both.

Instead, she closed her eyes. Not that it helped; she still saw all things the air touched and moved. Her Elemental form was taking over again. She closed the hand that wasn't being held by her brother into a tight fist. She waited for the bull to finish its second charge as she didn't want it hurt.

When she was sure it was at a safe enough distance, she released her fist. The pulse moved the hairs of the bodies lying on the ground but passed right over them. The shadows that were still standing were destroyed completely. She shut their mouths and eyes, causing the smoke to be trapped in the dying bodies.

The sonic boom of the pulse blast shook the foundations of the buildings in the village, bricks falling from the church tower, the bells ringing in the vibrations. The Manor house shook violently.

**

The demons were closing in on Jude. She hunched over Tenney, holding him tightly to her, wishing she could tell him the things she wanted to. She kissed his face, whispered an apology, and turned her face, un-cowed, to her attackers.

The ground shook and the church bells rang.

**

Meg used the momentum of the house to deliver another punishing blow to Gallagher's stomach. He doubled over, the dagger loosening in his hand. She made a grab for it, but he tossed it high, the gold and red shining unnaturally bright as it spun in the air.

A black hole opened above it. A smoky hand reached down, grabbed it, and pulled it in. The portal closed, leaving only the natural night in its place. Gallagher laughed, putting his head back as far as his malformed neck would allow. He opened his jaw wide, and the demon left, flying out into the night.

Meg could do nothing for the man. He had been dead the moment Gallagher had singled him out. She quickly turned to Stace and pulled the machete out of his neck. His spine was almost completely severed. With the toe of her boot, she pushed the girl's body off him, then removed the body's zipped top. She tied it around Stace's neck, trying to hold together the cords and sinews as much as possible.

Meg lifted him up and carried him to the roof's edge. She leapt from the roof, landing softly even with the extra weight. Placing Stace safely out of sight near some bins at the back of the house, she cast her senses out to the field. Hedge was stirring. He was okay.

She began to run in the opposite direction from her son and went looking for Jude and Tenney.

**

Jude wasn't going to give these bastards the satisfaction of hearing her scream. She wouldn't scream. She wouldn't. But her resolve was weakening.

They came closer, their stench overpowering. A hand reached out for her, grabbing her by her hair. The giant pulled her off Tenney and held her aloft, this time her feet really were dangling. She wrapped a hand around his arm, trying to relieve some of the pain and the follicular stress on her scalp.

She thought she would finally pass out.

Then there was a bright flash.

A shining sword cut the giant's head off.

There were screams as the other demons were struck down.

And then warm hands carried her back to Tenney and placed her next to him. Those same hands rested on her head, and she felt the sensation of healing coming through the fingertips.

Jude began to come to fully, returning to the world. A face looked at her through the lightest gold-coloured eyes she had ever seen. He was inspecting her, his perfect quiff moving as he watched her like a bird of prey taking in its target before deciding to attack or not.

"Hmmmm," she thought she heard him murmur.

Meg called out to them. The face looked away. The figure stood up, his own light reflecting off his gold armour and the blood on his sword. He opened golden wings and vanished in another flash of light.

Meg ran over to her, holding her face, bringing her back fully to reality with a bang. "Who was that?" Jude asked.

"That was Paul," Meg uttered, as if a man with golden wings saving them was more of a hindrance than a blessing.

"Who?"

"The angel Stace met in a church today. Though you'll know him better as Raphael."

"WHAT?" There was yet another mythological creature for Jude to wrap her mind around. "As in the *Arch*angel?" If she hadn't already been sitting by Tenney, a hand on his chest feeling his shallow breaths, she felt sure she would have dropped to the floor. She looked down at him. His eyes were still swirling, blue.

"We've already told you about them," Meg said straightforwardly as she concentrated on checking Tenney over, patting his cheek trying to bring him back.

Jude felt sure that she had never heard mention of Angels in all the stories Meg and Stace had liked to tell them. "When, exactly, have you mentioned angels?" she demanded to know.

"They are the Councillors, the soldiers of the Creator."

Chapter 36

"What's wrong with him?" Jude asked.

Meg looked up at her and considered her answer quickly. They didn't have much time.

"He's between worlds again. With Aura."

Jude rubbed her face. "You mean he's dying?" Meg nodded.

"Yes. If we don't get them back soon, their bodies will die, and their spirits will be lost to us forever. Aura will become her element completely and Tenney will just be," she saw Jude's face pale, but she needed to know what was happening, "gone." Jude dipped her head.

"So, we've got to get them back. How do we do that?"

"When it happened at the weekend, Stace said that it was like they just made the choice. We have to hope they make the same choice now. And the only way to do that is to bring them together, physically. Remind them of this world. Give them something to live for." She stared deeply into Jude's eyes, yellow eyes meeting brown.

"Do you love him, Jude?"

She wiped away a slow tear as it rolled down her cheek.

"Yes," she whispered.

**

The spirits were fading, only their connection through their clasped hands giving them any form of reality. The air called to her, and a light beckoned him, tempting them away. There was so much fear and danger in this world. So much loss. Heartbreak. Disappointment. Pain. To give it all up, to move on, was too seductive. They looked at each other, their familiar features blurry and indistinct.

"I think I could keep you with me," she said. *"We can be whole, together. Forever. Nothing need separate us again."*

He looked at her. *"But you don't know that, do you?"*

She looked away, unable to lie to him.

**

Meg ran to find Aura and Hedge in the field. The first light of dawn was peeking over the trees.

Back at the gate, Jude leaned across Tenney, looking down into his face, fearing that she too might be dragged down into his swirling blue eyes. She gently pushed his hair off his forehead. His body was getting cold, his breathing becoming shallower.

Another tear fell from her eye, landing in his.

He blinked.

**

Something hit the spirit's face, running into his eye. His sister felt him start, in surprise.

"What's happening?" She felt his grip slacken.

He looked away from her, back towards the large house. His free hand floated to his lips as he felt a kiss. He remembered being kissed. *"Jude…"*

She tried to hold on to him, tried to keep him with her. Then he turned back to her. His megawatt smile beamed down upon her, anointing her.

"Love, Aura," he said. *"We forgot about love. Think about Mum, Dad, Sammy. Think about me, our love for each other."* He was facing her now, becoming more substantial, colour starting to define his features again. He held both her hands, lightly in his fingers. *"Think of Hedge."*

She gasped as a pleasant pain pierced her heart. *"Hedge?"*

She looked around. The wolf was crawling towards her body. He lay down beside her, his nose resting across the back of her head as she lay face down in the mud. She felt her hair stir as he breathed warmly upon her.

Then, in her mind's eye, she saw emerald, green eyes, looking at her like no one, not even Tenney, had ever looked at her. She remembered human bodies becoming like one.

She remembered love.

The spirits separated.

**

Whoomph.

Sounds assaulted him.

Whoomph.

Next came smell—the early morning dew, and the dirt beneath the gravel. The sharp tang of freshly spilt blood. And he smelt lilies, mixed with fresh grapefruit, finishing softly in a scent that was only her.

He could smell her.

Whoomph.

Then feeling returned. He felt the stones digging into his back. He felt her weight as she leant over him.

He felt her lips as she kissed him back to life.

Whoomph.

He could hear her, calling him back.

He opened his eyes. The sunlight streaked pink across the early morning skies. A bird flew over them, looking down at them. A peregrine falcon, his mind told him, randomly. Slowly, he lifted his hand and stroked the back of her head as it lay on his chest. Her eyes were closed, so he whispered to her, "My heart would hear her and beat, were it earth in an earthy bed; my dust would hear her and beat, had I lain for a century dead…"

Jude gasped and opened her eyes. He had returned to her! Her eyes were red-rimmed, wet with tears, and all she could do was stare at him. He pushed himself up slightly, resting on his elbows, and cupped her face, stroking her tears with his thumbs.

He brought her face to his and kissed her. He kissed her until they both truly believed that he had come back, that he had chosen life. That he had chosen her.

He kissed her to remember the physical world, the reason why he came back.

When they pulled apart, fractionally, her lips bruised from the intensity of his kiss, she looked at him, his beautiful hazel eyes staring back at her.

"Where's Aura?" he whispered into her hair. "And why are we surrounded by decapitated bodies?"

**

They ran together around the side of the building. Above them, the bats were returning to their roosts in the cavities of the old barn at the rear of the manor house, which acted as a garage of sorts. Jude ran on, but Tenney slowed. Something in the shadows had caught his eye.

A boot, at the end of a leg clad in black jeans, poked out from behind the bins. Tenney approached carefully. He pushed aside the bins and recoiled backwards, his hand over his mouth as he gagged.

Jude, realising he wasn't with her anymore, doubled back and found him retching in the cobbled yard. "What's wrong?" she cried, desperate in case he was going to leave her again. She rubbed his shoulders. "Tenney?" she asked, the anxiety and fear in her voice making him turn to look up at her.

He wasn't ashamed to let her see the tears freely falling from his eyes. He stood up, took her hand, and wordlessly led her to the leg. Stace was sitting, glassy dead eyes staring outwards, propped up against the wall of the house. There was a mass of blood down the front of his dark hoodie. His mouth was slack, his skin even paler than before. But it was the bloody top tied around his neck, crudely holding it together, that stood out.

Jude gasped aloud, her hand going to her mouth as her eyes widened. "I thought he couldn't die!" she whispered, shocked to her core.

"So did I," Tenney whispered back to her.

The morning sun's first rays hit his leg, touching a piece of exposed skin on the ankle.

"Tenney, look!" said Jude, pointing. "He's getting sunburn... How can he get sunburn if he's dead?" Tenney forced himself to hunker down closer, wiping his mouth and eyes, trying to look beyond the bloodied corpse in front of him, forcing himself to think objectively.

"Does Meg know?"

Jude shrugged. "I don't know. She didn't say much, just that she had to get back to Aura and Hedge." Jude decided to tell Tenney later about the Archangel's visit. She was still trying to process his arrival into her growing mental bestiary. The mention of Aura drove Tenney to make a decision.

"We need to keep him in the shadows until we tell Meg. She'll know what he wanted. How he wanted to be…" he trailed off. The thought that someone as strong and wise as Stace could be taken down seemingly so easily made him re-evaluate a lot of things. He needed to reach his sister and finish helping her to reconnect with him and the physical world.

Together, with as much respect for their fallen leader as they could give him, Jude and Tenney pushed Stace closer to the wall. Jude found an old tarpaulin in the barn, and they covered him, protecting his still sensitive skin from the morning light.

With a last look at the motionless shape, and a silent goodbye, they ran towards the field.

**

Aura stirred in the mud. Her mind was delirious from the loss of blood and her return to the solid world without Tenney beside her. Hedge lay at her side, keeping her conscious by touching her face with his cold, wet nose and licking her eyes if she shut them for too long. Then strong arms scooped her up and carried her away from the bull and his cows, away from the bodies in the field, trampled by the 2000-pound animal or pulverised by the blast that had seemingly come from nowhere.

She was carried through a small gate towards the back door of the church. Aura was lowered to the floor, her protector wolf standing guard, as the person effortlessly broke the lock and pushed the door open. She was again lifted up and placed gently on a pew.

Cool, cold water splashed her face and ran into her mouth. She smelt disinfectant as the person broke open a first aid kit and poured liquid onto some gauze. She cried out as the liquid was dabbed gently upon the cut on her chin, stinging and adding to the burn. She closed her eyes, wanting to succumb to the oblivion that called her as her human body began shutting down.

"Aura? Aura?"

Warm hands on her face.

A smell she recognised. Someone was calling her. Someone she had to listen to. She tried to roll over. She just needed five more minutes, and then she would get up. Only five.

The hands ran over her face again. She felt her shoulders being lifted, placed on a lap. Instinctively, she rolled into him. She placed a hand on his top and mumbled, "just five more minutes…"

**

Tenney ran straight into the church, Jude close behind him. Meg was leaning over Aura, dabbing something on her face. No, he recalled the sudden pain he had experienced. She was dabbing something on her chin.

Meg looked up as they entered, unsurprised to see him there. When she realised that Aura was slowly reviving, she knew that Tenney would be too. Their connection with each other was so strong that even distance didn't matter anymore. They had found their way back without being in close physical proximity. However, when she saw how weak Aura was, she knew that she had to get her undercover, somewhere Tenney would find them easily and where she could treat the vicious wounds on Aura's face and leg.

"She's cut her chin and the back of her leg badly," Meg informed him.

"I know," said Tenney, kneeling beside her, running his hands gently over Aura's face while observing her pale skin and her blue-veined eyes. Hedge whined beside him, never taking his eyes off Aura. He looked at the wolf and noted the bloody gash through matted fur on his ribs. "Why is she so ill if all she did was cut herself?"

Meg answered him, her centuries of experience patching up wounds giving her a better understanding of the body's workings than most modern doctors.

"Because it was barbed wire, and she fell in cow shit and mud. And because she left her body to defeat the demons." Meg clenched her jaw, anger pouring off her in waves at the fact that, again, they had almost lost her. She went to work on Aura's leg, disinfecting it and bandaging it. Aura barely stirred.

Jude watched from the sidelines, waiting to be told what to do. She looked up when a beam of light came through one of the windows, highlighting a golden angel. She turned her eyes to him, determined to understand why he had helped them. Helped her. She ran her hand over the top of her head. It was like the giant had never grabbed her there. There didn't seem to be any hair loss or bruising or swelling. Her neck had a mild, residual soreness where he had held her. But her scalp? Nothing.

She watched the angel in the window, silently beseeching it for answers, when a cloud rolled over the sun, and the angel faded away. As the window dimmed and the radiance lessened, she felt certain that there was something about Raphael that was familiar. Something about him that suggested they had met before…

"Aura? Aura?" Tenney whispered, his voice making Jude turn away from the window and look at him. Aura seemed to waken slightly at the sound of his voice. Gently, he brushed her hair, matted with muck, away from her face. He lifted her slightly and rested her head on his lap. "…five…nutes mor…" he heard her mumble as she turned towards him.

"Meg?" Jude spoke up. "We found Stace's body. We're so sorry."

"Did you move him?" Meg replied tonelessly. This night was a disaster. And she was alone to deal with the repercussions. For a little while yet. But a lot can happen in 24 hours, she thought reflectively.

"No," replied Jude. "Well, only so he was out of the light of the sunrise."

"Good." Meg wiped her hands on her trousers and stood up fluidly. "We have some work to do, you and I. Tenney, what time does your family leave for work and school in the morning?" Meg was all efficiency now.

"8, 8:30-ish. Why?"

"You can't take Aura home like that, too many questions will be asked. We need to try to ensure that none of us can be linked to this place. It's just nearly 7 now. You have to take Aura somewhere, keep her warm while you replace your father's key. Then look after her until you can get her home unseen. She won't die now that she's with you. Focus on the connection; give her some of your strength."

He nodded, already feeling the cord strengthen between him and his twin. "What will you do?"

"Jude and I have to bury Stace before your father and the owners return. We need to ensure there is nothing around to incriminate any of us. We won't have time to dispose of the bodies, but I'll give one of them the machete," Meg said, her eyes narrowing. Jude's eyes widened when she heard the word 'machete.' "We'll put it in the hands of one of the men in the field. The police will think it was a robbery gone wrong by a group of smack heads."

Jude couldn't fault her. That would be the conclusion she would have reached had she been first on the scene and was ignorant of the supernatural side to the proceedings.

"We'll meet you tonight, at the Lodge, okay?" Meg turned to the door, expecting Jude to follow her. "You'd better go," she said to Tenney. "I think Hedge will go with you. I don't think much will separate him from Aura at the moment." And with that, she grabbed Jude's arm and walked out of the church. Jude cast one last, desperate look at Tenney before exiting.

Tenney looked down at his sister, and then at the wolf. He suddenly felt very tired. He was giving Aura energy, and he felt the peace of the church beginning to weigh on his already burdened shoulders.

"Well, buddy," he said to Hedge, trying to shake the soporific effects of the building from his mind. "Let's go."

He picked up the first aid kit and rested it on Aura's stomach. Then, with great care not to cause more damage to her leg, he put one of his hands under her thighs and wrapped the other around her shoulders. He lifted her up, held her close so that her head rested on his shoulder, and carried her away.

Chapter 37

The day dawned brightly, with regular people going about their daily business. Cars left the village for the drive to Gloucester, a journey that typically took 20 minutes but could stretch to an hour and a half during the early morning rush hour, with traffic bottlenecking at Highnam and Over. Delivery vans drove through the village towards the town, while secondary school children grudgingly walked to the bus stop to catch their ride to schools scattered across the Forest and in Gloucester. None of them noticed the black wolf or the man carrying the young woman towards the front of the terraced houses.

Hedge had discovered all the hidden paths a wolf could take, allowing him to watch the Wiseman house without being seen. Confidently, he led Tenney and Aura home. They moved slowly, Tenney taking extra care not to jolt or stir the sleeping body in his arms. Exhaustion was etched on his face as he staggered forward. The wolf, now turned back to him, fidgeted on his front legs, anxious for these humans to reach safety.

Tenney's haggard face glistened with a sheen of moisture as he looked out from under his brow. He licked his lips as Aura stirred slightly. Taking a deep breath, he mustered the last of his physical energy and concentrated on giving her what remained of his spiritual reserves. He walked on.

As they approached the Barracks, the wolf stopped, alerted by a sound. His ears and nose twitched. Quickly, he led them through a gap in the hedgerow and into a field. Sam walked past on his way to catch the school bus, his ears covered by headphones and his head down, thumbs moving over the screen of his phone. Tenney watched him from the shadows, a part of him filled with concern for his semi-reclusive brother. Aura whimpered into his jacket, causing Sam to stop and look up. After a small shake of his head, Sam returned to the glow of his phone screen. Tenney breathed a sigh of relief as Sam showed no further sign of having heard them.

Ordinarily, on any other day, carrying his slight sister would have been easy. But today, he was overwhelmed with feelings of devastation, bereavement, and concern. Stace was dead, and his sister was injured and semi-conscious. Stace's blood wouldn't be able to provide another miracle cure—not that he wanted that for Aura. The blood lust was all-consuming, and it affected him still, though he didn't admit it to Jude and had tried, in vain, to keep it from Aura. For one such as her, he did not know what she would be able to do. He did not want her to ever find out. To carry the guilt that she may—no, that she would want to—kill the people she loved to get their lifeblood.

And so, he tried to heal her through their unique bond. Unique even for creatures such as them, or so they had been told. He could already feel her improving, although he would not be satisfied until he had cleaned the filth of the field and of that night from her.

As they approached the Barracks, he lead them to the old shed half hidden within the thick hedgerows. It was sometimes used as a hangout by the youths in the village. Tenney kicked in the rotten door, leaving it swinging off its rusty hinges. The wolf pushed past, nose to the ground, making sure it was safe. He growled, hackles raised, and crouched low, pointing with his whole body towards the shadows at the back of the space.

"What is it, Hedge?" Tenney asked, supporting Aura as the door frame supported him, ready for one of the smoke demons to appear from the shadows. Hedge tensed up his muscles and pounced savagely, catching a large brown rat between his jaws. He shook it and dropped its lifeless body to the floor. Then he sat on his haunches. If he had been a normal dog, he would have looked quite proud of himself, Tenney thought.

Everyone knew what went on in the shed. Tenney had used it himself on the odd occasion when necessity called for it, with Aura waiting anxiously in his room until he was finished. But none of the neighbours did anything to stop the kids. The consensus among the parents was that at least they knew where their kids were likely to be, so they could be dragged out if needed or kept a subtle eye on at other times.

There were some musty old sleeping bags in another corner. They weren't ideal, but they were all they had to keep warm. Tenney kicked them about to ensure there were no bottles, needles, or more rats hidden in their folds. Gently, he lowered Aura down. Hedge came and lay next to her, giving her his body warmth. Tenney went back to the door and propped it shut, enclosing them in semi-darkness.

He fingered the key in his pocket. They were too late to return it where Samuel had left it, but he had another idea. Walking around to the back of the house, he carefully opened the gate, praying its squeak wouldn't alert anyone to his presence. Creeping as far as he could up the garden path without the dogs hearing or the parents seeing him, he threw the key, watching as it thudded against the door. He crouched behind the greenhouse and watched. Samuel stepped out, a piece of toast and marmalade in his mouth, looked around, and muttered something to

Martha. As he turned back to the warmth of the kitchen, his foot kicked the keys. With a puzzled look on his face, he scooped them up, looked back down the garden, and returned to his breakfast.

Tenney rubbed his hand down his face. His father was going to have a very bad day. He felt guilty about that. But he hadn't asked the demons to come, hadn't asked for the bloodbath. Hadn't wanted Stace to die… He shook his head. He couldn't think of these things. Not right now. He had to get Aura well and get her home without arousing any suspicion. Then come up with another story to explain why their children had come home from a night out with more injuries. He crept back to the shed.

Hunkering down beside Aura, Tenney gently scooped her up as though she were a child asleep. Hedge, preoccupied with eating the rat, didn't seem to notice his own wound. In the dimness of the shed and under the darkness of his coat, it was hard to tell what was going on. Tenney felt the grubby bandages on his wrists. They were still bruised, and the burns from the ropes were raw, but he was healing. His neck was stiff and tender to the touch where the giant's hands had bruised him. He was certain there would be large purple contusions when he next looked in a mirror.

All these thoughts, mixed with guilt, threatened to drown him. He felt the tiredness creeping in. Looking down at his sister, he removed his jacket, leaving only his long-sleeved rugby shirt between him and the autumn-winter chill. He propped her up and sat behind her, letting her head rest on his chest, her legs between his. He covered her with his jacket to help stop her shivering. She continued to sleep. Hedge shifted closer, his huge, hairy body warming them both. Soon, Tenney felt his eyes begin to close, and he fell into a fitful nightmare.

**

Jude and Meg were burying Stace. Stace, the immortal, who couldn't die. Jude being lifted by the giant, shaken until her neck snapped. His heart breaking. His fears from the night manifested themselves in his dream.

And then the vision changed. He saw Hedge, half human, half wolf, fully dead. Meg, enraged by grief, running at the demon-men, only to be mown down by a hundred different weapons. Jude was rushing to get somewhere, anywhere away from him, fear burning brightly in her eyes as she looked back at him. A flash of golden light. Everyone was dead because he couldn't save them.

He saw rivers of blood flowing from him. He was lying in it, his unseeing eyes staring upwards as a winged figure flew over. The ruby dagger protruded from his heart. Stace was staring down at him, shaking his head in disappointment. The faint outlines of a bridge in the distance, and Aura screaming... Screaming so loudly...

He woke up with a start. Aura was in his lap, still asleep but thrashing as she screamed out in terror as she shared his dream. He held her tighter to his heart, letting her hear its frantic beat as he forced it to slow, to calm down. He put a hand on her matted hair, lowered his head to hers, and whispered softly to her. She slept on, calm and safe, soothed by his voice.

Hedge's ears perked up. His head moved around. Tenney looked at his watch. 8:32 a.m. From the driveway, he heard his mother's soft American voice echo.

"Another all-nighter then. I do wish they would tell us if they were staying out." He felt another stab of guilt in his gut.

"I'm sure they're fine, Love." Good old Dad. "We mustn't forget that they are adults; they have their own, er, friends." Tenney realised that his Dad probably hadn't told Ma about the entirety of their awkward conversation. God, Tenney thought, was that really only yesterday evening? The world for him had shifted again on its axis, and he wasn't sure how much more he could take.

He thanked God that Jude didn't demand more of him than he was able to give. That she kind of understood that if he had anything to give, Aura would always be the first to get it. But he realised with a start, as he finally admitted it to himself, Jude was a very, very close second.

He was shocked by the intensity of his feelings for her. No girl or woman had managed to tempt him back, willingly, more than a few times. She was like a drug to him. The more he took, the more she gave to him, and the more he needed her.

Thinking of Jude brought yet another stab of guilt as he was then forced to think about her grisly task back at the Manor and the dig. She shouldn't even have been involved, but it was like some 'higher power' had ordained they should meet, that she should save him from himself. That she should come to the Forest and pursue a relationship with someone like him, one which some people—including his own mother—would struggle to understand.

He closed his eyes and forcefully banished the thoughts from his head, returning to the present and listening to the sound of a car door closing, followed by his father's car engine's distinctive spluttering noise as it struggled to start on a cold morning. He heard it's tyres crunch on the gravel as his dad reversed from their driveway, his mother presumably in the passenger seat, and then drove down the track, away from their hidden children, and away to their soon-to-be very bad days.

Tenney waited another five minutes, then summoned the last ounce of his dwindling strength to lift Aura and the first aid kit. He carried her out of the garage and around to the back gate, pushing it open with his hip. Hedge sat on the grass beneath their bedroom windows, watching as Tenney awkwardly fished out the keys from his pocket and let them in. In a blur of black, white, and brown, Bo and Jess shot past him to the newest object of their affection, rubbing their heads against the face of the wolf.

Tenney called the dogs back indoors and shut the door with his foot, all the while supporting Aura in his shaky arms. He gently laid Aura on the sofa in the kitchen and encouraged the dogs to follow him to their beds, tossing a treat at their feet. Swinging his sister back into his arms, he began to climb the stairs and head to the bathroom.

The house was very quiet. He could hear Jess scrabbling the blankets in her bed as she created a little nest to sleep in; the ticking of his father's old Grandfather clock in the dining room; the buzz of the boiler and the percolating noise of the coffee pot. He could hear Aura's soft, slightly wheezy breathing.

He gently lowered her onto the bathroom mat and began running warm water into the bath. It wasn't so long ago that she had nursed him here, cleaning his wounds and easing his pains after his trance-like walk, and then crawl, to the Fort. Again, he wondered how this had happened.

Tiredness was making him see things differently. He couldn't see the good; all he could see was that his sister was suffering, and he felt powerless and useless. Idiotic even. He felt torn in too many directions between being a brother, a son, a lover, a friend, and a protector. He felt the little bomb in his head begin to tick as his defences were lowered. Deep in his soul, he felt the blood lust withdrawal start to gnaw at his insides. Desperate, he sought out Aura's calming inner voice, finding only garbled, incoherent nonsense as her brain responded to the fever that had started in her body.

Tenney's knuckles turned white as he leaned on the edge of the bath and told himself to get a grip. He told himself it was exhaustion. He'd feel better when she felt better. Running a hand through his hair, he turned back to his sister.

She was finally awake, watching him. His mind probe had nudged her, helping to bring her back to consciousness as she naturally responded to his desperation. He smiled down at her and helped her to sit up. Gently, he removed her muddied watch, placing it on the sink, and then he took off the two jackets—his and hers.

Her t-shirt was soaked in blood and stuck to her skin. She cried out when he tried to remove it. Her jeans weren't much better, having adhered to the wound behind her knee. So, he removed her shoes and socks, and gently lifted her up again, placing her into the warm water still fully clothed.

The shock of the water on her feverish body was too much, and she clung to him, trying to get out again. Tenney disentangled himself from her, took off his boots and socks, and slipped into the water behind her, fully clothed. His presence in the tub soothed her, and she lay back against him.

"The old moon laughed and sang a song," Tenney whispered two verses of another poem, one their parents read to them as they drifted off to sleep, calming her further. *"As they rocked in the wooden shoe, And the wind that sped them all night long Ruffled the waves of dew...."*

Aura fell asleep again, lulled by the words, the warmth of the water and the sound of his heartbeat.

**

They had been happy, living in ignorance. As long as they weren't apart for long, they were content, just the two of them, living only for each other. He knew it sounded selfish, but he had always believed it was more selfish to deny the connection, to act like they weren't closer than most siblings. On some subconscious level, he had always known they were one person in two bodies, that Aura, in the womb, could only be Aura because of his DNA and soul.

He helped her out of the brackish water, sitting her on the lidded toilet and wrapping her in a towel. Then he proceeded to empty the tub and began refilling it with clean water. He took off his soaked jeans and quickly went to their rooms to fetch her robe, a pair of jogging bottoms, and a clean t-shirt for himself. His mind was a whirl of how things should have been, could have been, if he had never left to go to Lincoln.

Tenney helped to remove her ruined clothes and the sodden dressing on her chin. The cut was deep and jagged. He winced at the memory of the shared pain. It had hurt her. A lot. He looked at the cut on her leg; it too was bad, but not quite as deep, not quite as vicious. He clenched his jaw in frustration. He was the one who got the hurts, bore the brunt of their pains; his was the body that was marred by old and new scars. He could take it. Aura should never have received these. He should have been with her.

But if he had been with Aura, Jude would be dead. The choices left up to him were impossible to make. He wished that Hedge wasn't a slave to the wolf, that he was human and could have helped Aura with more ease. Instead, he was hampered by a handicap that wasn't of his making.

Aura still hadn't spoken, mentally or verbally, but she was listening to his thoughts; he could feel her on the periphery.

"It's not good, Aur," he started to say. They had always been honest with each other. "I'll clean it and the leg as best as I can, but you may need to get your chin stitched up. You'll probably need antibiotics as well for the fever."

She nodded her ashen face once and looked away. "Can you get back in the water? I'll wash the muck out of your hair." He tried to smile again. Gingerly, she stood up, using him as support, and stepped into the water. He washed her hair and her back as she huddled in the tub.

When she was finally clean, he tenderly dried her, wrapped her in her dressing gown, and redressed the wounds. Tidying the bathroom and wrapping their ruined clothes in one of the towels, he carried his bundle of clothes and boots in one arm, the other wrapped around Aura's waist.

They walked to his room. He pulled back the covers of his bed, and she climbed in. In the distance, he heard the sirens of the police cars as they arrived at the Manor House. It was nearly 10 a.m. His dad would've found the disastrous scene and called the cops. He hoped that Jude and Meg had gotten away in time.

Tenney looked out of his window as he drew the curtains closed. The wolf was still sitting there, his shining green eyes fixed on the window. He nodded once. She was okay. Hedge blinked, stood up, and moved away, leaping over the gate, back to the woods. He understood that Hedge would need to feed and rest to allow his speeded-up healing to happen and regain his energy. Tenney also knew that in a few hours' time, there would be green eyes staring up at the window again. He felt strangely reassured for the first time that morning.

Turning back to his sister, Tenney noted that she had begun to look better. The dressing on her chin was clean and white, and her eyes were more focused, clearer. She watched him as he came back to her. He slipped between her and the wall, pulling the duvet over them, cocooning them, and shutting out the world. She moved her back towards his chest, and he wrapped his arms around her.

"You know, it's not so bad," she whispered.

"What?"

"Knowing what we are."

"Have you been reading my thoughts again?" he teased her gently.

He felt her smile in response. "I can always feel your thoughts. They are always in my head, like a constant background hum. They've always been there, even before we knew how to recognise them. Before we learned to use the skills. That's why I couldn't breathe when you went away. Because suddenly the reason to breathe had gone. But now, we are strong enough to keep the connection even over hundreds of miles. And for that alone, I will always be grateful to Meg and Stace, and to Hedge, for teaching us about our true selves."

She felt his arms tighten around her. He knew exactly what she meant. Knowing was a powerful thing. It told them why they were so different from other people, why Aura never quite fitted in. Why he got so rage-filled and depressed.

It had also brought Hedge and Jude into their lives. He knew that for all the heartbreak, neither of them would change that.

"You're right," he whispered back, his mouth close to her ear. "It's not all bad."

"I'm glad you went to Lincoln, Ten…" she mumbled as she began to fall back to sleep. Tenney looked up and marvelled at her indomitable, positive nature. He held her closer and placed his chin on the top of her head.

Tenney finished the poem, *"Wynken and Blynken are two little eyes, And Nod is a little head..."*

Then he fell into a dreamless, healing sleep.

**

Sam couldn't concentrate. His maths teacher had asked him several times to stop daydreaming. He stared out of the window, replaying the events of that morning in his mind. He swore he felt eyes watching him as he walked down the lane towards the bus stop, Imagine Dragons thumping their tunes through his headphones as he typed a message to Theo.

In the seconds of quiet between tracks, he thought he heard Aura whimpering in pain. There was definitely something dodgy going on with his half-brother and sister.

Chapter 38

Aura woke up with a gasp. She blinked rapidly, rubbing her eyes with her fingers, trying to dispel the memory of the shared dream in the garage, which had skittered around her subconscious as she slept. She saw his blood, pooling across the grass… His blood was her blood…

Her head ached and her mouth was dry, but she felt better. The fever had broken, likely due to the energy he had given her to heal. It had been a foolish thing to do, as she had felt him weaken, but still, he gave to her. He had always been like this, giving all of himself to save her. She shivered despite his body warmth behind her and the duvet that covered them.

She would have done the same for him when he had a concussion, but Stace had been right. The energy it would have taken to heal such a severe wound would have killed them both; she understood that now.

Thoughts of Stace caused her to reflect on snippets of conversation she had overheard in her delirium. Surely Meg and Jude weren't burying Stace. He couldn't die. She felt certain she had misheard. At the back of her mind, she felt grief readying itself like a wave to wash her away if she let it. She decided it could stay where it was until she had absolute proof that their mentor had died. Behind her, she heard Tenney snore. The sound made her smile, and she rolled over.

He was lying on his back, his right arm still under her head, fingers dangling over the side of the bed. His left arm was flung over his head and across his eyes. His left leg was propped up on the foot, as though, even when asleep, he was ready to leap into action to defend her. He often adopted this pose when he was truly, deeply asleep. She saw his chest rise with each deep breath and heard the small snore that accompanied it.

It was one of the few times she could see his one and only tattoo, hidden under his upper arm between his armpit and elbow. Lines from the family poem. Lines that meant something to him, something he kept hidden and close to himself.

Gently, she placed her hand on his strong heart. Its beat was regular, nothing stopping it. No dagger. No blood loss. His fingers twitched slightly as she touched him. She smiled at his humanness, his physicality. Oh, how she loved him, this brother who was so much a part of her she wasn't always sure where she ended, and he began. Her other half, the keeper of her soul, her tether to the world.

Her own heart started to beat in rhythm with his as she tried to return some of the energy he had given her. She felt a warming glow under her hand as he absorbed it. She realised then that he was utterly exhausted. She wondered when the last time was that he had slept so deeply, so dreamlessly, without worrying about her or Jude. She smiled a little as she thought of Jude. He would say, smiling that megawatt smile of his, that the sort of worrying he had with Jude was a good, fun worry. But it still disturbed his sleep.

She knew, from their connection, that when he was with someone in that way, he gave them everything, his full attention. Until they were finished, and he could return to her again. But that in itself was exhausting. And with Jude, a person he was falling in love with, that giving of himself to her was a hundred times more.

Her brother, the giver. She reached up and gently kissed the tips of his fingers, noting the rope burns on his wrists. He must've taken the dressings off this morning after they got wet, she thought. The burns were still ugly red welts and yellowing bruises, but the healing process had begun, the welts scabbing over nicely.

Then she looked at his neck and the purple bruise in the shape of a giant hand, wrapped around him like a macabre scarf. His Adam's apple moved as he swallowed between the marks left by the thumb and fingers. Her hand gently ran over the contusions, feeling his beard stubble under her fingers. He smiled, his eyes moving under his eyelids as he began to dream.

Quietly, she slipped from the bed and padded gingerly to the bathroom.

It was still a bit of a mess. Mud on the linoleum and grime around the rim of the bath. Aura set to work, finishing putting the room to rights before she could bring herself to look in the mirror. She scrubbed the bath and the floor until she was satisfied that there was no evidence of their adventures in the night. Tenney will have to burn the ruined clothes, she thought.

When she was satisfied that the room was as it had been before they returned home, she finally stood at the sink and looked at her face. She saw the dressing on her chin. It was larger than she expected. Carefully, she began to peel it away, wincing as it pulled on the cut.

Nausea washed over her, and she quickly leaned over the sink. Her chin and the soft part under her mouth were bruised. Running from her bottom lip, over her chin and under her jaw, was an angry, zig-zagging cut. It wasn't closing as she had hoped. She remembered Tenney saying something about getting it stitched up, and she knew now that he was probably right.

She wasn't a vain girl, her seemingly moveable features meaning that she could never fully rely on her looks. But the disfigurement to her face still upset her. She felt herself begin to sob, all the shocks of the night beginning to overwhelm her.

"Aura?"

She turned around, unsurprised to see Tenney standing in the doorway, his eyes still sleepy, and his hair messed up. He walked in, closing the door behind him. Opening his arms wide, she went to him.

**

They were sitting on the sofa in the living room, drinking mugs of tea and watching an antiques programme on the telly when Sam came home from school. They heard him drop his bags at the door, the dogs greeting him, and then:

"What's happened to you? Ma's gonna be so pissed!" Tenney tensed at his brother's insensitivity, his emotions still too close to the surface. Aura placed a calming hand on his knee.

"I fell over, Sam," she said steadily, "and hit my chin and cut my leg."

"Are you okay?" Sam thought back to the whimper of pain he thought he had heard that morning. He genuinely cared for his sister; she was always easier to get along with than his older brother. Sam had always looked forward to the times when he and Tenney got on, but those occasions were often few and far between. Aura was calm, serene even. She more often than not remembered to ask him about his day, whereas Tenney just seemed to ignore him.

Sam had to admit that most of the time he felt awkward around Tenney's charisma and confidence. It didn't help that at school, people still spoke about his brother like he was some sort of god, while Sam was the nerdy, shy younger brother.

"I'm fine, Sammy. We're just waiting for the emergency clinic to start this afternoon so Ten can take me to the doctors for a quick check-up." She smiled at him, trying to reassure him, all the while conscious that Tenney was quietly fuming beside her.

"Okay," said Sam, still unsure. "If you're sure you're going to be okay, I'll just, ya know…"

"Yeah, Sam. Go and play on your little games," Tenney said coldly. Aura slapped his knee, not too softly.

"Ignore him, Sam. He's exhausted." She smiled again and watched as Sam, head down and shoulders drooping, exited and made his way to the stairs.

"Well, that was mean!" she rebuked Tenney. He just put his head in his hand, resting his elbow on the arm of the sofa. His other arm, across Aura's shoulders, squeezed her to him.

After another half an hour, their parents arrived home, coming down the garden and through the back door. They saw their mother supporting their father. His face was crestfallen, and he looked like he was carrying the weight of the world. Their mother's face showed her shock.

-*Ready?* Tenney asked Aura. She nodded.

**

Sam: *Theo? Are you there?*

Theo: *Hey Sammy. I'm here. Whassup?*

Sam: *T is being a dick. A is hurt, maybe badly.*

Theo: *What happened?*

Sam: *Dunno. Remember when I told you about thinking I heard A this morning? Something's definitely going on and I don't know what it is. But it made T more of a wanker than before.*

Sam: *Theo??*

Theo: *We should meet up, yeah?*

Sam sat back from the computer screen. His heart began to race. A slow smile spread across his face.

Sam: *Yeah.*

Theo: *Soon. Will be in touch. See ya, Sammy.*

**

Martha walked Samuel through the front door and into the heart of the house. He was almost mute with shock and stress. She had received a phone call at the school from his assistant, Nick, asking her to get to the dig ASAP. Fortunately, one of her friends was about to leave and offered to give her a lift.

The site was swarming with police. Yellow tape was everywhere. She gasped, putting a hand over her mouth when she saw the body bags and the tents, the men and women in coveralls scouring the area near the woodpile. A policeman stopped her and asked who she was. After she mumbled who she was there to see, he escorted her to Samuel.

He walked her around to the front of the house. One of the Smith-Frobishers was raving to another officer outside, making all sorts of threats. People were around one of the dining room windows, brushing powder over the sill. In the cow field towards the church, there were more men and women, covered head to toe with masks over their mouths, walking around more of the white tents. There was more yellow tape.

Samuel was sitting in the entrance hall of the Manor, his head in his hands. Martha ran to him, crouching in front of him, placing her hands on his knees. "Samuel!" she cried, "what's happened? What's going on?"

He raised his head, and she gripped his hands.

"I came on site this morning," he started. "There were all these men, these bodies…" He trailed off. Horror struck Martha full in the gut.

She pulled him to her in a hug, "Oh, my darling!" she began saying.

"It gets worse, Martha."

She sat back a bit and looked at him in shock. "How can it get any worse, Samuel?" she asked, disbelief running through her words.

"The dagger. I discovered later, during the police sweep of the house." He stopped, drawing a tearful breath. "It's gone, Martha. Someone stole the dagger."

They had had to wait all day, interview after interview with the police and then representatives of the University. It was a tornado of activity. Samuel, in shock, struggled to answer the easiest of questions. Finally, they let her bring him home, where she planned to get him a nice mug of sweet tea and make him a relaxing warm bath. And then, when he was feeling better, they would discuss what was going to happen next.

Within seconds of walking through the door and seeing her older children, that plan went out of the window.

"Family meeting!" she shouted. "Everybody! Kitchen! NOW!"

Obediently, they followed her to the kitchen table, Sam rushing down the stairs. The dogs retreated to their beds, knowing when it was better to stay away from the humans and keep quiet. They sat around the circular kitchen table and watched Martha carefully place her hands upon its surface as she composed herself.

She looked up at her family. Her husband looked broken, the highs of the days before followed by a crash no one could have foreseen. It would take time, patience, and the love and support of his family to help him through this phase.

Next, she turned her head to Sam. Her youngest son, pale, with bags under his eyes. He had his father's straight brown hair, without the curl that Tenney's had. He stared back at her with brown eyes that seemed too big for his teenage face. He was thin and shorter compared to his father and brother. She worried about him, despite what she said to Samuel, that this was just a phase. He wasn't making real friends, meeting real people, or seeing the beauty in the real world. She knew he struggled with the closeness of the twins, often feeling ostracised, alone, and lonely. She wished with all her heart that Tennyson had shown more than the occasional interest in his brother.

Thinking of her oldest child brought him into focus next. He leaned back in his chair on two of its legs, making his legs jump and twitch as he struggled to contain whatever pent-up aggression he was feeling inside. His arms were defensively crossed over his chest. She saw the painful marks around his wrists that had been hidden under the bandages and wept inside for him.

To her, they looked like rope burns, ropes that he had had to fight free from. She knew he was a fighter; all through secondary school, she received warnings about his behaviour. She remembered being called into the school during the twins' first term in their very first year, her son black-eyed and with bruises on his knuckles, but sitting there in the office looking very much as he did here in their kitchen—fully justified in his actions. When she asked him what had happened to bring her to the headmaster's office, he told her that they had taken Aura away from him. When she asked the head teacher what he meant, she was shown Tenney's schedule. He didn't share a single class with his sister throughout the whole week. She respectfully asked the head teacher to put them in the same classes, and his behaviour improved. Until they were separated again. She shook her head to clear the memory. She had tried to make peace with their relationship a long time ago.

Martha looked up his body to his head held proudly, his chin jutting out slightly as he dared her to say the wrong thing. Beneath the stubble from a few days of not shaving, she saw new bruises coming around from the back of his neck. She narrowed her eyes and looked closer. They looked like finger and thumb marks, from a very large hand. Too big for the policewoman to have inflicted.

There was more here than rough bedroom games. Something he wasn't divulging to her. But she was certain that Aura was in on the secret.

Aura was sitting as though Tenney was a magnet that she was drawn to. She naturally leaned towards him, although they didn't touch. Martha took a good look at her daughter.

She was pale, a lot paler than usual. Her eyes had a slight sheen across them, and she squinted like she had a headache. Her hair seemed lank, like all the life had left it. She looked small, fragile. On her sweet face was an ugly white dressing. Martha felt sure that she had seen her limp as she walked to the table.

She took another calming breath. "Right," she began, matriarch of her small family. "First thing first. There has been an incident at Dad's dig. Several bodies were found, in various degrees of," she swallowed and stammered slightly, "er, destruction. Police think that it was a drug-related incident. It will be on the news, so be prepared for questions. OK? But don't tell anyone anything." They all nodded.

"Secondly, the priceless ruby dagger was stolen. How they found the safe is anybody's guess. Apparently, the door was ripped off by something very strong." The twins shared a glance. Samuel frowned slightly when he saw it.

"If you hear anything, or know anything, you must tell us or a police officer. OK?" Again, they all nodded.

"And thirdly – Aura, what the *hell* has happened to your face?"

Aura shifted in her seat, Tenney's chair legs came down and he sat forward. *Battle lines being drawn,* Martha thought.

"I fell," she said weakly. "We'd met up with some of our friends in the pub. We decided to go for a walk, and we had to climb a fence, and I er, fell off, landed in the mud."

"Where were you Tenney?" Martha asked her son; her tone was harsher than she had intended.

He flicked his eyes to Aura. "With Jude." he said.

"OK. We'll be having a chat about that soon, mark my words. Aura, have you had any treatment for the wound?"

"We were just about to go to the emergency clinic," Tenney said, moving to stand up. Martha stopped him with one hand up.

"No. You will stay here. I will take Aura."

The twins shared another glance again. Sometimes it felt like they could communicate silently, the way they would instinctively know what the other was about to do, where the other one was.

"Ok." said Tenney, finally giving in after a few tense moments.

"Aura, get your coat. Tennyson, make Dad a strong, sweet tea. Sam, no more computers tonight. I want to see you downstairs, with the family when we return for supper. OK?" And with that last issued 'OK', the family were dismissed.

**

Tenney stood at the kettle, waiting for it to boil on the hob, playing absently with the tea bag, talking silently with Aura. She was in the waiting room, Mum trying to mine her for more information.

-Stay strong, he told her.

"Son?" Tenney jumped. He hadn't heard his father come in. He turned to him, gave a small smile, and leaned back against the counter.

"Tea's nearly ready, Dad. I'll bring it through for you if you like?"

"No, son," said Samuel. He really did look terrible, and the guilt began to twist in Tenney's gut again. "I thought we might have a chat."

Samuel stood still, his hands in his pockets, but Tenney could sense that he was struggling to hold back his temper. Tenney pushed himself up straight and crossed his arms again, forming a barrier between them.

Samuel was always slow to anger; Tenney had only seen it a few times in his whole life. This was the first time that he had ever seen it directed solely at him. His eyes positively burned with it.

"What is it, Dad?" he asked carefully.

"Yesterday, I swore I put the safe key in my bag," Samuel said, his voice trembling with barely suppressed rage. "Yet this morning, I find it lying by the back door."

"Okay…" said Tenney.

"I want you to tell me, no bullshit, no more lies. What happened last night?"

"We went out."

"All night?"

"I was with Jude."

"So where was your sister?"

"With some other friends."

Samuel stepped closer to his son, removing his hands from his pockets and looking Tenney squarely in the eye. He pushed his finger into Tenney's chest, stabbing him repeatedly as he made each statement.

"So you're telling me that your sister, the one person you have been surgically attached to for the last 21 years; the sister who couldn't cope with your move to Lincoln, the one YOU chose over a bright future; you are telling me that you left her 'with some other friends', in a field where she was injured whilst you spent the whole night shacking up with a woman god only knows how many years older than you?"

Tenney swallowed. He was shocked by the venom in his father's voice. He looked down at the floor, his face red.

"Don't lie to me, Tenney. Were you at the dig last night?"

Tenney went cold, as he felt Aura gasp. He looked up. His father was so close to him that he could see the blood vessels, bright red and bulging in his eyeballs. He was past the point of stress, and paranoia was feeding his wrath.

"No," said Tenney.

"I said. DO. NOT. LIE. TO. ME!" Spittle flew from Samuel's mouth as he enunciated each word. "There were bodies in the cow field. Did you know that? Trampled by the bull, others bitten by a large dog. The rest were pulverised by a blast that shook the village. Forensics are still finding parts of them all over the land. The detectives think they may have been chasing someone. There were smaller footprints in the mud, a place where a small person fell. Blood on the barbed wire. Pieces of blue stretchy denim caught in those barbs. And I come home to find my daughter has the wounds that a fall on barbed wire would cause."

Tenney shuffled his feet. He opened his mouth to speak. "No," Samuel said, quieter this time. "You do not get to talk yet. I have not finished." Tenney clenched his jaw, his fists tightening.

-*Calm*! Aura pleaded.

"And then the officers went to the church. More blood, several muddy footprints. These officers are clever folks. I overheard one of them say that a hiking boot, size 13, belonging to a male, average height of 6'4" to 6'5", carrying something or somebody, walked in and out of the church. Those same footprints were found heading back up the hill into the village. Black canine hair found on the same route and inside the church. They lost the trail due to the gravel, but it seemed they were headed up the lane to our house."

Tenney kept his mouth shut, but now he stared his father in the eyes, defiantly.

The kettle boiled on the stove, filling the kitchen with steam and its piercing whistle.

"And then I find this, behind the bathroom sink, encrusted with cow shit, mud, and blood." From his pocket, he pulled out Aura's watch. They had forgotten it. After Aura had seen her face in the mirror, Tenney had been more concerned with her wellbeing. It must have fallen. "*Dammit*!" he thought.

-*It's ok!* He heard Aura's voice clearly in his mind. -*We'll be home soon. Just hold on!*

"We weren't there, Dad. We don't know anything about what happened."

"I DO NOT BELIEVE YOU!" Samuel shouted again, brandishing the watch in Tenney's face. He looked like his heart had broken, like Tenney had let him down in the worst possible way.

Maybe I have, thought Tenney. I will never be able to make it up to him.

"Dad?" Sam stood in the doorway, a quivering Bo in his arms. Samuel turned to him.

"Go upstairs, Sam. Don't come back down until your mother comes home. Take the dogs with you. I need to speak to Tennyson alone."

Sam was visibly distressed to hear his brother and father arguing. Shock shone out of his face, tears rolling down his cheeks. He turned and bolted with the dogs to his room, slamming his bedroom door behind him. The heavy bass of his music reverberated through the floorboards.

Samuel turned back to Tenney. He sobbed, trying to hold back the tears. "You know, son, I thought we had a close, honest relationship. From the moment I held you in my arms, you were my boy. *Mine*." The poignancy of those words was lost on Tenney.

"My first child. And then I learn things that will break your mother's heart if she ever found out. And I realise, I don't know you at all. Not. At. All." He turned away slightly and wiped his eyes. "You have broken my heart, Ten. I don't think I will ever be able to trust you again. You have put your sister in unimaginable danger. You keep coming home with different bruises and scrapes, and now rope burns and pressure bruises from a strong grip around your neck. The sex games excuse won't wash with me, son." He sounded exasperated, tired, his fingers pinching the corners of his eyes above his nose.

"If I learn that you were at the dig last night, and you were involved and that you got your sister involved, you will not be welcome here again." He dropped the watch to the floor at Tenney's feet. "You have broken my heart, Tenney," he repeated as he walked away, his head bent, a defeated man.

Tenney rubbed his face. He felt his eyes burn with unshed tears.

-Aura? He knew she had witnessed the argument through his eyes and ears. She would think on her feet and back him up to Mum. He ached to see her, to make sure she was okay. But he couldn't stay in the house. Not at the moment.

-I've got to go. I'll be okay. I'll come home tomorrow. Hopefully, Dad will have calmed down.

-I know. Be safe, Ten. I love you.

-Love you too.

He switched off the stove, the room immediately quietening down as he walked out of the kitchen. He found his trainers and jacket, slipping out of the house into the cool evening air.

**

Sam: *When shall we meet?*

Theo: *Halloween? I'll be in your neck of the woods. I've heard there's going to be some fireworks in Bristol.*

Sam: *Great!*

Theo: *Can't wait to meet u Sam.*

Sam: :)

Chapter 39

By the time Martha and Aura arrived home, Sam was in his room, his music loud enough to be heard all the way down the lane. Samuel and Tenney were nowhere to be seen. Martha rushed up the stairs, entered Sam's room, and told him to turn the music off and go downstairs. He could choose the film that she was determined to make the whole family watch together.

Next, she entered the room she shared with Samuel. He was lying on the bed in a semi-foetal position, arms wrapped tightly around his body. She sat beside him, resting a hand on his shoulder.

"Tenney and I had a fight," he said simply. Her poor, sweet, gentle husband, she thought. Her heart broke for him, for the distress he felt. She massaged his arm, letting him speak in his own time.

"He went out. We probably won't see him until tomorrow." Samuel wiped his eyes. "It's been a shit day all round really."

"I know."

"And then I go and accuse Tenney of putting his sister in harm's way. Of being at the site last night."

"Oh, Samuel, my darling, no," she said soothingly. "Aura told me what had happened. They were at the Fort. It was in one of the fields there that she fell."

"What have I done?" Samuel cried, desolation sweeping over him as he finally realised, he had allowed his fears for his children, the shock of the theft, and all the deaths at the Temple to grow into paranoia. He had pushed away his son, a man, it was becoming abundantly clear to him, that he knew very little about. The only thing he was sure of was Tenney's sense of righteousness, his impassioned anger. It would take him time to fully trust his father again, if Samuel realised as he recalled Tenney's admission the night before the dagger was lost to them, he ever really had to begin with. Something had shifted, and the gulf between them felt insurmountable.

Martha hugged him to her breast, letting his tears soak her top. "Tenney knows you are under a huge amount of stress. He'll come around. He loves you, and tomorrow you can both forgive each other. It'll be alright, my love."

She felt him nod as he hugged her back tightly, his chin digging into her as though he needed to bury himself deep in her love for him.

"Aura's okay. The doctor had one of the nurses put a few stitches in her chin, and they cleaned up her face and leg. She's got some antibiotics to fight any lingering infections and has been told to rest for a few days. But she's okay."

"Thank God," he replied simply.

"We're going to watch a film of Sam's choosing. Do you want to come down and join us?" she asked him, gently smoothing back his hair, her touch easing some of the tension from his brow.

"In a bit, love. I just need to regain my equilibrium." Martha nodded, kissed him on the mouth, and joined her children downstairs.

**

Aura was curled up on the sofa, a mug of hot chocolate in her hands, with three more steaming mugs on a tray on the coffee table. One of the dogs was sprawled across her lap, snoring peacefully. Sam had the controller in his hand, flicking through a vast array of films until he found one he was happy with. Aura shifted slightly to make room for her mother, who sat between her and Sam. She handed Martha a mug and leaned back, resting companionably against her shoulder.

"So, what are we watching?" she asked.

"X-Men," Sam replied.

"So, what's that all about then?" She smiled as both her children groaned in exasperation.

**

Tenney waited outside the hotel for Jude. She walked out of the front door, kissed him lightly on the corner of his mouth, and led him to her Jaguar. They drove into the woods to the Lodge, where Meg and Hedge were waiting for them outside.

"How is Aura?" Meg asked Tenney as he got out of the car.

"She's okay. She's home now," Tenney replied. Hedge looked at his mother, cast another glance at Tenney, and slunk off into the night.

"Where's he going?" Jude asked.

"To sit in our garden probably." Tenney smiled down at Jude, half his mind with Aura, telling her not to be surprised if she spotted green eyes in the garden, and warning her not to let Dad see Hedge. A black dog would only lend credence to his suspicions.

They all walked into the Lodge and sat in the semi-warmth of the sitting room. Tenney told them all about Aura's recovery, their shared dream in the shed, and his fight with his father. Jude rested her hand in his, squeezing his fingers.

"So, what happened after we left?" Tenney asked.

"We did what we said we would do," Meg replied matter-of-factly. "We fixed the scene. We couldn't do much for the two on the roof. Hopefully, they will be discovered, and if they're not, an anonymous tip-off will be sent to the cops." The way Meg said it, Tenney and Jude were certain that this wasn't her first cover-up.

"I'm sorry about Stace," he said meaningfully.

Meg started. She looked confused, as if Tenney had said something completely alien.

"Thanks, I guess. But there's not much to be done until tomorrow night. So, I suggest the only thing we can do is get some sleep, then we can all meet here tomorrow night to discuss what to do next."

Tenney got to his feet, helping Jude up. Meg didn't seem remotely grief-stricken; her comment didn't make any sense to him. Tenney thought she would be out there hunting down the demons who had killed her friend, especially a friend she had known for a lifespan which no human could fathom.

"Okay, tomorrow night," he said, deciding that exhaustion was making him misinterpret what he was seeing and feeling. He and Jude bid their farewells to Meg and walked back to the car.

"So, what did you do with Stace?" he asked her.

"Meg was adamant he be buried quickly and deeply. We found the mound of waste earth beside the dig and buried him there. It is probably the one place the cops wouldn't think to look." He marvelled at her ability to take part in something so grim and distressing, breaking laws she had sworn to uphold to keep them safe.

"Thank you," he said simply.

"I got the impression that Meg would try and move him tomorrow night, but I don't know if that's such a good idea. The police will be there for a while yet. I would give it a week, at least. But she kept saying 'no, he'll move tomorrow.'" Jude shrugged her shoulders slightly, like she too found Meg's behaviour odd.

"I think it must be shock. I mean, they've been friends for near enough two millennia. Imagine that kind of grief, huh?" She gave him a nervous smile, shook her hair back, and opened the door of her car.

Tenney looked back at the solitary light in the Lodge before climbing in beside her. She drove them back to the hotel, and without a word, led him inside.

**

A breeze brushed her cheek. Jude stirred, sticking a hand out across the bed. She felt nothing but empty sheets. Alarm made her sit up and scan the room. The window was open, the curtain wide. Tenney had positioned the rattan armchair so he could sit and look out into the night.

Silently, she got out of bed and moved behind him. She felt him purr as she ran her fingers through his hair, down his neck, and across his broad shoulders. His hands gripped the chair's armrests, but he stayed still and let her work her magic.

Bending down, she lightly kissed his ear, then kissed the finger marks the giant had left on his neck. It was like she was trying to kiss him better. Tenney shut his eyes, wanting to tell her that it was working, but not wanting to break the spell she was casting over him.

Suddenly, as her hands moved down his chest, he turned in the seat, grabbing her waist and pulling her over the back of the chair, onto his lap. She lay across him, her head resting on his shoulder. He nudged her nose with his, and when she raised her mouth, he kissed her.

**

Before he carried her back to the bed, they talked. They shared memories and asked questions to learn more about each other. Jude felt his fingers as he lightly stroked her spine, up and down, setting her nerves tingling.

"You guys really like poetry, don't you?" she said.

"You worked that out all by yourself?" he teased her. She pinched him and laughed. "Mum used to read us poems instead of fairy tales. Said it would give us a better understanding of the real world. She said that fairy tales weren't real. I would challenge that now, after all we know."

"Why 'Maud' in particular?"

"You know what, I don't know for sure. I think Mum was recommended it by some old guy when she studied in America. Warning a young student against the perils of falling in love, I guess. Obviously didn't work, she met Dad that year and before she knew it, she was married with twins."

Jude swallowed and looked away in case he saw the secret his parents had shared with her in her eyes. He lifted his hand to her chin and gently turned her back to face him.

"What is it?" he asked softly.

She looked back at him and said, "'*It is better to have loved and lost, than never to have loved at all.*' Isn't that Tennyson?" she whispered. He stroked the hair away from her face and smiled broadly.

"It is." She settled back onto his chest.

"My dad was very proud of his American roots," he felt her smile. "He always had bikes; I couldn't remember him without one. He was a highly skilled mechanic. Always tinkering, at work and at home. Engine parts scattered everywhere. It drove Mum half crazy. I think she would have all the bike and car parts in the world in her house now if it meant he was alive again." She paused, and Tenney waited for her to pick up her story again.

"When he first moved over here to be with my Mum, he missed his bikes so badly. She bought him a Harley Davidson as a first wedding anniversary present. I still don't know how she afforded it. Before Dad died, alongside her reporting, she volunteered for a homeless charity, organising soup kitchens and such. She always said, 'You don't need lots of money, Jude, just enough for a roof over your head. You'll always be rich with the amount of God's currency we have in our family.'" She smiled again.

"I remember sitting on Dad's lap as he rode around the streets behind our house. Highly illegal, of course. But it's my favourite memory, leaning back against him, feeling him there, knowing he was keeping me safe. It was so much fun!"

"Why didn't your mum move to the States?"

"She would've. But she's afraid of flying."

"How'd they meet then?"

"He'd come over here for a bike tour, working as a mechanic. He told me that when he saw Mum, he knew she was the only one for him. I miss him so much." The breeze from the open window caught a lock of her hair and blew it towards him, sending out the smell of lilies and grapefruit. He hungrily breathed her in.

"What's God's currency?" he asked, resting his face next to hers.

"Why, love, of course."

**

Dawn's light came through the still open window, gently waking her. Jude hadn't spent a full night with Tenney before, at least not in bed, together like this. She took the opportunity to observe him while he was still, fast asleep.

He lay on his back, his left leg bent at the knee and resting lightly on the foot. His right leg was out straight, with a slight twist at the ankle where he was relaxed. They were athletic legs, coated in a layer of dark hair over his apparently perennial tan. The sheet covered his waist, but only just. One small tug and she would see everything.

Her eyes moved up past his waist, past the old and new bruises and scars on his body. Like his legs, his torso was finely sculpted, athletic. Strong. His still young muscles clearly defined. There was a small freckle beneath one of his nipples.

Next, she saw the dark hair of his armpit; his left arm was flung over his face, obscuring all but his cupid's bow lips and strong, stubbled chin and jaw. Underneath his arm was a tattoo, a few lines written in black calligraphy handwriting. The characters were small, tucked between the muscles. A private tattoo, only for him and those he chose to show, close to his heart. She was amazed she hadn't looked at it closely before. She looked closely at it now. Another poem? she thought.

The writing was so small and tightly joined together as it slanted towards his elbow; it was hard to make out. But she was curious. Gently, she leant across him and ran a finger down the tattoo. His right hand, spread out on the bed, fingers pointing towards where she had been lying, twitched. Then moved up and rested in the small of her back, his finger lightly making circles there.

She kept her finger on his tattoo. She could see him smile under his arm. "Who wrote this?" she asked.

"Tennyson," he replied from under his arm.

"What does it say?" she shifted a little on his chest, her hand wrapped lightly around his arm, her thumb making similar movements over the tattoo as the ones his fingers made on her back.

Without moving his arm from his eyes, he recited the words by rote: "'*From the meadow your walks have left so sweet, That whenever a March wind sighs, He sets the jewel-print of your feet, In violets blue as your eyes, To the hollows in which we meet, And the valleys of Paradise.*'

"I thought of Aura when I first heard it," he explained. "Even before we learned of her, er, history, I always thought of her as the wind, a breeze that supported me, held me up. Held me together when I felt I was losing control. She has a strength that not many people can see. But, if you're not careful, it feels like she will slip away from you and be carried off." His shoulders shrugged a little, causing his hand to travel further up her back so now his fingers traced the outline of her shoulder blade.

"It's a bit more from Maud," he added almost as an afterthought.

"Ohhhh," she laughed, "more Maud!" She drew the name out, so it hung in the air.

Quickly, using his foot to push him over, he laid her back on the bed, his full weight pressing down on her, his hazel eyes staring down into her brown ones.

"Yeah," he said, roughly. "More Maud…" And he kissed her and he loved her.

Chapter 40

The last days of October promised good weather, clear and bright. Halloween was a week away, along with the convention and fireworks party at Clifton. Aura lay in her bed and rested her hand on the bedroom wall. Gently, she tapped on it; tap tap tap-tap-tap tap.

Nothing.

Tenney had stayed out all night. Her palm spread out on the dividing wall, imagining that he was on the other side.

-Aura?

-Hey.

-You ok?

-Uh huh. You? She felt him smile and stretch, the warmth of another body beside him. She chuckled.

-Hedge stayed in the garden all night.

-Did Dad see him?

-I went out, on the pretext of getting some fresh air, and sat in the shadows with him for a while.

-I'm sorry he's not with you properly, Tenney said, heartfelt.

-Me too. She tried to hold in the sob, but it was impossible now to hide anything she felt from him.

-I'm coming home! She felt him begin to move, extricating himself from his lover's arms.

"No!" she exclaimed. The word escaped her lips as quickly as it echoed in her mind. She didn't want to ruin his time with Jude, but a small, selfish part of her wished he would ignore her protestations, choose her as he had so many times before, and come home. She quickly dampened that thought before it could grow into something ugly.

-I'll hop in the shower and head over, ok?

-No, Ten. Seriously, I'm fine.

-I need to speak to Dad anyway, he said. He went quiet for a while, and when he was back, she felt the water splashing on his head.

-Jude says hey, laughter in the background.

-Hey back, Jude. Tell her I'm sorry for dragging you away.

-She's cool.

-Ten?

-Yeah?

-Don't rush, ok. He smiled. She didn't think Jude would let him rush off anyway. They did sound happy, and if Tenney was happy, then she was happy. She *was* happy.

Aura pushed back the duvet and slipped from the bed, walking in bare feet to the bathroom. She looked at her face in the mirror, then twisted around to look at her leg. The doctor had told her to keep the bandages on for at least a week. Absently, she wondered if Stace would teach her how to morph her face, like Hedge had seemed to think she could do...

The breath went from her lungs as she remembered that Stace was dead. The man, she couldn't think of him as anything but a man, who had become their mentor was gone. As she felt the grief she had pushed back begin to swarm forward, threatening to make her crumple, she heard a knock on the bathroom door.

"Aura, love? Are you ok?"

It was her dad. She opened the door and went into his arms. He held her tight, soothing her. Telling her it was ok. Everything was going to be ok. He would make things ok, he promised her, though he had no way of knowing what it was he promised her.

**

"AURA?" Tenney burst through the front door. Martha stepped out of the kitchen, her dressing gown wrapped around her, a mug of coffee in her hands.

"Nice of you to come home," she said, semi-sarcastically.

Tenney ran his hand through his hair. She noted the bags under his eyes; his tiredness was palpable.

"Ma, I'm sorry, but I've got to find Aura." She didn't have time to say anything more as Tenney rushed past her and ran up the stairs two at a time. Martha shook her head at her son's strange behaviour and returned to the kitchen. Bo circled her legs, wagging his tail and looking up at her longingly. Martha moved back to the bottom of the stairs and called up to him.

"Tenney? Don't be long! This dog is desperate for a good walk!"

"No worries, Ma!" he called back as he disappeared down the landing.

He found Aura with their dad in their parents' bedroom. Samuel had his arm wrapped around her as she rested her head on his shoulder. As soon as Tenney had felt her cry out in grief, his body responded to her pain. He had apologised to Jude, who he left in the shower, quickly dressed, and ran home.

He stood in the doorway, unsure if his father would welcome his presence, but he was desperate to comfort his twin.

"It's alright, son." Samuel, dressed in his t-shirt and bed shorts, his hair and beard messed up, still looked drawn, haggard, and sleep-deprived, but he wasn't angry anymore. "I'm sorry about last night. It was a pretty awful day. I shouldn't have taken it out on you."

Tenney shifted his weight from foot to foot. He didn't know where to put his hands, eventually opting for his pockets, rolling his shoulders up and forward as he looked down at his feet. His throat was choked up. He nodded, finally looking at Samuel.

"I'm sorry too," he said, coughing a bit to help clear the emotional blockage.

Aura rolled her eyes, wiping away a stray tear at the same time.

"Men," was all she needed to say, astounded at how few words they needed to use when making up. She gave Samuel a kiss on his cheek, another small hug, and stood up. "Thanks, Dad," she said.

Tenney moved to let her past, gave a small smile and a little wave to his dad, and followed her to her room, shutting the door behind them.

"I'm sorry you left Jude like that," she said. Tenney flopped down on her bed. He was sorry too; it had been about to get interesting. But he'd make it up to her later, he thought, smiling. Aura threw her top at him.

"Stop thinking so loudly! I really don't need to see that image!"

He laughed long and loudly, the tension leaving his body. He rolled over and propped himself up on his elbow, his head resting on his hand. "How's the leg?"

"It's okay," she said, showing him the long bandage running behind her knee before pulling on some thick tights and her skirt. "Why?"

"Fancy walking up to town with me and Bo? I want to go to the bookshop."

Aura grinned at him, cocking her eyebrow. She knew exactly what he was going to buy and approved wholeheartedly.

"Yeah, alright," she agreed, quickly adding a proviso, "so long as we can get a bacon butty for breakfast?"

"Deal!"

Slowly, Tenney, conscious of Aura's limp, walked up the hill towards the town with his sister and their little dog. About halfway, they spotted Hedge, his loping form coming casually across a field to join them. To the casual passer-by, he looked like a large black German Shepherd, trained well enough not to need a leash (unlike the terrier, who kept stopping as he found new and exciting smells).

Aura rested one hand in Hedge's fur, her fingers penetrating it to feel his skin underneath. Her other arm was linked through Tenney's.

Now she was truly happy.

**

Jude looked at herself in the mirror, checking that her hair was adequately scraped back so it wouldn't interfere with her bike helmet. Satisfied, she picked up her backpack, helmet, and keys, and left her room to ride into Gloucester.

She was heading into the city to find a dress for the fireworks party in a week's time. She had considered taking the Jag, but that morning she felt a bike ride would help dispel some of the excess frustrations Tenney had left her with. She also wanted to feel close to her dad. After their intimate conversation the night before, memories had been conjured up, and she needed to do the thing her dad loved. She needed to ride her bike, as fast as she legally could.

As she passed the reception counter, the porter beckoned her over. In his hands was a package wrapped in brown paper, her name written on the front, and a letter.

The writing looked familiar, and she remembered the scribbled note from Tenney atop the party invitation. Walking out of the hotel and towards her bike, she opened the package. Inside was a book – *The Complete Works of Alfred, Lord Tennyson*. A page had been dog-eared – *Maud: a Monodrama*. She smiled again.

Turning to the front. She saw inside, in the same handwriting as on the paper bag, the opening line to another poem was scrawled:

i like my body when it is with your body. It is so quite new a thing....

Jude felt herself blush a little as she read line of poetry by E.E. Cummings. At the end of it, Tenney had added another note, confirming that it was him who had sent the book to her. It read:

It's not Tennyson, but I think it says it all. Love, T x

Jude closed the book and held it to her chest. She beamed.

Underneath the package was another, more official-looking letter. It was from Gloucestershire Constabulary. As she walked forward, she slipped her finger under the envelope flap.

It was a request to go to Gloucester Police Station for the transfer interviews. 10 a.m. on the 31st of October. She only had until that date to decide whether to stay and build a new life here or return to Lincoln and all that was familiar.

**

The local newspaper board outside the village shop carried the headline:

MASS MURDER AT MANOR!

Tenney ducked into the shop, handing Aura the dog's lead. Hedge had disappeared again as soon as they neared the village. When Tenney came out of the shop, he had several papers tucked under his arm.

"It's gone national as well," he said. "Come on, we can't go home yet. We need to know what people are saying." She nodded.

They walked to the park near the estate, stopping at the road to let a large van pass before crossing over. When they reached the park, they sat on the swings, Aura with a paper while Tenney scrolled through the news stories on his phone. All the headlines carried similar front-page headlines to the one plastered across the local paper:

BODIES FOUND AT FOREST DIG!

ARCHAEOLOGY DIG DEATHS!

MACHETE ATTACK IN QUIET GLO'SHIRE VILLAGE.

They all told the same thing, in various degrees of elaboration: a drug deal gone wrong, heroin found in the pocket of one of the dead, decapitation, mutilation, body parts, the Bulls attack, the machete discovered in the hands of a dead man. As they read, Aura noted Tenney rubbing his neck where the giant had gripped him.

Then there was the strange earthquake that shook the village the same night.

Now it was her turn to feel unsettled. She had vague recollections of their time in the *inter duo mundos*. She shuddered as she thought how easy it would have been to disregard the physical world and become a monster.

Her father's name caught her eye in the *Daily Mail*:

'Prominent local archaeologist from Bristol University, Dr. Samuel Wiseman, had, only two days ago, made the discovery of his life. At the feet of the statue dedicated to the Roman goddess Sabrina, he found a very rare dagger, wrapped in the material of a Celtic noble woman's dress. That same priceless artefact was discovered to have been stolen by one of the perpetrators who escaped.

'Police believe that the men were intoxicated by drink and drugs, and in their inebriation fought together. Police are asking for any witnesses to come forward. If you were there, or saw anything, please call the Serious Crime Division of Gloucester Constabulary on the number below. Police would particularly like to speak to the two women seen entering and leaving the site that morning.

'The University offered no comment, but it is believed that Dr. Wiseman will be taking compassionate leave due to stress after making the grisly discovery yesterday.'

"Tenney, we need to warn Jude and Meg," she showed him the story. "And make sure Dad's okay."

Tenney nodded, agreeing before he asked her another question.

"Aura," he said, dropping the paper under his feet. "Do you remember much from that night?"

"Bits and pieces," she replied.

"Do you regret coming back?"

She thought on the question. Taking his hand in hers and swinging lightly, she looked over to him through the chains.

"No. We must always come back, Tenney. We can't give in to the temptation, the power, of staying there. I don't know if I would be able to keep you with me for one. And think of the pain we would cause the people we love if we chose that option, effectively dying in their eyes. Unimaginable. We must always choose life, no matter how hard it can be."

He looked away, over towards the edge of the park where they could see the forested hill fort. Green eyes sparkled at them from the undergrowth.

"You really love Hedge, don't you?" he asked.

"As much as you love Jude," was her simple response. "You haven't told her, have you?"

"I don't think I really admitted it to myself until last night. I never thought I would be able to love someone like that."

"I know. Me either."

"What are we going to do, Aura?"

"We are going to live, Tenney. Live and love." She smiled at him. He turned back to her and mirrored her completely.

Chapter 41

They heard the crowds before they saw them. In the relatively short time they had been in the park, news crews, reporters, villagers, and neighbours had all congregated outside the front of their house. A hubbub of activity. Tenney recognised Debbie, her voice lively as she chatted animatedly to a man with a recorder, no doubt spinning a web of lies.

His whole body tensed up as he pulled the dog's leash taut, causing Bo to become tense as well. Aura paled at the sight. There was their home, the curtains drawn tight, and a couple of police officers standing guard outside, stopping people from knocking on the door. She looked up at Tenney and noted his steely, determined eyes.

Someone on the edge of the crowd turned around and looked at them. Aura breathed a small sigh of relief. It was Jude. She walked over, dressed ready to go out on her bike, her helmet slung over her arm, a bag on her back.

As she approached them, she gently turned them around, walking them towards the track that led behind the house.

"Better not go that way," she warned them solemnly. "I was about to go to Gloucester when I saw the crowds walking up the lane. I tried to get in, see if you were okay. But the officers turned me away."

"How long have they been there?" Tenney asked. He was looking straight ahead, his jaw clenching and unclenching as he struggled to hold in his emotions. Jude could feel his muscles, tight beneath the sleeve of his hoodie.

"Just under an hour, I guess. How long have you been out?"

"Longer than that. We left fairly early. When we walked past the shop, we saw the headlines, so I got some of the papers. We've been at the park reading them."

They approached the back gate. A reporter and a man with an SLR camera stood by a solitary policeman. The constable saw the trio coming up the track and stopped them with one hand up.

"Sorry, no visitors. The family aren't taking any callers." Jude blanched when she saw Tenney square up to the officer. He stood a good few inches above the man, radiating anger and ferocity. His jaw was clenched, and his eyes burned with a barely contained rage.

Before he could make the situation worse, Jude pushed between them.

"My name is Police Constable Jude Marcello, Lincoln police force. These are Tennyson and Aura Wiseman; they live here and would like to go home."

She immediately regretted saying their names so loudly in front of the reporter who had found his way back here. Straight away, his photographer started taking pictures, whilst he stuck a recorder under Tenney and Aura's noses, asking inane questions. Then the reporter seemed to register their names, linking them to a previous story a few weeks back.

"Hey – aren't you the 'miracle twins?'" He used his fingers to make air quotes around the word "miracle." "Twins who brought each other back from the brink of death? Yeah," he said, more confident now, "yeah, that's right! You are! So how do you feel – your family being linked to death again?"

The ferocity Tenney was sending out from every pore of his body as he turned from the policeman to the reporter would have made a wise man cower in fear. His muscles tensed, and his fists clenched at his sides. He pushed Aura behind him towards Jude, who gripped his sister's upper arms to steady her. Tenney stepped into the reporter's personal space, using his full height to intimidate. His breath was heavy, and his eyes were dark with fury. He didn't utter a word, just glared down at the reporter as if he were scum.

Eventually, the reporter realised he had overstepped, lowering his voice recorder. The long-lensed camera continued clicking in Tenney's face. Casually, Tenney lifted a hand, still imposing his indomitable will, and grabbed the camera by its lens, yanking it from the reporter's hands. The strap around the reporter's neck pulled taut. Tenney ripped it over the reporter's head, pulling him off balance.

From the house, they heard a door open. Samuel rushed out. "It's okay, Officer!" he shouted down the garden path. "Those are my children and their friend. Let them in!" The officer, keeping a careful eye on Tenney, stepped aside and ushered them through. Tenney moved back a few paces and casually tossed the camera into the dense hedgerows which marked the periphery of the hill. The reporter and his cameraman gaped, open-mouthed, as Tenney stepped towards them again and growled, "No comment." He turned, placing himself between Aura and Jude, wrapping them in his long arms, and walked the girls and the dog up the path.

Samuel quickly got them inside, locking and bolting the door behind them. He leaned back against it, breathing a sigh of relief. Aura had her head buried in Tenney's chest, her hand clenching and unclenching his top. He turned to his father.

"What the hell?" he asked coldly, his voice a low growl.

Samuel blanched slightly, his heart pounding with the same shock Tenney had felt the day before when faced with his father's rage. Jude thought he looked terrible. She remembered the happy man from the twins' birthday, full of life and optimism, spinning his wife around the kitchen as he serenaded her with poetry. This man was a shadow of that man. He looked up and seemed to notice her properly for the first time.

"Hello, Jude," he said quietly. "You'd best come through. We're in the kitchen." Tenney rubbed Aura's back and led her down the corridor, Jude following. Samuel brought up the rear. They found Martha and Sam in the kitchen. Martha was still in her dressing gown, and Sam had slumped down in his seat, trying to make himself look small, Jude thought. They weren't alone.

Martha leapt up when she saw Tenney and Aura. The three of them embraced, her relief palpable having them back home safely. She took Aura from Tenney's arms, brushed the hair from her face, and then looked her all over. Aura's eyes were red-rimmed, wet from the tears shed and unshed. She tried to smile at her mother but couldn't quite manage it.

Jude watched Tenney. She saw how hard it was for him to let someone else look after Aura. His tell, running his hands through his hair until the long strands stood up straight, betrayed his anxiety. His eyes darted around the room, never settling, as if he were searching for threats.

Samuel pushed past her and sat next to Sam at the table. Martha pulled out a chair and made Aura sit down. Tenney leaned on the kitchen work surface behind his sister, his posture tense and protective. It was only then that Martha spotted Jude. She froze, one hand tightened into a fist. Jude was about to make her excuses, leave quietly and quickly.

She turned towards the door.

"Hey!" she heard Tenney call out. "You're not going anywhere! Ma - don't blame Jude – none of this is her fault. She can help us make sense of what's going on, help us move forwards. Translate the cop jargon," he said, casting a sideways look at the two interlopers in their kitchen.

They couldn't be anything but detectives.

Jude gave him a small smile, grateful for his support. She turned back to Martha.

"Let me help you, Mrs. Wiseman." Out of respect for her, she had reverted back to using her title. Martha looked her up and down and considered what Tenney had said.

"Tenney's right. You can stay." She turned back to the table, sat beside her daughter, and held her hand.

Jude took a deep breath, held out a hand to the first detective, and introduced herself, giving her rank and number. "I'm on, er, leave…" she ended the introduction.

"My name is DCI Mike Gwynne. This is DC Nora Crane. We were just giving Mr. and Mrs. Wiseman an update on the incident. We've suggested that they might want to spend a few nights in a hotel, in the city maybe, just until things quieten down a bit."

Gwynne was a man in his late 50s, Jude guessed. Slightly portly, but experienced, although she thought he probably hadn't had many crime scenes like this to deal with in the Forest of Dean. The other one, Crane, was a younger woman, gaunt-looking and serious. She watched everything, taking notes without saying a word. Jude knew she would have to be careful, keep everything professional, so that Crane didn't catch any irregularities. She wished she could pass that message on to Tenney, but she didn't have that connection which he shared with Aura.

Tenney still radiated repressed fury. An emotion like that made people think less clearly, and she was worried he would inadvertently say something that would make the officers take a closer look at his alibi. It would be better if he said nothing at all. With that in mind, Jude moved and stood next to Tenney, seeing Martha flinch as she saw her lean against her son.

Jude had done it on purpose. It was partly to keep him in line if she sensed he was about to react. But also, just to let him know that she was there for him. She felt him relax slightly against her.

"What have you learnt so far?" she asked. She was in full cop mode now. She knew exactly how to proceed.

"We're still searching the property. We think that the thief may have climbed out of a window and escaped across the roof. The guy must've been like a monkey. It's one hell of a climb up there." Gwynne tutted and shook his head in disbelief. "We have a cherry picker, and forensics will be heading up there as we speak. But so far, the conclusion is that it was a twofold operation. The first was the theft of the artefact. The second a drugs deal gone very wrong."

"Are you looking for anyone else?"

"Only the two women seen this morning, but the description of them is hazy. Not even enough to tell you age, race or hair colour. So, unless they come forward, that's a dead end." Gwynne didn't notice Jude tense slightly when he mentioned the two women, but Crane's gaze narrowed.

Jude forced herself to relax again.

Gwynne continued, "A large black dog was also seen, so we're checking all the local dog owners as well."

Aura twitched. The sharp eyes of Crane again caught it. "Are you okay, Miss Wiseman?" she asked, a little suspiciously. "Do you know someone with a dog like that?"

Aura stared up at her, wide-eyed. A slight breeze ruffled Jude's hair. Uh oh! she thought, Aura's feeling trapped! Tenney looked sharply at his twin, even more aware of her current state. He turned to the Detective Constable.

"My sister has been unwell, and we've all had a nasty shock. So back off!" he growled the last words.

Crane looked suitably abashed. Jude softly rested a hand on his arm. She would've suggested that Martha take Aura upstairs, but she sensed that if Aura went out of the room, Tenney really would be uncontrollable.

The breeze died down as Aura composed herself. "I have seen a dog like that. It belongs to someone from the town. Don't know who though." She lied fluidly. Jude wondered if Tenney was telling her what to say.

Crane scribbled in her notebook.

"Can you think of anything else, Mr. Wiseman?" Gwynne asked. Samuel shook his head. No. He couldn't think of anything.

"Have you made a decision about what you're going to do? Whether you stay here or go to a hotel?"

Martha looked at her husband, her children. She nodded. "Yes, we'll go to Gloucester. Stay in a hotel there. I'll phone Sam's school. I'm sure this qualifies as special circumstances, and they'll let us take him out for a few days, especially this close to the half-term break. We could make a holiday of it! Spend some time together." She tried to smile, make it sound positive.

All of her children became animated, talking at once, imploring their mother to reconsider. Martha held her hands up!

"Whoa there!" she said. "One at a time! Sam?"

"I'm meeting a friend next week. I can't miss it!" Martha looked at her son's earnest face. She had never heard him talk so passionately about meeting someone in the real world and she felt bad to dash his hopes, to ruin his week.

"I'm sorry, Sam. You'll have to rearrange it. There will be plenty of time to meet up with friends after all this is past us. You'll enjoy it more without any of this," she waved her hands in the air to signify the current situation. To solidify her position, she played the "You're only 16, you stay with us," card.

Next, she looked at her elder children.

"We're staying here," Tenney said simply. His voice didn't brook any argument.

"I'd prefer it if you came with us," Martha replied, but she knew she couldn't force them to come. They were 21, adults. Old enough to make their own mistakes.

"We're staying," Tenney said again.

Martha wondered when her son had gotten so cold.

Aura was a bit more diplomatic. She looked at her mother, rested a hand on her arm. "We'll stay, Ma. Keep an eye on the house." Jess chose that moment to jump up at Martha, resting her front feet on her thigh. Aura laughed a little, it was perfect timing from their elderly pet! "And who will look after the dogs if we're not here?" she asked.

Martha stroked the dog's head and long ears. She smiled back at her daughter.

"Okay," she grudgingly submitted. "But you have to phone me, three times a day – at least! Keep us updated on everything. We'll phone round the hotels, find some rooms, and let you know where we are. If either of you change your minds, then you come join us, ya hear?" She stroked her daughter's cheek.

Sam pushed his chair back, the legs scraping loudly and painfully on the floor. "That is so unfair!!" he shouted. "Why can't I stay with them?"

Samuel had finally had enough, his temper flaring again. "SAM!" he slammed a hand on the table, making everyone in the room jump. "Your mother has spoken. You are coming with us because you are still a child. You will stay with us because we are your parents. That is final. Now, go and pack. Tell your friend you're sorry, you'll have to arrange to meet another time."

Sam angrily pushed his chair over, barely missing Jess's tail as it hit the floor. The dog yelped and darted under the table.

"HEY!" Tenney shouted at him, scooping the quivering dog up into his arms. His voice was a mix of anger and concern, his protective instincts flaring.

Sam had hot tears in his eyes. "Fuck off, Ten." He turned and stamped up the stairs, slamming his bedroom door with a force that rattled the house.

Martha put a hand over her mouth and closed her eyes, slumping back in her chair. The weight of the situation seemed to press down on her shoulders. Samuel turned to his other children, his expression stern but weary.

"You will behave when we are away. You will inform us as to your whereabouts. You will not, under any circumstances, go anywhere near the Manor or the Temple. Do I make myself clear?" His quietly forceful voice was more effective than if he had shouted. Both Tenney and Aura nodded, their faces set in determined lines.

He turned to his wife. "Martha, go and get dressed and packed. I'm thinking Gloucester is too close. You always said you wanted to visit Stratford upon Avon. We'll try the hotels there, try and get a suite so we can keep an eye on Sam. You're quite right, we'll make it a holiday." He moved to stand wearily up. "Everything will be better when we get home," he said quietly, hopefully.

Martha leaned over the table and squeezed his hand, her eyes filled with a mixture of sadness and determination. She made her excuses to the Detectives, apologised for Sam's outburst, and walked to the door.

When she reached the door frame, she rested her hand against it and tapped her fingers before turning. "Jude, may I have a quick word with you?"

Jude nodded, suddenly nervous as she followed Martha out of the kitchen. They stopped in the hallway; Martha's arms were firmly crossed over her chest, her eyes hard and unyielding.

"I don't know what sort of relationship you have with my boy, or where you may think it is going. But I want you to remember, he is 21. Impressionable and as far as I know, the only girl he has ever hung around with is his sister."

Jude hid her gasp of surprise – Martha really didn't know about Tenney's past experiences. She wanted to say that Martha should be warning her about Tenney! But she wasn't going to ruin her rosy-eyed view of her son. He could shatter that impression all by himself, if Martha ever decided to talk to him like the man he is, and not the boy he was.

"If you ever hurt my son again, physically or emotionally, I won't care that you're a cop. You won't know what's hit you." Jude looked suitably contrite, remembering that Tenney had told Martha that it was sex games that had caused the ligature marks on his wrists. "But that being said, they will need someone to keep an eye on them. So, I'm going to trust you. I'll give you my cell number. You call me if anything, *anything*," she stressed the word again, "gives you cause for concern."

"You can bank on it, Mrs. Wiseman." Jude's voice was steady, but inside she felt a mix of fear and determination. Martha turned to the stairs, she put one hand on the banister about to pull herself up.

"It's Martha. Mrs. Wiseman makes me think of my mother-in-law." And with that, she left Jude and went to get ready to leave.

**

Things moved quickly after that. Samuel had found a nice hotel near the centre of Stratford. He booked a small suite with two bedrooms and a sitting room. They packed up, Sam looking miserable the whole time. Finally, it was time for them to go. They kissed Tenney and Aura goodbye, ensuring that they would keep their promises and contact them regularly. Martha looked meaningfully at Jude.

Then the Detectives ushered them out of the back door, past the reporters who had quadrupled whilst they had been inside and escorted them off the property.

The house was very quiet.

Tenney crossed his arms and looked at the two girls. His eyes were intense, filled with a mix of determination and lingering anger.

"Right then," he began, his voice steady but low. "What's the plan?"

Chapter 42

The journey to Stratford-Upon-Avon fell quiet very quickly. Martha's mind was firmly back in the Forest, with her older children. Samuel, exhausted from the events of the day before followed by a sleepless night, had to use all of his concentration to drive.

Sam sat in the back, his headphones firmly over his ears, shutting out any conversation his parents might have wanted to start, if they had been inclined to do so. He watched the scenery fly past, the familiar sights on the road to Gloucester, and then up into the Cotswolds and beyond.

Dad had been promising Mum a trip to Stratford for ages. Shakespeare fitted in with her love of poetry and prose, and Elizabethan plays. The thing was, Sam had never imagined that he would be dragged along with them.

He grudgingly acknowledged that things at home weren't great, that Dad had had a shock. The reporters and police outside the house were intrusive. But why did he have to suffer for it? He wasn't the one gallivanting off all night doing God-only-knows-what with God-only-knows-who. Not like Tenney and Aura.

He knew that they sneaked out in the night and back again in the morning. He had seen them go several times when they were meant to be 'grounded'. He had followed them on occasions, seen their strange friends at the fort. He shuddered as he remembered seeing Tenney drink the other man's blood. And yet, they had been rewarded for their disobedience. Whereas he, the son who didn't really cause any concern, his father's true son, was forced to spend a week with his parents, hiding away miles from where he really wanted to be.

Sam felt angry, hurt, and hugely disappointed. He'd never met Theo, never spoken to him, not properly; all their conversations were in texts, emails, or in the fantasy war games chat room. But their friendship through the game had seemed to grow and deepen. He had never been able to talk so freely to someone before, in total confidence.

Surreptitiously, he brought up the picture on his phone, the one that Theo had sent him. His heart clenched involuntarily, a mix of excitement and fear swirling inside him. Theo's short, curly blond hair and bright blue eyes seemed to glow from the screen, his skin radiant with the warmth of the sun. Theo looked like he enjoyed the sunshine as much as he enjoyed the computer, and had told Sam that he loved BMX and skateboarding just as much as playing games online.

Theo had mentioned he was 17, having celebrated his birthday at the beginning of September. Born in Italy but raised in Scotland, he lived with his father and brother. His father was constantly traveling, leaving them at home with their uncle and cousin. But his dad had finally agreed that Theo could visit him over half term, meaning he would be closer to the Forest of Dean and could meet Sam – if that was what Sam still wanted.

Catching a glimpse of his own reflection in the car window, Sam quickly turned away. His straight brown hair, too long in the fringe, lacked Tenney's natural curl and flick. He could never wake up with effortless 'bed-hair' like his brother. The hair framed a pasty face, acne dotted his nose, chin, and forehead. It wasn't as bad as some of his friends, but he was still conscious of it. He wore dark clothes, t-shirts with heavy metal and nu-metal bands on, pockets big enough to carry his phone, his Beats headphones around his neck. He wasn't an athlete; his skills lay in the digital world. Ask him anything to do with computers, and he could answer it. That was where he made friends, where he could create his personality, be the person he thought he should be rather than the person he was.

As he looked back at Theo's picture, a warmth spread through him, mingled with a pang of longing. He couldn't, wouldn't, admit it, but Theo was more attractive to him than anyone he'd ever met. The thought of meeting him in person filled him with both hope and dread. He squirmed slightly, trying to push the feelings down, but they bubbled up, undeniable and strong.

Maybe it was a good thing not to meet Theo. He wasn't sure if he could bear it if Theo rebuffed him. A small voice inside him whispered his other fear – Theo's picture was too perfect, too golden. What if 'Theo' was some sad, middle-aged bloke looking for kicks? Sam quickly shook that fear from his mind. Theo was his friend. He wouldn't do that to him.

His phone vibrated in his pocket; the music dimmed slightly as the tone sounded in his ears. He looked at the screen and gave his first smile since this whole debacle started.

Theo: *Hey Sam, I've got an idea how we can still meet up on Thursday, if u r still game?*

Sam looked at the backs of his parents' heads, smiled, and keyed in his response, hitting send before he could change his mind.

Sam: *Tell me what to do.*

**

Some of the reporters were still hanging around outside the house, despite witnessing the Wisemans leaving the property with suitcases. They decided to wait it out until night fell, then go and find Meg at the Lodge.

Aura stifled a huge yawn, causing her wound to pull uncomfortably under the dressing. The three of them were sitting on the sofa, Tenney in the middle with the dogs across his lap. The TV was on, another of Sam's Marvel films. *Thor*, if she remembered correctly. Tenney turned to look at her. She yawned again.

-I'm knackered, she said silently.

"I think I might go grab some shut eye," she said for Jude's benefit. She patted Tenney on the cheek and asked him to wake her if she overslept. She left them to the film as she climbed the stairs, the blue cord following her, keeping the link open with Tenney.

**

Tenney could feel the cord, sensing when Aura was in bed, her eyes shutting as she drifted off, a dream forming in her subconscious. Silently, he whispered her poem, *Wynken, Blynken, and Nod one night, sailed off in a wooden shoe…* When he was sure she was away, he turned to Jude, nestled under his arm, engrossed in the film as Thor sat in the café smashing mugs of coffee, shouting "ANOTHER," and then giving a goofy smile to Darcy. Tenney smiled almost as goofily as Chris Hemsworth when Jude laughed at the absurdity of the film.

Gently, he shifted Jess and Bo off his lap. Jude seemed to read his thoughts and responded as he began to touch her thigh, moving her around so he lay over her.

"Hey!" she protested. "I was watching that…" He smiled, kissing her to stop her complaints. When he let her have a breath, she spoke again; "What about Aura?" That devilish smile slowly crept across his features.

"She's fast asleep… dreaming," he whispered as he kissed her jaw, her ear, the pulse in her neck.

Jude was too caught up in the moment to protest any further. "Oh, well, that's ok then…"

**

Aura's eyes closed, she heard the poem whispered softly at the back of her head, as she drifted off…

"Aura?" A new voice, coming from behind her as she lay on her side in her bed. It was a lovely voice; one she hadn't expected to hear for another few weeks. She smiled as a hand wrapped over her waist and moved under her t-shirt. His hand was warm as he stroked her belly.

She could feel him, spooning her back, fitting himself to her contours, breathing on her neck softly. She moved her hand down so her fingers linked with his.

"I didn't think I would get see you properly before the full moon," she whispered, her eyes still shut.

"I'm always with you Aura," Hedge replied. He kissed her neck.

She moved her body back so she was as close to him as she could be. She felt him lean across her. Suddenly conscious of her face, she burrowed deeper beneath the covers, tucking her head down.

"What are you doing?" he asked, a small laugh echoed in his voice.

"I've hurt myself." She whispered. "I don't want you to see me, not yet. I'm not ready for that."

She felt his hand leave hers. For a moment she thought he was going to leave her. She lay very still, hardly daring to breathe in case he heard her panic. But his hand moved up her body, and gently touched her face. She felt his thumb skirt her dressing, oh so tenderly. He rested it on the corner of her mouth.

"Does it hurt?" he asked. She nodded, yes it does.

His thumb lingered on the corner of her mouth, stroking the part that wasn't swollen and bruised. Gently he kissed her, his lips barely touching hers, somehow finding the only part that wasn't damaged.

She felt him kiss her along her cheek to her ear, his breath warming her. "A man had given all other bliss, And all his worldly worth for this, To waste his whole heart in one kiss Upon her perfect lips." The words sent a shiver all down her spine.

The air around her vibrated, shaking the row of houses to their foundations.

He whispered once more, his lips so close to her ear that each movement felt like a kiss. "I love you Aura, whatever shape I come in. Whatever shape you *come in. Nothing hidden, remember? Speak to Stace…"*

She finally opened her eyes. There was a flash of green. And then he was gone. *A dream* she thought, a tear rolling down her cheek.

Outside in the early evening light, a wolf howled.

**

Tenney knocked softly on Aura's door before entering. He found her curled up tightly, her body wrapped around a pillow. Her face was pale, eyes red-rimmed from crying, hair and clothes dishevelled.

He moved to the bed, placed a steaming mug of tea on her bedside table, and sat beside her. She didn't move for the longest time, his hand resting gently on her shoulder. The silence was interminable for him. He berated himself for his selfishness, for getting caught up in the moment.

"It's not your fault," she whispered.

"I should have thought, Aura. I'm so sorry. It felt like you were having a good dream, and I just got carried away. I should have held back." She heard the anger in his voice, tinged with disgust at his perceived selfishness.

Slowly, she disentangled herself from the pillow, sat up, and looked him in the eye. She saw the pain he believed he had caused her as clearly as if she were looking in a mirror. He saw her swirling blue eyes, never the same hue at any one time. They seemed to merge with the tears that threatened to fall.

Aura didn't touch him; she just looked at him. She knew he battled with the choices of his heart. Just as she knew that he would choose her above anyone else, even if that was the wrong choice. The feelings of her heart, the choices, the heartbreak, mirrored his completely.

They should have felt closer, but the guilt they each carried at the thought that somebody else could make them feel so happy was beginning to drive a wedge between them.

She wiped her eyes, remembering the time before he left, when they had sat on this bed together, completely comfortable, happy with their place in this world, united and whole.

"Where's Jude?" she finally asked.

He breathed out a long sigh, like he had been waiting for her to give him permission to exhale. He gave a nervous, small twitch at the corner of his mouth. He'd never been nervous with her before. She felt a fresh surge of tears well up inside her.

"She went back up to the hotel… to get some stuff together for tonight's meeting with Meg, have a shower, you know, that sort of thing."

"What happened?" she asked, as if she didn't know.

"I sensed you were upset, and we felt the house shake. Then I heard the wolf howl. He knows when you're suffering too, I guess. Jude says I get a look on my face when I know you're hurting." He looked down at the covers, his fingers fiddling with the duvet.

Aura sobbed. She felt lost, weightless.

Tenney looked back up at her, his face turning bone white with shock. He quickly knelt upon the covers and gathered her into his arms, holding her tightly to his chest.

"Don't go, don't go, don't go!" he begged over and over. She looked over his shoulder and down at her hands. They were almost translucent, the pink colours of the bedding shining through the ethereal blue hue.

She gasped aloud, and he held her tighter still. "Don't go, don't go," he said and thought it all at the same time. Somehow, she managed to grab his t-shirt, gripping it tightly between her fists, grounding herself, re-tethering herself to her soul.

Tenney gingerly began to release her when she started to feel more substantial again but didn't fully let go of his grip. Fear was now etched on his face. "Don't go, Aura, please. I'm sorry!"

This time, she enveloped him in the hug.

-*I'm here, I'm here,* she told him silently.

"What happened?" he asked, fear etched in his voice.

"It felt like we had drifted apart, like we weren't in step anymore. Like I was nothing but air. Lost." She sniffed against his shoulder.

"We're okay, Aur, we're okay. We are just starting a new path, but we're still together. Still walking in the same direction. I'll never leave you. I promise."

"Love sucks, huh?" she tried to joke. He held her tightly to him, rocking her gently as they focused on the bonds that prevented them from falling apart.

They sat together, watching the night set in through her window. "How long was I asleep?" she finally asked. It had felt like only minutes, but the room had darkened considerably since she first shut her eyes.

"About three hours," he answered.

Aura was shocked. "Three hours?" she asked in disbelief, looking at his grinning, self-satisfied face.

"Yeah," he confirmed, smiling at the memory. "It was pretty epic." He laughed as she hit him lightly on the chest. She put her head back over his heart and settled again to the sound of its rhythm.

"Was it a good dream?" he asked, teasing her with a smile she could feel.

"It was, until I figured out it was only a dream. It felt so real." He made a comforting noise and rubbed her arm. "I should have figured it out before, though. He quoted Tennyson to me."

"Really? Which one?"

"Launcelot talking about Guinevere's lips. It was very sweet, really. But just before he left me," Tenney felt her shudder, "Hedge told me to speak to Stace. That was probably the shock that made me wake up."

She paused.

"I admit, this last day, I haven't really been able to process the fact that Stace is really gone. We've only known him, in this life, for a short time. But he's helped us figure some things out, given us answers we never even knew we had questions for. And poor old Hedge, in his current state, probably doesn't even realise anything's happened."

Tenney stayed silent. He knew she didn't need platitudes or false assurances. Just the fact that he was there, with her, giving them the time and space they needed to reconnect properly. Alone, with no distractions—happy ones or otherwise. He tethered her back to the world.

"Did Jude like the book?" she asked, letting him know that his relationship was as important to her as it was to him.

"Yeah, she loved it," she felt him relax slightly under her head. She could sense the small smile as he thought of Jude. Aura held his shirt, trying not to think of Hedge and his absence that wasn't an absence. Tenney's hand stroked her arm soothingly. He exhaled, long and deep, causing the hair on the top of her head to move with the breath.

"When Hedge is here properly, we'll have to all do something fun. Normal. The four of us together."

He was letting her know that her relationship was just as important to him as it was to her. She gripped his top tighter, a small tear escaping from her eye. He caught it with his thumb, and they watched the same phenomenon they had experienced in the hospital.

Tenney's skin absorbed the tiny drop of water.

"I'd like that," she replied, happier at last.

His phone in his pocket suddenly vibrated, breaking them from their trance. He pulled it out and checked the message. "That's Jude," he said. "She's on her way back. It's time to head up to the Lodge. You good to go?"

She nodded and looked up at him. "Let's go."

**

It was two nights after the events at the Manor House. A small group of local teenage boys couldn't resist taking the girls they were trying to impress up there to see if they could sneak past the coppers and pretend to spot some ghosts.

'Everyone' at school knew that a good way to impress girls was to be their hero if they were scared. And a good way to scare them was to take them to a haunted house. They had all grown up in the village, knowing the stories of ghostly figures who walked the grounds, haunting the building and the relatively recent re-discovery of the Roman Temple. The site held a new, dangerous allure after the events of the previous nights.

They were a group of three boys, around 16 years old, and two girls of a similar age. The leader of the group, Jace, was already on the cusp of declaring one of the girls, Courtney, his girlfriend. He just needed to prove himself to her. Then, when they returned to school, he would have a new status as 'one of the first'. He'd be as famous as that kid who left when he was still in the second or third year. What was his name, Benny? Kenny? Something like that. He'd be a legend!

And so, he and his small but loyal group of mates set out to impress the girls with their courage. Full of bravado, he assured them it was a perfect plan.

They saw parents ushering young children home from a party at the village hall. That had been them once, not so many years ago, when they were still kids. Now they had more to prove, more guts. They laughed, egging each other on, flirting clumsily with the girls. Finally, they saw the large house loom up out of the darkness, at the very edge of the village. Each of them stopped, none willing to confess to the small fearful feeling that grew in their bellies. Jace hid his shaky hands in his pockets and strode forward, an act of confidence that had his friends following him.

They crept up to the edge of the field that skirted the property, between the house and the church. They were all giggling nervously behind him. One of his friends shone his torch underneath his chin, making a ghoulish noise, while the girls play-screamed.

The big bull and his cows had been moved by the farmer earlier that day. All that stood in the field were the white tents and a bored-looking copper. Bored, but his eyes were scanning the field. He spotted the torchlight and shooed them away. Jace knew another way in. He was a proper local, after all.

It was a longer walk, but safer. They went up the lane, past the drive entrance, and into the field on the other side. Keeping low behind the wall, they crept along until they reached the bank which cut through the property. The ancient row of sweet chestnuts swayed in the breeze that had begun to pick up. They found a part of the stone wall that had crumbled, making it easy to clamber over.

After helping the girls, who still giggled nervously, Jace led them and spotted the Temple. Courtney, her arm looped tightly around her reluctant friend's arm, encouraged her to carry on with them.

They hid behind one of the ancient trees and observed the activity at the house. Lights were on, a cherry picker raised up to the roof. Two people dressed in head-to-toe coveralls carefully carried what looked like a body bag across the roof, giving a thumbs up when they were ready to be lowered. On the ground was a second body bag.

The kids gasped, laughing nervously. They hadn't really expected to see actual evidence of the deaths. They shrank back from the bank and retreated towards the relative safety of the Temple.

No one stood watch there; the site was virtually untouched. The evidence of the archaeologists' work was scattered around them. They saw the ditches and the tent connected to a generator. Nearby stood a porta cabin.

Jace spotted the pile of dirt next to one of the excavation sites. He clambered up to the top of it, dancing about, waving a can of lager in the air, crowing to the crescent moon. Dark clouds rolled over the sky, a rumble of thunder threatening in the distance, adding to the ambience of the moment.

Jace was loving the attention and the atmosphere, feeling all-powerful, unstoppable. He took a swig from his can, spitting some of it out when suddenly the ground beneath him moved. He stopped, his friends laughing at him. Still unused to alcohol, he thought it was the drink making the world spin. He laughed with them and began dancing again.

This time, the earthen mound shook and pushed upwards. Jace fell backwards, causing his friends to fall about with cackles of glee at his clumsiness. Lightning spread across the clouds, lighting the ground below.

The cackles of laughter soon turned to cries of alarm and fear as the flash of light revealed a bone-white, bloodless hand breaking through the surface. The peel of thunder drowned out the screams as the hand grabbed Jace's ankle.

Jace wet himself and pulled back, trying to break the unbreakable hold. The hand then became an arm, then a shoulder, followed by a mud-encrusted head.

But it was the face that caused Jace to pass out in fear.

Blood-red eyes flashed in the night, a bright red scar across its neck.

And long fangs protruded straight from the monster's gums, dripping with saliva as it screamed at the kids – "RUN!!"

Chapter 43

The sound of blood flowing through the bodies of the children called out to the exsanguinated creature, tempting it to replenish what it had lost. A part of its consciousness that wasn't yet given over to the primordial need to drink told it that these were not the right prey. It stretched out its hand from the grave towards the body on the ground and turned its head to the others, their screams drowned out by the rolling thunder.

"RUN!" it shouted, before it was tempted to chase them. Through the reddened haze of its eyes, it saw them take off. Slowly, it pulled the rest of its dirt and blood-encrusted body out of the grave.

They had abandoned the one who had fainted to the monster.

The dark clouds rumbled as the raindrops started to fall, thick and heavy. The storm grew in intensity as the creature leaned over the body and inhaled the smell of the life-renewing liquid flowing strongly through the child. It was mixed with the sweet tang of urine that had stained his jeans.

The creature's fangs throbbed in time with the heartbeat pulsating through the unconscious body beneath it. The vein in the boy's neck, his head thrown back as he hit the earthen mound, throbbed in time with the strong pulse found in the bodies of the young. It could see the blood as it was pumped around his body and brain. It sang to the creature, beckoning it to bite, to drink its fill…

A low, insistent growl stopped it. Green eyes met red, a flash of sharp white teeth through a snarled lip, the tongue pushing against them as the black wolf warned the creature off. The creature moved backwards, crouching low over its prey, its sharp nails digging deeply into the clothes possessively, scratching the warm flesh underneath.

The wolf, blacker than the night, only its eyes and teeth visible under the storm clouds, crept closer, snarling ferociously. Its ears lay flat against its head as it held its head low. The green eyes remained fixed on the creature in front of it.

The creature mirrored its adversary. They stared at each other for what felt like an eternity, each one weighing up the other's strengths and weaknesses. Time stretched like elastic, the crackle of electricity popping in the air, the thick clouds obscuring the moon. A bolt of lightning came down from the heavens, striking the temple. It acted like a whiplash, snapping the tension between the two creatures with a loud bang, and they leapt at each other. They met mid-air in a clash of furious energy, teeth, and immense power and strength.

The thunder rolled above them, the lightning offering glimpses of the maelstrom of activity as black fur and bone-white skin moved together to ascertain supremacy.

To find the weaker. And dominate them.

The creature began to tire. The loss of blood it had suffered from its initial wound, and then in the slow regeneration the earth offered it, meant that ultimately it was no match for the wolf. The creature, with its last ounce of strength, made one last attempt to bite through the wolf's thick mane of hair, to reach its spine and sever it. The wolf twisted so that the creature landed on its back beside the still unconscious body of the boy.

The wolf crawled up the creature's body, as the creature had done to the boy.

The green eyes stared deep into the red, communicating to the starving being beneath it.

Green eyes flashing in the night…

… Blue eyes swirling with trust and love…

He *knew* this wolf.

The red eyes began to retreat, leaving a single shard of greeny brown. A dart of hope for the wolf. Slowly, its eyes never leaving the creature, the wolf began to retreat from atop its body. The rain continued to fall on the oversensitive skin of the creature, reminding it of its weakness, its hunger… Every pore screamed out for blood.

The boy stirred slightly, moaning. The cold rain had begun to revive him. The creature moved its head to look at him. The wolf growled softly in its throat.

Not him, not here… it seemed to say to the creature.

The wolf backed a few more steps away, moving its head as though beckoning the creature, asking it to follow.

The boy's hand twitched, his fingers flexed.

Jace came to, the rain splashing on his face. He struggled to remember what had happened and groggily called out to his friends. There was no answer.

His clothes were soaked through, his chest felt bruised, and his clothes had been torn, as though he had been mauled by a lion. Jace struggled to sit up. It was still dark; the temple site was eerily quiet. Nothing moved or called out in the night. The clouds obliterated the moon and the stars.

Staggering to his feet, clutching his side with one arm wrapped around him, he made his way off the mound. His bruised ankle gave way under him as he caught it in the recently upturned earth, a depression where there had once been a hole. Jace fell again, hitting the red mud with a splat.

Then, all at once, it all came back to him. The strong hand wrapped tight around his ankle, the creature pulling itself out of hell. Red eyes and sharp fangs as it looked hungrily at the boy.

Jace's screams alerted one of the police officers as he walked up the driveway.

The officer didn't see the dark shadows of the wolf and the Nightwalker.

**

A dark street. Houses with the lights off.

All except for one.

A raised voice.

Male.

A begging, pleading voice, followed by the sound of a fist hitting flesh.

Female.

The harsh cries of a terrified child.

The wolf sat in front of him, blocking his path forward. The only way was up the pathway to the house. And so that was the way the creature walked.

The wolf stayed at the end of the path, waiting and watching.

The creature lifted a dirty hand, fingernails black from clawing through the dirt, and knocked on the door.

The crying stopped.

Heavy footsteps echoed down the corridor. Then the door swung open violently, releasing the fumes of alcohol, cigarettes, and unwashed bodies.

And the residual tang of blood.

The man was big. His girth was almost as wide as the doorway, and not just from fat. Beneath the glutinous wobble was a strong layer of muscle. He was tall, his balding, scarred head rising a good foot above that of the creature who stood opposite him. The creature's sharp eyes zoomed in straight away to the bloodied knuckles, noting that it wasn't this man's blood, but another's that coated the back of his hands. He carefully sniffed the air. Not one person's blood, but three.

"What the fuck do you want, fucker?" the man eloquently asked the stranger.

He was careful not to look up too soon, wanting this person to feel real fear, a slow realisation that his crimes had caught up with him and death was knocking on his door.

"I heard a noise," he croaked, his throat dry from his time in the ground. "Thought I should just check things were okay here."

The man laughed. Behind him, a petite woman stood cradling a small child in her arms, trying desperately to make it stop crying. The creature looked at her through his half-closed lids. He saw her blackened eyes, the swollen split lip. The child was bleeding from its ear, whimpering on its mother's shoulder.

"Jim?" she asked quietly.

'Jim' moved across the door, obliterating the creature's sight of the woman. He eyed the diminished, pale, sickly-looking man in front of him, assuming he was one of the drugged-up, homeless layabouts that migrated down from the town. Someone who had no right to stick their grubby nose into his business. *The coward can't even look me in the eye*, he thought maliciously. Jim rolled his shoulders back and balled his fists as he started to step out of the house, pulling the door to behind him.

Big mistake, the creature thought.

He had forgotten who he was.

What he was.

For over 90 years, he had lived one of his happiest, quietest lifetimes with Aura and Ingrid. Lived the life of a scholar. A professor. A man of peace. Only killing wild animals to survive. And then, in the 21 years between, he had become a seeker again, his time taken up looking for Aura and Tenney. There had been no time to hunt the ultimate prey, get the ultimate fix.

Apart from the filthy blood of the possessed.

It had been over 350 years since his last burial and regeneration. He struggled to remember why. He vaguely recalled a battle in the north of England during the Civil War. A demon on horseback caught him unawares and cut him through from behind. He remembered clawing his way out through the mass of bodies in the communal death pit.

The demon hadn't lived for long after his reanimation.

But now he realised that over a century of peace and fairly easy living meant he had forgotten, no, *denied*, what he really was.

He hadn't been on guard, hadn't been prepared. Raphael had warned him. And he had lost his head. Almost literally.

The wolf had led him well by coming here. By leading him to this bad man.

Jim shoved the creature down the rain-soaked path, his rancid breath stinking of rotten teeth, alcohol, and cigarettes. It assaulted the creature's senses. But he let himself be manhandled into the shadows, away from where the woman might see them. He heard a dog's bark from the house.

He was totally unaware of what the man was saying, hearing only the steady throb of the man's heart, strong despite his abuse of his own body. The creature felt nothing but the burn firing throughout him as the man pushed him towards the darkest part of the path.

When they were in the dark, away from prying eyes and innocent ears, Jim shoved the creature once more, expecting him to fall back as he had done. Instead, it felt like he was pushing against the face of a cliff. Immovable and ancient. He tried again. When the man didn't move, didn't even flinch, the thug raised a fist, putting all his strength into his arm and smashed it down into the creature's bony sunken cheek.

The bones in Jim's hand were pulverised by the impact. His knuckles breaking through to the surface. He screamed. Somewhere behind him the creature heard a door creak open, the woman calling again for Jim. A large dog pushing past her. It was probably the only creature in the world stupid enough to want to try to stop his master's death.

It hurtled down the pathway, barking manically.

Time slowed again for the creature. Each beat of the man's heart reverberated through its body, in the dark he could see every bead of rain on the man's face; his bloodied hand, this time covered in his own gore, shone in the creature's eyes. He savoured the ecstatic feeling that he knew would come, the orgasm of release as he knew he would feel no guilt for the life he had to take in order to live.

A life lost in order to save those he loved. Another chance to become a player in the greater fight that was coming.

The wolf, a creature of the supernatural had been strong enough to defeat the Nightwalker in his weakened state. But a mere human, no matter how strong he was by *human* standards, stood no chance against such a creature, whatever state of nourishment it was in.

Jim finally began to acknowledge this fact.

Then he heard the creature moan softly as though anticipating a moment of pure ecstasy.

The man shuffled uselessly backwards.

A solitary light came on from a house nearby. It was enough for the man to see the blood red eyes for the first time. They stared lasciviously, hungrily down at him through the skull like face. In slow motion he saw the wet mud in the man's hair and the bone white skin shining through from underneath. He saw his own blood smearing the creature's cheek where he had hit him. A flash of red on white, making the eyes glow brighter. He saw the creature's mouth open wide. The fangs descended from the upper palate of his mouth, sharp, dangerous.

Real.

Jim screamed again and his body reacted as so many had before when they knew their end was coming in shocking supernatural violence.

But the creature didn't care. Finally, after an age of waiting, in a flash of speed, he pounced on the man and wrapped one wasted hand around the man's throat. Despite his weakened condition and his marginally shorter stature, he lifted the man up so his feet were dangling several inches above the wet ground.

As the lightning danced through the clouds, the creature finally stopped toying with his prey and pulled the man down. He fastened his mouth around the artery in the man's neck severing it and tasted the sweet liquid as it flowed down his throat.

It had all taken seconds for the man to realise he was about to die. In that time the creature had only been half aware of the dog as it ran down the path. Finally, it reached them and leapt towards him, teeth barred, a mad look in its eyes.

A greater creature leaping from the shadows, took the dog down. The wolf tore out its throat, killing the dog almost instantly.

The creature and the dying body fell together to the ground. He lifted the man's torso up and held him as close as a lover, his mouth suctioned over the wound his teeth had made. The life force pulsed through him, revitalising him, restoring his sense of self, confirming his role in this world.

There was no blood on the ground as the creature drank, all the blood was sucked deep into the belly of the beast.

Lucidity began to return to the creature. He began to remember.

His teeth were weapons in war, used for slashing, ripping. A tool.

But this had been a different need, a need for self-preservation. This had been his choice, to take a life so that others may stand a better chance of living.

He thought of the small family in the house. Their terror, their blood spilt by this oppressor, this tormentor and bully who lay beneath him. He felt this was a justifiable kill. Not all monsters were the ones who stalked the dark or were slaves to the moon. Not all monsters had the excuse of demonic possession. Some monsters were purely human.

One life for potentially millions, a good sacrifice of a life destined for the destruction of innocents. A choice which had to be made if his role in this was to be fulfilled. He had to be what he once was. He couldn't lose his head again.

He was an immortal soldier, a leader of men and creatures of myth.

He was a mentor, scholar. A Father figure.

He could give life through pain.

He could give death.

He drank until there was no blood left in the body. His strength returned and he stood up, fluidly. His body had filled out again, muscles clearly defined through his wet shirt; his eyes lost their redness. His fangs retracted back into his mouth satisfied at last, completing the human disguise he wore. He stretched, cracked the muscles in his neck, and walked to the house.

He broke open the door with one twist of the handle and stepped inside. He smelt the rank air and followed the scent of blood to the decrepit living room. He found the woman cowering behind the sofa in the corner with the small child in her arms. Beside her was the beaten and abused body of an older girl.

He knelt down, felt for the girl's pulse. It was there, but it was weak. She felt cold. He grasped the woman's chin, stared into her bruised purple rimmed eyes like a hawk staring at a mouse.

"He won't be back." he said, nodding towards the door. "Do you love your children?" The woman, still shaking badly, nodded an affirmative.

"You must phone for an ambulance. Save your children. You will never see him again. No one will ever see him again." She nodded once more utterly stupefied.

He rose up to his full height, turned and walked back out the house.

Grabbing the drained corpse by its collar with one hand and the remains of the dog with the other, he dragged them away through the night. The reanimated man knew all the ways a person can dispose of a body and it never be discovered. The black wolf padded silently beside him as he finished his grisly task.

The man now knew exactly *who* he was, who his wolf-companion was. He knew where he needed to go. There was a new determination in his eyes.

When he had destroyed the evidence of death, Stace and Hedge began to walk home towards the Lodge.

The General was back.

Chapter 44

They walked the now familiar night path to the Lodge. The freedom of being able to leave the house without lies, half-truths, or silence—creeping past their slumbering family—mixed with the rebalancing of their relationships, gave the trio a feeling akin to lightness. A lightness many would still consider a burden, tied to the grief they felt waiting to kick in when they were united in their band of misfits. A grief for the missing leader of their troop.

As they drew closer, the happy chatter dwindled to a muted hum, and finally to nothing. Anxiety at what they would find at the Lodge encroached into the light.

The Land Rover had been moved and was now parked in the shadows of the house. Aura felt a twist of longing in her belly when she saw it, knowing the owner would not be in it. Jude, her arm linked through Aura's, gave her a squeeze. She smiled at the thought that from these crazy weeks, she had found someone she could call a friend. She returned the squeeze.

Behind them, Tenney whistled, and from the shadowed ferns, Jess and Bo came. The older one steadily made her way while the younger sprinted towards them. They had debated leaving the dogs at home, but to Tenney and Aura, they were as important a part of their lives as any family member. The thought of leaving them alone at night in a quiet, empty house, after they had been alone so many times recently, was too much for Aura to bear.

He re-leashed them, and they approached the battered front door.

A small light shone from the window of the sitting room at the front of the house. They had quickly discovered that this room was the most waterproof and kept most of the drafts out. A fire had been lit in its fireplace. They could see a figure sitting in front of the flames, watching them dance and sing. The trio took a deep breath, unsure how Meg was going to react.

It was a given that she had seen and witnessed countless deaths. But to lose someone who had walked beside her for so many years… Well, to the three relatively short-lived beings, the thought was intolerable. With this in their minds, they let themselves in.

**

Meg had heard the trio and their dogs from quite a way down the track. She noticed the change in their tone as they approached the house. *They don't know!* she thought, a little mischievously. She sat in front of the roaring fire and waited for them.

The door into the room creaked open. She didn't turn around. The temptation to drag out their awkwardness was too great. She hadn't felt so playfully naughty in a while. God only knew when she would have the opportunity for a little fun again.

The events at the Manor told her that something was happening. Something the demons had been planning since the dawn of time was only now beginning to play out. The Councillors were mobilising, as proven by Raphael's intervention, not once, but twice in as many days.

She wondered, as she had over the last night and day, why he had saved the girl, Jude. The most obvious reason was the growing affection between her and the Tether; her almost Elemental-like power to influence him. But why the Archangel decided that was enough of a reason to save her didn't quite sit right with her. The only other reason she could think of seemed highly implausible. It was a very rare phenomenon, maybe happening once in 500 years. The consequences if her suspicions were realised could be dire. There had already been one such phenomenon in the last 200 years. To have two so close together should have been unheard of.

She pushed the puzzle to the back of her mind when she heard Tenney give a little cough into his hand, a human mannerism to gently alert someone of their presence in a time of great upset and grief. She turned slowly and looked at them over her shoulder.

The littlest dog wasn't fooled, she thought. He stood there, pulling gently at the end of his lead, tail wagging furiously. Meg clicked her tongue once, Tenney dropped the leash, and the dog ran to her side, immediately rolling onto his back in the ultimate submissive gesture.

He was rewarded with a good scratch of his tummy. Seeing his happiness, the older dog walked tiredly over, collapsing between Meg and the fire, quickly falling asleep.

It was too much for Aura, who ran forward, knelt beside Meg, and wrapped her arms around her shoulder. She began murmuring condolences in her ear, telling her how sorry she was. Meg awkwardly tapped Aura's shoulder as she tried not to smirk, conscious of the other two watching her closely.

But her sharp ears had picked up a new sound moving stealthily through the trees. She caught the tang of human blood spilt, the strong hearts of the pair. One beat with the eternal power of an animal in its youth; the other beat more slowly, but it was powerful once again.

Tenney and Jude came and sat by Meg and Aura, who was still clinging to her in the awkward embrace. *If it had been anyone else,* Meg thought, *I would have extricated myself from them by now.* All the incarnations of this Elemental had been like a daughter to her.

As Tenney rifled through his backpack, she heard the pair draw closer to the house.

"Tea?" he asked her, holding out the silver flask.

Meg looked up at him and noted his confusion as she beamed at him. Her eyes sparkled in the fire's light, betraying her happiness and relief.

"Meg?" he asked, unable to hide his shock at seeing the woman he had believed to be broken by grief looking so happy. "Are you OK?" he finished, looking quickly at Jude.

"Of course she is." A gruff voice from the doorway. "She is just aware of the amount of work we have to do if we are going to get you three battle-ready."

The three of them fell back in shock as they saw the spectre of Stace framed in the doorway.

Meg couldn't help but laugh, pushing Aura gently away from her. "It's about bloody time! I was worried Hedge hadn't found you and you had slaughtered half the village!"

**

The newly resurrected Stace had disappeared again to shower and change out of his tattered, blood- and mud-encrusted clothes.

Tenney, Aura, and Jude turned towards Meg, full of disbelief. Tenney led the way with some not-so-gentle questioning, his voice reverberating around the room as Meg stared him down, her arms crossed over her chest. She understood that he needed to vent, to release some of the rage that lay beneath his surface; so, she watched him unblinkingly as he allowed it to bubble up. All his instincts screamed that he needed to protect his sister from any more hurt, and this overwhelming need was exacerbated by the bombshell of grief cancelled.

Jude, quietly fuming as she paced the floor, began to reconsider, for the hundredth time, just how much of this new world she really didn't understand. Silently, she considered again exactly how much more she could cope with. Aura just sat there as still as a statue, silent, her face pale. The wolf leaned against her, supporting her side; the little dog curled up in her lap, snoring softly.

When Stace finally reappeared, cleaned and ready, it was Aura, waking from her trance-like state, who stood up and slapped him, before falling into his arms, tears of joy streaming from her eyes. The sound of her palm hitting hard flesh cut Tenney off mid-tirade and stopped Jude's pacing.

"I think it's time you all know more about our kind," Stace said solemnly as he held Aura to him.

Gently, he disentangled her from him and walked her to the fireplace. He sat her down and folded himself next to her, letting her lean against him. He saw Tenney's jaw tick; his eyes harden, as they flickered to his sister and the nightwalker. Those same eyes cleared slightly as the twins communicated silently, Aura placating her brother. He turned to Jude and held out a hand to her, and together they sat down facing Stace and Aura.

Meg sat to Stace's right, Hedge the Wolf spread his great bulk out behind the three supernatural's, acting like a bolster of a sofa. Jess and Bo lay beside him.

"Nightwalkers and Moon Cursed are born when the Elementals manifest into the physical and have relations with a mortal," Stace began. "That much you know. Creatures such as me have the dubious honour of being fathered by Metal.

"We need to be buried, cut off from air, water, and fire, and cocooned in the attributes of our father and his closest sister, Earth, to become a Nightwalker after Martyrdom. Elements of different ores can be found throughout the whole of the earth, in the smallest patch of soil. Metal is the easiest association for my father, but in fact, he is master of all the fruits of the earth—metals, gems, oils, lava. So long as I am reburied, I cannot die, because my body is re-energised by these fruits."

"If that's the case," said Tenney, curious and spotting an obvious flaw, "then why are you allergic to sunlight? Why do you drink blood?"

"I am a creature of the ground, and all the fruits of earth are formed in darkness. My curse exemplifies that which killed me when I am in the sunlight. Fire killed me, so fire weakens me. The Sun is the greatest source of natural fire in this galaxy; therefore, the sun will always weaken me."

Stace paused, allowing them to absorb this information and reconcile it with the folklore surrounding his kind. He was the oldest progeny left of the Elementals after his kind were purged, the forefather of modern vampire lore. When he judged that they had comprehended what he had told them, Stace continued.

"My killing teeth are as hard as diamonds. I am as fast as the lava that flows beneath the Earth's surface. I am as strong as steel. My heart is strong but beats slowly, and I require very little air to live.

"My skin is like the armour a knight used to wear, but like any armour, it has weak points. Sharpened blades thrust or sliced through my skin with enough strength will still penetrate. My body cannot produce new blood like a human's. When I am cut badly enough, I lose blood.

"My touch is cold, and my complexion pale. Humans start to notice the differences, and it is harder for me to move about incognito through the world. Because of this, I need to regularly replace the blood I lose. I need refuelling, re-humanising; and the only way to do this is to take warm blood from another.

"The blood I take to stay strong and keep on the mask of humanity is transformed in my body. I heal quickly, and that same blood can heal another. But that person then runs the risk of becoming beholden to the blood lust."

Tenney shifted awkwardly at the unpleasant reminder of his experience, his hidden craving for more.

"Usually, animal blood will suffice, but occasionally, after I have lost most of my reconstituted blood, as I did on the roof of the manor, only human blood will return me to my original strength and faculties." He paused and looked away, his eyes turning sad. "It is something I do not like to do."

They each wondered who had lost their life to give Stace back his.

Jude was intrigued. "So, what about werewolves then?" she pondered aloud, looking toward Meg.

Meg blinked her yellow eyes, and Hedge lifted his head. Jude felt suddenly as though she was in the crossfire of green and yellow lasers, and she shifted on her butt, dropping her gaze before Meg or Hedge did.

"I am the daughter of Earth," Meg said simply. "The moon acts like a Tether to the earth, a twin connected eternally but separated forever. It influences the way the earth works, the pull of gravity, the waves on the shore…

"When I was human, before I learned about my ancestry, I relished the feel of the land, the beauty of the countries I passed through. When I fell to Martyrdom, taking my boy with me, my allegiance was moved to that of the moon's pull. We are slaves to it, in the literal sense. We have no control over the changes that our bodies go through during the full moon cycle." Hedge shifted imperceptibly closer to her, and subconsciously Meg's hand moved through his black pelt.

"Like Stace, we heal quickly, especially at night. And we retain the agility, heightened senses, and strength of our wolf forms." Aura turned her head to look over her shoulder at the wolf behind her. With one hand, she mirrored Meg and stroked Hedge's flanks as she searched for the knife wound he had received trying to defend her. Aura found nothing—no scarring or scabs, just healthy skin beneath the thick fur. She then recalled his agility and effortlessness as he climbed up to Jude's bedroom window.

"Are there other creatures?" Jude asked.

Tenney turned to her, concern showing on his face. She sounded stressed. He noted the tightening of her lips, the small crease between her eyes.

He watched her carefully.

Meg looked quickly at Stace. "There are," she began, "but they are rare."

"What are they?"

Meg shifted uncomfortably. "Each Elemental, before and after the Tethering, possesses the power to pass on unique genes, which are only triggered after violent death. All, except for Air." They all turned to look at Aura, who had squirmed as she considered the children past versions of her may have had.

"Air has never begot a child," Meg said simply.

Aura looked confused. "What do you mean?" she asked carefully.

Stace continued from Meg's revelation. "Air has always been associated with purity, with etherealness and the insubstantial. In your original Elemental state, you have no physical body, and no desire to be trapped within a skin. You had no means of carrying a child. That inability to carry another inside you has been passed down through your physical incarnations. I have been with you for all your human lives, and I have never witnessed you birth anything."

Aura swallowed as she realised that she would never be a mother, never experience that which many women took for granted.

Jude stifled a sob. She felt that she could understand some of Aura's grief at not becoming a parent as she thought about the toxic medicine which kept her arthritis at bay but robbed her of bearing new life. She hadn't shared this with Tenney, but she felt his eyes on her as she related to Aura. She knew he felt torn between her and Aura. Both needed his support, but there was little he could do to help them, except be near to them.

Stace continued, looking between Aura and Tenney, seeing the struggles both of them were enduring. "Unlike the other Elementals who have some form of physicality about them, air is just that. Air. So, when you were tethered, you took on the flesh, bones, and blood of your twin. You share their very soul and genes."

"The fact that you two are not identical twins and different genders is unheard of, and something I do not yet understand," Stace shook his head slightly. "But your connection is very strong. Because you share the same genetic material, your souls so intricately intertwined, you and Tenney share amplified characteristics. The other Elementals and their Tethers do not share these characteristics to the same degree. They find it easier to be apart for a time. The rage, the extreme panic, and the sense of loss when you are apart happen slowly for them, so long as they are reunited regularly.

"This is why you need to keep your mental channels open and your connection clear." Stace needed to emphasise his next sentence. He needed to ensure that they understood what he had to say to them. "When you die, Tenney, and your body is returned to the earth or cremated, Aura will cease to be. Only Meg, Hedge, and I will remember her. And then she will be reborn again. Hopefully."

Tenney didn't know why, but the word 'hopefully' hung ominously in the air. He knew instinctively that things were different with this tethering, but he had held on to the hope that Aura would always be in the world, in one form or another. 'Hopefully' had cast a doubt in his mind.

Stace paused again, before looking solemnly at the twins. "Air is nothing without their Tether, and their Tether is broken without Air."

**

Jude stepped outside, a conflict of emotions running through her. This new world was once again becoming too much for her to handle. The love she was experiencing, a love she had never believed she would have after so many years of being alone, was overwhelming enough. Add in the complication of the difference in age, and she knew in her heart that it wasn't destined to last.

Yes, she looked younger than her years, and in many ways, her experiences—or her lack of experiences—in her life only compounded it. But one day, age would catch up with her. She would finally look her age, and he would always be near enough a decade younger than her.

The complications piled up in her mind.

The connection between Tenney and Aura was stronger than she had believed. Aura was literally made from Tenney. If Tenney died, and when his body was returned to the earth, Aura would cease to be, moving on to become her next self. Or maybe just ceasing altogether. Her heartbreak at his death, the strength of their tether, might mean that he would be her last connection to the world. There would be no more Air in human form. If what she was inferring from Stace and Meg was true, then that possibility heralded potentially apocalyptic consequences for the world if Aura became her true self before her time was up.

Meg's confession that there were more supernatural creatures, ones previously consigned to fairy tale books and her mother's fertile imagination, were real made her want to scrub her mind clear, go back in time to before all this and live in blissful ignorance once again.

Added to these revelations was the knowledge, and the hope, that in a few days' time she would learn something about her vanished mother. To get any information, she needed to be with it, on the ball. Prepared for whatever she would find at Clifton.

That had to be her priority.

It had to be.

She rubbed her face furiously. "Get a grip, Jude!" she told herself angrily.

"Hey," he said from behind her.

Hastily, she wiped her face, surprised to see her hands wet. She pushed back her long, curly hair, and forced a smile to her face. She could do this. She was a cop, a professional. She had to get her priorities straight.

Mum first, love life second. Potential supernatural wars way, way down in third. Concentrate on the real world!

Turning to look at him, she felt her conviction waver. He stood there, hands in his pockets, eyes peering at her from under his brown fringe. She longed to run her hands through his hair, pull him close to her. Make believe that none of this mattered.

Instead, she stood rigid, her arms wrapped tightly around her body. He stepped closer to her.

"Tenney," she began, cross at herself for the awkwardness in her voice. "I can't do this anymore. You and I, it's fun, but I never banked on getting so involved. Ya know? I mean, jeez, I'm nearly 30 years old. You're barely 21. And now all this 'stuff' that's going on, it's, well…" she swallowed, "it's just too much." She felt a sob rise in her throat, so she quickly stopped talking.

He stepped closer still; she could smell him, his animal spice, the scents that were purely him; the scent that spoke right into the very heart of her. She tried to step back, holding up a hand to fence him off.

Quickly, his hand shot out and his long, dexterous fingers wrapped around her hip, holding her close to him, ignoring her futile attempt to ward him off.

"Bull shit," he said.

His face was so close to hers that she felt his breath caress her skin as he spoke those two words.

"What?" she spluttered.

"Bull. Shit." This time he enunciated each word. "I know this is overwhelming. Freaky even. But it's not a reason to leave me. Age doesn't matter when you love someone."

"Wh… wh… what?" she stammered, too shocked by his words to say much more.

"I thought you were a cop, someone good at reading the clues, reading people," he teased her softly, gently tipping her chin up to make her look at him. He looked deep into her eyes. "Aura figured it out ages ago. Way before I could admit it to myself." His thumb stroked the side of her face, resting on the corner of her lips. She felt his caress and instinctively leaned into his hand.

"I'm in love with you, Jude. I think I have been since Lincoln. And I know you love me too. It is because of that certainty that I know we can make this work."

Jude kept her arms crossed around her body; her fists clenched tightly. It was a barrier between him and her rapidly beating heart. A pointless shield against the words which were striking her heart and her mind with permanent, longed-for scars.

An owl hooted in the dark trees and a fox barked. The cool night air added to the shiver already beginning to course through her, her adrenaline peaking.

He wrapped his other hand around her hip, pulling them together, closing the gap. She shivered again.

"I'll help you find your mum," he said softly. "Stace has promised to help us perfect the long-distance telepathy stuff. Going to Bristol for the party will be a good opportunity to test it out." He pulled her closer still, his nose tracing the outline of her cheek. She closed her eyes and felt herself relax into him, her body betraying her yet again.

"As for this 'stuff'," he waved one of his hands across the clearing, encompassing with one gesture all of the revelations of the last month. "I'm scared too. I'm scared for Aura; scared for myself. And I'm scared for you. But you make me want to fight the demons outside and the demon that lives inside me. You make me stronger, and Aura senses it.

"If it wasn't for you, we'd be so wrapped up in ourselves, we wouldn't care about what the rest of the world was going to go through. You give me the reason to see beyond my sister and myself. Only you." He brushed a loose curl from her face. Jude closed her moist eyes, shutting out the intense look in his hazel ones, hoping that some darkness would help her to see clearly.

"Aura's in love with a man who is pushing 2000, and most of that time he's not even human. What's 8 or 9 years, huh? I'll still think you are the most beautiful woman when you're 80. I will still love you." He kissed her eyelids and the space between them, erasing the crease of anxiety and doubt which had been there before. The warmth of his breath spread from her temple down through her body, filling her heart with something fresh. Something true.

"I am so in love with you, Jude Marcello," his whispered voice quavering with emotion.

Jude finally opened a clenched fist and rested it on his heart. She felt it beat once, twice. Three times. Steady, comforting. Her own heart slowed to match its rhythm.

She tilted her chin up and opened her still damp eyes to look up into his beautiful face.

"I love you too," she whispered, simply and meaningfully.

He kissed her then, putting all the love he felt for her into that embrace as he held her close, their bodies moulding together. For the first time since her father had died, Jude felt a wholeness engulf her body, mind, and soul. Finally, she felt as though somebody wanted—no, *needed*—her. She belonged to someone, and he was wholly hers. With absolute certainty, she now knew where her home and her heart lay.

Chapter 45

Before dawn could send Stace back into the shadows, he led the motley crew up to the summit of the fort.

Aura considered her companions: their regenerated, powerful leader; the wolf who walked in her human skin, and the beast she loved deeply, but with whom she could only truly be with for two short days a month when he wore his humanity.

Then there was the Tether, her beloved twin brother. Her beginning; the other half of her soul. He walked easily, hand in hand with the human he had fallen wholly in love with. In the shadow of the black wolf, the spaniel padded along, her brown eyes watching her people, her small nose twitching, and the bases of her long silky ears rising above her head as she listened to all the sounds in the dark woods. The terrier skittered around them, happily moving between them all but silently taking cues from his new pack leader, the wolf's calm demeanour translating down to the small dog.

And then there was herself, Aura, the ancient Elemental that apparently united them all. She stifled a yawn, Tenney turning to her instinctively with a look of concern as her face registered the pain as her cut lip and chin were stretched by the movement. She smiled at him and waved.

-I'm okay!

He nodded once at her, failing to mask the concern in his eyes, before turning back to look up the path and whisper to Jude. Aura was pleased that Tenney had finally admitted to Jude how he felt. She watched them together; noticed how secure they now seemed with each other. The connection that they had formed together would only strengthen his connection to her, and subsequently, her connection to the world.

Hedge loped smoothly beside her, his lithe, sinuous body rolling as he kept pace with her. Aura thought about his strength to be able to withstand this strange separation and held on to it like a talisman which gave her the strength to endure. She counted the nights until she could be with him properly again as she held his coarse mane of hair in her closed fist.

They crested the hill and came upon the now familiar clearing. They walked through the meadow towards the flat rocks, where Meg quickly started a fire. Hedge lay down beside her right-hand side, leaning into her and sharing his body warmth. Tenney mirrored Hedge;

sitting on Aura's left, instinctively leaning against her, shoulder to shoulder. His free arm was snaked around Jude's waist, pulling her tight to him.

Stace and Meg looked at the foursome, each one supporting the other. It felt right somehow, the four of them, together. United by a common cause.

United by love.

Werewolf, Elemental, Tether, and human. The dogs by their feet, asleep as the flames roared.

Stace.

Aura looked at him. The yellow and red of the flames danced off his porcelain white face, eyes watching her from the shadows the light created. He sat so still, barely breathing. But she knew his mind was working. She wanted to ask him again how it was possible for him to be here now. The only evidence of his near decapitation was the incredibly thin red line at his throat, which seemed to be disappearing with every minute of his return to strength.

"You need to stop thinking completely like a human. Considering only human limitations," he had told her earlier that night when Tenney had left them to find Jude. "You are an immortal being, who has been a fundamental part of this world since its conception. If you want to live, you must accept that."

His words reverberated around her head, but she still didn't fully understand them. All she had to go on were this life's experiences and a couple of hazy memories Hedge had helped her to recall. There was a part of her that thought those memories were nothing but her active imagination, a fantasy to please him. The memories of Glevum could just be a result of her knowledge of Roman life in the city, passed down to her by her father.

She felt herself shiver, whether from the cold, the tiredness, or just a deep, strange sadness, she didn't know. Tenney wrapped his right arm around her and held the two women he loved best in the whole world close to him, unwilling to forsake either of them. Aura's head, bending to his shoulder, found its usual resting place, and she began to feel better.

"Hedge said that I should be able to change my appearance," Aura said to Stace and Meg, wanting to begin to do something productive, anything that might stop her mind from turning in circles with questions unanswered or unready to be accepted.

Meg, who was sitting beside Stace, picked up a piece of wood and began pulling the bark off.

"Of course you can," she said simply. "We've all seen the dragon."

Aura fidgeted, feeling embarrassed as she became aware of her vanity. "Yeah, I know," she replied, "but that's not what I meant." Aura had begun to twist the hem of her fleece around her thumb as she let the awkwardness enshroud her.

-Why is this so hard? she asked Tenney desperately.

Tenney cast a sidelong glance at her before turning back to Meg and Stace.

"What she wants to know is, can she fix her face?" he asked. For once, she was grateful for his bluntness.

"Of course you can," Meg repeated, as if it were the most natural thing in the world to change one's appearance. "But what you have to ask yourself is, do you want to?" Aura looked between the two mentors, a frown line appearing between her eyes. Why wouldn't she want to fix the disfigurement? She had thought that Meg would understand her desire not to stand out too much in society, her desire to blend in and go unnoticed.

Aura could feel Tenney about to stand up for her, his mind probing her thoughts, reading her emotions as though they were his own. But before he could utter a word, Meg continued.

"You have to think what the humans in your life will think if, suddenly, you're all healed up. Perfect again. How will you answer those questions?" Meg looked at her, her yellow eyes focusing their beams on her face searchingly. She pointed the de-barked wood at her. "You always have to think of the consequences." They all heard the stress on the word *always*; they all saw Meg's fingers tense slightly around the wooden shard.

"It was the automatic, gut reaction to things that sent you and Tenney to the *inter duo mundos* not once, but twice. This would be a good time to learn to think, quickly, about what might happen to you and to those around you, if you give in to your powers and act without considering as many of the outcomes as possible."

"It's only a cut!" Tenney said heatedly.

"Yes, but it's an obvious cut, which for a human would take weeks to heal, and then it would scar. Aura can't go home with a wound like that vanished as though it had never happened." Her yellow eyes moved back to Aura. "If you can learn to control your physical body, you will find it easier to control your Elemental body."

"But," said Stace, finally breaking his silence, "we can teach you to heal the wound on your leg."

Since Stace's return to life, Aura had been clad in jeans, the only visible evidence of the injury to her leg being the limp as she walked. Stace had not seen her in anything that would show the bandage, and it hadn't been mentioned in his presence. She naively began to wonder how he knew about the cut.

Then she noticed his nostrils flare slightly. It hit her like a punch to the gut as she truly accepted what Stace was. He is a nightwalker, an immortal, ancient beyond belief. A bona fide vampire. A drinker of blood.

Human blood.

This man, this Creature, could read their bodies better than an x-ray or a CT scanner. He could see their hurts as though they stood before him naked. Through his senses of smell and hearing, he was able to detect even the slightest change in their blood, the rhythm of their heartbeats. His eyes, she realised, watched their pulses as they rose in their necks.

Aura felt her cheeks flush as she let the shame swell up in her, realising how badly she had underestimated him. And Meg. Hedge as well. She had thought of them as human, with unfortunate side effects. But human nonetheless.

Only now was she beginning to understand what he had meant back at the Lodge.

They weren't human. And neither was she.

She had to stop thinking as a human and start thinking as an Elemental. She squared her shoulders, sat upright. Tenney, reading her thoughts, confirming with her what she was discovering, let her draw away from him slightly.

"Okay," she said, a new determination rising within her. "Teach me."

**

Meg held out one of the two mirrors she had brought with her to the summit. Aura had rolled up the leg of her jeans, and gingerly pulled off the dressing. Tenney watched her closely, ready to leap in, protect her.

"TENNEY!" Stace barked at him. "Relax. She's fine. Concentrate on lending her some of that excess energy you have been blessed with. Focus on supporting her and not on protecting her."

Tenney ground his teeth and narrowed his eyes at Stace. An animalistic part of him wanted to growl at Stace. Tell him exactly where he could go. He probably would have, if he hadn't felt Jude's hand on his thigh, squeezing it gently. He felt the warmth and comfort of her hand seep up his body; the rage and need to protect which had begun to cloud his mind put back in its place, if only for a time.

He rested his hand over hers, interlocking his fingers with hers. She left her hand where it was, gently rolling her fingers like a wave across his jeans. Tenney breathed in and closed his eyes, seeing Aura through his mind's eye and not his physical ones. Aura shone at him, a light blue beacon. She looked like a thermal image that soldiers used in the films to see through walls. Only brighter, warmer somehow despite the coldness of her blue light. He saw the cords between them and gasped. He had known they were there, had felt them, but this was the first time he had seen them so clearly.

-You ok? She asked.

-Uh huh. You?

-Yeah. It's an ugly wound though.

Tenney let his mind's eye travel down her leg and saw a puckered slash of white marring the blue light of her skin. He tensed. Jude's fingers rolled over his thigh, and he relaxed.

Carefully he began to pour energy into his sister.

-WHOA! She cried out silently. *-Steady Ten – you need to keep some for yourself remember! Just a trickle will do.* He felt her smile, heard her laugh softly as he eased off. *-That's better. Thanks.*

"Hold the mirror at your leg so you can see the cut clearly." Meg instructed from the physical realm. He saw Aura do as instructed. "Now, see the particles of air around you. You already know you have control over them. Use them to knit your skin back together."

Aura concentrated. Tenney heard her breathe in and out, could feel her anxiety that it wasn't working. He heard Stace tell her to relax, and he saw the tension in her shoulders. He breathed with her, using his lungs to slow hers down. Aura relaxed.

Her light grew brighter, and he saw her lean back, no longer looking at the mirror or the wound, but at the movements in the air around her. Her head was tilted back as though in ecstasy, her mouth opened in a gasp. A moan. She shuddered. She shimmered.

There was a blazing, radiant flare of light at her leg. To Tenney it looked like the flash of light just before an eclipse of the sun; it was almost too blindingly bright to look at. Tenney automatically shielded his face and felt Jude dig her fingers into his leg as she too gasped in surprise. The blackness that was Hedge sat upright, his head cocked, ears batting forwards and back. Jess whimpered a little and he felt her warm little body nestle against his side.

Finally, Tenney blinked open his eyes trying to shift the small flashes of light that still played over his retinas. He saw the residue of the light as it faded around her leg. Aura then raised her head, and looked at him, smiling joyfully.

"How did you do that?" Stace asked. He too sounded surprised at the power she had demonstrated.

She tore her eyes off her brother. "It wasn't just me," she replied. "Tenney helped."

All the eyes of the little group turned to stare at Tenney.

**

Stace and Meg had sent the two couples off in separate directions, each pair with one of the mirrors, to practice their telepathic communication from a distance. They heard the laughing, the giggles, the sneaked kisses from Tenney and Jude when they thought no one was paying them any attention.

"They need to be much further apart for this to work," Meg said solemnly, avoiding the part of this night's conversation she was dreading.

"I know. Tenney will be going to Bristol soon to help Jude to find her mother. That should be far enough. An interesting experiment," Stace replied, a small smile on his lips, his scholarly side showing through the hard soldier he had been presenting since his return.

God, she was glad he was back. It had been such a long time since his last revival; her paranoia told her that he might not be able to do it. That he had forgotten how to do it. Ever since their time in America, he had been different, softer somehow.

They needed the General. They had needed the General ever since they had found the twins again. She was saddened that it had taken his death for him to finally, fully and intentionally, let that side out again. She wouldn't like to be the demon that had tried to kill him when Stace got his hands on her again.

But mostly she was just glad for him to be beside her again. She was lost when they weren't together. Even in those times when they had had to separate, she didn't feel right until they were working together again. Raising Aura's different incarnations, teaching her and her sister-tether how to live in this strange, unmerciful world.

Thinking of Aura as a child and all her many, and varied twin sisters brought back the part of the conversation she was trying to avoid. Her shoulders hunched forward as she wrapped her arms around herself and brought her knees up to her chest.

"They really aren't a normal pairing, are they?" she finally said.

"No. They're not," Stace said gravely.

"Aura was always so much more dominant in her past lives, her Tether only really having nominal power over her. Do you remember? How her sisters were more like an anchor, only really there to keep her tied to the world?" Stace nodded his head. He did remember.

"But this time they seem to be more equal. I didn't think the Tether could walk with her in the *inter duo mundos*. And his rage, it's so palpable, so quick. If they can't control it, they will never have lives apart from each other. He will kill an innocent, or himself. And nobody will be able to stop him, no matter how strongly he loves them."

Stace clenched his jaw, understanding that they were both thinking of Jude and Hedge, and the conundrum they faced. If they stayed in Tenney and Aura's lives, so closely entwined by the bonds of love, their lives were in danger should the twins be forcibly separated. Or the twins may make the wrong choice when faced with saving the ones they loved. But Tenney and Aura were more stable, happier when they were with their partners; it was different from the other times Aura and Hedge had been together.

This time her Tether loved someone as much as she loved Hedge. They were more equal. They were stronger when the four of them were together.

He ran a hand through his hair, down his face. His tell when something was troubling him.

"There has never been an Elemental so deeply entangled with their Tether. There has never been a Tether able to help create the light show we witnessed tonight or walk with their sibling between realms and bring them back to the world. I honestly think that Aura would not have been able to do it if Tenney hadn't been there. Think back," his hands had become animated as he began to get caught up in his discoveries and new understandings. Meg watched his long, cold fingers as they danced through the air.

"All the times she changed form, it was either to protect him or she was in a deep dream state. Or when she walked in the *inter duo mundos* or caused the sonic blasts, it always had something to do with him. I think we were underestimating them when we said that she would be nothing without Tenney." He paused.

"If Tenney is killed, or commits suicide, or is separated from her for too long even with their strong communication links, she will falter. When he dies and after he is returned to the earth at his burial, she will cease to exist in a human body." He stopped suddenly, his hands falling to his lap as he turned to Meg. She saw the fearful solemnity in his eyes. "I fear this is her last life. Air will rampage, uncontrolled by its physical form. Nothing will stop her as her grief will be unendurable, even if she will not remember why she grieves."

"What about her love for Hedge? That is as strong as Tenney's is for Jude. We've both seen how Jude is able to calm Tenney. Maybe after a few more full moons together, they will have that same tie that the other two share?" Meg was clutching at straws, trying to hold on to some form of hope.

Stace turned to her, his face sad. "Meg, can you not see that they are already at that point in their relationship? When have you ever seen the Wolf willingly enter a building? Or stay so long around humans? At the end of the day, however, the love the twins have for each other will always win out. They are one and the same. One cannot exist without the other.

"All of the Elementals who are still a part of the world are probably experiencing a new path, a new, stronger, more unusual Tethering. Choices will have to be made. I just pray that when that time comes, Aura and Tenney and the other Elementals and Tethers choose the right one for the world, and not just for themselves."

They heard the laughter as the foursome gave up and instead engaged in a spot of tag, the terrier yipping happily around their legs, Tenney using every opportunity to grab Jude, who laughed out loud and playfully slapped his hands away. The flush on her warm brown skin betraying her delight and her desire to be touched that way.

Hedge was circling Aura like a force field, preventing the others from tagging her. But Aura was having no trouble keeping the others away from her when Meg saw her control the air to make Tenney rise slightly from the ground when he tried to tackle her from behind, sending him sprawling in the trampled grass. Meg couldn't help but laugh as Bo leapt on his master, smothering him with his small body.

The older dog, sleeping happily beside the fire, opened one eye and looked reprovingly at Meg, making her laugh louder still.

They all seemed so happy in each other's company, so accepting of their differences. She knew that Stace was right about her son and Aura, and she worried about how it would affect him when Aura became one with the air again. How would an immortal wolf-man manage in the world without Aura's physical self somewhere in it? She realised now how cruel it had been separating them for so many centuries. Maybe if she had allowed them to meet in each lifetime, all of this could have been avoided, or at least made more bearable.

Meg breathed a sigh and felt Stace wrap his brotherly arm around her shoulders, pulling her into his side. They watched the four children— for they were children to her and Stace— together in the glow of the fire's light. Their children. That was how she felt about them, even Jude, she realised with some astonishment.

Oh, how she wished she could protect them from what was to come.

Chapter 46

The Wiseman's time in Stratford-Upon-Avon had begun strained. Each of them was tired and barely talking. Sam reread Theo's messages for the hundredth time. He knew what he had to do; he just wasn't sure it would work.

As they got out of the car at The Falcon Inn, after a trip to Anne Hathaway's house, they staggered towards the doors leading to the reception area. Sam glanced at his parents. His father looked marginally better for being away from Denebury, but his mother appeared worn out. *Worrying about the others,* he thought, unable to hide the small worm of bitterness.

Sam stowed his phone in his pocket and walked up to Martha. He held out his hand. "Here, Ma, let me carry that," he said, taking her bag. He turned away, not unaware of the look of shock that spread across her face.

He had to admit, from the outside, it did look kinda cool. The Falcon Inn was a long, low black-and-white Tudor building sitting at a crossroads in the heart of the town. It faced the street opposite a small church called The Guild Chapel. Down the street, he could see the lights reflecting off the river Avon and the roof of the Royal Shakespeare Company theatre. Sam looked left and saw more Tudor houses, shops, bars and hotels.

His dad began talking animatedly, pointing out interesting facts about the street and the buildings, trying to make this trip feel like a real, pre-planned, much-longed-for holiday.

The three entered the hotel. Samuel retrieved their key, and they climbed the stairs to the first floor and their suite of rooms. Suddenly, his dad left to retrieve some forgotten bauble from the car and Sam was left alone with his mother.

They both fidgeted, unused to the slow-growing feeling of detachment that had crept unknowingly between them. Martha wrapped her arms around her body, gave him a small smile, and quickly looked away. Sam, unused to beginning conversations, thought back to Theo's advice:

Theo: *Treat it like a mission in the Game. Act like you want to be there with them. Enjoy the few days you will spend just you & them, no Halves to distract their attention from you. Be helpful, courteous. Don't spend hours on your tablet or phone, at least not when you're with them. You'll see them relax. Trust me.*

He had smiled when Theo first started calling his brother and sister the Halves. Somehow, it made them more bearable, less perfect. Sam drew in a breath. "Are you okay, Ma?" he asked, as though it was the most natural thing in the world.

Martha started at her usually shy, quiet boy, speaking to her unprompted. It shocked her out of her stupor, reminding her that she had three children, not just two. And the youngest one was here, with her. She felt her heart swell a little; she still had one child who needed her.

She reached out to her teenager, rubbing a hand up his arm reassuringly. "I'm fine, love," she answered. "I'm just wondering whether it's too soon to phone Tenney, see how they're doing." She looked away again, reaching into her pocket and fingering her phone, not seeing the hurt that flared up behind her child's eyes. Sam clenched his jaw, cut to the quick that she was still only thinking about the others. He couldn't quite hide the hurt in his voice when he replied that she should do what she thought was best. Martha was too caught up in her own worries to hear it anyway, as she pulled the phone out and hit Tenney's speed dial.

Samuel walked back in, still smiling in a parody of the Cheshire cat as Martha was talking to Tenney. Sam saw her shoulders relax as she was reassured that everything was okay. Martha smiled at Samuel, who also breathed out in relief.

She hung up. "Aura's fast asleep and Tenney's watching a film with Jude. All perfectly harmless, they're just relaxing. Nothing to worry about." She said the last part as though it had been Sam and Samuel who had been worrying about them, and not her. "Right then!" she decreed, clapping her hands together. "Shall we go and get some supper or what?" And with that, she led the two of them out of the suite.

And so began Sam's mission: give his parents three great days with him. Be the perfect son. And then, Wednesday night, suggest that they might like to spend Thursday on their own, maybe go and see a play. Tell them he'll be fine, that he has homework to do before heading back to school.

Then, when they leave Thursday morning, he was to walk to the train station and catch the first available train to Bristol. He could then make his way to The Clifton Suspension Bridge.

And he would finally meet Theo, the person who had become so much more than a friend in his heart.

His heart began to beat rapidly, a mix of excitement and nervous anticipation flooding through him.

**

Aura, Tenney, Jude, and Hedge spent the next few days together. Their days were filled with training from Meg and Stace, perfecting their telepathy, Aura's shapeshifting, and Tenney's fighting skills. Jude laughed every time Meg tripped Tenney or slipped his punch only to land a blow in his ribs.

But he improved. Jude had to admit his natural athleticism meant he learned the moves quickly, his excessive energy aiding his fast recovery. Soon, he had Meg dancing on her tiptoes as he caught her unawares a few times.

Stace watched them from the shadows, working mainly with Aura, teaching her about meditation and feeling connected to the world, not just to Tenney—or Hedge. Jude had overheard Stace talking to Aura about the times she felt connected to the world when she wasn't with her brother. Aura had blushed sweetly, burrowing her still-scarred chin into her woollen turtleneck. The wolf shifted closer to her, and Aura leaned against him.

"When I'm with Hedge," she had admitted. Stace looked at her, needing to know more. She had shifted again. "You know," she cocked her head at the great black beast, "when he's himself and we're… together…" At that, she raised her eyebrows and looked pointedly at Stace.

Jude had smiled broadly and laughed quietly when she saw the ancient vampire's eyes widen in understanding. She thought she saw him pale further, which she had been sure should have been an impossibility. From across the clearing, Tenney had stopped his swordplay with Meg and shouted, unhappy with the direction the conversation had taken. Meg used his distraction against him and executed a perfect back leg sweep, sending him sprawling yet again to the ground, gladius point aimed directly at his heart.

"Congratulations. Game over. You're dead. Don't be distracted. Let Aura fight her battles. You fight yours."

This time Jude laughed out loud, restraining Bo from leaping on Tenney as he was prone to do when he was on the ground.

They were happy, she realised, enjoying the company each other could provide. She gave Tenney and Aura the space they needed to stay connected, and she was pleasantly surprised to find that she wasn't jealous of their closeness. Ever since that night, when Tenney had told her he loved her, she had been filled with a new sense of confidence. Of belonging. Of hope.

At quiet times, she would consider her impending interview with Gloucester Police. She ran through all the questions they might ask her about that night at the Manor House, her time at the Lincoln Force, or even her reasons for staying so long in Gloucestershire. Tenney had picked up a few times on her apprehension. She just kissed him, patted his cheek, and sent him back for more pummelling from Meg.

But she was worried about it. She was also anxious about the possible revelations of the Bonfire Night party at The Avon Gorge Hotel. The days were moving so quickly, it would soon be upon them. She hoped beyond hope for a real, clear lead on her mother. She wanted, at this time of joy and love, to share some of it with her estranged parent.

Her only parent.

Thinking of her absent mother naturally caused her to remember her dad, his wonderful Bronx accent as he gave her his advice on how to handle Rae.

"She's an exotic creature, Honey. She needs to be treated gently, with care and love. But she is stronger than either you or I could ever realise or imagine. One day she will tell you her story, her sacrifices for us. And then you'll understand her distance. But know this, my precious girl; she loves you with her whole heart."

Jude remembered his arms wrapped around her as he held her in his lap after one particularly trying time when her mother had ignored her. He had kissed her on her forehead, wiped away her tears. When Rae had returned to them from her mental prison, she insisted on tucking Jude up in bed, telling her stories of werewolves and vampires, angels and demons.

She shivered at her mother's accuracy in her stories now that she knew the truth of the world. Again, she wondered if Rae knew more than she let on. It was one of the many reasons she needed to find her, to ask her what she knew about this turn of events. Jude was determined to get some real answers from her mother.

At night, Aura stayed at the Lodge, close to Hedge, even though all she could do was lie beside him. She said she slept better knowing he was there, even if she couldn't be with him as they both wanted. The differences between Hedge the Man and Hedge the Wolf became more apparent the more time they spent together.

When he was a wolf, he was 100% wolf, although cleverer than a beast ought to be, and semi-domesticated by his devotion to Aura. But when he was a man, he thought like a man, acted like a man—just one with unusual eating habits and heightened agility, strength, and senses.

So, Jude and Tenney left them together, returning either to his family home or her hotel, where they were as close as two people could be, cementing this new love for eternity.

**

The chill of the hard winter to come settled ominously over the ancient woodland. The animals prepared themselves for the next few months: the fallow and roe deer finishing the rut; badgers, foxes, and squirrels settling into their setts, dens, and nests; hedgehogs beginning their hibernation. The boar migrated deeper into the darkest parts of the forest.

The air was full of the natural silence that beckons the coming season, the anticipation of snow and storms. The British soil was settling and preparing itself for the long sleep, ready for the spring. Overhead, a solitary, silent barn owl flew by, a flash of white. Pipistrelles and long-eared bats danced through the sky, chasing their prey, competing with the greater horseshoe bats from the Manor House's barn.

A badger, looking for any last morsel of food, snuffled through the undergrowth. Its sensitive nose twitched, scenting the animals that had passed there before as it carried on, unconcerned by its surroundings. It went further into the undergrowth and stopped short. A movement in the shadows, something darker than the night. The badger turned around and quickly sped away.

Gallagher, clad in a new body and using the shadows as a cloak, had been watching the group as they moved around the clearing of the ancient fort, learning more about them as they interacted with each other. Discovering their weaknesses, their strengths. He wondered at the strength of the Elemental and the Tether. He was curious about the power the human woman held over them.

He felt quite confident that his presence was going undetected by them. Even the lycanthropes, clad in human and wolf-skins, were unaware of him, so caught up were they by the others, their main focus. Only the ordinary creatures of the world avoided his darkness.

At night, the Nightwalker, newly regenerated after his death at the Manor, hunted the larger animals, rebuilding his strength. Gallagher followed him, assessing his strength, realising that he would be the most dangerous of the group when it came to the fight. Their past history meant that Gallagher had witnessed first-hand Placidus's strength, power, and intelligence.

But he had also learned how to watch him from afar. He knew him as well as he knew any being in heaven, earth, or hell. These nights, he used his innate understanding of Placidus to keep one step ahead of him, remaining downwind and using the portals if the Nightwalker came too close or caught his scent on the breeze.

Made from pure darkness, the portals had first opened when two ancient cities fell to two of the mightiest angels. Many of the demons who were bred in these cities had used these gateways to flee, lying in wait and returning to the earth when it was their time to enter the fight. Gallagher twitched in anticipation. The time was finally near. They had waited for an eternity, skulking in the darkness, using human bodies to move freely in this world. Soon, they could claim their rightful places and show their true forms, making slaves of humanity for eternity.

The Nightwalker stirred from his feast of the boar he had taken down. Blood dripped from his mouth as his head twisted around, trying to work out where his instincts were screaming for him to look.

Gallagher silently turned on his heel. He strode soundlessly through the undergrowth until he found a patch of inky blackness. He stepped through it…

…and walked out of the tunnel at the remains of the nineteenth-century Iron Works situated nine miles across the Forest from the site of the Fort. He surveyed the site before him from one of the terraces of the stepped ruins. Behind him rose the grey stone of the old buildings; below him were the works ponds, now dried up, and an expanse of grass, partially taken over by the dense woodland surrounding it.

Dotted all over the area were the possessed, more than had ever congregated in one place since the destruction of their home. An army of stolen bodies; a legion of warriors preparing in their own ways for the coming battle, and he was their Legate. Their leader. In his hand, he twisted the ruby dagger, *Χερουβείμ Στιλέτο*, the weapon that would bring about his enemies' downfall.

He smiled viciously, savouring the prospect of defeating his old enemy, and moved down into the orgy of writhing bodies.

Tomorrow night would mark the dawn of a new era, one shrouded in shadows.

* *Cherouveím Stiléto* - Χερουβείμ Στιλέτο *"Χερουβείμ"* (Cheroubin) refers to cherubim, which are heavenly beings or angels, and *"Στιλέτο"* (Stiléto) means stiletto or dagger.

Chapter 47

The morning of Halloween and the night of the party had finally arrived, crisp and chill, the sun hanging low in the morning mists that had seeped up from the valley below. Jude rifled through her wardrobe, pulling out her police uniform. She breathed in deeply as she looked at it on its hanger, considering all that it had stood for—her pride when she wore it and the (sometimes begrudging) respect she received from the people she helped or arrested.

She thought of her old Commander, remembering how he had almost insisted she stay in Gloucestershire. He had swept away any trace of the incidents with Tenney at the train station and the cathedral. Then, he had given her the choice: transfer to the Gloucester force or return to Lincoln. What would her friend and partner Ellie say if she were here? Would she tell her to follow her head or her heart?

Her tummy filled with butterflies. Anxiety threatened to swamp her as she thought of the two events scheduled for today. She shook herself, got a grip, and began to redress as a policewoman again.

Tenney had left only moments earlier to spend time with Aura before they left for the party that night. She had told him that she was going to Gloucester to get a party dress for tonight; she didn't want him to worry unnecessarily about the police interview. She looked at herself in the mirror. Her old self, the one she had left in Lincoln, stared back at her.

Her long, curly brown hair was scraped back in a tight, neat bun, and the uniform sat on her like an old glove, its familiar reassuring lines not quite failing to hide her curves. She did intend to finally go dress shopping after the interview, and with that in mind, she packed some civvies in her rucksack.

One last look in the mirror, checking she looked presentable and professional. She zipped up her jacket, grabbed her bag and car keys, and left the hotel room.

The Jaguar took her through the village, past the lane which led to the Wisemans' terraced house and the Fort, then past the chip shop, inn, and village store. At the small roundabout, she cast her eyes right, towards the Manor house. There was still a police presence there, the archaeologists asked to keep away from the site for at least another week.

Since the discovery of two more bodies on the roof – one of whom, it was confirmed, had been a well-respected and well-liked cameraman who worked for the BBC - compounded with the hysterical kid's story about witnessing the living dead rising from the earthen mound by the Temple, the police still had a lot of work to do. As far as she knew, they had put the boy's tale down to a vicious prank by some other youths in the week before Halloween. The boy's bruises were probably from twisting his ankle as he passed out from the drink he had consumed.

The fact they looked as though they had been made by claws proved nothing, according to the police report. Those poor children would never know how close to the truth they were.

She turned left and drove away from the place of death, the church zipping past her on her right, the primary school and estate across the road from it. Next was the steep road that led down from the village, around a sharp bend.

As she drove through the canopy of leaves, the road widened out, the woods giving way to rolling fields. The sight before her never failed to take her breath away. Laid out in front of her, before the road curved around again and again, was the Severn valley. The mighty river curved down from the Welsh mountains, which lay beyond Gloucester, to the Bristol Channel and the sea.

Behind it were the Cotswolds, and in the middle of the valley, shining in the reflection of the early winter sunlight, Gloucester Cathedral stood out like a beacon. If she had had time to stop and really look, she would have seen the distinctive boxy shape and tall white chimney of the hospital, the rows of dock warehouses now luxury apartments at the repurposed fashionable Quays.

The floodplain fields surrounded the city on all sides, interspersed by the river and the canals. Villages were dotted about, bisected by the main roads. She knew that this land was prone to flooding when the river burst its banks, sometimes during the bore, when a wave flowed up from the estuary. This land really was ruled by Sabrina, she thought almost reverently as the next bend stole the view from her sight.

Jude wondered what it would have been like for Meg and Hedge to live here, to grow up in these hills, this valley, 2000 years ago. It was almost too overwhelming a prospect for her human mind to comprehend, and yet she knew now that she did believe what they told her of their past entirely and unquestionably.

In fact, after Tenney's admission of his feelings, the things she had seen and done since he blasted into her life, she realised that she really did believe them. Suddenly the world was full of possibilities—she began to think about a TV series she had watched, where the tagline was

'Endless Wonder.' And that was exactly the phrase she wanted to use to describe the way she felt at this very moment.

The world was full of endless wonder, and with Tenney, she was going to experience it wholeheartedly. Whatever the outcome of today's interview and tonight's party, she knew she had a place where she belonged.

With Tenney. He was her home. He held her heart like no one had before, and no one would again.

She smiled, positive about the future for the first time in her life. It was at that moment that she decided definitely to hand in her notice at Lincoln constabulary, find a home and accept whatever new job role they offered her in Gloucestershire.

She would give this fledgling relationship a real go, see what happened. Build a new life for herself, and when she found her mother again, she would bring her to live here, in these healing hills, away from the claustrophobia of living in a city. A place where perhaps they could mend their relationship, get to know each other again. Properly. As adults.

Yes, she thought. Endless wonders. Endless possibilities.

At the T-junction, she made another left, and this time drove along the banks of the river, following its twists and turns through the villages of the valley, and into Gloucester.

**

Tenney and Aura sat together at the top of Pen y Fan. Aura was wrapped up against the chill in the thick sleeping bag Tenney had carried. Beanies were pulled down low over their heads, covering the tops of their ears. They sat close to each other, Tenney's arm drawing his sister into his side as she rested her head in her natural spot. They had decided to try out the dragon flight again, to see if they could do it without stress, anxiety, or separation as a trigger.

They had flown for miles, revelling in the opportunity it presented them to be truly alone. They felt freer flying through Aura's element, high above the clouds. Instinctively, they both chose the mountain as their point of destination. It carried memories of a camp the school had organised for them when they were 14. They remembered trekking up here by foot with their classmates. The view had been marred by cloud. But today, using her powers, Aura willed the cloud cover to part so they could see the view. Aura had told Tenney about how Stace had run here with her the first time she had consciously transformed.

They looked north, and in the distance, over the rolling desolate landscape, they could see Brecon itself sitting in the hills.

-*It's quite beautiful, isn't it?* Aura thought.

-*Yeah. Shame we didn't get to see it the first time after we trekked all that way,* Tenney laughingly replied.

-*Do you remember the blisters on my feet when we got back to the camp? They were so gross!*

-*Remember them?* he replied, almost despairingly. -*I had to share your pain, you couldn't handle it by yourself! And that was all subconsciously, before we knew what we were doing.*

She shifted in his arms, nudging him slightly in his ribs with her elbow. With the playful jolt, he felt her shiver. He held her closer and said out loud, "You're getting cold. Maybe we should think about heading back?"

She shook her head vehemently. "Na ah, watch this. Meg taught me something new whilst you were, ahem, with Jude." This time it was his turn to pinch her lightly through the sleeping bag. "Oi!" she cried out in fun, "do you want me to show you or not?"

"By all means," he replied, laughing, feeling truly happy.

Aura closed her eyes. He watched her, her small heart-shaped face, the jagged scar Stace had forbidden her from healing in case it raised too many questions. He could see the blue veins under her light skin. Her nose wrinkled slightly in concentration. And then, around him, he felt the air shift and grow marginally warmer. It came from the south, warming their backs.

"What the?!" he said, looking around.

"Shhhhhhh!" she admonished. She brought one hand out of the bag and rested a fingertip on his temple. "Close your eyes," she ordered.

He did so. Immediately, he saw what she could see. All the different currents of air moving around them, in different colours. A rainbow of continuous movement. The majority of colours were blues and greens, icy cold hues. But interspersed in them were oranges, reds, and yellows. He gasped in amazement. Using her mind, Aura was choosing which air current she wanted to move around them. Selecting one of the few warm colours, she was calling it

369

to her to warm them. She manipulated it so that it formed a bubble of comfortable heat around them, taking the chill away.

When she was satisfied that they would be comfortable for a little while yet, she removed her finger from Tenney's head and opened her eyes. The vision was slow to fade in his eyes, a hazy memory of it lingering after she broke the physical connection.

"Wow," was all he needed to say, looking at her beaming, radiant face.

They sat there looking at the view, the warm bubble of air keeping the worst of the mountain's chill from them. They were together, at peace. All too soon, they knew it was time to head back.

Effortlessly, Aura transformed into the blue dragon, breathing warm air around Tenney, sending the southerly wind back on its course. He collected the sleeping bag and leapt onto her back. She grew the ties and held him firmly onto her.

-Ready?

As Tenney settled onto Aura's back, he felt the powerful muscles beneath her scales ripple with anticipation. The moment she sprang into the sky, he was enveloped in a rush of exhilaration. The ground fell away rapidly, and the wind whipped past his face, carrying with it the scent of pine and earth. The sensation was unlike anything else—an intoxicating blend of freedom and power.

-Aura – fly home via Gloucester! Tenney asked her. He sensed her glee as she instinctively knew why he would want to go that way.

The air around them grew colder as they ascended, but Aura's warm breath created a cocoon of comfort. He could feel the rhythmic beat of her wings, each powerful stroke propelling them higher and faster. The world below became a patchwork of greens and browns, rivers snaking through the landscape like silver threads.

As they soared above the clouds, the sun bathed them in a golden light, casting long shadows across the billowing white expanse. The sky stretched endlessly in every direction, a vast canvas of blue. The sensation of flight was both thrilling and serene, a perfect harmony of speed and stillness.

Tenney felt every movement Aura made, from the subtle shifts in her wings to the powerful thrusts that sent them rocketing forward. The air currents danced around them, and he could sense Aura's connection to the elements, guiding them effortlessly through the sky. The dragon's eyes, sharp and keen, scanned the horizon, while Tenney's heart pounded with a mix of awe and joy.

When Aura performed a somersault, the world spun around them in a dizzying blur, and Tenney's laughter echoed through the sky. The sensation of weightlessness, followed by the rush of gravity pulling them back, was exhilarating. It was a dance of freedom, a celebration of their bond and the incredible power they shared.

As they descended towards Gloucester, the landscape came into sharper focus. The winding river, the patchwork fields, and the distant city all seemed to welcome them. Aura's bellow resonated through the air, a triumphant call that made Jude, driving back to Denebury, look up and smile. For a moment, they were all connected, sharing the magic of the moment.

Aura momentarily broke cover, and Tenney laughed and waved as Jude waved up at them. With a final burst of speed, Aura shot back up into the atmosphere, leaving the world below behind. They soared above the clouds once more, the sky their playground, the wind their constant companion. It was a sensation of pure, unadulterated freedom, a reminder of the endless possibilities that lay ahead.

**

Sam couldn't believe that Theo's plan was working! He had played the dutiful son all week, being attentive and trying not to roll his eyes when his mother insisted on talking about the Halves, asking him over and over whether she should phone them or text them. But by Wednesday night, she seemed easier, more relaxed.

A few times, he had caught Dad looking at him, like he suspected something. But Sam just smiled and asked him questions about Stratford, which would be guaranteed to distract Samuel from his suspicions.

They were coming to the end of their week, with only two more nights before heading back on Saturday. "I'll be fine!" he had insisted as he suggested that his dad might like to take Mum to the theatre. He'd done some research and found a modern-ish play at the RSC. His mum had squirmed slightly, confessing that there were a few more places she would like to visit outside of the town. Maybe head north to Warwick …

And so, on Thursday morning, Sam happily waved his parents off. As he saw their car disappear down the street, he ran back up to his room. He finished checking he had everything he would need and wrote a note to his parents explaining that he'd got a call from a schoolmate. He had to go home early to finish a joint piece of school coursework.

It was really important. He was sorry. He'd see them on Saturday.

Sam left the note on their bedside table, ignoring the small niggle of doubt and apprehension that wormed in his gut. If he was forced to admit it, he had actually enjoyed his week with his parents. He had enjoyed spending time with them, without the direct competition from his brother and sister. But he was desperate to meet Theo.

Finally, this thought hardened his resolve as he tightened the straps on his backpack, cast his eye once more over the two-roomed suite, clenched his jaw, and left.

And now he was on the train, heading south. He had several hours to kill before he met Theo, but he wasn't bothered. He felt happy now that he had decided what he was going to do. Sam checked his phone once more, memorising the route he would have to walk from the last station at the Clifton Downs to The Avon Gorge Hotel.

Theo had insisted the grounds behind the hotel were the best place to see the fireworks. He'd said there would be a party; a group of his mates, fellow kids of parents who worked for his father, would be there too.

He said it would be epic.

He said he was looking forward to meeting Sam. Sam felt his face tighten from the smile he could no longer suppress.

As the train rumbled on, he felt his phone vibrate. It was a text message.

C u soon Sammy!

Sam's smile broadened. He could no longer contain his glee.

**

Aura double-checked Tenney's bag, making sure he hadn't crumpled the black-tie suit he'd borrowed from their neighbour down the road. She knew she was fussing, but this was a big moment for her. For both of them.

Tenney, in the same pair of jeans and the thick winter fleece he'd worn on Pen y Fan, smiled up at her as he pulled on his black boots. He opened his mind and spoke to her.

-Hey, this is good for us, remember?

-Yeah, I know. I'll just miss you, that's all.

-One night. Nothing will happen. And you can reach me anytime. You're keeping that cord open, right?

In her mind's eye, she saw the strongest cord which connected their soul, the one which connected her heart to Tenney. It was bright blue and strong. She was getting used to seeing these strange, wormy entities which kept her grounded through Tenney to the world.

Playfully, she mentally tugged on it.

-Oi! Felt that! he thought.

She just laughed.

"Ready?" she asked as he stood up.

"Ready."

**

Tenney walked down the road to Jude's hotel and knocked on her door.

"Hold on!" she called through the door.

A couple of seconds later, she opened the door, dressed in her skintight bike leathers. Tenney let out a groan as he took in her shape, perfectly sculpted by the dark clothing. He wrapped his hands around her waist, resting them on her hips and pulling her in closer. He gave her a kiss which left her imagination reeling at what he wanted to do, if they had had enough time.

Playfully she slapped him away. "Get off you idiot," she laughed. "We've got to go!"

Tenney groaned again and tried to think of things that would be deemed as being highly un-erotic.

She moved around the room, and over her shoulder she said: "Nice air show today by the way! Good job it was quiet on the roads. I don't think the other cars would have known what to make of you guys when you suddenly appeared out of thin air!" She was smiling as she said it.

"They'd have just thought they saw a weird plane or something. I'm realising that ordinary people are very good at only seeing what they want to see and creating something plausible for the things they don't believe!" He wasn't bothered. All he could think about was the fun night they had in front of them.

Aura's cord was still strong. It was just like she was there with them, only she stood behind him so he couldn't see her. Only sense her. She was also helpfully putting images of toads and warts in his mind, trying to help dampen his arousal. It wasn't really working. He rubbed his eyes.

Jude caught the action, and immediately came up to him, resting two hands on his chest, "You ok?" she asked concerned. Ever since his head injury she was always suspicious when he screwed his face up like that.

"Yeah," he said, explaining what Aura was trying to do. Jude just laughed, pressed herself against him, aggravating him, and kissed him softly on the mouth.

"Hold on, it'll be worth it when we get there!" she winked. His face turned red, as he tried to cool himself down. She turned away again walking to the wardrobe. A clothes bag was hanging there, holding her dress for that evening. In a smaller bag she had everything else that she would need. "Can you fit that and my shoes in your bag?" she said nodding at the bits and pieces on the bed.

"Yeah," he replied. "Why are we taking the bike and not the jag?" he asked, eyeing all their luggage.

"Coz the bikes more fun, and tonight, I feel like celebrating!" She couldn't quite hide the gleam of excitement in her eyes. Tenney wondered if there was something more going on than just the anticipation of the party and the hopeful, reconciliation with her mother. *If* there were any clues as to her mother's whereabouts.

Tenney watched Jude as she went into the bathroom, fixing earrings to her ears. He put what she asked in his bag and slung it over his shoulder, so it rested on his hip. He picked up Jude's backpack and slipped that over his shoulders, tightening the strap. Next, he carefully folded the clothes bag and attached it to the straps.

"Let's do this." Jude said, stepping from the bathroom.

He smiled and laughed, bowing slightly as he opened the door to let her through.

**

Tenney and Jude sped up the A48 towards Chepstow, the wind whipping past as they crossed the Old Severn Bridge. He savoured every second of holding onto Jude's waist, feeling the warmth of her body through her skintight bike leathers. She wriggled backwards, fitting perfectly between his legs, making him smile beneath his helmet. The ride felt all too brief as they arrived at The Avon Gorge Hotel, its grand facade overlooking the majestic Clifton Suspension Bridge.

Upon arrival, Tenney quickly touched base with Aura, letting her know they had arrived safely. He felt her smile through their connection, sharing the breathtaking view of the gorge and the bridge through his eyes.

Jude approached the reception desk and gave her name. The staff, recognising her, promptly escorted them to one of their finest suites. She inquired about Mr. Glendower and was informed that he eagerly anticipated meeting her at the evening's party and fireworks display.

Once alone in their suite, they exchanged a glance, then looked at the inviting bed.

"We've got less than 40 minutes, Cowboy," Jude teased, her eyes sparkling with mischief. "Can you manage it?"

Before she could finish her sentence, Tenney was already unzipping her bike leathers, pushing her gently onto the bed.

**

Forty-five minutes later, after a shower to wash off the grime of the road and the extra sweat they had created, they started to get dressed for the evening. Jude eyed Tenney up and down in his borrowed dinner suit. He wore black trousers that fit perfectly around his legs. His black jacket hung over the back of the chair, waiting to be put on. The white shirt had black buttons down the front, and he was struggling endearingly with his black bow tie.

"Come here," she said, reaching up to his neck to tie the tie for him, smoothing it out. She placed her hands on his chest, tapping him lightly with her fingers. "Gorgeous!" she said, kissing him.

Jude took a quick look at the time on her phone. "We're gonna be so late!" she groaned. Tenney just laughed and walked back into the bathroom.

Closing, but not locking the door, he looked into the mirror. He braced himself on the sink and closed his eyes. It was time to try the new communication. At the Fort, it had only been partially successful. Meg had surmised that it was because they were too close in proximity and the need wasn't great. Tenney could feel the beginnings of the rage scratching at him, begging him to let it take over, promising him that he would feel better if he just gave in.

The cord was still strong between them; he could still feel her, but the physical distance weighed down on him. Despite feeling euphoric and satiated by his time with Jude, it had only been a happy distraction. Now, he needed Aura. He needed to know that they were okay. That he was okay. That he could go down to the party and not fly off the handle, ruining everything for Jude. He exhaled and closed his eyes.

-Aura?

-I'm here. Having fun? She answered him quickly and clearly; it was like she was standing right beside him. He let out a relieved breath and tried to bring some jocularity to his feelings.

-You bet! They both laughed.

-I'm by a mirror. Wanna try this?

-Sure – hold on... Aura went dark. For a few seconds, he couldn't feel her. His grip on the sink intensified, his knuckles whitening, his palms sweaty.

-I'm back! I'm in the "cloakroom" at the Lodge. Hedge is here too. He sensed her make the speech marks over the word cloakroom. Amazingly, since acquiring the building, Stace had made great strides in making the place habitable. But the bathrooms were obviously quite low on his list. The downstairs cloakroom, larger than the twins' rooms at home, held an old loo, sink, and an overlarge mirror, mottled at the edges and warping slightly in the middle. But it was perfect for this experiment.

-Ok, ready to try this.

-Yep.

Tenney opened his eyes and looked in the mirror. He laughed with joy. Instead of seeing his own reflection, he saw his sister, smiling and laughing with him. Behind her was the familiar run-down, damp, mouldy space of the lodge's cloakroom. Hedge was lying across the door, his great black body barring it from entry by anyone outside the room. The reflection of his striking green eyes never once left Aura, following her constantly, his ears twitching to discern any changes in her voice, her heart rate, her breathing.

There was a vivid blue cord of light connecting them through the mirror. Tenney felt elated!

-*It worked!*

Aura was laughing and crying all at the same time.

-*You look very handsome!*

-*Ah, these old things? I wear these every day...* Tenney joked, running his finger around the inside of the collar, looking uncomfortable. Aura laughed at his gag.

-*I bet Jude looks beautiful?*

-*Dunno. I left her in the room in her undies. I thought she was beautiful in just those, but I don't think she would have appreciated me saying that... She's quite nervous.*

-*I'm not surprised. Stay linked, Tenney, so I know you're okay?*

She seemed worried. He placated her gently, promising not to leave her.

-*What are you doing tonight?*

-*Gonna sneak out past Stace and Meg. Sit with Hedge. It's a clear night tonight, we may see some fireworks from the top of the Fort. I rang Mrs. Morgan not long ago – the dogs are fine and apparently enjoying watching repeats of Midsomer Murders!* They had asked their neighbour if she wouldn't mind dog-sitting for one night, a request the old lady eagerly agreed to, virtually snatching the leashes from Tenney's hands when he had dropped them off.

-*Promise me you'll be careful, okay?* She looked at him meaningfully, cocking an eyebrow. The reprimand was softened by her smile.

- *'Course I'll be careful.* He was amazed at her strength as she tried to hide her sadness. - *Love you, Sis.*

-*Love you too. Have fun tonight. I'm so glad this worked!*

-*Me too, see you tomorrow.*

He saw the mirror shimmer, and then he was looking back at himself in the hotel bathroom. He tamped down the feelings of separation and went to the bathroom door.

When he came out, he stopped dead in his tracks.

She wore a long, green column dress, ruffled over the hips and hanging off one toned shoulder, leaving the other bare. She looked uncomfortable but beautiful, like a Greek goddess.

He walked up to her, taking her newly manicured hands in his. She nervously bit her bottom lip and looked down, her cheeks showing a blush as she tried to hide her awkwardness. To make her believe him, he lifted her chin and made her look straight into his eyes.

"I've never seen anything quite like you tonight. You take my breath away." He cupped her chin in his hands. She could feel his warm breath caress her face. He gently kissed her, careful not to smudge her lipstick. Then, taking her hand, he led her from the room and down to the party.

Chapter 48

People were mingling everywhere as the couple walked down the stairs. Waiters and waitresses moved gracefully through the crowd, balancing trays of champagne and delicate finger foods. This was a whole new experience for Tenney, and he suspected that Jude hadn't been to many parties like this either.

They stood on the landing, gripping each other's hands as they surveyed the mass of people swarming below. The heat from the bodies below rose up the stairs towards them. Tenney was desperate to loosen his bow tie; he ran a finger around his collar, feeling the small beads of sweat forming there. He felt Jude squeeze his hand, as much to reassure herself as him. He felt Aura sending him positive vibes, though he wished she could send a cool breeze as well.

Tenney and Jude looked at each other, and he momentarily forgot about his discomfort as he took in the sight of her again. She really did look gorgeous, her hair cascading down her back in soft, black curls and natural ringlets. The green dress clung in all the right places, and the colour, one that would wash out most people's complexion, served to heighten the warm browns in her skin. As she smiled up at him, the light reflected off her shiny lipstick. Her dark eyes were like warm pools of honeyed chocolate, framed by mascara and subtle eye shadow. He thought he might like to drown in them one day…

Tenney slipped his arm around her waist, proud to be escorting such a beautiful woman—his beautiful woman—to the party. He wanted to show her off, but also carry her back to the room and keep her all for himself.

"Ah, Officer Marcello!" The Scottish voice broke Tenney from his reverie. He felt his jaw clench slightly at the interruption. Jude patted his chest and turned to the intruder.

"Mr. Glendower," she said. So, this was the mysterious man she had met a few weeks ago, Tenney thought. He took his eyes from her and looked in the direction of her gaze. A thin, older gentleman, as tall as Tenney, stood before them. His eyes crinkled with pleasure as he took in Jude, the grey in them flashing with interest. Tenney instinctively tightened his hand on her waist, pulling her closer. He leaned down and whispered in her ear.

"Stay close, okay?" There was something off about this man. Something he didn't trust. He felt her subtle nod in agreement before she introduced them.

"May I introduce my partner, Tennyson Wiseman." Despite his discomfort, Tenney felt a shard of warmth in his heart as she publicly claimed him as her equal, her partner. He quickly stored the feeling, held out his hand to Glendower, and waited for him to reciprocate.

Glendower tore his eyes from Jude to Tenney, only then apparently realising that she had brought a plus-one. He looked shocked, a bit taken aback as he looked Tenney up and down. It was starting to get awkward, Tenney holding his hand out to the man. Glendower just assessed him, and then, just as Tenney considered withdrawing the handshake, the older man clasped his hand.

Two things happened simultaneously: first, Tenney experienced a sudden onslaught of information, hitting him like waves of the sea, too many to process, a series of clips assaulting him like a deranged movie reeling past his eyes.

The second thing that happened was that he felt like he was drowning, that the same waves of information were dragging him down into an abyss. He could smell and taste the salt of the ocean, hear the waves crash above him. Tenney felt lost at sea.

Somewhere far away, he felt Jude shaking him, calling his name over and over, trying to bring him back to the moment. Back to dry land.

With a great force of will, he dropped Glendower's hand. As he did so, he realised his own had become thick with sweaty, salty moisture. Staggering back, weak and lightheaded, he loosened the bow tie, letting it hang limply from his neck.

Jude was calling his name through a thick wad of air. Inside his mind, he felt Aura's concern. Suddenly, Tenney doubled over; he was sure that he had somehow swallowed seawater and was going to be sick. He coughed, surprised that nothing came up.

People were parting around him, sneering down their noses. He heard Glendower snap his fingers, call some waiters over, and tell them to help the young man to the bathroom and to stay with him until he had recovered. He bristled slightly at being referred to as a young man, and then Jude was no longer touching him as he was being half-walked, half-dragged to the toilets.

He tried to call out to Jude, but his throat was still too thick with brackish water to utter more than a gurgle. He looked back over his shoulder and saw Glendower ushering her away to the terrace.

Jude desperately looked back as the bathroom door closed between them.

**

Sam could see the lights of the hotel in the distance. He had just finished an awkward conversation with his mother, finding a quiet spot to talk to her away from any noises that might suggest he was someplace else, and not at his friend's house or the family home with his siblings.

She demanded to speak to Tenney or Aura. He had to think quickly, telling her some cockamamie story about them going to the cinema. He reassured her that he was okay and told her to enjoy the play. He wasn't too surprised when she told him they were coming back that evening after the play. He would have to ensure he was home before they were, but he felt sure he could get a lift back with Theo or someone from the party. Nothing could ruin this night! After hanging up, he let the stress out in a long breath, counted to three, and began walking again.

As his anticipation rose, he picked up his pace. The walk from Clifton Down station hadn't been too far, but it had been a long day, and he should have been tired. Now that he was near his destination, all he felt was a giddy excitement.

The hotel was on the right-hand side of the road, cars pulling up to its front door, letting out rich-looking partygoers. He could hear a string quartet's music playing through the doors as they opened. On the opposite side of the street and running away from the hotel itself were the characteristic white terraced Georgian houses typical of this affluent area.

A white wall ran from the hotel and down the street. Theo's instructions had been to look out for the sign saying, 'Clifton Rocks Railway.' He had said there was a small road that ran behind the hotel, called Princes Lane. Sam was to follow the lane to its end, and then he could make way down to the trees, and just a few meters from that spot there would be a glade. Theo assured him that he would be there, waiting for him.

Sam found the lane exactly as Theo had described it. He cast one more look at the bright lights of the hotel and its party and began to walk down the dark lane towards his friend.

He heard laughter coming from the terrace above him, the string music louder here. He kept his head down, a tight fist wrapped around his backpack's straps, the other clutching his mobile, debating whether to call Theo or not. His heart was beating quickly as the adrenaline and excitement coursed through him. He was so lost in his own decisions, his own thoughts, that he didn't see the shape rise out of the shadows.

**

Jude felt Glendower's cold hand press into the small of her back as she was propelled away from Tenney and out onto the terrace. She was dreadfully concerned about him. She had never known someone to turn green so quickly without being on a ferry in a choppy ocean. Glendower, too, had looked a bit sick as he shook Tenney's hand, but he managed to recover his composure quickly.

"Officer Marcello, I assure you my staff members are taking the best possible care of your young friend. I'm sure he will be quite recovered and will be back to join us soon." Glendower's attempt at reassurance didn't quite ring true, his smile not reaching his eyes.

A figure emerged from the crowd on the terrace.

"Miss Marcello, a pleasure to meet you again." Frommes the butler bowed stiffly from his waist.

"Ah, Frommes, a glass of champagne for our esteemed guest and a quick word if you don't mind."

"Certainly, sir." Frommes clicked his fingers once, and a waitress appeared with a tray of champagne glasses topped up with softly bubbling liquid. Jude took a glass, sipping it gently as she kept one eye on the doorway, looking out for Tenney.

Glendower's hand still lingered on her back, making her feel more and more uncomfortable. She gently shifted away, anxious not to seem rude, but desperate not to be touched anymore.

"Thank you," she said, raising the glass.

Glendower inclined his head slightly. "Please excuse me, Officer Marcello. I will be back in a moment." He stepped away, Frommes following him, their heads bent close together.

Jude turned around in a circle. She could see the bridge, the crowds on the other side waiting for the fireworks. It was all lit up, the last of the traffic being let over before the bridge was shut for the display. She continued to turn around until she was facing the door again. The only view she was really interested in involved Tenney walking back to her. Her stomach clenched with anxiety, all her senses screaming at her. She told herself it was just worry, for

Tenney, and for the reason they were here—to learn more about her mother's disappearance. She hoped Glendower would return quickly, tell her what she wanted to hear, and then she and Tenney could get back on the bike and return to her lovely, simple bedroom in her cozy hotel in Denebury.

She shivered a bit, wishing she'd brought a shawl with her to fend off the chill coming from the Avon Gorge. She drank some more champagne and waited.

**

Glendower's voice was low and harsh as he spoke to the demon masquerading as his manservant. "You didn't tell me the Tether would be here!" he whisper-shouted. "The bastard nearly sucked all the air out of my lungs!"

"We weren't completely sure that she would bring him or that he could be away from the Elemental like this. But now he is here, it is one more bargaining chip, one more obstacle that can be eradicated. What did you feel when you touched him?" Frommes couldn't quite hide the curiosity in his voice.

Glendower composed himself again. "He's strong, their connection is like nothing I've ever felt before. Stronger even than my own. But he is also woefully undertrained. It was quite easy for me to get the better of him, but I'm not sure I could do it again once he has learned all the tricks of a Tethered person. I also felt danger; it lies within him, just under the surface. He uses a lot of his energy just keeping it held in. Restraining it. Most of it is subconscious. You could use that against him if you should ever need to."

There was a part of Glendower that rebelled against giving Frommes so much information. It stuck in his throat, making him swallow, his Adam's apple moving rapidly up and down his neck.

"Remember our bargain, Humphrey," Frommes drawled. "If you don't give us what we want, we will kill her, turn her into an undine. And then what would your brother do?"

The thought of his brother Dominic turned Humphrey Glendower pale. He had promised him that they would get her back, but now the price was almost too high. He knew that Dom was close; he could feel him, but they hadn't seen each other in over a year. Humphrey didn't know how broken Dominic was going to be after months of captivity and anxiety for his lost daughter. He made a new resolve: finish this, get his niece back, repair his brother. Live in peace again.

All he had to do was give the demon what he wanted. Even if it was the life of one of his own kind. Was he really prepared to allow them to kill a fellow Tether?

**

"Spare some change, Sonny?" the tramp croaked. He had long, grey, scraggly hair and a beard that reached below his waist. A thick, woollen hat, reminiscent of those worn by sailors, was pulled low over his head. There was some evidence of its once vibrant turquoise-green colour, the hat had become grimy and faded from years of exposure to the elements. His voice was soft through parched, cracked lips.

Sam eyed the dirty hand stretched out from the battered coat. He struggled not to show the repulsion he felt at the smell the man exuded. Carefully, he reached into his jeans pocket and pulled out a few pound coins, dropping them into the grasping hand.

The tramp quickly pulled the coins to his chest, almost as though he was afraid that Sam would snatch them back. He was muttering under his breath.

Sam began to walk away. The man called after him, a thank you. "Take care now, Sonny!" he said. Sam shook his head slightly. He was hearing things. The 'Sonny' had sounded an awful lot like Sammy.

Chapter 49

Tenney retched over one of the bathroom sinks, his hands braced on either side. The jacket, so lovingly folded by Aura, now lay crumpled in a pile at his feet. The bow tie hung loosely around his neck; the top few buttons of his shirt hastily undone. It felt as though he was drowning, salty water rising from his belly and gushing from his mouth in a torrent.

The sink was empty despite his heaving. It still felt as though he had an ocean rolling about inside him. Aura's voice was competing with the images that still flooded through his brain. He couldn't hear her properly. It was like she was calling to him through water. He was panicking, he knew he was panicking. He took a deep breath, relieved to feel clean air and not acrid seawater.

He concentrated on the breath, the air around him. When his shaking began to subside, with some trepidation, he turned the tap on and splashed his face. The cold, clean water refreshed him. As his mind cleared, one image began to reveal itself.

Glendower stood alongside another man, identical in every way. They looked happy together. Whole. Twins? Tenney thought. With his eyes still closed, he tried to call up more images, piecing together the clues for the answer that was so close, yet remained elusive.

He clawed at the images, the memory of the water. Suddenly, a turquoise monster rose up in his mind's eye. Mottled light reflected off its massive scales, its huge fangs. Its tongue flickered out, gill-like protrusions on its sinuous neck moving in time with the tongue. It was dragon-like, but without wings, its legs ending in massive flippers. Its mouth was open, and as it shot towards him, ready to swallow him whole, Tenney fell back in shock. The creature was so terrifyingly real.

-*TENNEY*! He clutched his head as his sister's scream finally penetrated his mind.

-*I'm here! I'm here!*

-*Ten? What was that?* Tenney should have realised that Aura would've experienced everything he had.

-*I don't know.* He was in shock. Carefully, he pulled himself back up to the sink, bracing himself once again.

-*I'm coming,* she said.

Tenney shook his head – *No, we'll come back. Just let me get Jude. We can be home in an hour.* He began to move away, but he could still feel his sister's anxiety.

-Are you near a mirror? he asked her.

-Yeah, we didn't go far up to the fort before I felt something terribly wrong happen to you. She sobbed. His heart clenched as he felt her love for him fly over the miles, connecting them.

The mirror shifted in front of his eyes, finally revealing Aura, her wide blue eyes moving frantically through a tear-stained face as she looked for him. He tried to smile reassuringly and gave a little wave. Behind her, Hedge stalked across the room. He looked bigger, the hair on his neck sticking up, his mouth caught in a low growl. Meg or Stace were knocking on the door, asking if everything was okay.

Tenney began to speak, to reassure her that they would soon be home, when Aura's mouth opened wide, and she pointed behind him. *-TENNEY*! She screamed again – *BEHIND YOU!* But the warning came too late. One of the waiters who had helped him away from the party raised a crude cudgel and dropped it heavily against the back of Tenney's head.

The last thing he saw before he passed out was Aura, her mouth wide, her skin turning to scales, her eyes flashing blue fire. Stace had broken the door down and had his arms around her rapidly growing frame. He was manhandling her out of the room.

The last thing he heard was her scream as it changed into the dragon's roar.

**

Jude drank the last drops of the champagne; the bubbles were simultaneously popping and caressing her tongue and mouth. She was feeling almost euphoric. As she drained the glass, a waiter helpfully appeared, removing the empty glass from her hand and quickly replacing it with a full one.

She was watching the door.

Why was she watching the door? There was something, no, someone important. Someone she was waiting for… Tenney! She thought, shaking herself out of the stupor a little. The alcohol was hitting her hard tonight. She took another sip of the delicious, fruity wine.

"Jude," a soft, sultry Scottish voice behind her.

She turned away from her vigil, Tenney forgotten again.

"Mr. Glendower!" she replied, a little too happily she felt. She mustn't lead him on, someone might be upset…

Glendower smiled down at her; he gently stroked his hands up and down her upper arms. His touch felt like a warm wave on a hot, sunny beach. She closed her eyes and imagined herself in the Caribbean, lying on a white beach, the waves washing around her naked body as she lay with Tenney… *Tenney*!

In shock, she opened her eyes wide again and quickly stepped away from Glendower, turning back to the door. Why did she keep forgetting him? What was wrong with her?

"Jude," Glendower repeated her name again. "Are you enjoying the champagne?" It would have been rude if she didn't take another sip and reply to him. He was her host, after all. As the liquid coursed through her system again, she felt that same warm fuzzy feeling, her mind clouding over once more.

"It's lovely, Mr. Glendower." She replied, happy again.

"I'm so glad you are enjoying it. We send some of our own water to Champagne to be added to some of their bottles. This is a Glendower Springs Champagne."

"It's magic champagne…" Jude giggled, drinking more of the golden fluid.

"It certainly is, Jude." Glendower gently placed a hand on her lower back and turned her away from the door and towards the view from the terrace. "I do so hope you don't mind me calling you Jude. I have a feeling you and I will be seeing a lot of each other, and I want us to be close," he drew her into his side, "friends."

She felt his breath as he uttered the last word. Involuntarily, she felt a small stirring inside her. She smiled up at him, confused by the feeling, and yet unsure why she should feel uncomfortable. If anything, all she really felt was a little merry, woozy, drunk even. She giggled girlishly again.

"I think the fireworks are about to start, and we have a lot to discuss." He moved her towards the balustrade, his fingers skimming her hips. Jude was powerless to stop him.

**

The dragon paced anxiously outside the Lodge. The Nightwalker had gotten her out before she had become too large and broke through the walls and ceiling. Torn clothing littered the ground around her. Between her mighty forelegs, a white orb throbbed with a bright white light, beating in time with her heart. She roared loudly, impatient. Finally, the Nightwalker and the she-wolf emerged. They carried bags and weapons. The black wolf was pacing around her legs, unafraid of her size, her strength, or her whiplashing tail.

The two humanoids leapt effortlessly onto her back despite their baggage. The Nightwalker was stronger again now that the sun was setting over the horizon. The she-wolf sat behind him, her legs gripping his hips, her hands loose around his waist.

The dragon rose up into the sky. The black wolf looked up at her and leapt, covering the distance in a single bound. A part of her, her human self, marvelled at his power. Her mighty fore claws caught him gently mid-air and carried him close to her body. Close to her thudding heart.

The dragon and her passengers turned in the air, flying east towards the mighty river, and then south towards her soul.

**

Sam had searched the area. It was like a small woodland, with some open glade-like spaces. He wondered if Theo and his friends were in a different glade. Maybe he had got the directions wrong? But no, he was sure he hadn't. Everything matched what Theo had said. Sam had grown up in much larger, denser woodland, and he knew that he had covered the whole area. There were no signs of a party anywhere. Below him ran a busy road, and then the Avon Gorge, flowing out to sea.

Sam turned around. He could feel the panic in his belly. The whole area was empty. The only signs of life were coming from the party at the hotel.

He felt like a prat. Ashamed, he bashed a tear from his eyes. He began to consider what to do. He couldn't stay here, alone. Like the total idiot he was.

Why did he trust Theo? Everyone said, be careful about who you meet online. It was rammed down their throats at school, his parents almost daily giving him gentle reminders about the risks of befriending people that way.

He struck his head. He was so angry with himself. With Theo, if that was even his name. How could someone be so cruel, offer so much hope only to dash it so spectacularly?

There was a sudden explosion as an array of multi-coloured lights across the sky broke him from his trance. The fireworks on the bridge were starting.

Dejectedly, he wandered over to the edge of the gorge and watched them.

As Sam walked, he pulled his phone out of his pocket and dialled his sister's number. The phone rang and rang until he heard Tenney's voice jokingly asking him to leave a message, Aura's squeals as she tried to stop him adding 'big sloppy kisses' at the end.

It only made him feel more alone.

Next, he dialled Tenney's number. It too rang on, a similar message at the end. Sam couldn't stop the tears now. He looked at his phone, tempted to throw it into the water below. His thumb scrolled through the list of names. Marcello, Jude… He paused, his thumb hovering over it.

Tenney had given him the number – 'just in case mind!' he had warned Sam. He had been spending so much time with the policewoman lately, it kinda had made sense. Now she might be Sam's only hope of getting out of this mess.

Sam hit the name and heard the dial tone. Above him, from the terrace, he heard a distinctive pop song. It was distinctive because it jarred with the string music of the party.

He looked up. Long black hair hanging over shoulders and a green dress appeared. She was fumbling with her bag, struggling to get it open and find the phone. She looked half-cut, but Sam experienced a surge of hope – Jude was here - and if she was here, then Tenney might be too. Didn't he say something about a party? Sam couldn't quite remember; he had adopted a sort of ennui as far as his brother and sister were concerned.

He wanted to shout up, wave his hands, but she looked so unsteady on her feet, he was half afraid that she would fall over the low barrier between her and the drop to the field. He began to walk back to the access road, determined to gate crash the party and find Jude or his brother.

As the ringing stopped and Sam heard the answerphone message, she pulled out her mobile and appeared to shake her head as she realised, she had reached it too late.

Hands circled around her waist; a grey head of a tall, much older man appeared over her shoulder. She dropped the phone back into her bag, unconcerned with who might have been phoning her.

Sam clenched his jaw. The night was getting better and better. Not only was he stranded, stood up by a false friend, he had just discovered that his brother's girlfriend was cheating on him.

Sam's feelings of rejection were overwhelming. The sting of betrayal from Theo, someone he had trusted and hoped to connect with, cut deep. It wasn't just the embarrassment of being stood up; it was the crushing realisation that he had been duped, that his trust had been misplaced. The warnings from his parents and teachers echoed in his mind, amplifying his sense of foolishness and self-reproach.

As he watched the fireworks, the vibrant colours and loud bangs seemed to mock his inner turmoil. The festive atmosphere of the hotel party contrasted sharply with his isolation and despair. Each unanswered call to his siblings deepened his sense of abandonment. The familiar voices on the voicemail, once comforting, now felt like a cruel reminder of his solitude.

Seeing Jude, his last hope, in the arms of another man, shattered him further. The sight of her, seemingly carefree and intimate with someone else, felt like a final blow. It wasn't just about her; it was about the cumulative weight of the night's disappointments. The rejection, the loneliness, the betrayal – it all converged, leaving Sam feeling utterly forsaken and adrift.

**

Through the champagne haze, Jude felt her bag vibrate and heard her distinctive ring tone. She disengaged herself from Glendower and fumbled with the clasp of her bag. Resting the bag on the balustrade, with fingers that felt too big and clumsy for her hand, she finally managed to pull the phone out, just as the vibrations stopped and the song ended. The screen read 'missed call'.

Glendower snaked up behind her again, his hands encircling her waist. Instinctively, and because her legs felt like jelly, she leant back against him. He carefully swept her long hair over her shoulder, lowering his nose to her shoulder blade, greedily inhaling her scent.

She closed her eyes and rested against him. "Tenney…" she purred. The fireworks were firing off all around her, their noise running through her, their light making her skin change colour. She felt warmth spread through her. Confusion and euphoria mingled inside her, making her pliant and susceptible. He whispered into her ear, his breath tickling her lobe.

It felt like she was swimming in thick water; the voice was simultaneously far away and coming from inside her. The hands were moving over her like waves.

Temptation swarmed her. No more worries, no more supernatural challenges. She could be free by enslaving herself to this man, to this feeling.

-Jude! Suddenly her eyes shot open. She looked around for the voice.

-JUDE!

She felt her senses begin to return to her slowly. Shocked at Glendower's proximity to her, she stepped forward. Leaning out over the terrace, she felt sure the voice was coming from out there, across the gorge.

-JUDE!

It was growing insistent, and it sounded like the person who called to her was in a lot of pain. She heard it once more, stronger than before.

– JUDE!!

"Mum?" she called out, finally recognising the timbre of the voice.

Suddenly the music stopped, and the party guests all turned to face her. She spun around as an icy feeling crept up her spine. Glendower stood before her, his hands behind his back, and a look of disappointment on his face. Next to him was Frommes and another man. She hadn't comprehended the power that radiated from the butler until this moment. Dressed in dark clothing, he looked incongruous against all the bright party frocks of the guests.

She moved back against the terrace's barrier, her head whipping around at all the faces watching her. Their eyes were changing, becoming dark. Cold fear began to seep through her. *Demons*! she realised too late.

"Jude, I don't know how you broke out of the water hypnosis," said Glendower. "We were hoping to question you whilst you were still under its spell. You must hold more power than we assumed."

"Never mind!" Frommes spoke up. He had lost all trace of his servitude, and now Jude realised who the real boss was in their relationship. "We can get more information from Her if her spawn is awake and screaming."

"Wha… wha…" she stammered. She swallowed as she realised who was missing from beside her. "Where's Tenney?"

The man behind Frommes smiled cruelly. There was something about him that was eerily familiar, something that told her not to trust him at any cost. He nodded over the rail. Jude followed his eyes.

Below her, she saw two men dragging a third body between them, their hands under his armpits. She saw a flash of red blood glistening in the light of the fireworks as it mingled in the brown hair and down his white shirt. They were heading down the lane towards the grassy area that led to the gorge. Her heartbeat stopped before starting up again in a rapid staccato.

"TENNEY!" she cried out.

Desperately, she turned around, looking for any face that might help her. All the possessed jeered at her, their laughter echoing like a sinister chorus. Glendower stepped towards her, his eyes gleaming with malice. She flinched back, repulsed by him.

"Jude, let me help you," he said, his voice dripping with false concern.

"You bastard!" she spat at him, her voice trembling with rage. "Where are they taking him?"

He raised a hand to her face, his touch now cold and unwelcome. She turned away, her cheeks burning from outrage and despair. "He's just to ensure that you behave, collateral you could say."

Her eyes blazed with fury as she looked back at him. "You do know who he is, don't you? Who his sister is? We have some very powerful friends!"

The crowd laughed, a chilling sound that sent shivers down her spine. Glendower was the first to recover. "I confess, my associates hadn't told me, so it wasn't until I touched him that I realised what he is. Two of the Tethered cannot touch without some repercussion. We are the conduits for the Elementals' powers, and when two mix, those same elements battle internally for supremacy." Jude couldn't hide her shock.

"I will admit—if he had been properly trained, he could have overpowered me. Instead, I beat him. And now he is unconscious—alive, but unconscious. Which means his Elemental is either catatonic or losing their mind from the separation. You'll get no help from them, or from the vampire and wolves."

Jude felt her legs give out as he spoke, this time from the burden of understanding that no one would help her. She was alone. She clung to the balustrade for support, her knuckles white. Tenney was disappearing into the darkness. Rapidly, her mind began to work. She had to play for time, find out exactly what they wanted from her. Then maybe she could find some other help, but from where, she knew not.

"Ok," she began, her voice barely a whisper. "What do you want from me?"

Frommes spoke, his voice like gravel. "Why, all we want is a family reunion."

The demon stepped forward, his breath suddenly rancid as he gripped her arm, forcing her to look out at the bridge. A large explosion went off, lighting up the sky, showing the silhouette of the bridge as the firework spread out across the sky. Between the arches of one of the bridge's towers, a body was hanging by its arms.

Long skirts flapped around her legs, her black hair hanging down past her waist, blowing in the wind. Her outline was as familiar to Jude as her own. She knew that person.

"Mum…" she gasped. As the revelation of what she was seeing became a reality, she let out a piercing scream. Her legs finally gave out as she witnessed her mother's agony at the hands of these monsters.

**

Sam, hiding in a small copse of trees and bushes, heard the scream from the terrace. He had realised something was afoot when the music suddenly stopped. There was movement coming from the hotel. Afraid that he would be spotted, he hid. He didn't want trespassing to be added to the growing list of his concerns.

From his hiding place, he saw the men dragging the body from the lane towards the gorge. He watched as they carried him by. If he reached out far enough, he could have touched him. His heartbeat pounded frantically as he recognised his brother, totally unconscious between them. His mind reeled, unable to process what he was seeing. He sat back and shuffled deeper undercover. As the scream reverberated around the space, he felt a large branch under his hand. Subconsciously, his hand closed around it.

**

Tenney felt himself begin to stir. His painful eyes fluttered open. He saw grass and leaves moving below him, the toes of his posh shoes dragging through the ground, leaving furrows. *They're gonna be wrecked...* he thought, randomly.

Two pairs of strong hands were holding him up, preventing him from face-planting into the ground. He tried to shake his head, but pain coursed through it, reminding him of the last head wound he had received. He moaned as he realised why he felt so powerless.

Through his foggy senses, he heard one of the men laughing. They dropped him. He rolled over and saw the other one raise his foot to stamp down on Tenney's head, ready to send him back to oblivion. Weakly, he raised his hands up, a useless defence against the heavy boot.

He screwed his eyes shut, waiting for the impact.

But it never came.

The man collapsed beside him. The other one looked around and growled. Tenney quickly used the distraction to spin his legs around, taking the man's legs out from under him. As he dropped to the ground, a new figure appeared, a heavy branch-like club raised above his head. He brought it down upon the man's temple, knocking him out.

Tenney's saviour dropped exhausted to the ground. Shaking the last of the concussion off, Tenney dragged himself up into a kneeling position. He brushed the hair off his face, feeling the blood and the sharp pain from the wound the man had given him in the hotel's bathroom. He looked at the man who had saved him.

"Sammy!?!" he couldn't believe what he was seeing.

"Hey, Ten," replied his brother.

Chapter 50

Sam helped Tenney to his feet. In his other hand, he clung onto a bloodied branch.

"What are you doing here, Sam?" Tenney asked, his voice a mix of confusion and concern. "I thought you were still in Stratford with Mum and Dad."

Sam looked abashed, staring at his foot as he ground his toe into the grass.

"SAM!" Tenney grabbed his shoulders, shaking him to get him to answer.

Sam raised his head. His face was pale white, streaked with tears. Suddenly, he looked every inch of his sixteen years, a frightened kid. Tenney pulled him into his arms and held him close. Eventually, Sam raised his empty hand and returned the hug, gripping onto Tenney's shirt as he finally let himself cry onto his brother's shoulder.

One of the men at their feet began to stir. Tenney gently disengaged himself from his sibling, walked up to the man, and stamped on his head, rendering him unconscious again. He grabbed him under his armpits and pulled him under some bushes. Sam watched as his brother calmly went about his business.

Tenney looked up at him. "A little help, Sammy?" Together, they hid the two men deep under the trees. Tenney figured they'd be out for a little while. Sam had hit the second man well, a red welt rising between his eyes. The first had the print of Tenney's shoe on his jaw.

He crouched down and peeled back one of the men's eyes. They were black. He let the eyelid drop closed. "Shit," he whispered under his breath. Closing his eyes, he tried to contact Aura. Her mind was reeling, uncontactable as she flew over land and water. He knew where she was heading, and he needed to be there, waiting for her.

"Ten?" Sam's small voice reminded him of his obligations. Fluidly, his head wound forgotten as he tried to work out the series of events that led to this moment, he stood up. Sam couldn't see Aura as a dragon. That would be too difficult to explain. He needed to get him away, somewhere safe where he could get him after he had sorted this mess out.

He strode over to his brother, grasped him by his upper arm, and began to march him back towards the hotel. Jude could keep an eye on him.

"Right," he said, his voice brokering no argument from Sam, "talk. Tell me how the hell you got here, and why you're here. No lies, Sammy. This is bloody serious."

Sam looked up at Tenney, his eyes wide with fear and guilt. "I… I followed Theo. He said he had a plan to meet here tonight. I… I didn't know you'd be here too…"

Tenney's grip tightened on Sam's arm. "You shouldn't have come, Sam. This is dangerous."

"I know," Sam whispered, tears welling up again. "I just wanted to meet Theo."

Tenney sighed, his anger melting into concern. "Alright, we'll figure this out. But you need to stay close to me, understand?"

Sam nodded, his face pale but determined. "I understand."

**

Cold water splashed on her face, reviving her. Jude spluttered as it drenched her, the icy shock jolting her senses awake. Clammy hands hoisted her up into a sitting position. Black eyes stared at her menacingly. She raised a hand to cover her nose as his rancid breath washed over her.

"Hello, little angel," said a familiar, raspy voice.

"Gallagher!" she said, recognition and understanding finally hitting her. He laughed, licking his lips as he stepped away.

He was replaced by Frommes, all semblance of the butler gone. He looked like a monster, his black eyes mad, his lips drawn tight. He gripped her by her chin, his cold, skeletal fingers digging painfully into the soft flesh of her cheeks. Swiftly, he backhanded her across her mouth. She tasted blood on her tongue and heard Gallagher cry out in glee.

Frommes still had her face in a vice-like grip. With a strength that belied his height and stature, he lifted her to her feet. Pulling her face close to his so she could hear every word, he spoke, "You will tell us how they do it?"

She was confused. "How who do what?" Her words were thick, her mouth damaged from the blow and the hand that was clamped around her.

He twitched his head, and one of his minions placed a chair behind her. He pushed her down on it as another began to tie her arms to its armrests. Gallagher walked behind her and held her head between his hands, squeezing her if she struggled against her bonds.

Frommes paced in front of her, his hands behind his back. "Tell me everything you know about them."

"Who? The Elementals?" she asked, still confused. Surely Frommes knew enough from working with the Tether-betrayer, Glendower. She wondered where his brother was, what had happened to make them separate and betray their own kind in such a heinous way.

Gallagher's thumbs moved around behind her head and pressed into the top of her spine. Her vision clouded as a sharp pain travelled down her spine and up through her head. She cried out again. Gallagher released the pressure but kept his hands and thumbs in place, ready to reapply the force if she answered badly again.

Frommes stopped walking. "Bring me the stones," he demanded.

A demon scurried forwards in a slinky, pink satin dress. Jude felt sorry for the human whose skin the creature wore. Only now did she see that all of the 'guests' were fit, healthy, and above all, young men and women. Jude guessed she couldn't have been more than 18 or 19 before she was stolen away.

The girl carried an ornate box, something treasured jewellery would be kept in. Frommes took it from her, and the creature moved away, almost bowing reverentially as she stepped backwards. Frommes walked back up to Jude. He crouched in front of her, fingering the box.

"When the world was created, weapons were made that could defeat even the most powerful of beings. You have heard of the ruby dagger, The Cherubim Blade? Hmm?" He was talking to her like he was a teacher, and she the student. Subtly, she nodded her head, as much as Gallagher would allow her.

"Well, three stones were made that would incapacitate and debilitate the strongest warriors. The Seraphim Stones. But, like the dagger, they were lost. For millennia, they passed into myth. Until the time when they were needed again, and then the Earth relinquished them to us. You should have heard her screams as we took them from her." His eyes clouded over in something akin to ecstasy as he remembered the sound, like he was recalling a beautiful piece of music.

Jude felt bile rise in her throat.

Carefully, his clawlike fingers opened the box, revealing two gemstones with an indentation where a third one should have sat. They were each burning with an inner glow. Their proximity to her made her feel weak, sick. They hummed, their power surrounding her until… snap, the lid closed. The feeling passed as quickly as it had come upon her.

"We waited for the next Fall." Jude realised he wasn't talking about Autumn. The way he said Fall made it sound like a significant event, a rare occurrence. "We had narrowly missed the last one. But creatures such as they are predictable, fallible. We knew it would happen eventually. And it did. 30 years ago, one of them came to earth, tied themselves to a human and cursed themselves to a hundred years of mortality."

Jude felt her body clench, a cold dread settling in her stomach. "Who fell?" she asked, her voice barely a whisper, afraid of the answer. Frommes stepped back, opening her line of sight to the bridge. Another burst of colourful fire illuminated the sky, and her mother's body was lit up.

"Why, an Angel of course!" said Frommes gleefully, his eyes gleaming with malevolent delight.

**

Tenney didn't know what to think of his brother's story. Anger and sympathy battled within him, but disbelief overshadowed everything. How could someone as clever as Sam be so idiotic?

"But why, Sam? If you knew there was a risk that this 'Theo' would be bogus, why would you leave Mum and Dad and disobey them? Do they even know you're here?" Tenney's voice was a mix of frustration and concern.

Sam shook his head, staring at the ground, shame written across his face. He could feel the weight of Tenney's disappointment pressing down on him.

"Where do they think you are? At home? With me and Aura?" Tenney pressed on, his voice rising. Sam nodded, a small, almost imperceptible movement. "So, you were going to make us implicit in all this then? Without even asking us?"

Sam stopped suddenly, his head snapping up to meet Tenney's gaze. Anger flared in his eyes, replacing the shame. "It's so easy for you, isn't it? You're their golden boy, Tenney can do no wrong!" Sam's voice was bitter, each word dripping with resentment. "I know you and Aura sneak out most nights. I know the stories they tell about you at school. I know everything. I even know…" Sam's voice broke, and he stopped himself from revealing the biggest secret about the twins' paternity.

"What?" Tenney asked coldly, suspicion creeping into his voice. "What do you know, Sam?"

Sam wiped an angry, hot tear from his eye. He shouldered past Tenney, his backpack adding weight to his shove. "Nothing," he muttered, striding up towards the lane.

Periodically, they heard laughter from the terrace, a stark contrast to the tension between the brothers. The night was cool, the air filled with the scent of damp earth and distant music. Tenney ran his hand through his hair again and strode out after his brother. As Tenney reached out to stop Sam, to ask him what he meant once and for all, they heard Jude scream.

Both brothers stopped and looked up. "JUDE!" Tenney cried out. He made to get past Sam when a figure appeared before them.

The tramp stepped out from the shadows. "You can't go up there, Sonny," he croaked, holding a dirty hand out to stop him.

Tenney actually growled and ran at the man, desperation fuelling his every step. The tramp slowly raised his hands, as though summoning something from the ground. The earth shook violently, fissures opening in the tarmac. Water poured out from the cracks, winding around Tenney's ankles and legs like thick, watery ropes.

The tramp opened his eyes. "You can't go up there, Tennyson," he said again.

Tenney turned around as far as he could in his watery bindings. "SAM!" he yelled desperately. "RUN!"

Before the tramp could raise the water to stop Sam, he had sprinted into the darkness of the trees.

Tenney turned back to the tramp. "You must be Water," he said, his voice steady despite the fear gripping him.

The tramp inclined his head. "And you are the Tether to my sister, Air. So, we are basically family." As he finished his introduction, his body began to shift, ripples of water cascading over him. He grew in size, transforming into a turquoise leviathan with a wide-jawed head and long, sharp teeth. Instead of wings, it had a long, vicious tail with barbs down its length. At the end of its two legs were clawed and webbed feet.

The tramp had become the leviathan from the Glendower's watermark.

He picked Tenney up in his jaw and carried him down to the gorge.

**

Jude struggled again to make sense of what he told her. An Angel? And he implied that her mother was the aforementioned angel… She felt herself laugh. Frommes, surprised by her response, turned around.

"You honestly think that my mother is an angel?" she scoffed. "She's afraid of flying, you utter moron!"

Frommes nodded at Gallagher again. He squeezed her head once more. Jude cried out. In the distance, she thought she heard Tenney, but she was insensible, barely able to hold on to consciousness. Gallagher finally released the pressure.

"Your mother doesn't fly because she is banned from the skies!" Frommes shrieked. "The longer she hangs there, in mid-air, with the stone around her neck, the more tortured she becomes. So, you are wasting time by not telling me what I want to know!" He slapped her again. Her hands clenched into fists, the ropes digging into her skin on her arms.

Frommes raised his hand once more. As it arched down, Glendower stopped him. Frommes glared angrily at the Tether.

"How dare you!" he spat, red-faced.

"Dominic has the boy!" Glendower stated. "We need to move fast before it's too late!" He looked down at Jude, pity on his face. She spat blood on his shoe and looked away.

Frommes grabbed her face once more, turning her to look at him. "Tell me how they can keep their bodies, and why they are welcomed back when they have served their penance? Tell me why He forgives them, and casts us into shadow?"

A loud bellow echoed down the gorge. Frommes looked up, startled as he peered into the distance. The fireworks had caused the skies to become foggy with smoke. The crowds, believing the bellow to be an indicator of more amazing displays in the skies, collectively looked up. He heard them ooh and ahh.

Turning to Glendower, he dropped Jude's face and grabbed him by his lapels.

"You said that she would be incapacitated by his unconsciousness!" Before Glendower could reply, Frommes opened the box, pulling out a chain with a yellow moonstone at its end. He draped it around Jude's shoulders so that it hung on her chest, touching her skin.

Immediately, Jude felt all her strength leave her. She saw the skin where the stone lay turn white, blue veins appearing. She felt faint.

As she drifted in and out of reality, she heard snippets of conversation, orders by Frommes. "Have you got the dagger?.. the portal…. End this!"

Gallagher scooped her up, and she was engulfed in the darkest black she could imagine. No sight. No sound. No smell. Weightless and drifting.

She was sure she was dead.

Chapter 51

The crowd cheered as the dragon flew over them, roaring, blue steam shooting from its mouth. Two figures sat astride its powerful back; it cradled another creature in its fore claws.

It would be the talk of the town, even after the coming events. Many would speculate at the amazing show the fireworks organisers had put on. Some claimed it was video projection or drones, others immense animatronics or puppetry. The sceptics said that the developers had watched too many hours of *The Lord of the Rings*, and they were trying to produce something akin to the fireworks display Gandalf put on for the Hobbits.

All agreed that the Clifton Suspension Bridge Trust would be hard-pressed to top it at next year's fireworks display.

**

Sam hid once again in the undergrowth. He flattened himself to the ground as the monster carried Tenney away. He pushed himself up and ran after the creature. He stumbled in his haste down the decline, rolling over and over. He barely managed to stop himself before he hit the road that ran parallel to the River Avon.

Fortunately, it was quiet, the traffic stilled by the display on the bridge. The monster ran over the lanes and jumped out over the water.

A loud roar reverberated down the gorge, echoing off the cliffs. Sam covered his ears. A second terrifying, mythical creature swooped down. Two people leapt gracefully from its back; a third dog-like animal dropped from its claws.

The dragon, for that was the only way he could describe it, beat its wings, roared again, and shot out after the first, wingless behemoth. Before it could hit the water, the dragon raked its claws down its back. The first creature screamed in pain, rearing its head back, releasing Tenney up into the air.

Sam saw his brother's body flung high. The creature spun underneath him, splashing down into the water. The dragon pirouetted into the sky and plucked Tenney out of mid-air before gravity dragged him down to certain death.

Sam screamed, "NOOOO!"

The dragon flew off with his brother.

**

Stace and Meg landed safely in an area of green beside the observatory. They looked around, quickly assessing the situation. Portals began opening around them. Stace turned to the bridge. With his sharp eyes, he immediately spotted the body hanging from the bridge, another portal opening below it.

"Meg!" he called out. Meg turned to him, blades in each of her hands, her stance ready to fight. Stace simply pointed to the bridge. Meg nodded once, as Stace ran, faster than light, to the second point of the battle.

Meg felt the great black shape of her son as he joined her. "Are you ready, Hedge?" she asked quietly. He growled in response, his hackles up. The demons emerged from the portals. Meg released a war cry which would have chilled the marrow of a regular person's bones.

The mother and son leapt into the fight.

**

Tenney was falling. One minute he had been in the mouth of the Leviathan, the next he'd felt a judder run up through the creature's body, one of its teeth nicking his skin. And now he was falling towards the black water and the mouth of the monster once again.

He closed his eyes, thought of Jude. Thought of Aura.

And then – wham – she had him. Giant dragon claws held him gently against her breast. He saw her heart, glowing within her. He placed a hand over it, and he was transported back to her room.

They were sitting together on the bed, hugging and crying.

"You're ok! You're ok!" she cried repeatedly.

"I am, I am, I am..." he replied, stroking her head, kissing her temple.

He pulled back slightly and looked into her blue eyes, blue like violets. He laughed. She felt so real, here in their sanctuary. The tattoo's words came to his mind:

'From the meadow your walks have left so sweet, That whenever a March wind sighs He sets the jewel-print of your feet, In violets blue as your eyes, To the hollows in which we meet And the valleys of Paradise.'

The wind had brought her back to him. He remembered the dragon, her jewel-like skin, the sacred space in between – the inter duo mundos *- where they could be together, their connection strengthening. Being with her was like being in paradise, for him.*

She drew him close to her. She was his sister. His best friend. His confidant. His twin. And now he truly understood it. She really was his soul.

"Ten?" she whispered.

"Yeah," he replied, wanting to stay like this forever.

"We've got to go back, they need us."

"I know."

"Ten?"

"Yeah?"

"I love you."

"I love you too."

When he opened his eyes again, he was caught between Aura's claws. She flew him towards a clearing where Meg and Hedge were battling a horde of demons. He squeezed one of her talons gently, stroked her mighty paw.

Softly, she released him. He turned and waved to her before running to join the fight. Meg threw him one of her blades. Aura felt pride as she saw how well he fought.

Then she saw a black blur as Hedge shot past her. He was amazing, using only teeth and claws to take down enemy after enemy, gutting them, ripping and shredding. Meg whirled like a dervish, spinning around. Nobody could stop her or the bite of her blade.

With three mighty beats of her wings, Aura pushed herself back into the air. Her fight was elsewhere, with another creature. She headed back down the gorge to meet her Elemental brother.

**

Jude felt a cold wind slice through her as she was jolted back to consciousness. She was still cradled in Gallagher's arms, her body weak and trembling from the stone's mysterious power. But now, instead of the terrace, they were on a bridge. The black nothingness had somehow transported them here.

She shuddered, both from the chill and the haunting memory of the void that had swallowed her. From her vantage point in the enemy's arms, she could see her mother's bare feet dangling above her, a sight that sent a fresh wave of horror through her.

Glendower stood nearby, his face ashen. He kept glancing over the edge of the bridge at the frothing water below, then back at her. His eyes were filled with a torment she couldn't understand.

"I'm sorry," he muttered, his voice barely audible. Jude couldn't tell if he was speaking to her or to some unseen presence. With a final, pained look, he climbed over the railing and plunged into the river below.

Frommes approached, yanking her head back by her hair. Jude could only manage a weak groan as pain shot through her scalp.

"We have your daughter!" Frommes shouted up to the crucified figure above.

Her mother's body twitched in response.

Frommes drew a dagger, its hilt devoid of the dreaded rubies. A small relief washed over Jude—this blade wouldn't sever her soul, only her life.

Gallagher's grip tightened as Frommes pressed the dagger's point into the soft flesh above her clavicle. Blood welled up and trickled down her skin. She cried out, but her voice was feeble.

The blade sank deeper, scraping against bone. Jude screamed, the sound raw and piercing.

Her vision blurred, the world around her flickering in and out of focus. Her mother seemed to vibrate above her, a ghostly figure in her agony. Frommes was shouting, demanding to know how to reclaim his former self, but the words were lost on Jude. Her mother was just a human, an ordinary woman. How could they do this to her, to them?

The pain in her shoulder intensified as Frommes twisted the dagger again. Blood sprayed across her face, and a black cloud began to rise beside her.

**

Stace ran, the scent of blood and the sound of a scream driving him forward. He heard a voice cry out, "No." It was a voice he hadn't heard in a very long time, and it spurred him to run even faster.

He took in the sight before him: Gallagher holding Jude, limp in his arms. Why was she here? he wondered. The smell of her blood was stronger now, flowing warm and rich and red. He saw the dagger protruding from her and the hand that twisted it.

Pure fury swelled up in Stace. "Frommes," he growled.

In one mighty leap, he drew his gladius and landed beside the trio. With a single, swift motion, he struck off the leader's head. Blood splattered over Jude. Stace spun around, his training and skills flooding back to him. He knew exactly who he was, what he was. He sliced through another demon as it charged forward.

Gallagher laughed, dropping Jude and summoning a portal. Before he disappeared into it, he pulled a golden dagger from a sheath hidden under his jacket and cruelly licked it. Stace's blade flew through the air, hitting nothing as the portal and the demon vanished.

Stace heard a laugh behind him. "Hello, Roman, we meet again!" It was the she-demon from the Manor.

Stace smiled darkly, his teeth elongating. He let his Nightwalker side take over completely.

The she-demon charged, overconfident from her previous defeat of him. As she leapt at his back, he knelt in Frommes' blood, pointing his second, longer blade up and under his arm. The demon landed on it, skewered but still alive. Stace withdrew the blade and spun up and around, faster than thought. He grabbed her by the throat.

She looked up into the red eyes of the oldest of the Nightwalkers, the mightiest and strongest of his kind. Using his hand to tighten around her throat, he forced her mouth shut. There would be no escape for this demon.

He lifted her single-handedly from the ground, her feet dangling in the air. He looked upon her like a lover, opened his mouth, and spoke as he smelled her blood, heard the beat of her heart as it pumped the joyous fluid around her body.

"My dust would hear her and beat; Had I lain for a century dead; Would start and tremble under her feet, And blossom in purple and red." He bit deeply into her carotid artery and drank her dry, trapping the demon in the dying mortal's body.

**

Jude stirred slightly on the bloodied ground, her mind swimming through a thick haze. Each heartbeat seemed to sap her energy, the seraphim stone's power draining her. The white patch on her breastbone had spread, creeping up her neck and down her belly, blue veins showing everywhere. She thought she heard Stace quoting *Maud*. Maybe it was just her wish for Tenney that made her hear the poem.

**

The battle raged on in the grassy clearing. The small group of three were winning, forcing the demons to retreat into the shadows. Suddenly, a new portal opened. Gallagher stepped out, languorously waving a ruby-encrusted dagger.

Tenney turned to face him. "Ready for the next round, Little Boy?" Gallagher taunted.

Tenney charged forward.

**

The dragon dived into the water, knowing she couldn't stay long in his realm. She streamlined her body, preparing for the confrontation. He swam up towards her, mouth wide, moving effortlessly through the water. They met in a burst of bubbles, claws outstretched, talon-webbed feet against those of a raptor. They danced a deadly dance underwater. Aura felt herself weakening as his element dragged her down.

A small splash behind them, from the bridge, caught their attention. The Water Elemental roared in outrage and tried to swim towards the body of the man. Aura seized the distraction, digging her claws into his flesh and scales. With a couple of powerful beats of her wings, she carried them up, up into her element, up into the air.

**

Stace dropped the corpse and looked down at Jude. She had passed out, but she was still alive. His eyes were drawn to the change in her skin colour, the pulsing yellow stone near her heart.

"Good God," he breathed through his bloodied lips. Suddenly, he understood why she was here, why she was so important. He looked up at the woman hanging from the bridge. His suspicions had been correct.

Kneeling by Jude, he ripped the chain from her neck and tossed it and the stone over the side of the bridge. Already, her skin darkened, returning to its normal colour. He left her and began to climb up to the woman.

**

Tenney was holding his own against Gallagher. The demon looked scared, realising that Tenney had learned some new moves since their last encounter. A movement behind Gallagher caught Tenney off guard. He narrowly parried the dagger as Gallagher thrust forward.

"Tenney!" Sam screamed. Tenney tried to get Sam to run—run away!

But Sam, seeing his brother fighting for his life, dashed forward, swinging his backpack above his head, screaming loudly. He hit Gallagher across the head, knocking him off balance. Gallagher shook his head, focusing on his new quarry. He ran at Sam, knife drawn, the point aimed straight for him.

He thrust forward and hit flesh. Sam gasped as Tenney pushed him away, blood soaking quickly through his white shirt. Gallagher crowed and disappeared.

Tenney smiled down at his brother and coughed, blood and spittle coming out of his mouth. He dropped down, Sam holding him in his arms.

**

Aura was winning! The Leviathan was weakening the higher they flew. She felt euphoric. Then, a sensation like a sharp blade cut through her. She cried out in pain, releasing the Elemental. He dropped back towards the water, and Aura fell uncontrollably behind him.

**

Stace reached the woman.

"Hey!" he shouted. "HEY!" She weakly turned her head, looking out through her long, lank hair.

"Placidus?" she whispered.

"Jude needs you! Your daughter needs you!" The second stone glowed from a choker, held tight at her throat.

"What?" she croaked. "Jude?"

"She's down there – she's dying!" he lied, hoping to shock her, to wake her up. "She needs you now!"

"What can I do, Placidus? I am nothing. I have nothing left to offer."

Stace was shocked by her dejection. Her wretchedness was more than simply the imprisonment of the stone. She was heartbroken, he realised, from being cut off from heaven and from her true love.

"What happened to you?" he asked.

"He died," she said simply, weakly. She seemed to sag further.

"But Jude is alive—and she needs you—RIGHT NOW!"

She shook her head. Stace groaned in despair. He looked up the river. In the distance, the first glow of the sun could be seen. He didn't have much time.

But with the sun's rise, he remembered Paul's words: "When you see my sister, tell her all she has to do is ask, and she shall receive."

"ASK HIM!" he cried out to her. "Ask him and he will give you your wings back!"

She looked at him again, like he was a madman. From below, they heard a loud, painful cry as Jude came to and tried to move, her wounded shoulder causing her unimaginable agony.

A tear rolled down the lady's face. She nodded and spoke in a language man did not know. The stone at her throat burst into stardust, spreading out into nothingness.

A ray of light hit her, suffusing her in its glow. Stace shielded his eyes as her brightness intensified.

**

Aura broke out of her free fall just in time. She flapped her wings, weaker now. She had to get to him. She had to save him!

She flew to the clearing.

Meg was applying pressure to his wound, Hedge pacing around them. A third person sat, arms wrapped tightly around his knees, rocking back and forth as he cried, his heart broken.

Aura landed, causing the boy to startle. She didn't care. She needed to get to him. She changed back to her human form, using the air to cover her body like a shroud, and knelt at Tenney's side.

Gently, she lifted his head onto her lap and stroked the hair from his face. He tried to smile at her, his megawatt smile dimmed. His eyes were filled with pain. He tried to speak, but only blood came out of his mouth.

"Shhhhh," she said, "I'm here now."

-*I'm scared.*

-*I know.*

-*Wait for me.*

-*I'll always wait for you, Tenney."*

-*I lov…"* Even his mental speech wasn't stronger than death. He slipped away from her, mentally, physically, and spiritually. Aura closed her eyes and tried to find him in the space between realms.

She searched everywhere for her lost brother.

He was truly gone.

**

Jude was in strong arms again, flying through golden light. She looked up, the pain in her shoulder gone, all her hurts healing. A beautiful, golden-hued face smiled down at her.

"Mum?" she asked.

"Hello, my darling."

"Where are we going?"

"To your friends, sweetheart."

"Okay," Jude whispered, snuggling against her mother's breast like she used to do as a child.

**

Stace reached the clearing and saw Aura keening over a body. He pulled Meg away.

"I'm sorry, Stace, it happened so quickly!" she began, tears rolling down her cheeks.

His face dropped in shock as he saw the body of Tenney, the boy who had radiated life a short time before, lying dead beside his siblings. He would grieve and plan later; for now, Meg needed to know about the development from the bridge.

"Shh, we'll come to that in time. We have another problem…"

A loud boom echoed as something landed in their midst. Bright golden light shone from the Being in the centre.

Meg's mouth dropped open. "Is that…?"

"Uh huh," said Stace.

The Being gently lowered Jude to her feet and watched as she ran to the fallen man, crying out in pain. The two women Tenney had loved most in the world washed his face with their tears.

The Being turned to Meg and Stace.

"She was in her hundred-year penance," Stace began to explain, "that was why we couldn't reach her. I should have figured it out when I was told her name by the kids. Raechael Garbling. It's an obvious pseudonym – an anagram. And Jude, well, Jude is her daughter."

"Then that means that Jude is a…"

"Yep," Stace replied, his jaw clenched, his hand running through his hair. "She's a Nephilim. And not just any Nephilim. She is the daughter of one of the most powerful Angels in existence."

The golden being walked forward, flexing her wings in the air. She smiled at Meg. "Hello, Margaret," she said.

Meg immediately dropped into a low kneeling bow. "Archangel Gabriel," she said with deep respect.

Chapter 52

Things moved quickly after the battle at the bridge, but then slowed down as the judiciary and police force meticulously went over the scene, collecting facts and evidence from the bodies. By the time the police arrived, Stace had whisked Aura, Sam, Meg, and Hedge away, leaving Jude with Tenney. Aura could barely look at her younger brother, knowing his presence had led to Tenney's, and subsequently, her own death. Stace hotwired a car, "probably one of the hotel's demon-guests," he justified, and drove them back to the Lodge.

He carried Aura to one of the refurbished rooms, laid her on her bed, and left Hedge with her. The great wolf stretched himself out along her front, letting her cry into his black fur.

In his own room, Stace quickly changed into another t-shirt, conscious that the next task required subtlety, delicacy, and empathy. A bloodied shirt would only serve to frighten and perplex the child.

Downstairs, Meg had made Sam a warm drink. Stace smelled the air—chamomile, he realised. The boy hadn't said a word since the events at the hotel. Stace still wasn't quite sure how Sam had managed to turn up there, or why he was there. Another mystery of the night.

But he had seen enough people suffering from extreme shock, where they entered a withdrawn state, trying to make sense of what they had witnessed, while afraid that if they opened up, they might witness something else.

He sat across from the boy, resting his hands on his knees, trying to adopt a less threatening pose.

"Your parents will have been told; you know. We will need to get you home and ready for their questions." The boy just stared down into his mug of tea, only a small tick under his right eye betraying the emotions he was feeling inside.

"What you experienced tonight, Sam," Stace tried to make the gravity of the situation clear to the boy, "you can't tell anybody. Not a soul, do you understand?"

Still no response. Meg stared out of the window; her arms wrapped around her waist.

"Sam," Stace tried again, "what you saw, with Aura," Sam flinched visibly at the mention of his sister's name, "you'll have to try and forget you saw it." Stace felt his voice catch in an unusual display of emotion. "Soon no one will remember Aura clearly, she will be lost in time. So will the dragon. It will all be as a bad dream."

"Your brother died in a mugging, trying to protect his girlfriend. You weren't there, Sammy, okay?"

At the mention of his nickname and his brother's death, Sam broke down. Meg quickly shot forward, taking the mug out of his hands and holding the boy close to her. She hummed the lullaby she sang to Hedge as a cub.

"Shhhh, shhhhh, shhhh," she cooed to him.

Sam said something indistinct into her shoulder. "What was that, honey?" she asked calmly.

"It was my fault. Tenney got in the way of the dagger protecting me. It's all my fault...." He cried and cried.

Aura stood in the doorway, a blanket around her shoulders, her wolf at her side. Her face was pale, her form slightly fuzzy around the edges as though she was struggling to stay in this world and not succumb to the *inter duo mundos*.

In her hand, she clasped her mobile phone.

"That was Dad. They've been told about Tenney. They're heading home. We're to meet them there." She didn't look at her brother, instead turning away and walking back to her room to collect her bag.

Meg helped Sam to his feet, supporting him as she steered him to the door. "I'll see them home," she said.

**

At the hotel, Jude waited with Tenney's body. She had called the police, saying her boyfriend had been attacked. Mugged. That there had been some kind of illicit party. They were the innocents who had happened to be in the wrong place at the wrong time.

She cradled him close to her, her tears mingling with the blood on his face. The dagger was long gone, off through a portal with Gallagher. Her heart burned with rage at the thought of the demon, at what he had done. The prophecy had come true. The dagger had separated a soul. Tenney and Aura's were irreparable, and now nobody knew what would come next.

She stroked his precious face, still so perfect despite the bump on his head and the blood around his mouth. She whispered words of love, told him that she would never forget him, that their time together had been perfect. She regretted nothing. Memories of their laughter, their shared dreams, and the warmth of his embrace flooded her mind, making the loss even more unbearable.

The hotel was dimly lit, casting long shadows that seemed to dance with the flickering light from a broken streetlamp. The air was thick with the scent of blood and the remnants of the fireworks, a stark contrast to the eerie calm that had settled over the grassy area.

When the police arrived, she reverted to her professional state, giving clear and concise answers to their questions. She recounted the version of events she, Stace, and Meg had hastily cobbled together. When they asked her what her profession was, she had told them.

"Soon to be newly appointed Detective Constable, Gloucestershire Constabulary," she said, her voice steady despite the turmoil inside.

That was what the interview at the station had been about. A promotion and a transfer from Lincoln to Gloucester. Her new beat was to be the Forest of Dean and Wye Valley area. She had been looking forward to telling the news to Tenney tonight, at the party. Telling him that there was an actual chance that they could give their relationship a real go. Maybe have a proper future together.

Her heart faltered when she realised that that future had been stolen from them.

Her mother, looking distinctly less angelic and dressed in more normal clothes, arrived to take her 'home'. She shepherded her daughter away from the scene of death. They passed Martha and Samuel Wiseman, a police officer trying unsuccessfully to placate them, giving them limited information. Martha broke down in her husband's arms as Tenney's covered body was wheeled past them.

Her own mother hid her in her arms. Jude couldn't speak to them. Not yet.

When they were a safe distance away from the humans, Gabriel, formerly Rae, set her wings free and carried her daughter back to her home.

She didn't have long to try to explain to her what had happened, but she would beg one more boon from her Creator. Ask him to let her stay until after the funeral. She had let Jude down so many times in her childhood, she didn't want to desert her now. She could empathise completely with the power of a broken heart.

Chapter 53.

The day before the start of the Full Moon.

It took a further two weeks before Tenney's body was released to be buried, the investigation and autopsy delaying his internment. His body lay, cold and mutilated, in the drawers of the morgue. Aura had endured the weeks, aware that her time was short, but wishing that she could disappear now, maybe find Tenney again. Somewhere. Somehow.

Martha was a wreck. She would sit for hours in one chair in any room and just stare forwards at nothing. And then, the next minute she raged at anybody who happened to be in the vicinity. Her grief was a volatile storm, unpredictable and consuming.

Sam avoided her, but she didn't notice, such was her grief. In fact, Sam went out of his way to avoid all of his family. He ignored his phone and computer, staying out of the house all day, only returning when the night drew in, afraid to be out in the dark. The shadows seemed to whisper his brother's name, a constant reminder of his loss.

It was left to Samuel to plan and prepare for the funeral. He used it to delay his own grief. He told himself that he needed to be strong. Hold his family together. When he was alone, he allowed himself to break down. He had lost his eldest son. His child, and he didn't know how any of them would survive it.

**

Jude scoured the news reports for stories about the events of that night. She was sadly unsurprised to read that the amazing fireworks display had received marginally more coverage than the murder of a young man, even one tenuously linked to other murders only weeks before. In a mere blink of a human's eye, between Tenney's death, Gabriel's rescue, and the police's arrival, the bodies of the demons slain by sword, tooth, and claw had disappeared. When she asked her mother what had happened to them, she had smiled enigmatically and simply said, "Your uncles have dealt with them."

Reading the headline to her mother, she said sarcastically, "I mean, who wouldn't think a light show which included a dragon would be of more interest than the death of a 21-year-old?"

Gabriel understood that anger was one of the steps of grief, and she let her daughter vent her frustrations. She knew that Jude needed to release the pent-up emotions, the rage and sorrow that threatened to consume her.

Using her connections, Jude had asked if any bodies had washed up on the banks of the Avon Gorge or been swept out to sea. None had been found. A few days later, the Glendower brothers, Humphrey and Dominic, appeared together on *This Morning*, talking about the tragic events at the Gorge and how they had hosted a party at which young Tennyson Wiseman was a plus one to his girlfriend.

Jude had thrown one of the cheap white hotel mugs at the screen when she saw them. The sight of their composed faces, their feigned sorrow, ignited a fury within her that she couldn't contain.

At night, she curled up to her mother and asked her questions about her heritage, what it meant now she was a Nephilim, the uncles she never knew she had. Her mother answered some questions directly, but for most, she remained magnanimous, only offering half answers or further questions. Gabriel wanted Jude to discover her own path, to understand her identity through her own experiences.

One thing she did set right in Jude's mind was her slow aging, how she looked younger than she was. Gabriel told her that the average life span of a Nephilim child was 300 years, sometimes longer if they were the child of one of the Archangels.

Jude asked her about the arthritis. Her mother explained that it was a result of her mixed blood – she was still human and would still experience human frailties and strengths. It was just that her life span would be longer than most.

As Jude sobbed herself to sleep, Gabriel never left her side. She held her daughter close, whispering soothing words, promising that she would always be there, no matter what.

**

Eventually, the day of the funeral dawned upon them. Perversely, after two weeks of rain and gloom, the day dawned bright, cold, and crisp. A beautiful day if it had been for any other occasion.

Samuel persuaded Martha into suitable clothes, made sure Sam didn't disappear, and prayed that Aura would show up after she went out for a walk that morning. She returned just in the nick of time. The hearse and the limousine were waiting outside the house, the street lined with mourners. Samuel wasn't sure, but he thought he saw a large black dog disappear behind the crowd as Aura walked towards him.

**

The coffin lay at the foot of the choir, facing the high altar in the church which sat at the heart of the forest, the same church where Stace had met with Raphael in his Paul guise. The church was full of people, friends from school, a gaggle of girls crying together in the corner. A strange woman with short hair and yellow eyes crept in and sat at the back. He wondered who she was, how she knew Tenney and why she seemed so familiar. Jude sat with her striking mother a few rows back.

She had eventually turned up at their door, tried to apologise, explain what had happened. Martha hadn't wanted to know, but Aura had invited her in. They had sat together in Aura's room for hours. He assumed it was a way for them to reminisce about Tenney.

Sam had returned home just as Jude left. His already pale son paled further, and ran up the stairs, keen to avoid the policewoman.

The family sat together in the front pew. The vicar intoned the order of service, Samuel was barely listening. But then he heard her call his name. It was time to give the eulogy.

He stood, untangling Martha's vice-like grip from his own, and patted his pockets for the piece of paper. He didn't need it. He had memorised all he wanted to say.

He walked to the lectern, his legs and hands shaking from the effort of holding it all together. He coughed into his hand, composed himself, and began.

"My son, Tenney," Samuel began, his voice trembling. He paused, gathering his strength. "My son, Tenney was a gregarious, passionate boy who grew into a gregarious, passionate man. His wit and intellect astounded us sometimes, as did his ability to see the positive in all things. Even if it meant that he had to crack an inappropriate joke to lighten the mood." A small titter rippled through the congregation.

"He was a lover of life, of people," Samuel continued, his voice breaking slightly. A girl in the back row, near the mysterious woman, cried out dramatically. Samuel coughed again, steadying himself. "He loved animals, especially his dogs, Jess and Bo. He loved being outside and he loved his family.

"His passionate nature meant that sometimes he was quick to anger, especially if he thought someone he loved was in danger or if they were being unfairly treated." Samuel felt a sob rising in his throat. He looked down at what was left of his family. At Martha, wasting away in her grief; Sam, who had chosen to close himself off from his family instead of grieving with them; and Aura, her wide blue eyes looking deeply into him.

"But the thing he loved the most, the only person who he felt truly happy and comfortable with, was his twin sister, Aura. From the moment they were born, you couldn't separate them for long without some type of disaster occurring." He gave a small, sad smile. How would his daughter cope without him? he wondered.

"Even when he met a lovely girl, he would still seek out his sister, as though the only way he could give himself to this person was if Aura approved and allowed him." His eyes drifted to Jude. "And she did, and…" he wanted to say, 'and he died because of it.' But he left it unspoken and hanging in the air. Jude knew what he wanted to say. They all knew. She looked down, patting tears from her eyes.

Samuel coughed once more. From another pocket, he pulled out a small, old blue book with a golden name embossed across the front. He turned to the marked page and looked up at the faces staring at him.

"Tenney was raised on poetry, so it seemed only right that I should read something from his namesake." He couldn't see the words through his tear-filled eyes. But he didn't need to see the words. They were engraved on his heart.

"Oh, let the solid ground

Not fail beneath my feet

Before my life has found

What some have found so sweet;

Then let come what come may,

What matter if I go mad,

I shall have had my day

Let the sweet heavens endure,

Not close and darken above me

Before I am quit…

**

Jude sat in the church, listening to the eulogy, the power of the words Samuel had chosen from *Maud* resonating deeply within her. She watched the family, her heart aching with each word. Her mother, her golden wings hidden from human eyes, sat beside her, holding her close. Tenney had been loved, deeply, wholly, and completely. Aura had understood it, because Aura too was in love. The veiled accusation had stung Jude to the heart. But she couldn't hide from the truth of it. He was only there, at the party, because of her.

As the procession followed the coffin from the church, Martha diligently avoiding Jude's eyes, Aura offering a small sad smile, Jude felt the weight of guilt begin to crush her. She looked up at her Angel Parent.

"Take me home," she whispered.

Gabriel nodded, her eyes filled with understanding and sorrow. She wrapped her arm around Jude's shoulders, guiding her gently out of the church. The sunlight outside was blinding, a stark contrast to the darkness that enveloped Jude's heart.

They walked in silence, the murmurs of the mourners fading into the background. Jude's mind was a whirlwind of emotions—grief, guilt, anger, and an overwhelming sense of loss. She felt as if she were drowning, unable to catch her breath.

When they reached a secluded spot, Gabriel unfurled her wings, their golden feathers shimmering in the light. She lifted Jude effortlessly, carrying her away from the pain and sorrow of the funeral.

As they soared above the trees, Jude buried her face in her mother's shoulder, tears streaming down her cheeks. She didn't know what the future held, but for now, she just needed to be away from it all, to find some semblance of peace in her mother's embrace.

**

Martha stood slightly apart from what was left of her family. The grief threatened to drag her down into the abyss with her firstborn. The clouds had finally begun to gather overhead, a sympathetic gesture for the mother who would have a permanent hole in her heart. She needed to be separate, to be alone, and to bear this burden of grief and guilt.

He was her son. From the moment she discovered the pregnancy, she felt this connection to him, and she knew that she couldn't abort him. Her parents disapproved, of course. Their rigid uprightness and attempts to seem perfect and proper didn't allow for a daughter with a child on the way out of wedlock, especially one who had shown such promise and been accepted to Harvard.

Samuel, dear, sweet, kind Samuel, who gradually became the love of her life, saved her that day when he bowed on one knee, a twisted hoop of grass in his outstretched hand, and asked her to marry him. His English mannerisms and good prospects appealed to her parents, and they were over the moon at the proposal, even though it would mean losing their daughter and grandchild to England. Samuel, from the moment she said yes, referred to the baby as 'his' or 'their' baby. And when Tenney was born, Samuel only ever thought of him as his son.

Of course, the surprise of Aura only sealed his love for these children. He would joke that maybe she was a gift of God, a blessing on their lives because of the sacrifices she had made to continue the pregnancy, to leave her home. But if Aura hadn't been born, maybe Tenney wouldn't have met Jude, he wouldn't have made that crazy dash across the country with a stranger to be beside Aura in the hospital. And he wouldn't have been at The Avon Gorge, he wouldn't have been killed… Quickly she shook that thought out of her mind. It's not her fault, it's not her fault… she repeated over and over, her new mantra so she could look at her daughter without wanting to scream and rage at her.

She looked across at the three of them, all huddled together, Samuel keeping a firm arm around Aura to stop her from collapsing. She would admit it now, in the darkest parts of her psyche. She was always jealous of the relationship between the twins, their closeness, and their inseparability. She would have loved for them to be normal, to show an interest in more than just themselves, and to have a proper mother-daughter relationship with Aura. She had always supported all three of her children, but now, she saw them as though through a veil, their brightness, their love shadowed and darkened. She thought she could never love them the same way again.

The coffin lowered into the hole, the vicar uttering the words, but the sound came to Martha as a buzz, unintelligible nonsense. Only Samuel reciting from Tennyson's poem had reached her through her pain, striking her heart. *Before my life has found, What some have found so sweet; Then let come what come may, What matter if I go mad, I shall have had my day.* She hoped he had found something sweet and grieved that his day had come so soon.

Finally, the rain came, a splash hitting her between her eye and her nose. It mingled with her silent tears. She turned her face to the sky and let it saturate her. *Maybe it will wash me away into the earth,* she thought.

She was told that for a suspicious death, the process had moved fairly quickly, due in no small part to the testimony of the policewoman (she refused to say her name) at the inquest. It was because of her that her child had been at the bridge that night, and not at home where he was supposed to be. She should have insisted that they all go to Stratford together, or that they stay. She could have stopped this!

She forgot that they were 21, adults with their own lives, their own minds. She didn't think about the fact she was already a married mother by their age. All she saw were her children, and she couldn't protect them when they had needed her the most. When *he* had needed her.

Earth was thrown onto the coffin, the sound of it hitting the wood a harsh reminder of the finality of it all. Each thud echoed in her mind, a cruel punctuation to her thoughts. She watched as the soil covered the polished surface, her heart breaking anew with each handful.

The rain intensified, soaking through her clothes, but she didn't care. She stood there, rooted to the spot, as if her presence could somehow keep Tenney closer to her. The mourners began to disperse, umbrellas popping open, but Martha remained, staring at the grave.

Samuel approached her, his eyes red-rimmed and filled with sorrow. He placed a gentle hand on her shoulder, but she didn't react. She was lost in her grief, her mind replaying every moment, every decision that had led to this point.

"Come on, love," Samuel whispered, his voice cracking. "We need to go."

Martha shook her head slowly, her eyes never leaving the grave. "I can't," she whispered back. "I can't leave him."

Samuel's grip tightened slightly, a silent plea for her to move, to come back to the world of the living. Tears streamed down Martha's face, mingling with the rain. She knew he was right, but the pain was too raw, too overwhelming. She took a deep breath, trying to gather the strength to take a step, to move forward.

"Please, Samuel," she whispered beseechingly. "I just need to be alone one last time with my boy." Samuel's hand squeezed her arm sadly once more. He nodded, and then his presence was gone. She watched him walk back to their surviving children.

**

Gabriel sat with Jude in the small cottage Stace had gifted her now that she was staying in the Forest. The cottage, nestled down a secluded track on a piece of land that included Denebury Lodge, was a haven of peace amidst the turmoil. Her daughter had finally fallen into a grief-filled sleep, exhausting herself from crying. Gabriel stroked her hair, kissed her sweet child's temple, and held her close within her arms.

"Oh, my darling," she whispered. "Sleep now, for you will need all your strength to cope with what is to come next." She knew that she would have to leave with the sunrise.

The room was dimly lit by the soft glow of a single lamp, casting gentle shadows on the walls. The scent of lavender from the garden wafted through the open window, mingling with the cool night air. Gabriel's heart ached for her daughter, knowing the trials that lay ahead.

As Jude slept, Gabriel's thoughts wandered to the challenges she would face. The Creator had granted her wings back, but it came with a heavy burden of responsibility. The return of her status, 70 years early, was unprecedented. She had to prove her worthiness, not just to Him, but to her brothers and to herself. The past weighed heavily on her, her grief for her lost soul mate and her remembered love for her child, a perfect mix of both her parents. A child born from the purest love.

She looked down at Jude, her heart swelling with love and protectiveness. "I will always be with you, my child," she murmured. "Even when you cannot see me, I will be there, guiding you, protecting you."

The night wore on, and Gabriel remained by Jude's side, her wings enveloping them both in a cocoon of warmth and safety. As the first light of dawn began to creep through the window, she knew it was time. She gently disentangled herself from Jude, careful not to wake her.

With one last kiss on her daughter's forehead, Gabriel stood and stretched her wings. She stepped outside into the cool morning air, the sky painted with the soft hues of sunrise. She took a deep breath, steeling herself for the reunion that was to come.

"I will return," she whispered to the sleeping world. "And when I do, I will be stronger, for both of us."

With a powerful beat of her wings, Gabriel took to the sky, leaving the cottage behind. Her heart heavy with the knowledge of the trials to come, but filled with hope for the future, she expanded her wings as her full glory burst from her. In a flash, she was gone.

**

Stace watched from the shadows, his eyes fixed firmly on Aura, waiting to see if she began the Fade. He didn't register anyone else. His grief was palpable. Normally, he didn't grieve the Tether; their lives were so fleeting, and they changed so regularly, grief was a wasted expense. But with Tenney, there was something about him, something different… For the first time in a long time, he allowed the pain of losing someone he cared about into his heart.

The black wolf sat on his haunches next to him. He watched her closely, his green eyes following her around the cemetery. The man, her father he assumed, his face obscured by the umbrella he held over his remaining children, led them away. She had one hand on Sam's shoulder as though she had to guide him, as though he was incapable of knowing what to do, where to go.

Silently, the wolf loped off, following the family, following the girl from the shadows. He knew that Hedge would stay near to her until the time came when the moon rose the following night, and he began to change. And then, provided Aura managed to hold on for long enough, she would find him, and God willing, they would be able to say their goodbyes. But he knew that as soon as the body was interred back to the earth, her time as this Aura was short.

He hoped she would find a way to be reborn. Become someone new, with new memories, a new sibling. It would start all over again. But this time was different; uncertainty shadowed everything. Half of her soul now lay cold in the ground, cut off from her by the dagger.

He forced himself to look at the sad group again. There was something about the man that made him think they had crossed paths before, but he had met so many humans that they all tended to become blurred, indistinguishable one from the other.

He should follow them too; he knew it was his duty. Meg was fulfilling her role, scouting out local pregnant women. But he felt himself rooted to the spot, under the tree, out of the weak sunlight and the soft rain. He turned back to the open grave. One figure remained standing there. She was drenched from head to toe, but she didn't raise her umbrella. Instead, she seemed to welcome the rain, as though it was the only thing that really mattered anymore.

The clouds parted slightly over the sun, the beam landing at Stace's feet. He stepped back, deeper into the shadows. The woman turned, alerted by the movement. She looked right at him, their eyes meeting through the droplets of water. She strode purposefully, ignoring the mud and the leaves, until she was only a few feet from him.

"Stace?" she whispered, unsure if her eyes were deceiving her.

Stace felt the shock radiate to his core. Martha Deakin stood in front of him, the only human woman in nearly two millennia who had stood a real chance of stealing his heart. Why was she here?

Pieces began to slot into place. Their surname – Wiseman. He remembered now his protégé had been Sam Wiseman, back when he was a professor in the States. He had been Martha Deakin's best friend.

Tenney's unusual name, named for Martha's favourite poet. He remembered she told him that night that if she ever had a son, he would be called Tennyson or Lancelot, from her favourite poem, *The Lady of Shalott*. He had turned her face to his, kissed her deeply, and made her swear that she would never name a child Lancelot. Instead, he had introduced her to *Maud*, whispering to her lines which made her body react more deeply to his touch.

He shook his head, the memories of that night coming back to him powerfully. So Tenney was Martha and Samuel's son. Maybe he had seen enough of Martha in the son to make him warm to Tenney. The Fates had played this game well, he thought.

"Who told you?"

Stace stopped. He looked directly at this woman he had loved for such a short time.

"WHO TOLD YOU?" Martha bellowed at him. Then, looking down and in a quieter voice, almost to herself, "I only told Samuel… No one else knew…"

"Told me what?" Stace asked, the first words he had spoken to her in over 20 years. She snapped her head up and looked at him again.

"Why are you here?" she demanded.

"I met Tenney and his sister a couple of months ago, by chance. They were very kind to me, helped me out. I didn't know they were your children. I am sorry for your loss." He turned as if to go, leave Martha to her grief. The half-truth sat uneasily upon his heart. But Martha would never have understood the reality. And he wanted to spare her the burden for a bit longer before she lost her daughter too. He wanted to tell her to go home, hug Aura, and tell her she loved her. But he couldn't. She could never know.

But Martha was unwilling to let him go. She called out again, as though she hadn't heard his explanation, or hadn't believed him. "Who told you?"

"Told me what?" he asked, slightly exasperated by her nonsensical questions.

"That they were yours. That my beautiful boy, lying cold and alone in the grave, was YOUR son?"

Shock hit Stace full force in the gut. Martha sobbed loudly. He turned back to her, his face showing the disbelief and dismay he felt. She was unable to hear his response. Unable to carry his burdens as well, she turned away, back towards the lych-gate and her diminished family.

Stace watched her leave, and then looked back at the hole. The banks of earth on either side of it, the men returning to finish burying the coffin and the body within.

The repercussions of Tenney's actions to save Sam hit him full force.

He was his son. And he had been martyred.

"Oh no…" he whispered.

Epilogue

First night of the Full Moon Cycle

The night drew in, the moon began its ascendance as it reached the first night of its fullness. From high atop the clock tower, four figures watched the cemetery below them. The grave had been covered with dark earth; the coffin obscured from sight under a settling mound of dirt. In the shadows, they saw the small movement of the creature that watched the grave.

"Do you think he will change?" the youngest of the four asked.

"Yes," came the surly reply of the oldest. The Archangel Michael turned to his brother. He had shaken off his human disguise and stood before them, all-encompassing. His word was law. His decree sacred. His foresight unmatched, even by that of his youngest brother. "Uriel, he has the nightwalker gene, and he martyred himself for the life of his human brother. He will change."

"This has never happened before. An Elemental cannot be Tethered to an immortal. It goes against everything we are trying to achieve, everything they have gone through." Uriel paced the tower's roof.

"Calm down, brother." A third, laconic voice spoke from the shadows as he leant against one of the balustrades, unafraid of the long drop down. Raphael pushed himself away and lithely walked towards Michael to share his vigil. "This is how it is meant to happen. You know that the Great Reckoning must come about soon, that the Elemental's choice is nigh. How the Elemental and her Tether deal with this will decide the fate of all mankind."

"And what of my daughter?" Gabriel spoke up, angry at how blasé her brother appeared. "She is not strong enough to lose a lover, only to find he is reborn a bloodthirsty killer!"

Raphael laughed softly at his sister's naivety. "Gabriel, you are still readjusting to the reclamation of your wings. You obviously are still harbouring human feelings towards your child. Soon those feelings will pass, and you can concentrate once again on the important things…"

Raphael swiftly stepped out of his sister's path as she flew at him. Uriel caught her mid-air and held her back.

"Sister! Look!" he said, nodding towards Michael. The muscles in his back had tensed, and the stone beneath his hands was crumbling as he watched what was taking place below them.

The three angels joined their elder sibling. The earthen mound was stirring, the sound of nails scratching on the wood, replaced by furious bangs, reverberated around the still, quiet graveyard. The shadowed figure strode forward, a sharp gladius hanging ready from one hand.

With a loud crash, a hand pushed through the wood of the coffin and the earth above it. It pushed the rest of its body up out of the ground with a loud wail of agony.

The nightwalker raised his sword arm, about to bring it down in a sweeping curve, determined to sever the head from the newborn vampire before he could feed and remain as he had become, for eternity.

The sword swung down faster than a human's eye could see it. Gabriel let out an involuntary gasp, ignoring Raphael's sneer at her apparent weakness. But before the blade cut through the flesh of the neck, it stopped.

The nightwalker dropped the sword before falling to his knees. He gathered up the writhing body of the boy and held him close to his heart, brushing the grave dirt from his hair, his face, and his clothes. He whispered quietly, offering calming words.

A fox, unaware of the danger, stalked its prey in the woods around the cemetery. The nightwalker gently laid the boy down, his body convulsing on the wet ground, as he sped faster than light after the animal, turning it from hunter to prey.

Returning within seconds with the stunned fox in his hands, he held the boy in his lap and gently severed the artery in the fox's neck. Warm blood pulsated from the creature and into the boy's mouth.

Seconds felt like hours before the boy finally latched onto the neck of the fox and drank until the animal was naught but a husk. The boy convulsed once as the final changes in his body took place. The angels knew that soon he would need another meal. A larger dose of blood. Human blood.

The nightwalker had made his decision. He had saved the boy but destroyed his soul.

The dagger's prophecy had been true. The soul and the body were irrevocably separated. *Perhaps forever*, thought Gabriel.

Stace, holding the revived but shocked Tenney close to his chest in a desperate embrace, looked up to the tower and saw the four figures on its roof. He defied them to challenge him, to remonstrate with him, to kill him for what he had let happen. As the Angels stepped away and vanished into four bursts of light, Stace cried out to the sky, the sound echoing around the valleys and mingling with the howl of the wolves as Meg and Hedge changed form.

"Αρχίζει! It begins!"

The rain fell heavily on the father and his son.

To be continued…

Poetry References

Maud: A Monodrama by Alfred, Lord Tennyson

Alfred Lord Tennyson (2008). *Selected Poems.* Penguin Classics.

Wynken, Blynken and Nod by Eugene Field

i like my body when it is with your body by E.E. Cummings

Philip, N. and Brent, I. (2004). *Best-loved poems.* London: Little Brown.

Thanks

I want to thank my own personal tribe of people who have been there when I have battled real and perceived demons and helped be a lifeline when all I could see was darkness.

My eternal thanks to my brother and sister, Matt and Ellie, for giving me the confidence to put my story out there and advise me every step of the way. And to my parents. Without your love, support, belief and encouragement I would have faltered long before now.

To Sarah, Stacey and Kate who read the book and loved it! Your friendships mean the world to me, and I am so grateful for the support and feedback you have offered. That is why I have dedicated Tethered to you!

To my nephews and niece – Noah, Ollie and Penny. I love you to the moon and back.

To the Royal Forest of Dean. A place which will forever be magical and mystical. Where the people and generous and loving. A place where you can rediscover the essence of what makes you, you.

To anyone suffering from low self-esteem, burnout or poor mental health. I hope you find your tribe who will support you and fight for you until you are strong enough to fight for them.

Love,

Hannah x